Andrew Kennedy Hutchinson Boyd

The Recreations of a Country Parson

Andrew Kennedy Hutchinson Boyd

The Recreations of a Country Parson

ISBN/EAN: 9783337427092

Printed in Europe, USA, Canada, Australia, Japan

Cover: Foto ©Andreas Hilbeck / pixelio.de

More available books at **www.hansebooks.com**

THE

RECREATIONS

OF A

COUNTRY PARSON.

BOSTON:

TICKNOR AND FIELDS.

M DCCC LXI.

RIVERSIDE PRESS:
PRINTED BY H. O. HOUGHTON,
CAMBRIDGE.

CONTENTS.

—◆—

CONTENTS.

CHAPTER I.

CONCERNING THE COUNTRY PARSON'S LIFE.

THIS is Monday morning. It is a beautiful sunshiny morning early in July. I am sitting on the steps that lead to my door, somewhat tired by the duty of yesterday, but feeling very restful and thankful. Before me there is a little expanse of the brightest grass. too little to be called a lawn, very soft and mossy, and very carefully mown. It is shaded by three noble beeches, about two hundred years old. The sunshine around has a green tinge from the reflection of the leaves. Double hedges, thick and tall, the inner one of gleaming beech, shut out all sight of a country lane that runs hard by : a lane into which this gravelled sweep of would-be avenue enters, after winding deftly through evergreens, rich and old, so as to make the utmost of its little length. On the side furthest from the lane, the miniature lawn opens into a garden of no great extent, and beyond the garden you see a green field sloping upwards to a wood which bounds the view. One half of the front of the house is covered to the roof by a climbing rose-tree, so rich now with cluster roses that you see only the white soft masses of fragrance. Crimson roses and fuchsias cover half-way up the remainder of the front wall; and the sides of the flight of steps are green with large-leaved ivy. If ever there was a dwelling embosomed in great trees and evergreens, it is here. Everything grows beautifully: oaks, horse-chestnuts, beeches: laurels, yews, hollies; lilacs and hawthorn trees. Off a little way on the right, graceful in stem, in branches, in the pale bark, in the light-green leaves, I see my especial pet, a fair acacia. This is the true country: not the poor shadow of it which you have near great and smoky towns. That sapphire air is polluted by no factory chimney. Smoke is a beauty here, there is so little of it: rising thin and blue from the cottage; hospitable and friendly-looking from the rare mansion. The town is five miles distant: there is not even a village near. Green fields are all about: hawthorn hedges and rich hedge-rows: great masses of wood everywhere. But this is Scotland: and there is no lack of hills and rocks, of little streams and waterfalls; and two hundred yards off, winding round that churchyard whose white stones you see by glimpses through old oak branches, a large river glides swiftly by.

It is a quiet and beautiful scene: and it pleases me to think that Britain has thousands and thousands like it. But of course none, in my mind, equal this: for this has been my home for five years.

I have been sitting here for an hour, with a book on my knee; and upon that a piece of paper, whereon I have been noting down some thoughts for the sermon which I hope to write during this week, and to preach next Sunday in that little parish-church of which you can see a corner of a gable through the oaks which surround the churchyard. I have not been able to think very connectedly, indeed: for two little feet have been pattering round me, two little hands pulling at me occasionally, and a little voice entreating that I should come and have a race upon the green. Of course I went: for like most men who are not very great or very bad, I have learned, for the sake of the little owner of the hands and the voice, to love every little child. Several times, too, I have been obliged to get up and make a dash at a very small weed which I discerned just appearing through the gravel; and once or twice my man-servant has come to consult me about matters connected with the garden and the stable. My sermon will be the better for all these interruptions. I do not mean to say that it will be absolutely good, though it will be as good as I can make it: but it will be better for the races with my little girl, and for the thoughts about my horse, than it would have been if I had not been interrupted at all. The Roman Catholic Church meant it well: but it was far mistaken when it thought to make a man a better parish priest by cutting him off from domestic ties, and quite emancipating him from all the little worries of domestic life. *That* might be the way to get men who would preach an unpractical religion, not human in interest, not able to comfort, direct, sustain through daily cares, temptations, and sorrows. But for preaching which will come home to men's business and bosoms; which will not appear to ignore those things which must of necessity occupy the greatest part of an ordinary mortal's thoughts; commend me to the preacher who has learned by experience what are human ties, and what is human worry.

It is a characteristic of country life, that living in the country you have so many cares outside. In town, you have nothing to think of (I mean in the way of little material matters) beyond the walls of your dwelling. It is not

your business to see to the paving of the street before
your door; and if you live in a square, you are not individually responsible for the tidiness of the shrubbery in
its centre. When you come home, after the absence of a
week or a month, you have nothing to look round upon
and see that it is right. The space within the house's
walls is not a man's proper province. Your library table
and your books are all the domain which comes within the
scope of your orderly spirit. But if you live in the
country, in a house of your own with even a few acres
of land attached to it, you have a host of things to think
of when you come home from your week's or month's
absence: you have an endless number of little things
worrying you to take a turn round and see that they are
all as they should be. You can hardly sit down and rest
for their tugging at you. Is the grass all trimly mown?
Has the pruning been done that you ordered? Has that
rose-tree been trained? Has that bit of fence been
mended? Are all the walks perfectly free from weeds?
Is there not a gap left in box-wood edgings? and are
the edges of all walks through grass sharp and clearly
defined? Has that nettly corner of a field been made
tidy? Has any one been stealing the fruit? Have the
neighbouring cows been in your clover? How about the
stable?—any fractures of the harness?—any scratches
on the carriage?—anything amiss with the horse or
horses? All these, and innumerable questions more,
press on the man who looks after matters for himself,
when he arrives at home.

Still, there is good in all this. That which in a dis-
ponding mood you call a worry, in a cheerful mood you
think a source of simple, healthful interest in life. And
there is one case in particular, in which I doubt not the

reader of simple and natural tastes (and such may all my readers be) has experienced, if he be a country parson not too rich or great, the benefit of these gentle counter-irritants. It is when you come home, leaving your wife and children for a little while behind you. It is autumn: you are having your holiday : you have all gone to the sea-side. You have been away two or three weeks; and you begin to think that you ought to let your parishioners see that you have not forgotten them. You resolve to go home for ten days, which shall include two Sundays with their duty. You have to travel a hundred and thirty miles. So on a Friday morning you bid your little circle good-bye, and set off alone. It is not, perhaps, an extreme assumption that you are a man of sound sense and feeling, and not a selfish, conceited humbug: and, the case being so, you are not ashamed to confess that you are somewhat saddened by even that short parting; and that various thoughts obtrude themselves of possible accident and sorrow before you meet again. It is only ten days, indeed : but a wise man is recorded to have once advised his fellow-men in words which run as follows, ' Boast not thyself of to-morrow, for thou knowest not what a day may bring forth.' And as you sail along in the steamer, and sweep along in the train, you are thinking of the little things that not without tears bade their governor farewell. It was early morning when you left : and as you proceed on your solitary journey, the sun ascends to noon, and declines towards evening. You have read your newspaper : there is no one else in that compartment of the carriage : and hour after hour you grow more and more dull and downhearted. At length, as the sunset is gilding the swept harvest-fields, you reach the quiet little railway station among the hills. It is wonderful to see it.   There is no village: hardly a dwelling in sight: there are rocky hills all round; great trees: and a fine river, by following which the astute engineer led his railway to this seemingly inaccessible spot.   You alight on that primitive platform, with several large trees growing out of it, and with a waterfall at one end of it: and beyond the little palisade, you see your trap (let me not say carriage), your man-servant, your horse, perhaps your pair.   How kindly and pleasant the expression even of the horse's back!   How unlike the bustle of a railway station in a large town!   The train goes, the brass of the engine red in the sunset; and you are left in perfect stillness.   Your baggage is stowed, and you drive away gently.   It takes some piloting to get down the steep slope from this out-of-the-way place.   What a change from the thunder of the train to this audible quiet!   You interrogate your servant first in the comprehensive question, if all is right.   Relieved by his general affirm-ative answer, you descend into particulars.   Any one sick in the parish? how was the church attended on the Sundays you were away? how is Jenny, who had the fever; and John, who had the paralytic stroke?   How are the servants? how is the horse; the cow; the pig; the dog?   How is the garden progressing? how about fruit; how about flowers?   There was an awful thun-derstorm on Wednesday: the people thought it was the end of the world.   Two bullocks were killed: and thirteen sheep.   Widow Wiggins' son had deserted from the army, and had come home.   The harvest-home at such a farm is to-night: may Thomas go?   What a little quiet world is the country parish: what a micro-cosm even the country parsonage!   You are interested and pleased: you are getting over your stupid feeling of

depression. You are interested in all these little matters, not because you have grown a gossiping, little-
minded man ; but because you know it is fit and right
and good for you to be interested in such things. You
have five or six miles to drive : never less : the scene
grows always more homely and familiar as you draw
nearer home. And arrived at last, what a deal to look
at ! What a welcome on the servants' faces : such a
contrast to the indifferent looks of servants in a town.
You hasten to your library-table to see what letters
await you : country folks are always a little nervous
about their letters, as half expecting, half fearing, half
hoping, some vague, great, undefined event. You see
the snug fire : the chamber so precisely arranged, and
so fresh-looking : you remark it and value it fifty times
more amid country fields and trees than you would
turning out of the manifest life and civilization of the
city street. You are growing cheerful and thankful
now ; but before it grows dark, you must look round out
of doors : and *that* makes you entirely thankful and
cheerful. Surely the place has grown greener and
prettier since you saw it last ! You walk about the
garden and the shrubbery : the gravel is right, the grass
is right, the trees are right, the hedges are right, everything is right. You go to the stable-yard : you pat your
horse, and pull his ears, and enjoy seeing his snug
resting-place for the night. You peep into the cow-
house, now growing very dark : you glance into the
abode of the pig : the dog has been capering about you
all this while. You are not too great a man to take
pleasure in these little things. And now when you
enter your library again, where your solitary meal is
spread, you sit down in the mellow lamplight, and feel

quite happy. How different it would have been to have walked out of a street-cab into a town-house, with nothing beyond its walls to think of!

This is so sunshiny a day, and everything is looking so cheerful and beautiful, that I know my present testimony to the happiness of the country parson's life must be received with considerable reservation. Just at the present hour, I am willing to declare that I think the life of a country clergyman, in a pretty parish, with a well-conducted and well-to-do population, and with a fair living, is as happy, useful, and honourable as the life of man can be. Your work is all of a pleasant kind; you have, generally speaking, not too much of it; the fault is your own if you do not meet much esteem and regard among your parishioners of all degrees; you feel you are of some service in your generation: you have intellectual labours and tastes which keep your mind from growing rusty, and which admit you into a wide field of pure enjoyment: you have pleasant country cares to divert your mind from head-work, and to keep you for hours daily in the open air, in a state of pleasurable interest: your little children grow up with green fields about them and pure air to breathe: and if your heart be in your sacred work, you feel, Sunday by Sunday and day by day, a solid enjoyment in telling your fellow-creatures the Good News you are commissioned to address to them, which it is hard to describe to another, but which you humbly and thankfully take and keep. You have not, indeed, the excitement and the exhilaration of commanding the attention of a large educated congregation: those are reserved for the popular clergyman of a city parish. But then, you are free from the temptation to attempt the unworthy arts of the clap-trap mob-orator, or to preach mainly to display your own talents and eloquence: you have striven to exclude all personal ambition; and, forgetting yourself or what people may think of yourself, to preach simply for the good of your fellow-sinners, and for the glory of that kind Master whom you serve. And around you there are none of those heart-breaking things which must crush the earnest clergyman in a large town: no destitution; poverty, indeed, but no starvation: and, although evil will be wherever man is, nothing of the gross, daring, shocking vice, which is matured in the dens of the great city. The cottage children breathe a confined atmosphere while within the cottage; but they have only to go to the door, and the pure air of heaven is about them, and they live in it most of their waking hours. Very different with the pale children of a like class in the city, who do but exchange the infected chamber for the filthy lane, and whose eyes are hardly ever gladdened by the sight of a green field. And when the diligent country parson walks or drives about his parish, not without a decided feeling of authority and ownership, he knows every man, woman, and child he meets, and all their concerns and cares. Still, even on this charming morning I do not forget, that it depends a good deal upon the parson's present mood, what sort of account he may give of his country parish and his parochial life. If he have been recently cheated by a well-to-do farmer in the price of some farm produce; if he have seen a humble neighbour deliberately forcing his cow through a weak part of the hedge into a rich pasture-field of the glebe, and then have found him

ready to swear that the cow trespassed entirely without
his knowledge or will; if he meet a hulking fellow
carrying in the twilight various rails from a fence to be
used as firewood; if, on a warm summer day, the whole
congregation falls fast asleep during the sermon; if a
farmer tells him what a bad and dishonest man a discharged man-servant was, some weeks after the parson
had found that out for himself and packed off the
dishonest man; if certain of the cottagers near appear
disposed to live entirely, instead of only partially, of the
parsonage larder; the poor parson may sometimes be
found ready to wish himself in town, compact within a
house in a street with no back door; and not spreading
out such a surface as in the country he must, for petty
fraud and peculation. But, after all, the country parson's great worldly cross lies for the most part in his
poverty, and in the cares which arise out of that. It
is not always so, indeed. In the lot of some the happy
medium has been reached; they have found the 'neither
poverty nor riches' of the wise man's prayer. Would
that it were so with all! For how it must cripple a
clergyman's usefulness, how abate his energies, how
destroy his eloquence, how sicken his heart, how narrow
and degrade his mind, how tempt (as it has sometimes
done), to unfair and dishonest shifts and expedients, to
go about not knowing how to make the ends meet, not
seeing how to pay what he owes! If I were a rich
man, how it would gladden me to send a fifty-pound note
to certain houses I have seen! What a dead weight it
would lift from the poor wife's heart! Ah! I can think
of the country parson, like poor Sydney Smith, adding
his accounts, calculating his little means, wondering
where he can pinch or pare any closer, till the poor

fellow bends down his stupified head and throbbing temples on his hands, and wishes he could creep into a quiet grave. God tempers the wind to the shorn lamb; or I should wonder how it does not drive some country parsons mad, to think what would become of their children if they were taken away. It is the warm nest upon the rotten bough. They need abundant faith; let us trust they get it. But in a desponding mood, I can well imagine such a one resolving that no child of his shall ever enter upon a course in life which has brought himself such misery as he has known.

I have been writing down some thoughts, as I have said, for the sermon of next Sunday. To-morrow morning I shall begin to write it fully out. Some individuals, I am aware, have maintained that listening to a sermon is irksome work; but to a man whose tastes lie in that way, the writing of sermons is most pleasant occupation. It does you good. Unless you are a mere false pretender, you cannot try to impress any truth forcibly upon the hearts of others, without impressing it forcibly upon your own. All that you will ever make other men feel, will be only a subdued reflection of what you yourself have felt. And sermon-writing is a task that is divided into many stages. You begin afresh every week: you come to an end every week. If you are writing a book, the end appears very far away. If you find that although you do your best, you yet treat some part of your subject badly, you know that the bad passage remains as a permanent blot: and you work on under the cross-influence of that recollection. But if, with all your pains, this week's sermon is poor, why, you hope to do better next week. You seek a fresh field: you try again. No doubt, in preaching

your sermons you are somewhat annoyed by rustic
boorishness and want of thought. Various bumpkins
will forget to close the door behind them when they
enter church too late, as they not unfrequently do.
Various men with great hob-nailed shoes, entering late.
instead of quietly slipping into a pew close to the door,
will stamp noisily up the passage to the further extremity of the church. Various faces will look up at you
week by week, hopelessly blank of all interest or intelli-
gence. Some human beings will not merely sleep, but
loudly evince that they are sleeping. Well, you gradually
cease to be worried by these little things. At first, they
jarred through every nerve; but you grow accustomed
to them. And if you be a man of principle and of sense,
you know better than to fancy that amid a rustic people
your powers are thrown away. Even if you have in
past days been able to interest congregations of the
refined and cultivated class, you will now show your
talent and your principle at once by accommodating your
instructions to the comprehension of the simple souls
committed to your care. I confess I have no patience
with men who profess to preach sermons carelessly
prepared, because they have an uneducated congregation. Nowhere is more careful preparation needed; but
of course it must be preparation of the right sort. Let
it be received as an axiom, that the very first aim of the
preacher should be to interest. He must interest, before
he can hope to instruct or improve. And no matter how
filled with orthodox doctrine and good advice a sermon
may be: if it put the congregation to sleep, it is an
abominably bad sermon.

Surely, I go on to think, this kind of life must affect
all the productions of the mind of the man who leads it.

There must be a smack of the country, its scenes and its cares, about them all. You walk in shady lanes: you stand and look at the rugged bark of old trees: you help to prune evergreens: you devise flower-gardens and winding walks. You talk to pigs, and smooth down the legs of horses. You sit on mossy walls, and saunter by the river side, and through woodland paths. You grow familiar with the internal arrangements of poor men's dwellings: you see much of men and women in those solemn seasons when all pretences are laid aside; and they speak with confidence to you of their little cares and fears, for this world and the other. You kneel down and pray by the bedside of many sick; and you know the look of the dying face well. Young children whom you have humbly sought to instruct in the best of knowledge, have passed away from this life in your presence, telling you in interrupted sentences whither they trusted they were going, and bidding you not forget to meet them there. You feel the touch of the weak fingers still; the parting request is not forgotten. You mark the spring blossoms come back; and you walk among the harvest sheaves in the autumn evening. And when you ride up the parish on your duty, you feel the influence of bare and lonely tracts, where, ten miles from home, you sometimes dismount from your horse, and sit down on a grey stone by the wayside, and look for an hour at the heather at your feet, and at the sweeps of purple moorland far away. You go down to the church-yard frequently: you sit on the gravestone of your predecessor who died two hundred years since; and you count five, six, seven spots where those who served the cure before you sleep. Then, leaning your head upon your hand, you look thirty years into the future, and

2

wonder whether you are to grow old. You read, through moss-covered letters, how a former incumbent of the parish died in the last century, aged twenty-eight. That afternoon, coming from a cottage where you had been seeing a frail old woman, you took a flying leap over a brook near, with precipitous sides; and you thought that some day, if you lived, you would have to creep quietly round by a smoother way. And now you think you see an aged man, tottering and grey, feebly walking down to the churchyard as of old, and seating himself hard by where you sit. The garden will have grown weedy and untidy: it will not be the trim, precise dwelling which youthful energy and hopefulness keep it now.

Let it be hoped that the old man's hat is not seedy, nor his coat threadbare: it makes one's heart sore to see *that*. And let it be hoped that he is not alone. But you go home, I think, with a quieter and kindlier heart.

You live in a region, mental and material, that is very entirely out of the track of worldly ambition. You do not blame it in others: you have learnt to blame few things in others severely, except cruelty and falsehood: but you have outgrown it for yourself. You hear, now and then, of this and the other school or college friend becoming a great man. One is an Indian hero: one is attorney-general: one is a cabinet minister. You like to see their names in the newspapers. You remember how, in college competitions with them, you did not come off second-best. You are struck at finding that such a man, whom you recollect as a fearful dunce, is getting respectably on through life: you remember how at school you used to wonder whether the difference between the clever boy and the booby would be in after days the same great gulf that it was then. Your life

goes on very regularly, each week much like the last.
And, on the whole, it is very happy. You saunter for
a little in the open air after breakfast: you do so when
the evergreens are beautiful with snow as well as when
the warm sunshine makes the grass white with widely-
opened daisies. Your children go with you wherever
you go. You are growing subdued and sobered; but
they are not: and when one sits on your knee, and lays
upon your shoulder a little head with golden ringlets,
you do not mind very much though your own hair (what
is left of it) is getting shot with grey. You sit down in
your quiet study to your work: what thousands of pages
you have written at that table! You cease your task at
one o'clock: you read your *Times:* you get on horseback and canter up the parish to see your sick: or you
take the ribbons and tool into the county town. You
feel the stir of even its quiet existence: you drop into
the bookseller's: you grumble at the venerable age of
the Reviews that come to you from the club. Generally,
you cannot be bothered with calls upon your tattling
acquaintances: you leave these to your wife. You
drive home again, through the shady lanes, away into
the green country: your man-servant in his sober livery
tells you with pride, when you go to the stable-yard for
a few minutes before dinner, that Mr. Snooks, the great
judge of horse-flesh, had declared that afternoon in the
inn-stable in town, that he had not seen a better-kept
carriage and harness anywhere, and that your plump
steed was a noble creature. It is well when a servant is
proud of his belongings: he will be a happier man, and
a more faithful and useful. When you next drive out
you will see the silver blazing in the sun with increased
brightness. And now you have the pleasant evening,

before you. You never fail to dress for dinner: living so quietly as you do, it is especially needful, if you would avoid an encroaching rudeness, to pay careful attention to the little refinements of life. And the great event of the day over, you have music, books, and children: you have the summer saunter in the twilight: you have the winter evening fireside: you take perhaps another turn at your sermon for an hour or two. The day has brought its work and its recreation: you can look back each evening upon something done: save when you give yourself a holiday which you feel has been fairly toiled for. And what a wonderful amount of work, such as it is, you may, by exertion regular but not excessive, turn off in the course of the ten months and a-half of the working year!

And thus, day by day, and month by month, the life of the country parson passes quietly away. It will be briefly comprehended on his tombstone, in the assurance that he did his duty, simply and faithfully, through so many years. It is somewhat monotonous, but he is too busy to weary of it: it is varied by not much society, in the sense of conversation with educated men with whom the clergyman has many common feelings. But it is inexpressibly pleasing when, either to his own house or to a dwelling near, there comes a visitor with whom an entire sympathy is felt, though probably holding very antagonistic views: then come the 'good talks' with delighted Johnson: genial evenings, and long walks of afternoons. The daily post is a daily strong sensation, sometimes pleasing, sometimes painful, as he brings tidings of the outer world. You have your daily *Times:* each Monday morning brings your *Saturday Review:* and the *Illustrated London News* comes not merely for the children's sake. You read all the Quarterlies, of course: you skim the monthlies: but it is with tenfold interest and pleasure that month by month you receive that magazine which is edited by a dear friend who sends it to you, and in which sometimes certain pages have the familiar look of a friend's face. You draw it wet from its big envelope: you cut its leaves with care: you enjoy the fragrance of its steam as it dries at the study fire: you glance at the shining backs of that long row of volumes into which the pleasant monthly visitants have accumulated: you think you will have another volume soon. Then there is a great delight in occasionally receiving a large bundle of books which have been ordered from your bookseller in the city a hundred miles off: in reading the address in such big letters that they must have been made with a brush: in stripping off the successive layers of immensely thick brown paper: in reaching the precious hoard within, all such fresh copies (who are they that buy the copies you turn over in the shop, but which you would not on any account take?): such fresh copies, with their bran-new bindings and their leaves so pure in a material sense: in cutting the leaves at the rate of two or three volumes an evening, and in seeing the entire accession of literature lying about the other table (not the one you write on) for a few days ere they are given to the shelves. You are not in the least ashamed to confess that you are pleased by all these little things. You regard it as not necessarily proving any special pettiness of mind or heart. You regard it as no proof of greatness in any man, that he should appear to care nothing for anything. Your private belief is that it shows him to be either a humbug or a fool.

In this little volume the indulgent reader will find
certain of those Essays which the writer discovered on
cutting the leaves of the magazine which comes to him
on the last day of every month. They were written, as
something which might afford variety of work, which
often proves the most restful of all recreation. They are
nothing more than that which they are called, a country
clergyman's *Recreations*. My solid work, and my first
thoughts, are given to that which is the business and the
happiness of my life. But these Essays have led me into
a field which to myself was fresh and pleasant. And I
have always returned from them, with increased interest,
to graver themes and trains of thought. I have not
forgot, as I wrote them, a certain time, when my little
children must go away from their early home: when
these evergreens I have planted and these walks I have
made shall pass to my successor (may he be a better
man!); and when I shall perhaps find my resting-place
under those ancient oaks. Nor have I wholly failed to
remember a coming day, when bishops and archbishops
shall be called to render an account of the fashion in
which they exercised their solemn and dignified trusts;
and when I, who am no more than the minister of a
Scotch country parish, must answer for the diligence
with which I served my little cure.

CHAPTER II.

CONCERNING THE ART OF PUTTING THINGS:

BEING THOUGHTS ON REPRESENTATION AND MISREPRESENTATION.

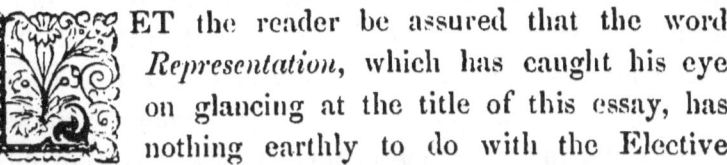

ET the reader be assured that the word *Representation*, which has caught his eye on glancing at the title of this essay, has nothing earthly to do with the Elective Franchise, whether in boroughs or counties. Not a syllable will be found upon the following pages bearing directly or indirectly upon any New Reform Bill. I do not care a rush who is member for this county. I have no doubt that all members of Parliament are very much alike. Everybody knows that each individual legislator who pushes his way into the House, is actuated solely by a pure patriotic love for his country. No briefless barrister ever got into Parliament in the hope of getting a place of twelve hundred a year. No barrister in fair practice ever did so in the hope of getting a silk gown, or the Solicitor-Generalship, or a seat on the bench. No merchant or country-gentleman ever did so in the hope of gaining a little accession of dignity and influence in the town or county in which he lives. All these things are universally understood; and they are mentioned here merely to enable it to be said, that this treatise has nothing to do with them.

Edgar Allan Poe, the miserable genius who died in America a few years ago, declared that he never had the least difficulty in tracing the logical steps by which he chose any subject on which he had ever written, and matured his plan for treating it. And some readers may remember a curious essay, contained in his collected works, in which he gives a minute account of the genesis of his extraordinary poem, *The Raven*. But Poe was a humbug; and it is impossible to place the least faith in anything said by him upon any subject whatever. In his writings we find him repeatedly avowing that he would assert any falsehood, provided it were likely to excite interest and 'create a sensation.' I believe that most authors could tell us that very frequently the conception and the treatment of their subject have darted on them all at once, they could not tell how. Many clergymen know how strangely texts and topics of discourse have been suggested to them, while it was impossible to trace any link of association with what had occupied their minds the instant before. The late Douglas Jerrold relates how he first conceived the idea of one of his most popular productions. Walking on a winter day, he passed a large enclosure full of romping boys at play. He paused for a minute; and as he looked and mused, a thought flashed upon him. It was not so beautiful, and you would say not so natural, as the reflections of Gray, as he looked from a distance at Eton College. As Jerrold gazed at the schoolboys, and listened to their merry shouts, there burst upon him the conception of *Mrs. Caudle's Curtain Lectures!* There seems little enough connexion with what he was looking at; and although Jerrold declared that the sight suggested the idea, he could not pretend to trace the link of association.

It would be very interesting if we could accurately know the process by which authors, small or great, piece together their grander characters. How did Milton pile up his Satan; how did Shakspeare put together Hamlet or Lady Macbeth; how did Charlotte Brontë imagine Rochester? Writers generally keep their secrets, and do not let us see behind the scenes. We can trace, indeed, in successive pieces by Sheridan, the step-by-step development of his most brilliant jests, and of his most gushing bursts of the feeling of the moment. No doubt Lord Brougham had tried the woolsack, to see how it would do, before he fell on his knees upon it (on the impulse of the instant), at the end of his great speech on the Reform Bill. But of course Lord Brougham would not tell us; and Sheridan did not intend us to know. Even Mr. Dickens, when, in his preface to the cheap edition of *Pickwick*, he avows his purpose of telling us all about the origin of that amazingly successful serial, gives us no inkling of the process by which he produced the character which we all know so well. He tells us a great deal about the mere details of the work: the pages of letter-press, the number of illustrations, the price and times of publication. But the process of actual authorship remains a mystery. The great painters would not tell where they got their colours. The effort which gives a new character to the acquaintance of hundreds of thousands of Englishmen, shall be concealed beneath a decorous veil. All that Mr. Dickens tells us is this: 'I thought of Mr. Pickwick, and wrote the first number.' And to the natural question of curiosity, 'How on earth did you think of Mr. Pickwick?' the author's silence replies, 'I don't choose to tell you *that!*'

And now, courteous reader, you are humbly asked to

suffer the writer's discursive fashion, as he records how
the idea of the present discourse, treatise, dissertation, or
essay flashed upon his mind. Yesterday was a most
beautiful frosty day. The air was indescribably exhilarating: the cold was no more than bracing; and as I
fared forth for a walk of some miles, I saw the tower of
the ancient church, green with centuries of ivy, looking
through the trees which surround it, the green ivy
silvered over with hoar-frost. The hedges on either
hand, powdered with rime, were shining in the cold
sunshine of the winter afternoon. First, I passed
through a thick pinewood, bordering the road on both
sides. The stems of the fir-trees had that warm, rich
colour which is always pleasant to look at; and the green
branches were just touched with frost. One undervalues
the evergreens in summer: their colour is dull when
compared with the fresher and brighter green of the
deciduous trees; but now, when these gay transients
have changed to shivering skeletons, the hearty firs,
hollies, and yews warm and cheer the wintry landscape.
Not the wintry, I should say, but the *winter* landscape, which conveys quite a different impression. The
word *wintry* wakens associations of bleakness, bareness,
and bitterness; a hearty evergreen tree never looks
wintry, nor does a landscape to which such trees give
the tone. Then emerging from the wood, I was in an
open country. A great hill rises just ahead, which the
road will skirt by and bye: on the right, at the foot of a
little cliff hard by, runs a shallow, broad, rapid river.
Looking across the river, I see a large range of nearly
level park, which at a mile's distance rises into upland;
the park shows broad green glades, broken and bounded
by fine trees, in clumps and in avenues. In summer-

time you would see only the green leaves: but now, peering through the branches, you can make out the outline of the grey turrets of the baronial dwelling which has stood there, added to, taken from, patched, and altered, but still the same dwelling, for the last four hundred years. And on the left, I am just passing the rustic gateway through which you approach that quaint cottage on the knoll two hundred yards off—one story high, with deep thatch, steep gables, overhanging eaves, and verandah of rough oak—a sweet little place, where Izaak Walton might successfully have carried out the spirit of his favourite text, and 'studied to be quiet.' All this way, three miles and more, I did not meet a human being. There was not a breath of air through the spines of the firs, and not a sound except the ripple of the river. I leant upon a gate, and looked into a field. Something was grazing in the field; but I cannot remember whether it was cows, sheep, oxen, elephants, or camels; for as I was looking, and thinking how I should begin a sermon on a certain subject much thought upon for the last fortnight, my mind resolutely turned away from it, and said, as plainly as mind could express it, For several days to come I shall produce material upon no subject but one,—and *that* shall be the comprehensive, practical, suggestive, and most important subject of the ART OF PUTTING THINGS!

And indeed there is hardly a larger subject, in relation to the social life of the nineteenth century in England; and there is hardly a practical problem to the solution of which so great an amount of ingenuity and industry, honest and dishonest, is daily brought, as the grand problem of setting forth yourself, your goods, your horses, your case, your plans, your thoughts and argu-ments—all your belongings, in short—to the best advantage. From the Prime Minister, who exerts all his wonderful skill and eloquence to put his policy before Parliament and the country in the most favourable light, and the Chancellor of the Exchequer, who does his very best to cast a rosy hue even upon an income-tax, down to the shopman who arranges his draperies in the window against market-day in that fashion which he thinks will prove most fascinating to the maid-servant with her newly-paid wages in her pocket, and the nurse who in a most lively and jovial manner assures a young lady of three years old that she will never feel the taste of her castor-oil, — yea, even to the dentist who with a joke and a smiling face approaches you with his forceps in his hand: — from the great Attorney-General seeking to place his view of his case with convincing force before a bewildered jury (that view being flatly opposed to common sense), down to the schoolboy found out in some mischievous trick and trying to throw the blame upon somebody else: almost all civilized beings in Great Britain are from morning to night labouring hard to put things in general or something in particular in the way that they think will lead to the result which best suits their views; — are, in short, practising the art of representing or misrepresenting things for their own advantage. Great skill, you would say, must result from this constant practice: and indeed it probably does. But then, people are so much in the habit of trying to *put things* themselves, that they are uncommonly sharp at seeing through the devices of others. 'Set a thief' to catch a thief,' says the ancient adage: and so, set a man who can himself tell a very plausible story without saying anything positively untrue, to discover the real truth under the rainbow tints of the plausible story told by another.

But do not fancy, my kind reader, that I have any

purpose of making a misanthropical onslaught upon poor
humanity. I am very far from desiring to imply that
there is anything essentially wrong or dishonest in trying
to put things in the most favourable light for our views
and plans. The contrary is the case. It is a noble gift,
when a man is able to put great truths or momentous
facts before our minds with that vividness and force
which shall make us feel these facts and truths in their
grand reality. A great evil, to which human beings are
by their make subject, is, that they can talk of things,
know things, and understand things, without *feeling* them
in their true importance — without, in short, *realizing*
them. There appears to be a certain numbness about
the mental organs of perception; and the man who is
able to *put things* so strikingly, clearly, pithily, forcibly,
glaringly, whether these things are religious, social, or
political truths, as to get through that numbness, that
crust of insensibility, to the *quick* of the mind and heart,
must be a great man, an earnest man, an honest man, a
good man. I believe that any great reformer will find
less practical discouragement in the opposition of bad
people than in the *inertia* of good people. You cannot
get them to feel that the need and the danger are so
imminent and urgent; you cannot get them to bestir
themselves with the activity and energy which the case demands. You cannot get them to take it in that the open
sewer and the airless home of the working man are such a
very serious matter; you cannot get them to feel that the
vast uneducated masses of the British population form a
mine beneath our feet which may explode any day, with
God knows what devastation. I think that not all the wonderful eloquence, freshness, and pith of Mr. Kingsley form
a talent so valuable as his power of compelling people to

feel what they had always known and talked about, but never felt. And wherein lies that power, but just in his skill to *put things* — in his power of truthful representation?

Sydney Smith was once talking with an Irish Roman Catholic priest about the proposal to endow the Romish Church in Ireland. 'We would not take the Saxon money.' said the worthy priest. quite sincerely; 'we would not defile our fingers with it. No matter whether Parliament offered us endowments or not, we would not receive them.' 'Suppose,' replied Sydney Smith, 'you were to receive an official letter that on calling at such a bank in the town three miles off, you would hereafter receive a hundred pounds a quarter. the first quarter's allowance payable in advance on the next day ; and suppose that you wanted money to do good, or to buy books, or anything else : do you mean to say you would not drive over to the town and take the hundred pounds out of the bank ?' The priest was staggered. He had never looked at the thing in that precise light. He had never had the vague distant question of endowment brought so home to him. He had been quite sincere in his spirited repudiation of Saxon coin, as recorded above; but he had not exactly understood what he was saying and doing. '*Oh, Mr. Smith.*' he replied, '*you have such a way of putting things!*' What a triumph of the Anglican's art of truthful representation!

One of the latest instances of skill in putting things which I remember to have struck me I came upon, where abundance of such skill may be found — in a leading article in the *Times*. The writer of that article was endeavouring to show that the work of the country clergy is extremely light. Of course he is sadly mistaken; but this by the way. As to sermons, said the lively writer (I don't pretend to give his exact words), what work is there in a sermon? Just fancy that you are writing half a dozen letters of four pages each, and crossed! The thing was cleverly put; and it really came on me with the force of a fact, a new and surprising fact. Many sermons has this thin right hand written; but my impression of a sermon, drawn from some years' experience, is of a composition very different from a letter — something demanding that brain and heart should be worked to the top of their bent for more hours than need be mentioned here; something implying as hard and as exhausting labour as man can well go through. Surely, I thought, I have been working under a sad delusion! Only half a dozen light letters of gossip to a friend: *that* is the amount of work implied in a sermon! Have I been all these years making a bugbear of such a simple and easy matter as *that?* Here is a new and cheerful way of putting the thing! But unhappily, though the clever representation would no doubt convey to some thousands of readers the impression that to write a sermon was a very simple affair after all, it broke down, it crumpled up, it went to pieces when brought to the test of fact. When next morning I had written my text, I thought to myself, Now here I have just to do the same amount of work which it would cost me to write half a dozen letters to half a dozen friends, giving them our little news. Ah, it would not do! In a little, I was again in the struggle of mapping out my subject, and cutting a straight track through the jungle of the world of mind; looking about for illustrations, seeking words to put my meaning with clearness and interest before the simple country folk I preach to. It was not the least like letter-writing. The clever writer's way of putting

things was wrong; and though I acquit him of any
crime beyond speaking with authority of a thing which
he knew nothing about, I must declare that his representation was a misrepresentation. If you have sufficient
skill, you may put what is painful so that it shall sound
pleasant; you may put a wearisome journey by railway
in such a connexion with cozy cushions, warm rugs, a
review or a new book, storm sweeping the fields without,
and warmth and ease within, that it shall seem a delightful thing. You may put work, in short, so that it shall
look like play. But actual experiment breaks down the
representation. You cannot change the essential nature
of things. You cannot make black white, though a
clever man may make it seem so.

Still, we all have a great love for trying to put any
hard work or any painful business, which it is certain we
must go through, in such a light as may make it seem
less terrible. And it is not difficult to deceive ourselves
when we are eager to be deceived. No one can tell how
much comfort poor Damien drew from the way in which
he put the case on the morning of his death by horrible
tortures: 'The day will be long,' he said, 'but it will
have an end.' No one can tell what a gleam of light
may have darted upon the mind of Charles I. as he
knelt to the block, when Bishop Juxon put encouragingly
the last trial the monarch had to go through: 'one last
stage, somewhat turbulent and troublesome, *but still a
very short one.*' No one can tell how much it soothed
the self-love of Tom Purdie, when Sir Walter Scott
ordered him to cut down some trees which Tom wished
to stand, and positively commanded that they should go
down in spite of all Tom's arguments and expostulations,
and all this in the presence of a number of gentlemen

before whom Tom could not bear any impeachment of his woodcraft; no one, I say, can tell how much it soothed the worthy forester's self-love when after half an hour's sulky meditation he thought of the happy plan of putting the thing on another footing than that of obedience to an order, and looking up cheerfully again, said, 'As for those trees, I think I'll *tak' your advice*, Sir Walter!' Would it be possible, I wonder, thus pleasantly to *put* the writing of an article so as to do away the sense of the exertion which writing an article implies? Have we not all little tricks which we play upon ourselves, to make our labour seem lighter, our dignity greater, our whole position jollier, than in our secret soul we know is the fact? Think, then, thou jaded man, bending over the written page which is one day to attain the dignity of print in *Fraser* or *Blackwood*, how in these words thou art addressing many thousands of thy enlightened countrymen and thy fair countrywomen, and becoming known (as Fielding puts it in one of his simply felicitous sentences) 'to numbers who otherwise never saw or knew thee, and whom thou shalt never see or know.' Think how thou shalt lie upon massive library-tables, in substantially elegant libraries, side by side perhaps with Helps, Kingsley, or Hazlitt; how thou shalt lighten the cares of middle-aged men, and (if thou art a writer of fiction) be smuggled up to young ladies' chambers; who shall think, as they read thy article (oh, much mistaken!), what a nice man thou art! Alas! all that way of putting things is mere poetry. It wont do. It still remains, and always must remain, the stretch and strain of mind and muscle, to write. Let not the critic be severe on people who write ill: they deserve much credit and sympathy because they write at

3

all. But though these grand and romantic ways of
putting the writing of one's article will not serve, there
are little prosaic material expedients which really avail
to put it in a light in which it looks decidedly less
laborious. Slowly let the large drawer be pulled out
wherein lies the paper which will serve, if we are allowed
to see them, for many months to come. There lies the
large blue quarto, so thick and substantial; there the
massive foolscap, so soft and smooth, over which the pen
so pleasantly and unscratchingly glides; *that* is the raw
material for the article. Draw it forth deliberately: fold
it accurately: then the ivory stridently cuts it through.
Weigh the paper in your hand; then put the case thus:
' Well, it is only covering these pages with writing, after
all; it is just putting three-and-twenty lines, of so many
words each on the average, upon each of these unblotted
surfaces.' Surely there is not so much in *that*. Do not
think of all the innumerable processes of mind that go
to it; of the weighing of the consequences of general
propositions; of the choice of words; of the pioneering
your track right on, not turning to either hand; of the
memory taxed to bring up old thoughts upon your subject;
of the clock striking unheard while you are bent upon
your task, so much harder than carrying any reasonable
quantity of coals, or blacking ever so many boots, or
currying ever so many horses. Just stick to this view
of the matter, just put the thing this way — that all you
have to do is to blacken so many pages, and take the
comfort of that way of putting it.

To such people as we human beings are, there is hardly any matter of greater practical importance than what
we have called the Art of Putting Things. For, to us,
things *are* what they *seem*. They affect us just according

to what we think them. Our knowledge of things, and
our feeling in regard to things, are all contingent on the
way in which these things have been put before us; and
what different ways there are of putting every possible
doctrine, or opinion, or doing, or thing, or event! And
what mischievous results, colouring all our views and feelings, may follow from an important subject having been
wrongly, disagreeably, injudiciously put to us when we
were children! How many men hate Sunday all their
lives because it was put to them so gloomily in their
boyhood; and how many Englishmen, on the other hand,
fancy a Scotch Sunday the most disagreeable of days
because the case has been wrongly put to them, while in
truth there is, in intelligent religious Scotch families, no
more pleasant, cheerful, genial, restful, happy day. And
did not Byron always hate Horace, put to him in youth
with the associations of impositions and the birch?
There is no more sunshiny inmate of any home than the
happy-tempered one who has the art of putting all things
in a pleasant light, from the great misfortunes of life
down to a broken carriage-spring, a servant's failings, a
child's salts and senna. You are extremely indignant at
some person who has used you ill; you are worried and
annoyed at his misconduct; it is as though you were
going about with a mustard blister applied to your mind:
when a word or two from some genial friend puts the
entire matter in a new light, and your irritation goes, the
blister is removed, your anger dies out, you would like to
pat the offending being on the head, and say you bear
him no malice. And it is wonderful what a little thing
sometimes suffices to put a case thus differently. When
you are complaining of somebody's ill-usage, it will
change your feeling and the look of things, if the friend

you are speaking to does no more than say of the peccant brother, 'Ah! poor fellow!' I think that every man or woman who has got servants, and who has pretty frequently to observe (I mean to see, not to speak of) some fault on their part, owes a deep debt of gratitude to the man, whoever he was, who thus kindly and wisely gave us a forbearing stand-point from which to regard a servant's failings, by putting the thing in this way, true in itself though new to many, that you cannot expect perfection for fourteen, or even for fifty pounds a-year. Has not that way of putting things sometimes checked you when you meditated a sharp reproof, and allayed anger which otherwise would have been pretty hot? Even when a rogue cheats you (though that, I confess, is a peculiarly irritating thing), is not your wrath mollified by putting the thing thus: that the poor wretch probably needed very much the money out of which he cheated you, and would not have cheated you if he could have got it honestly? When a horse-dealer sells you, at a remarkably stiff figure, a broken-winded steed, do not yield to unqualified indignation. True, the horse-dealer is always ready to cheat; but feel for the poor fellow, every man thinks it right to cheat *him;* and with every man's hand against him, what wonder though his hand should be against every man? Everything, you see, turns on the way in which you put things. And it is so from earliest youth to latest age. The old scholar, whose delight is to sit among his books, thus puts his library :—

My days among the dead are passed:
  Around me I behold,
Where'er these casual eyes are cast,
  The mighty minds of old:
My never-failing friends are they,
With whom I converse night and day. *

* Southey.

You see the library was not mere shelves of books, and the books were not mere printed pages. You remember how Robinson Crusoe, in his cheerful moods, put his island home. He sat down to his lonely meal, but *that* was not how he put things. No. ' Here was my majesty, all alone by myself, attended by my servants :' his servants being the dog, parrot, and cat. I remember how a wealthy merchant, a man quite of the city as opposed to the country, once talked of emigrating to America, and buying an immense tract of land, where he and his family should lead a simple, unartificial, innocent life. He was not in the least cut out for such a life, and would have been miserable in it, but he was fascinated with the notion because he put it thus : — ' I shall have great flocks and herds, and live in a tent *like Abraham.'* And *that* way of putting things brought up before the busy man of the nineteenth century I know not what sweet picture of a primevally quiet and happy life. I can remember yet how, when I crept about my father's study, a little boy of three years old, I felt the magic of the art of putting things. All children are restless. It is impossible for them to remain still, and we all know how a child in a study worries the busy scholar. All admonitions to keep quiet failed ; it was really impossible to obey them. Creep, creep about ; upset footstools ; pull off table-covers ; upset ink. But when the thing was put in a different way ; when the kind voice said, — ' Now, you 'll be my little dog : creep into your house there under the table. and lie quite still,' there was no difficulty in obeying *that* command : and, except an occasional bow-wow, there was perfect stillness. The art of putting things had prevailed. It was necessary to keep still ; for a dog in a study, I knew, must keep still, and I was a dog.

It must be a worrying thing for a great warrior or statesman, fighting a great battle, or introducing a great legislative measure, to remember that the estimation in which he is to be held in his own day and country, and in other countries and ages, depends not at all on what his conduct is in itself, but entirely on the way in which it shall be put before mankind — represented, or misrepresented, in newspapers, in rumours, in histories. How very unlikely it is that history will ever put the case on its real merits: the characters of history will either be praised far above their deserts, or abused far beyond their sins. 'Do not read history to me,' said Sir Robert Walpole, 'for *that*, I know, must be false.' History could be no more than the record of the way in which men had agreed to put things: and those behind the scenes, the men who pull the wires which move the puppets, must often have reason to smile at the absurd mistakes into which the history-writing outsiders fall. And even apart from ignorance, or bias, or intention to deceive, what a fearful thought it must be to a great man taking a conspicuous part in some great solemnity, such as the trial of a queen, or the impeachment of a governor-general, to reflect that this great solemnity, and his own share in it, and how he looked, and what he said, may possibly be put before mankind by the great historian Mr. Wordy! One can enter into Johnson's feeling when, on hearing that Boswell intended to write his biography, he exclaimed, in mingled terror and fury — 'If I thought that he contemplated writing my life, I should render *that* impossible by taking his!' It was something to shudder at, the idea of going down to posterity as represented by a Boswell! But the great lexicographer was mistaken: the Dutch-painter-like biography showed him exactly as he was, the great, little, mighty, weak, manly. babyish mind and heart. And not great men alone, historical personages, have this reason for disquiet and apprehension. Don't you know, my reader not unversed in the ways of life, that it depends entirely on how the story is told, how the thing is represented or misrepresented, whether your conduct on any given occasion shall appear heroic or ridiculous, reasonable or absurd, natural or affected, modest or impudent: and don't you know, too, what a vast number of ill-set people are always ready to give the story the unfavourable turn, to put the matter in the bad light; and how many more, not really ill-set, not really with any malicious intention, are prompted by their love of fun, in relating any act of any acquaintance, to try to set it in a ridiculous light? Your domestic establishment is shabby or unpretending, elegant or tawdry, just as the fancy of the moment may lead your neighbour to put the thing. Your equipage is a neat little turn-out or a shabby attempt, your house is quiet or dull, yourself a genius or a blockhead, just as it may strike your friend on the instant to put the thing. And don't we all know some people — not bad people in the main — who never by any chance put the thing except in the unfavourable way? I have heard the selfsame house called a snug little place and a miserable little hole; the same man called a lively talker and an absurd rattlebrain; the same person called a gentlemanlike man and a missy piece of affectation; the same income called competence and starvation; the same horse called a noble animal and an old white cow :—the entire difference, of course, lay in the fashion in which the narrator chose, from inherent *bonhomie* or inherent verjuice, to put the thing. While

Mr. Bright probably regards it as the most ennobling
occupation of humanity to buy in the cheapest and sell
in the dearest market, Byron said, as implying the
lowest degree of degradation —

> Trust not for freedom to the Franks, —
> They have a king *who buys and sells!*

And it is just the two opposite ways of putting the
same admitted fact, to say that Britain is the first
mercantile community of the world, and to say that we
are a nation of shopkeepers. One way of putting the
fact is the dignified, the other is the degrading. If a
boy plays truant or falls asleep in church, it just depends
on how you put it, or how the story is told, whether you
are to see in all this the natural thoughtlessness of boyhood, or a first step towards the gallows. ' Billy Brown
stole some of my apples,' says a kind-hearted man: 'well,
poor fellow, I daresay he seldom gets any.' ' Billy Brown
stole my apples,' says the severe man : ' ah, the vagabond,
he is born to be hanged.' Sydney Smith put Catholic
Emancipation as common justice and common sense : Dr.
McNeile puts it as a great national sin, and the origin of the
potato disease.   John Foster mentions in his *Diary*, that
he once expostulated with a great, hulking, stupid bumpkin, as to some gross transgression of which he had been
guilty. Little effect was produced on the bumpkin, for
dense stupidity is a great duller of the conscience. Foster
persisted: ' Do not you think,' he said, ' that the Almighty
will be angry at such conduct as yours?' Blockhead as
the fellow was, he could take in the idea of my essay : he
replied, ' That's just as A tak's ut!' But what struck
little Paul Dombey as strange, that the same bells rung
for weddings and for funerals, and that the same sound
was merry or doleful, just as we put it, is true of many

things besides bells. The character of everything we hear or see is reflected upon it from our own minds. The sun *sees* the earth look bright because it first *made* it so. You go to a public meeting, my friend. You make a speech. You get on, you think, uncommonly well. When your auditor Mr. A. or Miss B. goes home, and is asked there what sort of appearance you made, don't you fancy that the reply will be affected in any appreciable degree by the actual fact! It depends entirely on the state of the relator's nerves or digestion, or the passing fancy of the moment, whether you shall be said to have done delightfully or disgustingly; whether you shall be said to have made a brilliant figure, or to have made a fool of yourself. You never can be sure, though you spoke with the tongue of angels, but that ill-nature, peevishness, prejudice, thoughtlessness, may put the case that your speech was most abominable. Do you fancy that you could ever say or do anything that Mr. Snarling could not find fault with, or Miss Limejuice could not misrepresent?

Years ago I was accustomed to frequent the courts of law, and to listen with much interest to the great advocates of that time, as Follett, Wilde, Thesiger, Kelly. Nowhere in the world, I think, is one so deeply impressed with the value of tact and skill in putting things, as in the Court of Queen's Bench at the trial of an important case by a jury. Does not all the enormous difference, as great as that between a country bumpkin and a hog, between Follett and Mr. Briefless, lie simply in their respective powers of putting things? The actual facts, the actual merits of the case, have very little indeed to do with the verdict, compared with the counsel's skill in putting them; the artful marshalling of circumstances, the

casting weak points into shadow, and bringing out strong
points into glaring relief. I remember how I used to
look with admiration at one of these great men when, in
his speech to the jury, he was approaching some circumstance in the case which made dead against him. It was
beautiful to see the intellectual gladiator cautiously
approaching the hostile fact; coming up to it, tossing and
turning it about, and finally showing that it made strongly
in his favour. Now, if that was really so, why did it
look as if it made against him? Why should so much
depend on the way in which he put it? Or, if the fact
was in truth one that made against him, why should it be
possible for a man to put it so that it should seem to make
in his favour, and all without any direct falsification of
facts or arguments, without any of that mere vulgar misrepresentation which can be met by direct contradiction?
Surely it is not a desirable state of matters, that a plausible fellow should be able to explain away some very
doubtful conduct of his own, and by skilful putting of
things should be able to make it seem even to the least
discerning that he is the most innocent and injured of
human beings. And it is provoking, too, when you feel
at once that his defence is a mere intellectual juggle, and
yet, with all your logic, when you cannot just on the
instant tear it to pieces, and put the thing in the light of
truth. Indeed, so well is it understood that by tact and
address you may so put things as to make the worse
appear the better reason, that the idea generally conveyed,
when we talk of putting things, is, that there is something
wrong, something to be adroitly concealed, some weak
point in regard to which dust is to be thrown into too
observant eyes. There is a common impression, not one
of unqualified truth, that when all is above board, there

is less need for skilful putting of the case. Many people think, though the case is by no means so, that truth may always be depended on to tell its own story and produce its due impression. Not a bit of it. However good my case might be, I should be sorry to intrust it to Mr. Numskull, with Sir Fitzroy Kelly on the other side.

It is a coarse and stupid expedient to have recourse to anything like falsification in putting things as they would make best for yourself, reader. And there in no need for it. Unless you have absolutely killed a man and taken his watch, or done something equally decided, you can easily represent circumstances so as to throw a favourable light upon yourself and your conduct. It is a mistake to fancy that in this world a story must be either true or false, a deed either right or wrong, a man either good or bad. There are few questions which can be answered by Yes or No. Almost all actions and events are of mingled character; and there is something to be said on both sides of almost every subject which can be debated. Who does not remember how, when he was a boy, and had done some mischief which he was too honest to deny, he revolved all he had done over and over, putting it in many lights, trying it in all possible points of view, till he had persuaded himself that he had done quite right, or at least that he had done nothing that was so very wrong, after all? There was a lurking feeling, probably, that all this was self-deception; and oh! how our way of putting the case, so favourably to ourselves, vanished into air when our Teacher and Governor sternly called us to account! All those jesuitical artifices were forgotten; and we just felt that we had done wrong, and there was no use trying to justify it.

The noble use of the power of putting things, is when

a man employs that power to give tenfold force to truth.
When you go and hear a great preacher, you sometimes
come away wishing heartily that the impression he made
on you would last : for you feel that though what struck
you so much was not the familiar doctrine, which you
knew quite well before, but the way in which he put it,
still that startling view of things was the right view.
Probably in the pulpit more than anywhere else, we feel
the difference between a man who talks about and about
things — and another man who puts them so that we *feel*
them.   And when one thinks of all the ignorance, want,
and misery which surround us in the wretched dwellings
of the poor, which we know all about but take so coolly, it
is sad to remember that Truth does not make itself felt
as it really is, but depends so sadly for the practical effect
upon the skill with which it is put — upon the tact,
graphic power, and earnest purpose of the man who tells
it.   A landed proprietor will pass a wretched row of cottages on his estate daily for years, yet never think of
making an effort to improve them : who, when the thing
is fairly put to him, will forthwith bestir himself to have
things brought into a better state.   He will wonder how
he could have allowed matters to go on in that unhappy
style so long ; but will tell you truly, that though the
thing was before his eyes, he really never before thought
of it in that light.

   Some people have a happy knack for putting in a
pleasant way everything that concerns themselves.   Mr.
A.'s son gets a poor place as a Bank clerk : his father
goes about saying that the lad has found a fine opening in
business.   The young man is ordained, and gets a curacy
on Salisbury Plain : his father rejoices that there, never
seeing a human face, he has abundant leisure for study,

and for improving his mind. Or, the curacy is in the most crowded part of Manchester or Bethnal Green: the father now rejoices that his son has opportunities of acquiring clerical experience, and of visiting the homes of the poor. Such a man's house is in a well-wooded country: the situation is delightfully sheltered. He removes to a bare district without a tree:—ah! there he has beautiful pure air and extensive views. It is well for human beings when they have the pleasant art of thus putting things; for many, we all know, have the art of putting things in just the opposite way. They look at all things through jaundiced eyes; and as things appear to themselves, so they put them to others. You remember, reader, how once upon a time David Hume, the historian, kindly sent Rousseau a present of a dish of beef-steaks. Rousseau fired at this: he discerned in it a deep-laid insult: he *put it* that Hume, by sending the steaks, meant to insinuate that he, Rousseau, could not afford to buy proper food for himself. Ah, I have known various Rousseaus! They had not the genius, indeed, but they had all the wrongheadedness.

Who does not know the contrasted views of mankind and of life that pervade all the writings of Dickens and of Thackeray? It is the same world that lies before both, but how differently they put it! And look at the accounts in the Blue and Yellow newspapers respectively, of the borough Member's speech to his constituents last night in the Corn Exchange. Judge by the account in the one paper, and he is a Burke for eloquence, a Peel for tact, a Shippen for incorruptible integrity. Judge by the account in the other, and you would wonder where the electors caught a mortal who combines so remarkably ignorance, stupidity, carelessness, inefficiency, and dishonesty. As

for the speech, one journal declares it was fluent, the
other that it was stuttering; one that it was frank, the
other that it was trimming; one that it was sense, the
other that it was nonsense. Nor need it be supposed that
either journal intends deliberate falsehood. Each believes
his own way of putting the case to be the right way; and
the truth, in most instances, doubtless lies midway between.
But in fact, till the end of time, there will be at least two
ways of putting everything. Perhaps the M. P. warmed
with his subject, and threw himself heart and soul into
his speech. Shall we say that he spoke with eloquent
energy, or shall we put it that he bellowed like a bull?
Was he quiet and correct? Then we may choose between saying that he is a classical speaker, and that he
was as stiff as a poker. He made some jokes, perhaps:
take your choice whether you shall call him clever or
flippant, a wit or a buffoon. And so of everybody else.
You know a clever, well-read young woman: you may
either call her such, or talk sneeringly of blue-stockings.
You meet a lively, merry girl, who laughs and talks with
all the frankness of innocence. You would say of her,
my kindly reader, something like what I have just said;
but crabbed Mrs. Backbite will have it that she is a romp,
a boisterous hoyden, of most unformed manners. Perhaps Mrs. Backbite, spitefully shaking her head, says she
trusts, she really hopes, there is no harm in the girl —
but certainly no daughter of *hers* should be allowed to
associate with her. And not merely does the way, favourable or unfavourable, in which the thing shall be put,
depend mainly on the temperament of the person who puts
it — so that you shall know beforehand that Mr. Snarling
will always give the unfavourable view, and Mr. Jollikin
the favourable: but a further element of disturbance is

introduced by the fact, that often the narrator's mood is such, that it is a toss-up, five minutes before he begins to tell his story, whether he shall put the conduct of his hero as good or bad.

Who needs the art of putting things more than the painter of portraits? Who sees so much of the littleness, the petty vanity, the silliness, of mankind? It must be hard for such a man to retain much respect for human nature. The lurking belief in the mind of every man, that he is remarkably good-looking, concealed in daily intercourse with his fellows, breaks out in the painter's studio. And, without positive falsification, how cleverly the artist often contrives to put the features and figure of his sitter in a satisfactory fashion! Have not you seen the portrait of a plain, and even a very ugly person, which was strikingly like, and still very pleasant looking and almost pretty? Have not you seen things so skilfully put, that the little snob looked dignified, the vulgar boor gentlemanlike, the plain-featured woman angelic — and all the while the likeness was accurately preserved?

It seems to me that in the case of many of those fine things which stir the heart and bring moisture to the eye, it depends entirely on the way in which they are put, whether they shall strike us as pathetic or silly, as sublime or ridiculous. The venerable aspect of the dethroned monarch, led in the triumphal procession of the Roman Emperor, and looking indifferently on the scene, as he repeated often the words of Solomon, 'Vanity, vanity, all is vanity,' depends much for the effect it always produces on the reader, upon the stately yet touching fashion in which Gibbon tells the story. So with Hazlitt's often-recurring account of Poussin's celebrated picture, the *Et in Arcadiâ Ego.* As for Burke flinging

the dagger upon the floor of the House of Commons, and
Brougham falling on his knees in the House of Peers,
what a ridiculous representation *Punch* could give of
such things! What shall be said of Addison, often tipsy
in life, yet passing away with the words addressed to his
regardless step-son, 'See in what peace a Christian can
die!' We need not think of things which are essentially
ridiculous, though their perpetrators intended them to be
sublime: as Lord Ellenborough's proclamation about the
Gates of Somnauth, Sir William Codrington's despatch
as to the blowing up of Sebastopol, and all the grand passages in the writings of Mr. Wordy. Let me confess
that I do think it a very unhealthy sign of the times,
this love which now exists of putting grave matters
in a ridiculous light, which produces *Comic Histories of
England*, *Comic Blackstones*, *Comic Parliamentary De-
bates*, *Comic Latin Grammars*, and the like. Dreary
indeed must be the fun of such books; but *that* is not the
worst of them. Yet one cannot seriously object to such a
facetious serial as *Punch*, which represents the funny
element in our sad insular character. *Punch* lives by the
art of putting things, and putting them in a single way;
but how wonderfully well, how successfully, how genially,
he puts all things funnily! But to burlesque *Macbeth*
or *Othello*, to travesty Virgil, to parody the soliloquy in
Hamlet, though it may be putting things in a novel and
amusing way, approaches to the nature of sacrilege.
Sometimes, indeed, the ludicrous way of putting things
has served an admirable purpose; as in the imitations of
Southey's Sapphics and Kotzebue's morality in the
Poetry of the Anti-jacobin. And the ludicrous way of
putting things has sometimes brought them much more
vividly home to ' men's business and bosoms,' as in Syd-

ney Smith's description of the possible results of a French invasion. Nor has it failed to answer the end of most cogent argument, as in his description of Mrs. Partington sweeping back the Atlantic Ocean.

Do not fancy, my friend, that you can by possibility so live that ill-natured folk will not be able to put everything you do unfavourably. The old man with the ass was a martyr to the desire so to act that there should be no possibility of putting what he did as wrong. And when John Gilpin's wife, for fear the neighbours should think her proud, caused the chaise to draw up five doors off, rely upon it some of the neighbours would say she did so in the design of making her carriage the more conspicuous. When you give a dinner-party, and after your guests are gone, sit down and review the progress of the entertainment, thinking how nicely everything went on, do you remember, madam, that at that same moment your guests are seated in their own homes, putting all the circumstances in quite a different way: laughing at your hired greengrocer, who, (you were just saying) looked so like a butler; execrating your champagne, which (you are this moment flattering yourself) passed for the product of the grape and not of the gooseberry; and generally putting yourself, your children, your house, your dinner, your company, your music, into such ridiculous lights, that, if you knew it (which happily you never will), you would wish that you had mingled a little strychnine with the vintage so vilified. Still, it is pleasant to believe that there is no real malice in the way in which most people cut up their friends behind their backs. You really have a very kindly feeling towards Mr. A. or Mrs. B., though you *do* turn them into ridicule in their absence. After laughing at Mr. A. to

4

Mrs. B., you are quite ready to laugh at Mrs. B. to Mr. A. The truth appears to be, that all this is an instance of that reaction which is necessary to human beings. In people's presence politeness requires that you should put everything that concerns them in the most agreeable and favourable way. Impatient of this constraint, you revenge yourself upon it whenever circumstances permit, by putting things in the opposite fashion. I feel not the least enmity towards Mr. Snooks for saying behind my back that my essays are wretched trash. He has frequently said in my presence that they are far superior to anything ever written by Macaulay, Milton, or Shakspeare. I knew that after my dear friend's civility had been subjected to so violent a strain as was implied in his making the latter declaration, it would of necessity fly back, like a released bow, when ever he left me ; and that the first mutual acquaintance he met would have the satisfaction of hearing the case put in a very different way. And no doubt, if my dear friend were put upon his oath, his true opinion of me would transpire as nearly midway between the two ways of putting it respectively before my face and behind my back.

You are a country clergyman, let us say, my reader, with a small parish ; and while you do your duty faithfully and zealously, you spend a spare hour now and then upon a review or a magazine article. You like the thought that thus, from your remote solitude, you are addressing a larger audience than that which you address Sunday by Sunday. You think that reasonable and candid people would say that this is an improving and pleasant way of employing a little leisure time, instead of rusting into stupidity or mooning about blankly, or smoking yourself into vacancy, or reading novels, or listening

to and retailing gossip, or hanging about the streets of
the neighbouring county town, or growing sarcastic and
misanthropic. But don't you remember, my dear friend,
that although *you* put the case in this way, it is highly
probable that some of your acquaintances, whose proffered contributions to the periodical with which you are
supposed to be connected have been ‘ declined with
thanks,’ and whom malignant editors exclude from the
opportunity of enlightening an ungrateful world, may
put the matter very differently indeed? True, you are
always thoroughly prepared with your sermon on Sundays, you are assiduous in your care of the sick and the
aged, you have cottage lectures here and there throughout the parish, you teach classes of children and young
people, you know familiarly the face and the circumstances of every soul of your population, and you honestly give your heart and strength to your sacred calling,
suffering nothing whatever to interfere with *that :* but do
you fancy that all this diligence will prevent Miss Lem-
onjuice and Mr. Flyblow from exclaiming, ‘ Ah, see Mr.
Smith ; isn't it dreadful? See how he neglects his
proper work, and spends his time, his *whole* time, in writing articles for the *Quarterly Review !* It's disgraceful !
The bishop, if he did his duty, would pull him up ! ’

A striking instance of the effect of skilfully putting
things may be found in the diary of Warren Hastings.
The great Governor-General always insisted that his
conduct of Indian affairs had been just and beneficent,
and that the charges brought by Burke and Sheridan
were without foundation in truth. He declared that he
had that conviction in the centre of his being ; that he
was as sure of it as of his own existence. But as he
listened to the opening speech of Burke, he tells us he

saw things in a new light. He felt the spell of the way in which the great orator put things. Could this really be the right way? 'For half an hour,' says Hastings, 'I looked up at Burke in a reverie of wonder, and during that time I actually felt myself the most guilty being upon earth!' But Hastings adds that he did what the boy who has played truant does — he took refuge in his own way of putting things. 'I recurred to my own heart, and there found what sustained me under all this accusation.'

A young lad's choice of a profession depends mainly upon the way in which the life of that profession is put before him. If a boy is to go to the bar, it will be expedient to make the Chancellorship the prominent feature in the picture presented to him. It will be better to keep in the background the lonely evenings in the chambers at the Temple, the weary back-benches in court, the heart-sickening waiting year after year. And the first impression, strongly rooted, will probably last. I love my own profession. I would exchange its life and its work for no other position on earth; but I feel that I owe part of its fascination to the fragrance of boyish fancies of it which linger yet. Blessed be the kind and judicious parent or preceptor, whose skilful putting of things long ago has given to our vocation, whatever it may be, a charm which can overcome the disgust which might otherwise come of the hard realities, the little daily worries, the discouragements and frustrated hopes! How much depends on first impressions — on the way in which a man, a place, a book is put to us for the first time! Something of cheerlessness and dreariness will always linger about even the summer aspect of the house which you first approached when the winter afternoon was closing in, dark, gusty, cold, miserable-looking. What a difference it makes to the little man who is to have a tooth pulled out, whether the dentist approaches with a grievous look, in silence, with the big forceps conspicuous in his hand; or comes up cheerfully, with no display of steel, and says, with a smiling face, ' Come, my little friend, it will be over in a moment; you will hardly have time to feel it; you will stand it like a brick, and mamma will be proud of having such a brave little boy!' Or, if either man or boy has a long task to go through, how much more easily it will be done if it is put in separate divisions than if it is set before one all in a mass! *Divide et impera* states a grand principle in the art of putting things. If your servant is to clear away a mass of snow, he will do it in half the time and with twice the pleasure if you first mark it out into squares, to be cleared away one after the other. By the make of our being we like to have many starts and many arrivals: it does not do to look too far on without a break. I remember the driver of a mail-coach telling me, as I sat on the box through a sixty mile drive, that it would weary him to death to drive that road daily if it were as straight as a railway: he liked the turnings and windings, which put the distance in the form of successive bits. It was sound philosophy in Sydney Smith to advise us, whether physically or morally, to ' take short views.' It would knock you up at once if, when the railway-carriage moved out of the station at Edinburgh, you began to trace in your mind's eye the whole route to London. Never do that. Think first of Dunbar, then of Newcastle, then of York, and putting the thing thus, you will get over the distance without fatigue of mind. What little child would have heart to begin the alphabet, if, before he did so, you put clearly before him all the school and college work of which it is the beginning? The poor little thing would knock up at once, wearied out by your want of skill in putting things. And so it is that Providence, kindly and gradually putting things, wiles us onward, still keeping hope and heart, through the trials and cares of life. Ah, if we had had it put to us at the outset how much we should have to go through, to reach even our present stage in life, we should have been ready to think it the best plan to sit down and die at once! But, in compassion for human weakness, the Great Director and Shower of events practises the Art of Putting Things. Might we not sometimes do so when we do not? When we see some poor fellow grumbling at his lot, and shirking his duty, might not a little skill employed in putting these things in a proper light serve better than merely expressing our contempt or indignation? A single sentence might make him see that what he was complaining of was reasonable and right. It is quite wonderful from what odd and perverse points of view people will look at things: and then things look so very different. The hill behind your house, which you have seen a thousand times, you would not know if you approached it from some unwonted quarter. Now, if you see a man afflicted with a perverse twist of mind, making him put things in general or something in particular in a wrong way, you do him a much kinder turn in directing him how to put things rightly, than if you were a skilful surgeon and cured him of the most fearful squint that ever hid behind blue spectacles.

Did not Franklin go to hear Whitefield preach a charity sermon resolved not to give a penny; and was he not so thoroughly overcome by the great preacher's way of putting the claims of the charity which he was advocating, that he ended by emptying his pockets into the plate?

I daresay Alexander the Great was somewhat staggered in his plans of conquest by Parmenio's way of
putting things. 'After you have conquered Persia, what
will you do?' 'Then I shall conquer India.' 'After
you have conquered India, what will you do?' 'Conquer Scythia.' 'And after you have conquered Scythia,
what will you do?' 'Sit down and rest.' 'Well,' said
Parmenio to the conqueror, 'why not sit down and rest
now?' I trust young Sheridan was proof against his
father's way of putting things, when the young man said
he meant to go down a coalpit. 'Why go down a coalpit!' said Sheridan the elder. 'Merely to be able to say
I have been there.' 'You blockhead,' replied the high-
principled sire, 'what is there to keep you from saying
so without going?'

I remember witnessing a decided success of the art of
putting things. A vulgar rich man, who had recently
bought an estate in Aberdeenshire, exclaimed, 'It is
monstrous hard; I have just had this morning to pay
forty pounds of stipend to the parish minister for my
property. Now, I never enter the parish church (nor
any other, he might have added), and why should I pay
to maintain a Church to which I don't belong?' I omit
the oaths which served as sauce. Now, that was Mr.
Oddbody's way of putting things, and you would say his
case was a hard one. But a quiet man who was present
changed the aspect of matters. 'Is it not true, Mr. Oddbody,' he said, 'that when you bought your estate, its
rental was reckoned after deducting the payment you
mention; that the exact value of your annual payment
to the minister was calculated, and the amount deducted
from the price you paid for the property? And is it not
therefore true, that not a penny of that forty pounds

really comes out of your pocket?' Mr. Oddbody's face elongated. The bystanders unequivocally signified what they thought of him; and as long as he lived he never failed to be remembered as the man who had tried to extort sympathy by false pretences.

To no man is tact in putting things more essential than to the clergyman. An injudicious and unskilful preacher may so put the doctrines which he sets forth as to make them appear revolting and absurd. It is a fearful thing to hear a stupid fellow preaching upon the doctrine of Election. He may so put that doctrine that he shall fill every clever young lad who hears him with prejudices against Christianity, which may last through life. And in advising one's parishioners, especially in administering reproof where needful, let the parish priest, if he would do good, call into play all his tact. With the best intentions, through lack of skill in putting things, he may do great mischief. Let the calomel be concealed beneath the jelly. Not that I counsel sneakiness; *that* is worse than the most indiscreet honesty. There is no need to put things, like the Dean immortalized by Pope, who when preaching in the Chapel Royal, said to his hearers that unless they led religious lives they would ultimately reach a place 'which he would not mention in so polite an assembly.' Nor will it be expedient to put things like the contemptible wretch who, preaching before Louis XIV., said *Nous mourrons tous ;* then, turning to the king, and bowing humbly, *presque tous.* And it is only in addressing quite exceptional congregations that it would now-a-days be regarded as a piece of proper respect for the mighty of the earth, were the preacher, in stating that all who heard him were sinners, to add, by way of reservation, all who have less than a thousand a year.

Any man who approaches the matter with a candid spirit, must be much struck by the difference between the Protestant and the Roman Catholic ways of putting the points at issue between the two great Churches. The Roman prayers are in Latin, for instance. A violent Protestant says that the purpose is to keep the people in ignorance. A strong Romanist tells you that Latin was the universal language of educated men when these prayers were drawn up; and puts it that it is a fine thing to think that in all Romish churches over Christendom the devotions of the people are expressed in the selfsame words. Take keeping back the Bible from the people. To us nothing appears more flagrant than to deprive any man of God's written word. Still the Romanist has something to say for himself. He puts it that there is so much difficulty in understanding much of the Bible — that such pernicious errors have followed from false interpretations of it. Think, even, of the dogma of the infallibility of the Church. The Protestant puts that dogma as an instance of unheard-of arrogance. The Romanist puts it as an instance of deep humility and earnest faith. He says he does not hold that the Church, in her own wisdom, is able to keep infallibly right; but he says that he has perfect confidence that God will not suffer the Church deliberately to fall into error. Here, certainly, we have two very different ways of putting the same things.

But who shall say that there are no more than two ways of putting any incident, or any opinion, or any character? There are innumerable ways — ways as many as are the idiosyncrasies of the men that put them. You have to describe an event, have you? Then you may put it in the plain matter-of-fact way, like the *Times'* re-

porter; or in the sublime way, like Milton and Mr.
Wordy; or in the ridiculous way, like *Punch* (of design),
and Mr. Wordy (unintentionally); or in the romantic
way, like Mr. G. P. R. James; or in the minutely cir-
cumstantial way, like Defoe or Poe; or in the affectedly
simple way, like *Peter Bell;* or in the forcible, knowing way, like Macaulay; or in the genial, manly, good-
humoured way, like Sydney Smith; or in the flippant
way, like Mr. Richard Swiveller, who when he went
to ask for an old gentleman, inquired as to the health
of the ' ancient buffalo ;' or in the lackadaisical way, like
many young ladies; or in the whining, grumbling way,
like many silly people whom it is unnecessary to name ;
or in the pretentious, lofty way, introducing familiarly
many titled names without the least necessity, like many
natives of beautiful Erin.

What nonsense it is to say, as it has been said, that
the effect of anything spoken or written depends upon
the essential thought alone! Why, nine-tenths of the
practical power depends on the way in which it is put.
Somebody has asserted that any thought which is not eloquent in any words whatever, is not eloquent at all. He
might as well have said that black was white. Not to
speak of the charm of the mere music of gracefully mod-
ulated words, and felicitously arranged phrases, how
much there is in beautifully logical treatment, and beautifully clear development, that will interest a cultivated
man in a speech or a treatise, quite irrespective of its
subject. I have known a very eminent man say that it
was a delight to him to hear Follett make a speech, he
did not care about what. The matter was no matter; the
intellectual treat was to watch how the great advocate
put it. And we have all read with delight stories with

no incident and little character, yet which derived a nameless fascination from the way in which they were told. Tell me truly, my fair reader, did you not shed some tears over Dickens's story of Richard Doubledick? Could you have read that story aloud without breaking down? And yet, was there ever a story with less in it? But how beautifully Dickens put what little there was, and how the melody of the closing sentences of the successive paragraphs lingers on the ear! And you have not forgotten the exquisite touches with which Mrs. Stowe put so simple a matter as a mother looking into her dead baby's drawer. I have known an attempt at the pathetic made on a kindred topic provoke yells of laughter; but I could not bear the woman, and hardly the man, who could read Mrs. Stowe's putting of that simple conception without the reverse of smiles. Many readers, too, will not forget how more sharply they have seen many places and things, from railway engine sheds to the Britannia Bridge, when put by the graphic pen of Sir Francis Head. That lively baronet is the master of clear, sharp presentment.

I have not hitherto spoken of such ways of putting things as were practised in King Hudson's railway reports, or in those of the Glasgow Western Bank, cooked to make things pleasant by designed misrepresentation. So far we have been thinking of comparatively innocent variations in the ways of putting things — of putting the best foot foremost in a comparatively honest way. But how much intentional misrepresentation there is in British society! How few people can tell a thing exactly as they saw it! It goes in one colour, and comes out another, like light through tinted glass. It is rather amusing, by the way, when a friend comes and tells you a story which he heard from yourself, but so put that you hardly know it again. Unscrupulous putters of things should have good memories. There is no reckoning the ways in which, by varying the turn of an expression, by a tone or look, an entirely false view may be given of a conversation, a transaction, or an event. A lady says to her cook, You are by no means overworked. The cook complains in the servants' hall that her mistress said she had nothing to do. Lies, in the sense of pure inventions, are not common, I believe, among people with any claim to respectability; but it is perfectly awful to think how great a part of ordinary conversation, especially in little country towns, consists in putting things quite differently from the actual fact; in short, of wilful misrepresentation. Many people cannot resist the temptation to deepen the colours, and strengthen the lines, of any narration, in order to make it more telling. Unluckily, things usually occur in life in such a manner as just to miss what would give them a point and make a good story of them; and the temptation is strong to make them, by the deflection of a hair's breadth, what they ought to have been.

It is sad to think, that in ninety-nine out of every hundred cases in which things are thus untruly put, the representation is made worse than the reality. Few old ladies endeavour, by their imaginative putting of things, to exhibit their acquaintances as wiser, better, and more amiable, than the fact. An exception may be made whenever putting her friends and their affairs in a dignified light would reflect credit upon the old lady herself. *Then,* indeed, their income is vast, their house is magnificent, their horses are Eclipses, their conversation is brilliant, their attention to their friends unwearying and indescribable. Alas for our race: that we lean to evil rather than

to good, and that it is so much more easy and piquant to
pitch into a man than to praise him!

Let us rejoice that there is one happy case in which
the way of putting things, though often false, is always
favourable. I mean the accounts which are given in
country newspapers of the character and the doings
the great men of the district. I often admire the country
editor's skill in putting all things (save the speech of the
opposition M.P., as already mentioned) in such a rosy
light; nor do I admire his genial *bonhomie* less than his
art. If a marquis makes a stammering speech, it is sure
to be put as most interesting and eloquent. If the rector preaches a dull and stupid charity sermon, it is put
as striking and effective. A public meeting, consisting
chiefly of empty benches, is put as most respectably
attended. A gift of a little flannel and coals at Christmas-time, is put as seasonable munificence. A bald and
seedy building, just erected in the High-street, is put as
chaste and classical; an extravagant display of gingerbread decoration is put as gorgeous and magnificent. In
brief, what other men heartily wish this world were, the
conductors of local prints boldly declare that it is.
Whatever they think a great man would like to be
called, *that* they make haste to call him. Happy fellows,
if they really believe that they live in such a world and
among such beings as they put! Their gushing heart
is too much for even their sharp head, and they see all
things glorified by the sunshine of their own exceeding
amiability.

The subject greatens on me, but the paper dwindles:
the five-and-forty fair expanses of foolscap are darkened
at last. It would need a volume, not an essay, to do this
matter justice. Sir Bulwer Lytton has declared, in

pages charming but too many, that the world's great question is, WHAT WILL HE DO WITH IT? I shall not debate the point, but simply add, that only second to that question in comprehensive reach and in practical importance is the question — HOW WILL HE PUT IT?

CHAPTER III.

CONCERNING TWO BLISTERS OF HUMANITY:

BEING THOUGHTS ON PETTY MALIGNITY AND PETTY TRICKERY.

IT is highly improbable that any reader of ordinary power of imagination, would guess the particular surface on which the paper is spread whereon I am at the present moment writing. Such is the reflection which flows naturally from my pencil's point as it begins to darken this page. I am seated on a manger, in a very light and snug stable, and my paper is spread upon a horse's face. occupying the flat part between the eyes. You would not think, unless you tried, what an extensive superficies may there be found. If you put a thin book next the horse's skin, you will write with the greater facility: and you will find, as you sit upon the edge of the manger, that the animal's head occupies a position which, as regards height and slope, is sufficiently convenient. His mouth, it may be remarked, is not far from your knees, so that it would be highly inexpedient to attempt the operation with a vicious, biting brute, or indeed with any horse of whose temper you are not well assured. But you, my good Old Boy (for such is the quadruped's name). *you* would not bite your master. Too many carrots have you received from his hand; too

many pieces of bread have you licked up from his
extended palm. A thought has struck me which I wish
to preserve in writing, though indeed at this rate it will
be a long time before I work my way to it. I am waiting here for five minutes till my man-servant shall return
with something for which he has been sent, and wherefore should even five minutes be wasted? Life is not
very long, and the minutes in which one can write with
ease are not very many. And perhaps the newness of
such a place of writing may communicate something of
freshness to what is traced by a somewhat jaded hand.
You winced a little, Old Boy, as I disposed my book
and this scrap of an old letter on your face, but now you
stand perfectly still. On either side of this page I see a
large eye looking down wistfully; above the page a pair
of ears are cocked in quiet curiosity, but with no indication of fear. Not that you are deficient in spirit, my
dumb friend; you will do your twelve miles an hour
with any steed within some miles of you; but a long
course of kindness has gentled you as well as Mr. Rarey
could have done, though no more than seven summers
have passed over your head. Let us ever, kindly reader,
look with especial sympathy and regard at any inferior
animal on which the doom of man has fallen, and which
must eat its food, if not in the sweat of its brow, then in
that of its sides. Curious, that a creature should be
called all through life to labour, for which yet there
remains no rest! As for us human beings, we can understand and we can bear with much evil, and many trials
and sorrows here, because we are taught that all these
form the discipline which shall prepare us for another
world. a world that shall set this right. But for you, my
poor fellow-creature, I think with sorrow as I write here

upon your head, there remains no such immortality as
remains for me. What a difference between us! You
to your sixteen or eighteen years here, and then oblivion.
I to my threescore and ten, and then eternity! Yes, the
difference is immense; and it touches me to think of your
life and mine, of your doom and mine. I know a house
where, at morning and evening prayer, when the household assembles, among the servants there always walks
in a certain shaggy little dog, who listens with the
deepest attention and the most solemn gravity to all that
is said, and then, when prayers are over, goes out again
with his friends. I cannot witness that silent procedure
without being much moved by the sight. Ah, my fellow-creature, *this* is something in which you have no
part! Made by the same Hand, breathing the same air,
sustained like us by food and drink, you are witnessing
an act of ours which relates to interests that do not con-
cern you, and of which you have no idea. And so, here
we are, you standing at the manger, Old Boy, and I
sitting upon it; the mortal and the immortal; close
together; your nose on my knee, my paper on your
head; yet with something between us broader than the
broad Atlantic. As for you, if you suffer here, there is
no other life to make up for it. Yet it would be well if
many of those who are your betters in the scale of creation, fulfilled their Creator's purposes as well as you.
He gave you strength and swiftness, and you use these
to many a valuable end: not many of the superior race
will venture to say that they turn the powers God gave
them to account as worthy of their nature. If it come
to the question of deserving, you deserve better than me.
Forgive me, my fellow-creature, if I have sometimes
given you an angry flick, when you shied a little at a

5

pig or a donkey. But I know you bear me no malice; you forget the flicks (they are not many), and you think rather of the bread and the carrots, of the times I have pulled your ears, and smoothed your neck, and patted your nose. And forasmuch as this is all your life, I shall do my very best to make it a comfortable one. *Happiness*, of course, is something which you can never know. Yet, my friend and companion through many weary miles, you shall have a deep-littered stall, and store of corn and hay so long as I can give them; and may this hand never write another line if it ever does you wilful injury!

Into this paragraph has my pencil of its own accord rambled, though it was taken up to write about something else. And such is the happiness of the writer of essays: he may wander about the world of thought at his will. The style of the essayist has attained what may be esteemed the perfection of freedom, when it permits him, in writing upon any subject whatsoever, to say whatever may occur to him upon any other subject. And truly it is a pleasing thing for one long trammelled by the requirements of a rigorous logic, and fettered by thoughts of symmetry, connexion, and neatness in the discussion of his topic, to enter upon a fresh field where all these things go for nothing, and to write for readers many of whom would never notice such characteristics if they were present, nor ever miss them if they were absent. There is all the difference between plodding wearily along the dusty highway, and rambling through green fields, and over country stiles, leisurely, saunteringly, going nowhere in particular. You would not wish to be always desultory and rambling, but it is pleasant to be so now and then. And there is a delightful freedom about the feeling that you are producing an entirely unsymmetrical composition. It is fearful work, if you have a thousand thoughts and shades of thought about any subject, to get them all arranged in what a logician would call their proper places. It is like having a dissected puzzle of a thousand pieces given you in confusion, and being required to fit all the little pieces of ivory into their box again. By most men this work of orderly and symmetrical composition can be done well only by its being done comparatively slowly. In the case of ordinary folk the mind is a machine, which may indeed, by putting on extra pressure, be worked faster; but the result is the deterioration of the material which it turns off. It is an extraordinary gift of nature and training, when a man is like Follett, who, after getting the facts of an involved and intricate case into his mind only at one or two o'clock in the morning, could appear in Court at nine A.M., and there proceed to state the case and all his reasonings upon it, with the very perfection of logical method, every thought in its proper place, and all this at the rate of rapid extempore speaking. The difference between the rate of writing and that of speaking, with most men, makes the difference between producing good material and bad. A great many minds can turn off a fair manufacture at the rate of writing, which, when over-driven to keep pace with speaking, will bring forth very poor stuff indeed. And besides this, most people cannot grasp a large subject in all its extent and its bearings, and get their thoughts upon it marshalled and sorted, unless they have at least two or three days to do so. At first all is confusion and indefiniteness, but gradually things settle into order. Hardly any mind, by any effort, can get them into order quickly. If at all, it is by a tremendous exertion; whereas the mind has a curious power, without any perceptible effort, of arranging in order thoughts upon any subject, if you give it time. Who that has ever written his ideas on some involved point but knows this? You begin by getting up information on the subject about which you are to write. You throw into the mind, as it were, a great heap of crude, unordered material. From this book and that book, from this review and that newspaper, you collect the observations of men who have regarded your subject from quite different points of view, and for quite different purposes; you throw into the mind cartload after cartload of facts and opinions, with a despairing wonder how you will ever be able to get that huge, contradictory, vague mass into anything like shape and order. And if, the minute you had all your matter accumulated, you were called on to state what you knew or thought upon the subject, you could not do so for your life in any satisfactory manner. You would not know where to begin, or how to go on; it would be all confusion and bewilderment. Well, do not make the slightest effort. What is impossible now will be quite easy by and bye. The peas, which cost a sovereign a pint at Christmas, are quite cheap in their proper season. Go about other things for three or four days: and at the end of that time you will be aware that the machinery of your mind, voluntarily and almost unconsciously playing, has sorted and arranged that mass of matter which you threw into it. Where all was confusion and uncertainty, all is now order and clearness; and you see exactly where to begin, and what to say next, and where and how to leave off.

The probability is, that all this has not been done without an effort, and a considerable amount of labour. But then, instead of the labour having been all at once, it has been very much subdivided. The subject was simmering in your mind all the while, though you were hardly aware of it. Time after time, you took a little run at it, and saw your way a little farther through it. But this multitude of little separate and momentary efforts does not count for much ; though in reality, if they were all put together, they would probably be found to have amounted to as much as the prolonged exertion which would at a single heat have attained the end. A large result, attained by innumerable little, detached efforts, seems as if it had been attained without any effort at all.

I love a parallel case ; and I must take such cases from my ordinary experience. Yesterday, passing a little cottage by the wayside, I perceived at the door the carcase of a very large pig extended on a table. Approaching, as is my wont, the tenant of the cottage and owner of the pig, I began to converse with him on the size and fatness of the poor creature which had that morning quitted its sty for ever. It had been *shot*, he told me ; for such, in these parts, is at present the most approved way of securing for swine an end as little painful as may be. I admired the humanity of the intention, and hoped that it might be crowned with success. Then my friend, the proprietor of the bacon, began to discourse on the philosophy of the rearing of pigs by labouring men. No doubt, he said, the four pounds, or thereabout, which he would get for his pig, would be a great help to a hard-working man with five or six little children. But after all, he remarked, it was likely enough that during the months of the pig's life, it had bit by bit consumed and cost him as much as he would get for it now. But then, he went on, it cost us *that* in little sums we hardly felt ; while the four pounds it will sell for come all in a lump, and seem to give a very perceptible profit. Successive unfelt sixpences had mounted up to that considerable sum; even as five hundred little unfelt mental efforts had mounted up to the large result of sorting and methodizing the mass of crude fact and opinion of which we were thinking a little while ago.

Having worked through this preliminary matter (which will probably be quite enough for some readers, even as the Solan goose which does but whet the appetite of the Highlander, annihilates that of the Sassenach), I now come to the subject which was in my mind when I began to write on the horse's head. I am not in the stable now; for the business which detained me there is long since despatched: and after all, it is more convenient to write at one's study-table. I wish to say something concerning certain evils which press upon humanity; and which are to the feeling of the mind very much what a mustard-blister is to the feeling of the body. To the healthy man or woman they probably do not do much serious harm; but they maintain a very constant irritation. They worry and annoy. It is extremely interesting, in reading the published diaries of several great and good men, to find them recording on how many days they were put out of sorts, vexed and irritated, and rendered unfit for their work of writing, by some piece of petty malignity or petty trickery. How well one can sympathize with that good and great, and honest and amiable and sterling man, Dr. Chalmers, when we find him recording in his diary, when he was a country parish minister, how he was unable to make satisfactory progress with his sermon one whole forenoon, because some tricky and over-reaching farmer in the neighbourhood drove two

calves into a field of his glebe, where the great man
found them in the morning devouring his fine young
clover! There was something very irritating and annoying in the paltry dishonesty. And the sensitive machinery of the good man's mind could not work sweetly when
the gritty grains of the small vexation were fretting its
polished surface. Let it be remarked in passing, that the
peculiar petty dishonesty of driving cattle into a neighbouring proprietor's field, is far from being an uncommon
one. And let me inform such as have suffered from it
of a remedy against it which has never been known to
fail. If the trespassing animals be cows, wait till the
afternoon : then have them well milked, and send them
home. If horses, let them instantly be put in carts, and
sent off ten miles to fetch lime. A sudden strength will
thenceforward invest your fences; and from having been
so open that no efforts on the part of your neighbours
could keep their cattle from straying into your fields, you
will find them all at once become wholly impervious.

But, to return, I maintain that these continual blisters,
of petty trickery and petty malignity, produce a very
vexatious effect. You are quite put about at finding out
one of your servants in some petty piece of dishonesty
or deception. You are decidedly worried if you happen
to be sitting in a cottage where your coachman does not
know that you are ; and if you discern from the window
that functionary, who never exercises your horses in your
presence save at a walk, galloping them furiously over
the hard stones; shaking their legs and endangering
their wind. It is annoying to find your haymakers
working desperately hard and fast when you appear in
the field, not aware that from amid a little clump of wood
you had discerned them a minute before reposing quietly

upon the fragrant heaps, and possibly that you had overheard them saying that they need not work very hard, as
they were working for a gentleman. You would not have
been displeased had you found them honestly resting on
the sultry day : but you are annoyed by the small attempt
to deceive you. Such pieces of petty trickery put you
more out of sorts than you would like to acknowledge : and
you are likewise ashamed to discover that you mind so
much as you do, when some goodnatured friend comes
and informs you how Mr. Snarling has been misrepresenting something you have said or done; and Miss
Limejuice has been telling lies to your prejudice. You
are a clergyman, perhaps; and you said in your sermon
last Sunday that, strong Protestant as you are, you believed that many good people may be found in the
Church of Rome. Well, ever since then, Miss Limejuice
has not ceased to rush about the parish, exclaiming in
every house she entered, 'Is not this awful? Here, on
Sunday morning, the rector said that we ought all to
become Roman Catholics! One comfort is, the Bishop
is to have him up directly. I was always sure that he
was a Jesuit in disguise.' Or you are a country gentleman : and at an election-time you told one of your tenants
that such a candidate was your friend, and that you
would be happy if he could conscientiously vote for him,
but that he was to do just what he thought right. Ever
since, Mr. Snarling has been spreading a report that you
went, drunk, into your tenant's house, that you thrust
your fist in his face, that you took him by the collar
and shook him, that you told him that, if he did not vote
for your friend, you would turn him out of your farm,
and send his wife and children to the workhouse. For
in such playful exaggerations do people in small commu-

nities not unfrequently indulge. Now you are vexed
when you hear of such pieces of petty malignity. They
don't do you much harm; for most people whose opinion you value, know how much weight to attach to any
statement of Miss Limejuice and Mr. Snarling; and if
you try to do your duty day by day where God has put
you, and to live an honest, christian life, it will go hard but
you will live down such malicious vilification. But these
things worry. They act as blisters, in short, without the
medicinal value of blisters. And little contemptible worries do a great deal to detract from the enjoyment of life.
To meet great misfortunes we gather up our endurance,
and pray for Divine support and guidance; but as for
small blisters, the *insect cares* (as James Montgomery
called them) of daily life, we are very ready to think
that they are too little to trouble the Almighty with them,
or even to call up our fortitude to face them. This is not
a sermon; but let it be said that whosoever would learn
how rightly to meet the perpetually-recurring worries of
workday existence, should read an admirable little treatise by Mrs. Stowe, the authoress of *Uncle Tom's Cabin,*
entitled *Earthly Care a Heavenly Discipline.* The price
of the work is one penny, but it contains advice which is
worth an uncounted number of pence. Nor, as I think,
are there to be found many more corroding and vexatious agencies than those which have been already named.
To know that your servants, or your humbler neighbours, or your tradespeople, or your tenantry, or your
scholars, are practising upon you a system of petty deception; or to be informed (as you are quite sure to be
informed) how such and such a mischievous (or perhaps
only thoughtless) acquaintance is putting words into your
mouth which you never uttered, or abusing your wife and

children, or gloating over your failure to get into parliament, or the lameness of your horses, or the speech you stuck in at the recent public dinner; — all these things are pettily vexatious to many men. No doubt, over-sensitiveness is abundantly foolish. Some folk appear not merely to be thinskinned, but to have been (morally) deprived of any skin at all; and such folk punish themselves severely enough for their folly. They wince when any one comes near them. The Pope may go wrong, but they cannot. It is treasonable, it is inexpiable sin, to hint that, in judgment, in taste, in conduct, it is possible for them to deviate by a hair's-breadth from the right line of perfection. Indeed, I believe that no immorality, no criminality, would excite such wrath in some men, as to tread upon a corner of their self-conceit. Yet it is curious how little sympathy these over-sensitive people have for the sensitiveness of other people. You would say they fancied that the skin of which they have been denuded has been applied to thicken to rhinoceros callousness the moral hide of other men. They speak their mind freely to their acquaintances of their acquaintances' belongings. They will tell an acquaintance (they have no friends, so I must repeat the word) that he made a very absurd speech, that she sung very badly, that the situation of his house (which he cannot leave) is abominably dull, that his wife is foolish and devoid of accomplishments, that her husband is a man of mediocre abilities, that her little boy has red hair and a squint, that the potatoes he rears are abominably bad, that he is getting unwieldily stout, that his riding-horse has no hair on his tail. All these things, and a hundred more, such people say with that mixture of dulness of perception and small malignity of nature which go to make what is vulgarly called a person who 'speaks his mind.' The right way to meet such folk is by an instant reciprocal action. Just begin to speak your mind to them, and see how they look. Tell them, with calm politeness, that before expressing their opinion so confidently, they should have considered what their opinion was worth. Tell them that civility requires that you should listen to their opinion, but that they may be assured that you will act upon your own. Tell them what you think of their spelling, their punctuation, their features, their house, their carpets, their window-curtains, their general standing as members of the human race. How blue they will look! They are quite taken aback when the same petty malignity and insolence which they have been accustomed for years to carry into their neighbours' territory is suddenly directed against their own. And you will find that not only are they themselves skinlessly sensitive, but that their sensitiveness is not bounded by their own mental and corporeal being; and that it extends to the extreme limits of their horses' legs, to the very top of their chimney-pots, to every member of the profession which was honored by the choice of their great-grandfather.

You have observed, no doubt, that the mention of over-sensitive people acted upon the writer's train of thought as a pair of *points* in the rails act upon a railway train. It shunted me off the main line; and in these remarks on people who talk their mind, I have been, so to speak, running along a siding. To go back to the point where I left the line, I observe, that although it is very foolish to mind much about such small matters as being a little cheated day by day, and a good deal misrepresented now and then by amiable acquaintances, still it is the fact that even upon people of a healthful temperament such things act as moral blisters, as moral pebbles in one's boots. The petty malignity which occasionally annoys you is generally to be found among your acquaintances, and people of the same standing with yourself; while the petty trickery for the most part exists in the case of your inferiors. I think one always feels the better for looking any small evil of life straight in the face. To define a thing, to fix its precise dimensions, almost invariably makes it look a good deal smaller. Indefiniteness much increases apparent size; so let us now examine the size and the operation of these blisters of humanity.

As for petty malignity, my reader, have you not seen a great deal of it? There are not many men who appear to love their neighbours as themselves. No one enjoys a misfortune or disappointment which befals himself: but there is too much truth in the smart Frenchman's saying, that there is something not entirely disagreeable to us in the misfortunes of even our very best friends. The malignity, indeed, is petty. It is only in small matters. And it is rather in feeling than in action. Even that sour Miss Limejuice, though she would be very glad if your horse fell lame or your carriage upset, would not see you drowning without doing her very best to save you. Ah, poor thing! she is not so bad, after all. This has been to her but a bitter world; and no wonder if she is, on the surface, a little embittered by it. But when you get fairly through the surface of her nature, as real misfortunes and trials do, there is kindliness about that withered heart yet. She would laugh at you if you broke down in your speech on the hustings; but she would throw herself in the path of a pair of furious runaway horses, to save a little child from their trampling feet. I do not believe that among ordinary people, even in a gossiping little country town, there is much real and serious malice in this world. I cling to that belief; for if many men were truly as mischievous as you would sometimes think when you hear them talk, one might turn misanthrope and hermit at once. There is hardly a person you know who would do you any material injury; not one who would cut down your roses, or splash your entrance-gate with mud: not one who would not gladly do you a kind turn if it lay within his power. Yet there are a good many who would with satisfaction repeat any story which might be a little to your disadvantage; which might tend to prove that you are rather silly, rather conceited, rather ill-informed. You have various friends who would not object to show up any ridiculous mistake you might happen to make; who would never forget the occasion on which it appeared that you had never heard of the *Spectator* or Sir Roger de Coverley, or that you thought that Mary Queen of Scots was the mother of George III. You have various friends who would preserve the remembrance of the day on which the rector rebuked you for talking in church; or on which your partner and yourself fell flat on the floor of the ball-room at the county town of Oatmealshire, in the midst of a galop. You have various goodnatured friends to whom it would be a positive enjoyment to come and tell you what a very unfavourable opinion Mr. A and Mrs. B and Miss C had been expressing of your talents, character, and general conduct. How true was the remark of Sir Fretful Plagiary, that it is quite unnecessary for any man to take pains to learn anything bad that has been said about him, inasmuch as it is quite sure to be told him by some goodnatured friend or other! You have various acquaintances who will be very much gratified when a rainy day spoils the pic-nic to which you have invited a large party ; and who will be perfectly enraptured, if you have hired a steamboat for the occasion, and if the day proves so stormy that every soul on board is deadly sick. And indeed it is satisfactory to think that in our uncertain climate, where so many festal days are marred as to their enjoyment by drenching showers, there is compensation for the sufferings of the people who are ducked, in the enjoyment which that fact affords to very many of their friends. By taking a larger view of things, you discover that there is good in everything. You were Senior Wrangler : you just miss being made a Bishop at forty-two. No doubt that was a great disappointment to yourself; but think what a joy it was to some scores of fellows whom you beat at College, and who hate you accordingly. Some months ago a proprietor in this county was raised to the peerage. His tenantry were entertained at a public dinner in honour of the event. The dinner was held in a large canvas pavilion. The day came. It was fearfully stormy, and torrents of rain fell. A perfect shower-bath was the portion of many of the guests ; and finally the canvas walls and roof broke loose, smashed the crockery, and whelmed the feast in fearful ruin. During the nine days which followed, the first remark made by every one you met was, ' What a sad pity about the storm spoiling the dinner at Stuckup Place ! ' And the countenance of every one who thus expressed his sorrow was radiant with joy ! And quite natural too. They would have felt real regret had the new peer been drowned or shot : but the petty malignity which dwells in the human bosom made them rejoice at the small but irritating misfortune which had befallen.

Shall I confess it, *mea culpa, mea maxima culpa*, I re-joiced in common with all my fellow-creatures! I was ashamed of the feeling. I wished to ignore it and extin-guish it; but there was no doubt that it was there. And if Lord Newman was a person of enlarged and philosoph-ic mind, he would have rejoiced that a small evil, which merely mortified himself and gave bad colds to his tenan-try, afforded sensible pleasure to several thousands of his fellow-men. Yes, my reader: it is well that a certain measure of small malice is ingrained in our fallen nature. For thus some pleasure comes out of almost all pain; some good from almost all evil. Your little troubles vex you, but they gratify your friends. Your horse comes down and smashes his knees. No doubt, to you and your groom it is unmingled bitterness. But every man within several miles, whose horse's knees have already been smashed, hails the event as a real blessing to himself. You signally fail of getting into Parliament, though you stood for a county in which you fancied that your own influ-ence and that of your connexions was all-powerful. No doubt, you are sadly mortified. No doubt, you do not look like yourself for several weeks. But what chuckles of joy pervade the hearts and faces of five hundred fel-lows who have no chance of getting into the House them-selves, and who dislike you for your huge fortune, your grand house, your countless thoroughbreds, your insuffer-able dignity, and your general forgetfulness of the place where you grew, which by those around you is perfectly well remembered. And while it is true that even people of a tolerably benevolent nature do not really feel any great regret at any mortification or disappointment which befals a wealthy and pretentious neighbour, it is also certain that a greater number of folk do actually gloat over any event which humbles the wealthy and pretentious man. You find them, with a malignant look, putting the case on a benevolent footing. 'This taking-down will do him a great deal of good: he will be much the wiser and better for it.' It is not uncharitable to believe, that in many cases in which such sentiments are expressed, the true feeling of the speaker is rather one of satisfaction, at the pain which the disappointment certainly gives, than of satisfaction at the beneficial discipline which may possibly result from it. The thing *said* amounts to this: 'I am glad that Mr. Richman has got a taking-down, because the taking-down, though painful at the time, is in fact a blessing.' The thing *felt* amounts to this: 'I am glad that Mr. Richman has got a taking-down, because I know it will make him very miserable.' Every one who reads this page knows that this is so. Ah, my malicious acquaintances, if you know that the sentiment you entertain is one that would provoke universal execration if it were expressed, does not *that* show that you ought not to entertain it?

I have said that I do not believe there is much real malignity among ordinary men and women. It is only at the petty misfortunes of men's friends that they ever feel this unamiable satisfaction. When great sorrow befals a friend, all this unworthy feeling goes; and the heart is filled with true sympathy and kindness. A man must be very bad indeed if this is not the case. It strikes me as something fiend-like rather than human, Byron's savage exultation over the melancholy end of the great and amiable Sir Samuel Romilly. Romilly had given him offence by acting as legal adviser to some whom Byron regarded as his enemies. But it was babyish to cherish enmity for such a cause as that; and it was diabolical to rejoice at the sad close of that life of usefulness and honour. It was not good in James Watt, writing in old age an account of one of his many great inventions, to name very bitterly a man who had pirated it; and to add, with a vengeful chuckle. that the poor man was 'afterwards hanged.' No private ground of offence should make you rejoice that your fellow-creature was hanged. You may justifiably rejoice in such a case only when the man hanged was a public offender, and an enemy of the race. Throw up your hat, if you please, when Nana Sahib stretches the hemp at last! *That* is all right. He never did harm to you individually: but you think of Cawnpore; and it is quite fit that there should be a bitter, burning satisfaction felt at the condign punishment of one whose punishment eternal justice demands. What is the use of the gallows, if not for that incarnate demon? I think of the poor sailors who were present at the trial of a bloodthirsty pirate of the Cuban coast. 'I suppose,' said the one doubtingly to the other, ' the devil will get that fellow.' ' I should hope so,' was the unhesitating reply; ' or what would be the use of having any devil !'

But some real mischievous malice there is, even among people who bear a creditable character. I have occasionally heard old ladies (very few) tearing up the character of a friend with looks as deadly as though their weapon had been a stiletto, instead of that less immediately fatal instrument of offence, concerning which a very high authority informs us, that in some cases it is 'set on fire of hell.' Ah, you poor girl, who danced three times (they call it nine) with Mr. A. at the Assembly last night, happily you do not know the venomous way in which certain spiteful tabbies are pitching into you this morning! And

6

you, my friend, who drove along Belvidere-place (the fashionable quarter of the county town) yesterday, in your new drag with the new harness and the pair of thoroughbreds, and fancied that you were charming every eye and heart, if you could but hear how your equipage and yourself were scarified last evening, as several of your elderly female acquaintances sipped together the cup that cheers! How they brought up the time that you were flogged at the public school, and the term you were rusticated at Oxford! Even the occasion was not forgotten on which your grandfather was believed, forty years since, to have rather done Mr. Softly in the matter of a glandered steed. And the peculiar theological tenets of your grandmother were set forth in a fashion that would have astounded that good old lady. And you, who are so happily occupied in building in that beautiful woodland spot that graceful Elizabethan house, little you know how bitterly some folk, dwelling in hideous seedy mansions, sneer at you and your gimcracks, and your Gothic style in which you 'go back to barbarism.' You, too, my friend, lately made a Queen's counsel, or a judge, or a bishop, if the shafts of envy could kill you, you would not live long. It is curious, by the way, how detraction follows a man when he first attains to any eminent place in State or Church; how keenly his qualifications are canvassed; how loudly his unfitness for his situation is proclaimed; and how, when a few months have passed, everybody gets quite reconciled to the appointment, and accepts it as one of the conditions of human affairs. Sometimes, indeed, the right man, by emphasis, is put in the right place; so unquestionably the right man that even envy is silenced: as when Lord St. Leonards was made Lord Chancellor, or when Mr. Melvill was appointed to preach before the House of Commons. But even when men who have been plucked at the University were made bishops, or princes who had never seen a gun fired in anger field-marshals, or briefless barristers judges, although a general outcry arose at the time, it very speedily died away. When you find a man actually in a place, you do not weigh his claims to be there so keenly as if you were about to appoint him to it. If a resolute premier made Tom Spring a chief-justice, I doubt not that in six weeks the country would be quite accustomed to the fact, and accept it as part of the order of nature. How else is it that the nation is content to have blind and deaf generals placed in high command, and infirm old admirals going to sea who ought to be going to bed?

It is a sad fact that there are men and women who will, without much investigation as to its truth, repeat a story to the prejudice of some man or woman whom they know. They are much more critical in weighing the evidence in support of a tale to a friend's credit and advantage. I do not think they would absolutely invent such a calumnious narrative; but they will repeat, if it has been told them, what, if they do not know it to be false, they also do not know to be true, and strongly suspect to be false.

My friend Mr. C., rector of a parish in Hampshire, has a living of about five hundred a year. Some months ago he bought a horse, for which he paid fifty pounds. Soon after he did so, I met a certain malicious woman who lived in his neighbourhood. 'So,' said she, with a look far from benevolent, 'Mr. C. has gone and paid a hundred pounds for a horse! Monstrous extravagance for a man with his means and with a family.' 'No, Miss Verjuice,' I replied: 'Mr. C. did not pay nearly the sum you mention for his horse: he paid no more for it than a man

of his means could afford.'   Miss Verjuce was not in the
least discomfited by the failure of her first shaft of petty
malignity.   She had another in her quiver which she instantly discharged.   'Well,' said she, with a face of deadly
ferocity, 'if Mr. C. did not pay a hundred pounds for his
horse, *at all events he said he did!*'   This was the drop
too much.   I told Miss Verjuice, with considerable as-
perity, that my friend was incapable of petty vapouring
and petty falsehood; and in my book, from that day forward, there has stood a black cross against the individual's name.

Egypt, it seems, is the country where malevolence in
the sense of pure envy of people who are better off, is
most prevalent and is most feared.   People there believe
that the envious eye does harm to those on whom it
rests.   Thus, they are afraid to possess fine houses,
furniture, and horses, lest they should excite envy and
bring misfortune.   And when they allow their children
to go out for a walk, they send them dirty and ill-dressed,
for fear the covetous eye should injure them: —

At the bottom of this superstition is an enormous prevalence of
envy among the lower Egyptians.   You see it in all their fictions.
Half of the stories told in the coffee-shops by the professional story-
tellers, of which the *Arabian Nights* are a specimen, turn on malevolence.   Malevolence, not attributed, as it would be in European
fiction, to some insult or injury inflicted by the person who is its
object, but to mere envy: envy of wealth, or of the other means of
enjoyment, honourably acquired and liberally used.*

A similar envy, no doubt, occasionally exists in this
country; but people here are too enlightened to fancy
that it can do them any harm.   Indeed, so far from
standing in fear of exciting envy by their display of
possessions and advantages, some people feel much grati-

* Archbishop Whately's *Bacon*, p. 97.

fied at the thought of the amount of envy and malignity
which they are likely to excite. 'Wont old Hunks turn
green with fury,' said a friend to me, 'the first time I
drive up to his door with those horses?' They were
indeed beautiful animals; but their proprietor appeared
to prize them less for the pleasure they afforded himself,
than for the mortification they would inflict on certain of
his neighbours. 'Wont Mrs. Grundy burst with spite
when she sees this drawing-room?' was the remark of
my lately-married cousin Henrietta, when she showed
me that very pretty apartment for the first time. 'Wont
Snooks be ferocious,' said Mr. Dryasdust the book-col-
lector, 'when he hears that I have got this almost unique
edition?' Ah, my fellow-creatures, we are indeed a
fallen race!

Hazlitt maintains that the petty malignity of mortals
finds its most striking field in the matter of will-making.
He says:

The last act of our lives seldom belies the former tenor of them for
stupidity, caprice, and unmeaning spite. All that we seem to think
of is to manage matters so (in settling accounts with those who are
so unmannerly as to survive us) as to do as little good and plague
and disappoint as many people as possible.*

Every one knows that this brilliant essayist was
accustomed to deal in sweeping assertions; and it is to
be hoped that such cases as that which he here describes
form the exception to the rule. But it must be admitted
that most of us have heard of wills at whose reading we
might almost imagine their malicious maker fancied he
might be invisibly present to chuckle over the disappointment and mortification which he was dealing even
from his grave. Cases are also recorded in which rich

* *Table-Talk*, vol. i. p. 171. 'Essay on Will-making.'

old bachelors have played upon the hopes of half a dozen poor relations, by dropping hints to each separately that *he* was to be the fortunate heir of all their wealth; and then have left their fortune to an hospital, or have departed from this world intestate, leaving an inheritance mainly of quarrels, heart-burnings, and Chancery suits. How often the cringing, tale-bearing toady, who has borne the ill-humours of a rich sour old maid for thirty years, in the hope of a legacy, is cut off with nineteen guineas for a mourning ring! You would say perhaps, 'Serve her right.' I differ from you. If any one likes to be toadied, he ought in honesty to pay for it. He knows quite well he would never have got it save for the hope of payment; and you have no more right to swindle some poor creature out of years of cringing and flattering than out of pounds of money. A very odd case of petty malice in will-making was that of a man who, not having a penny in this world, left a will in which he bequeathed to his friends and acquaintance large estates in various parts of England, money in the funds, rings, jewels, and plate. His inducement was the prospect of the delight of his friends at first learning about the rich possessions which were to be theirs, and then the bitter disappointment at finding how they had been hoaxed. Such deceptions and hoaxes are very cruel. Who does not feel for poor Moore and his wife, receiving a lawyer's letter just at a season of special embarrassment, to say that some deceased admirer of the poet had left him five hundred pounds, and, after being buoyed up with hope for a few days, finding that some malicious rascal had been playing upon them! No; poor people know that want of money is too serious a matter to be joked about.

Let me conclude what I have to say about petty malignity by observing that I am very far from maintaining that all unfavourable remark about people you know proceeds from this unamiable motive. Some folk appear to fancy that if you speak of any man in any terms but those of superlative praise, this must be because you bear him some ill-will: they cannot understand that you may merely wish to speak truth and do justice. Every person who writes a stupid book and finds it unfavourably noticed in any review, instantly concludes that the reviewer must be actuated by some petty spite. The author entirely overlooks the alternative that his book may be said to be bad because it *is* bad, and because it is the reviewer's duty to say so if he thinks so. I remember to have heard the friend of a lady who had published a bitterly bad and unbecoming work speaking of the notice of it which had appeared in a periodical of the very highest class. The notice was of course unfavourable. 'Oh,' said the writer's friend, 'I know why the review was so disgraceful: the man who wrote it was lately jilted, and he hates all women in consequence!' It happened that I had very good reason to know who wrote the depreciatory article, and I could declare that the motive assigned to the reviewer had not the least existence in fact.

Unfavourable remark has frequently no earthly connexion with malignity great or petty. It is quite fit that, as in people's presence politeness requires that you should not say what you think of them, you should have an opportunity of doing so in their absence: and every one feels when the limits of fair criticism are passed. What *could* you do if, after listening with every appearance of interest to some old lady's wearisome vapouring, you felt bound to pretend, after you had made your escape,

that you thought her conversation was exceedingly interesting? What a relief it is to tell what you have suffered to some sympathetic friend! I have heard injudicious people say, as something much to a man's credit,
that he never speaks of any mortal except in his praise.
I do not think the fact is to the man's advantage. It
appears to prove either that the man is so silly that he
thinks everything he hears and sees to be good, or that
he is so crafty and reserved that he will not commit himself by saying what he thinks. Outspoken good-nature
will sometimes get into scrapes from which self-contained
craft will keep free; but the man who, to use Miss
Edgeworth's phrase, 'thinks it best in general not to
speak of things,' will be liked by nobody.

By petty trickery I mean that small deception which
annoys and worries you, without doing you material
harm. Thus it passes petty trickery when a bank pub-
lishes a swindling report, on the strength of whose false
representations of prosperity you invest your hard-won
savings in its stock and lose them all. It passes petty
trickery when your clerk absconds with some hundreds
of pounds. It indicates petty trickery when you find
your servants writing their letters on your crested note-
paper, and enclosing them in your crested envelopes. It
indicates that at some time or other a successful raid has
been made upon your paper-drawer. It indicates petty
trickery when you find your horses' ribs beginning to be
conspicuous, though they are only half worked and are
allowed three feeds of corn a day. Observe your coachman then, my friend. Some of your corn is going
where it should not. It indicates petty trickery when
your horses' coats are full of dust, though whenever you
happen to be present they are groomed with incredible
vigour: they are not so in your absence. It indicates

petty trickery when, suddenly turning a corner, you find
your coachman galloping the horses along the turnpike-
road at the rate of twenty-three miles an hour. It indicates petty trickery when you find your neighbours' cows
among your clover. It indicates petty trickery when you
find amid a cottager's stock of firewood several palisades
taken from your park-fence. It indicates petty trickery
when you discern in the morning the traces of very
large hobnailed shoes crossing your wife's flower-garden
towards the tree where the magnum bonums are nearly
ripe. But why extend the catalogue? Every man can
add to it a hundred instances. Says Bacon, 'The small
wares and petty points of cunning are infinite, and it
were a good deed to make a list of them.' Who could
make such a list? What numbers of people are practising petty trickery at every hour of the day! Yet, forasmuch as these tricks are small and pretty frequently seen
through, they form only a blister: they are irritating but
not dangerous: and it *is* very irritating to know that you
have been cheated, to however small an extent. How
inestimable is a thoroughly honest servant! Apart from
anything like principle, if servants did but know it, it is
well worth their while to be strictly truthful and reliable:
they are then valued so much. It is highly expedient,
besides being right. And not only is it extremely vexatious to find out any domestic in dishonesty of any kind;
not only does it act as a blister at the moment, but it fos-
ters in one's self a suspicious habit of mind which has in
it something degrading. It is painful to be obliged to
feel that you must keep a strict watch upon your stable
or your granary. You have somewhat of the feeling
of a spy; yet you cannot, if you have ordinary powers
of observation, shut your eyes to what passes round
you.

There is, indeed, some petty trickery which is highly
venial, not to say pleasing. When a little child, on
being offered a third plate of plum-pudding, says, with
a wistful, and half-ashamed look, 'No, thank you,' well
you know that the statement is not entirely candid, and
that the poor little thing would be sadly disappointed if
you took him at his word. Think of your own childish
days; think what plum-pudding was then, and instantly
send the little man a third plate, larger than the previous two. So if your gardener gets wet to the skin in
mowing a little bit of turf, in a drenching summer-
shower, which turns it, parched for the last fortnight, to
emerald green, tell him he must be very wet, and give him
a glass of whisky; never mind, though he, in his politeness, declares that he does not want the whisky, and is
perfectly dry and comfortable. You will find him very
readily dispose of the proffered refreshment. So if you
go into a poor, but spotlessly-clean little cottage, where a
lonely widow of eighty sits by her spinning-wheel. Her
husband and her children are dead, and there she is, all
alone, waiting till she goes to rejoin them. A poor, dog's-
eared, ill-printed Bible lies on the rickety deal-table
near. You take a large parcel which you have brought,
wrapped in brown paper; and as you talk with the good
old Christian, you gradually untie it. A well-sized volume appears; it is the Volume which is worth all the
rest that ever were written; and you tell your aged
friend that you have brought her a Bible, with great,
clear type, which will be easily read by her failing eyes,
and you ask her to accept it. You see the flush of joy
and gratitude on her face, and you do not mind though
she says something which is not strictly true — that it
was too kind of you, that she did not need it, that she
could manage with the old one yet. Nor would you

severely blame the brave fellow who jumped off a bridge
forty feet high, and pulled out your brother when he was
just sinking in a flooded river. if, when you thanked him
with a full heart for the risk he had run, he replied, in a
careless, good-humoured way, that he had really done
nothing worth the speaking of. The brave man is
pained by your thanks: but he thought of his wife and
children when he leaped from the parapet, and he knew
well that he was hazarding his life. And he is perfectly
aware that the statement which he makes is not consis-
tent with fact — but surely you would never call him a
trickster!

Mr. J. S. Mill, unquestionably a very courageous as
well as a very able writer, has declared in a recent publication, that, in Great Britain, the higher classes, for the
most part, speak the truth, while the lower classes, almost
without exception, have frequent recourse to falsehood.
I think Mr. Mill must have been unfortunate in his
experience of the poor. I have seen much of them, and
I have found among them much honesty and truthfulness,
along with great kindness of heart. They have little to
give away in the form of money, but will cheerfully give
their time and strength in the service of a sick neighbour. I have known a shepherd who had come in from
the hills in the twilight of a cold December afternoon,
weary and worn out, find that the little child of a poor
widow in the next cottage had suddenly been taken ill,
and without sitting down, take his stick, and walk away
through the dark to the town nine miles off, to fetch the
doctor. And when I told the fine fellow how much I
respected his manly kindness, I found he was quite unaware that he had done anything remarkable; 'it was just
what ony neibour wad do for anither!' And I could

mention scores of similar cases. And as for truthfulness, I have known men and women among the peasantry, both of England and Scotland, whom I would have trusted with untold gold — or even with what the Highland laird thought a more searching test of rectitude — with unmeasured whisky. Still, I must sorrowfully admit that I have found in many people a strong tendency, when they had done anything wrong, to justify themselves by falsehood. It is not impossible that over-severe masters and mistresses, by undue scoldings administered for faults of no great moment, foster this unhappy tendency. It was not, however, of one class more than another, that the quaint old minister of a parish in Lanarkshire was speaking, when one Sunday morning he read as his text the verse in the Psalms, 'I said in my haste, All men are liars,' and began his sermon by thoughtfully saying : —

'Aye, David, ye said it in your haste, did you? If ye had lived in this parish, ye might have said it at your leisure !'

There is hardly a sadder manifestation of the spirit of petty trickery than that which has been pressed on the attention of the public by recent accounts of the adulteration of food. It is, indeed, sad enough,

When chalk, and alum, and plaster, are sold to the poor for bread,
And the spirit of murder works in the very means of life :

and when the luxuries of the rich are in many cases quite as much tampered with; while, when medical appliances become needful to correct the evil effects of red lead, plaster of Paris, cantharides, and oil of vitriol, the physician is quite uncertain as to the practical power of the medicine he prescribes, inasmuch as drugs are as much adulterated as food. Still, there seems reason to hope that, more frequently than the *Lancet* Commission would lead one to think, you really get in the shops the thing you ask and pay for. I firmly believe that, in this remote district of the world, such petty dishonesty is unknown : and I cannot refrain from saying that, notwithstanding all I have read of late years in tracts, sermons, poems, and leading articles, of the frequency of fraud in the dealings of tradesmen in towns, I never in my own experience have seen the least trace of it.

Most human beings, however, will tell you that day by day they witness a good deal of indirectness, insincerity, and want of straightforwardness — in fact, of petty trickery. There are many people who appear incapable of doing anything without going round about the bush, as Caledonians say. There are many people who always try to disguise the real motive for what they do. They will tell you of anything but the consideration that actually weighs with them, though that is in most cases perfectly well known to the person they are talking to. Some men will tell you that they travel second-class by railway because it is warmer, cooler, airier, pleasanter than the first-class. They suppress all mention of the consideration that obviously weighs with them, viz., that it is cheaper. Mr. Squeers gave the boys at Dotheboys Hall treacle and sulphur one morning in the week. The reason he assigned was that it was good for their health : but his more outspoken wife stated the true reason, which was that, by sickening the children, it made breakfast unnecessary upon that day. Some Dissenters pretend that they want to abolish Church-rates, with a view to the good of the Church : of course everybody knows that their real wish is to do the Church harm. Very soft indeed would the members of the Church be, if they believed that its avowed enemies are extremely anxious for its welfare. But the forms of petty trickery are endless. Bacon mentions in one of his *Essays* that he knew a statesman who, when he came to Queen Elizabeth with bills to sign, always engaged her in conversation about something else, to distract her attention from the papers she was signing. And when some impudent acquaintance asks you, reader, to put your name to another kind of bill, for his advantage, does he not always think to delude you into doing so by saying that your signing is a mere form, intended only for the fuller satisfaction of the bank that is to lend him the money? He does not tell you that he is just asking you to give him the sum named on that stamped paper. Don't believe a word he says, and show him the door. Signing a promise to pay money is never a form; if it be a form, why does he ask you to do it? Bacon mentions another man, who ' when he came to have speech, would pass over that he intended most, and go forth, and come back again, and speak of it as a thing he had almost forgot.' I have known such men too. We have all known men who would come and talk about many indifferent things, and then at the end bring in as if accidentally the thing they came for. Always pull such men sharply up. Let them understand that you see through them. When they sit down, and begin to talk of the weather, the affairs of the district, the new railway, and so forth, say at once, ' Now, Mr. Pawky, I know you did not come to talk to me about these things. What is it you want to speak of? I am busy, and have no time to waste.' It is wonderful how this will beat down Mr. Pawky's guard. He is pre-

pared for sly finesse, but he is quite taken aback by downright honesty. If you try to do him, he will easily do
you : but perfect candour foils the crafty man, as the sturdy
Highlander's broadsword at once cut down the French
master of fence, vapouring away with his rapier. *You*
cannot beat a rogue with his own weapons. Try him
with truth : like David, he 'has not proved' that armour ;
he is quite unaccustomed to it, and he goes down.

Men in towns know that time is valuable to them ; and
by long experience they are assured that there is no use
in trying to overreach a neighbour in a bargain, because
he is so sharp that they will not succeed. But in agricultural districts some persons may be found who appear
to regard it as a fond delusion that ' honesty is the best
policy ;' and who never deal with a stranger without
feeling their way, and trying how far it may be possible
to cheat him. I am glad to infer, from the universal
contempt in which such persons are held, that they form
base, though by no means infrequent, exceptions to the
general rule. The course which such individuals follow
in buying and selling is quite marked and invariable. If
they wish to buy a cow or rent a field, they begin by
declaring with frequency and vehemence that they don't
want the thing, — that in fact they would rather not
have it, — that it would be inconvenient for them to
become possessors of it. They then go on to say that
still, if they can get it at a fair price, they may be
induced to think of it. They next declare that the cow
is the very worst that ever was seen, and that very few
men would have such a creature in their possession. The
seller of the cow, if he knows his customer, meanwhile
listens with entire indifference to Mr. Pawky's assevera-
tions, and after a while proceeds to name his price.

Fifteen pounds for the cow. 'Oh,' says Mr. Pawky, getting up hastily and putting on his hat, 'I see you don't want to sell it. I was just going to have offered you five pounds. I see I need not spend longer time here.' Mr. Pawky, however, does not leave the room: sometimes, indeed, if dealing with a green hand, he may actually depart for half an hour; but then he returns and resumes the negotiation. A friend of his has told him that possibly the cow was better than it looked. It looked very bad indeed; but it might be a fair cow after all. So the proceedings go on: and after an hour's haggling, and several scores of falsehoods told by Mr. Pawky, he becomes the purchser of the animal for the sum originally named. Even now he is not exhausted. He assures the former owner of the cow that it is the custom of the district always to give back half-a-crown in the pound, and refuses to hand over more than £13 2s. 6d. The cow is by this time on its way to Mr. Pawky's farm. If dealing with a soft man, this final trick possibly succeeds. If with an experienced person, it wholly fails. And Mr. Pawky, after wasting two hours, telling sixty-five lies, and stamping himself as a cheat in the estimation of the person with whom he was dealing, ends by taking nothing by all his petty trickery. Oh, poor Pawky, why not be honest and straightforward at once? You would get just as much money, in five cases out of six; and you would save your time and breath, and miss running up that fearful score in the book of the recording angel!

After any transaction with Mr. Pawky, how delightful it is to meet with a downright honest man! I know several men — farmers, labourers, country gentlemen — of that noble class, whose 'word is as good as their bond!' I know men whom you could not even imagine as taking

a petty advantage of any mortal. They are probably far
from being pieces of perfection. They are crotchety in
temper; they are rough in address; their clothes were
never made by Stultz; possibly they do not shave every
morning. But as I look at the open, manly face, and
feel the strong gripe of the vigorous hand, and rejoice to
think that the world goes well with them, and that they
find it pay to speak the truth, — I feel for the minute as
if the somewhat overstrained sentiment had truth in it,
that

An honest man's the noblest work of God!

I am firmly convinced that no man, in the long run,
gains by petty trickery. Honesty *is* the best policy.
You remember how the roguish Ephraim Jenkinson, in
the *Vicar of Wakefield,* mentioned that he contrived to
cheat honest Farmer Flamborough about once a year;
but still the honest farmer grew rich, and the rogue grew
poor, and so Jenkinson began to bethink him that he was
in the wrong track after all. A man who with many
oaths declares a brokenwinded nag is sound as a bell,
and thus gets fifty pounds for an animal he bought for
ten, and then declares with many more oaths that he
never warranted the horse, may indeed gain forty pounds
in money by that transaction, but he loses much more
than he gains. The man whom he cheated, and the
friends of the man whom he cheated, will never trust him
again; and he soon acquires such a character that every
one who is compelled to have any dealings with him
stands on his guard and does not believe a syllable he
says. I do not mention here the solemn consideration of
how the gain and loss may be adjusted in the view of another world; nor do more than allude to a certain solemn
question as to the profit which would follow the gain of

much more than forty pounds, by means which would damage something possessed by every man. All trickery is folly. Every rogue is a fool. The publisher who advertises a book he has brought out, and appends a flattering criticism of it as from the *Times* or *Fraser's Magazine* which never appeared in either periodical, does not gain on the whole by such petty deception ; neither does the publisher who appends highly recommendatory notices, marked with inverted commas as quotations, though with the name of no periodical attached, the fact being that he composed these notices himself. You will say that Mr. Barnum is an instance of a man who made a large fortune by the greater and lesser arts of trickery ; but would you, my honest and honourable friend, have taken that fortune on the same terms? I hope not. And no blessing seems to have rested on Barnum's gains. Where are they now? The trickster has been tricked — the doer done. There is a hollowness about all prosperity which is the result of unfair and underhand means. Even if a man who has grown rich through trickery seems to be going on quite comfortably, depend upon it he cannot feel happy. The sword of Damocles is hanging over his head. Let no man be called happy before he dies.

I believe, indeed, that in some cases the conscience grows quite callous, and the notorious cheat fancies himself a highly moral and religious man ; and although it is always extremely irritating to be cheated, it is more irritating than usual to think that the man who has cheated you is not even made uneasy by the checks of his own conscience. I would gladly think that in most cases,

> Doubtless the pleasure is as great
> Of being cheated as to cheat.

I would gladly think that the man who has done another feels it as blistering to remember the fact as the man who has been done does. It would gratify me much if I were able to conclude that every man who is a knave knows that he is one. I doubt it. Probably he merely thinks himself a sharp, clever fellow. Only this morning I was cheated out of four and sixpence by a man of very decent appearance. He obtained that sum by making three statements, which I found on inquiring, after he had gone, were false. The gain, you see, was small. He obtained just eighteenpence a lie. Yet he went off, looking extremely honest. And no doubt he will be at his parish church next Sunday, shaking his head sympathetically at the more solemn parts of the sermon. And probably, when he reflects upon the transaction, he merely thinks that he was sharp and I was soft. The analogy between these small tricks and a blister holds in several respects. Each is irritating, and the irritation caused by each gradually departs. You are very indignant at first learning that you have been taken in ; you are rather sore, even the day after, — but the day after *that* you are less sore at having been done than sorry for the rogue who was fool enough to do you.

I am writing only of that petty trickery which acts as a blister of humanity; as I need say nothing of those numerous forms of petty trickery which do not irritate, but merely amuse. Such are those silly arts by which some people try to represent themselves to their fellow-creatures as richer, wiser, better-informed, more highly connected, more influential and more successful than the fact. I felt no irritation at the schoolboy who sat opposite me the other day in a railway carriage, and pretended that he was reading a Greek play. I allowed him to fancy his trick had succeeded, and conversed with him of the characteristics of Æschylus. He did not know much about them. A friend of mine, a clergyman, went to the house of a weaver in his parish. As he was about to knock at the door, he heard a solemn voice within; and he listened in silence as the weaver asked God's blessing upon his food. Then he lifted the latch and entered: and thereupon the weaver, resolved that the clergyman should know he said grace before meat, *began and repeated his grace over again.* My friend was not angry; but he was very, very sorry. And never, till the man had been years in his grave, did he mention the fact. As for the fashion in which some people fire off, in conversation with a new acquaintance, every titled name they know, it is to be recorded that the trick is invariably as unsuccessful as it is contemptible. And is not a state dinner, given by poor people, in resolute imitation of people with five times their income, with its sham champagne, its disguised greengrocers, and its general turning the house topsy-turvy,—is not such a dinner one great trick, and a very transparent one?

The writer is extremely tired. Is it not curious that to write for four or five hours a day for four or five successive days, wearies a man to a degree that ten or twelve daily hours of ploughing does not weary the man whose work is physical? Mental work is much the greater stretch: and it is strain, not time, that kills. A horse that walks at two miles and a half an hour, ploughing, will work twelve hours out of the twenty-four. A horse that runs in the mail at twelve miles an hour, works an hour and a half and rests twenty-two and a half; and with all that rest soon breaks down. The bearing of all this is, that it is time to stop; and so, my long black goosequill, lie down!

CHAPTER IV.

CONCERNING WORK AND PLAY.

NOBODY likes to work. I should never work at all if I could help it. I mean, when I say that nobody likes work, that nobody does so whose tastes and likings are in a natural and unsophisticated condition. Some men, by long training and by the force of various circumstances, do, I am aware, come to have an actual craving, a morbid appetite, for work; but it is a morbid appetite, just as truly as that which impels a lady to eat chalk, or a child to prefer pickles to sugar-plums. Or if my reader quarrels with the word *morbid*, and insists that a liking for brisk, hard work is a healthy taste and not a diseased one, I will give up that phrase, and substitute for it the less strong one that a liking for work is an *acquired taste*, like that which leads you and me, my friend, to like bitter beer. Such a man, for instance, as Lord Campbell, has brought himself to that state that I have no doubt he actually enjoys the thought of the enormous quantity of work which he goes through; but when he does so he does a thing as completely out of nature as is done by the Indian fakir, who feels a gloomy satisfaction as he reflects on the success with which he has laboured to weed out all but bitterness from life. I know quite well that we can bring ourselves to such a state of mind that we shall feel a sad sort of pleasure in thinking how much we are taking out of ourselves, and how much we are denying ourselves. What college man who ever worked himself to death but knows well the curious condition of mind? He begins to toil, induced by the love of knowledge, or by the desire of distinction ; but after he has toiled on for some weeks or months, there gradually steals in such a feeling as that which I have been describing. I have felt it myself, and so know all about it. I do not believe that any student ever worked harder than I did. And I remember well the gloomy kind of satisfaction I used to feel, as all day, and much of the night, I bent over my books, in thinking how much I was foregoing. The sky never seemed so blue and so inviting as when I looked at it for a moment now and then, and so back to the weary page. And never did the green woodland walks picture themselves to my mind so freshly and delightfully as when I thought of them as of something which I was resolutely denying myself. I remember even now, when I went to bed at half-past four in the morning, having risen at half-past six the previous morning, and having done nearly as much for months, how I was positively pleased to see in the glass the ghastly cheeks, and the deep black circles round the eyes. There is, I repeat, a certain pleasure in thinking one is working desperately hard, and taking a great deal out of oneself; but it is a pleasure which is unnatural, which is factitious, which is morbid. It is not the healthy, unsophisticated human animal. We know, of course, that Lord Chief-Justice Ellenborough said, when he was about seventy, that the greatest pleasure that remained to him in life, was to hear a young barrister, named Follett, argue a point of law; but it was a highly artificial state of mind, the result of very long training, which enabled the eminent judge to enjoy the gratification which he described: and to ordinary men a legal argument, however ably conducted, would be sickeningly tiresome. If you want to know the natural feeling of humanity towards work, see what children think of it. Is not the task always a disagreeable necessity, even to the very best boy? How I used to hate mine! Of course, my friendly reader, if you knew who I am, I should talk of myself less freely; but as you do not know, and could not possibly guess, I may ostensively do what every man tacitly does, make myself the standard of average human nature, the first meridian from which all distances and deflections are to be measured. Well, my feeling towards my school tasks was nothing short of hatred. And yet I was not a dunce. No, I was a clever boy. I was at the head of all my classes. Not more than once or twice have I competed at school or college for a prize which I did not get. And I hated work all the while. Therefore I believe that all unsophisticated mortals hate it. I have seen silly parents trying to get their children to say that they liked school-time better than holiday-time; that they liked work better than play. I have seen, with joy, manly little fellows repudiating the odious and unnatural sentiment; and declaring manfully that they preferred cricket to Ovid. And if any boy ever tells you that he would rather learn his lessons than go out to the play-ground, beware of that boy. Either his health is drooping, and his mind becoming prematurely and unnaturally developed; or he is a little humbug. He is an impostor. He is seeking to obtain credit under false pretences. Depend upon it, unless it really be that he is a poor little spiritless man, deficient in nerve and muscle, and unhealthily precocious in intellect, he has in him the elements of a sneak ; and he wants nothing but time to ripen him into a pickpocket, a swindler, a horse-dealer, or a British Bank director.

Every one, then, naturally hates work, and loves its opposite, play. And let it be remarked that not idleness, but play, is the opposite of work. But some people are so happy, as to be able to idealize their work into play ; or they have so great a liking for their work that they do not feel their work as effort, and thus the element is eliminated which makes work a pain. How I envy those human beings who have such enjoyment in their work, that it ceases to be work at all! There is my friend Mr. Tinto the painter; he is never so happy as when he is busy at his canvas, drawing forth from it forms of beauty: he is up at his work almost as soon as he has daylight for it; he paints all day, and he is sorry when the twilight compels him to stop. He delights in his work, and so his work becomes play. I suppose the kind of work which, in the case of ordinary men, never ceases to be work, never loses the conscious feeling of strain and effort, is that of composition. A great poet, possibly, may find much pleasure in writing, and there have been exceptional men who said they never were so happy as when they had the pen in their hand: Buffon, I think, tells us that once he wrote for fourteen hours at a stretch, and all that time was in a state of positive enjoyment ; and Lord Macaulay, in the preface to his recently published *Speeches*, assures us that the writing of his *History* is the occupation and the happiness of his life. Well, I am glad to hear it. Ordinary mortals cannot sympathize with the feeling.

To *them* composition is simply hard work, and hard work is pain. Of course, even commonplace men have occasionally had their moments of inspiration, when thoughts present themselves vividly, and clothe themselves in felicitous expressions, without much or any conscious effort. But these seasons are short and far between: and although while they last it becomes comparatively pleasant to write, it never becomes so pleasant as it would be to lay down the pen, to lean back in the easy-chair, to take up the *Times* or *Fraser*, and enjoy the luxury of being carried easily along that track of thought which costs its writer so much labour to pioneer through the trackless jungle of the world of mind. Ah, how easy it is to read what it was so difficult to write! There is all the difference between running down from London to Manchester by the railway after it has been made, and of making the railway from London to Manchester. You, my intelligent reader, who begin to read a chapter of Mr. Froude's eloquent *History*, and get on with it so fluently, are like the snug old gentleman, travelling-capped, railway-rugged, great-coated, and plaided, who leans back in the corner of the softly-cushioned carriage as it flits over Chat-moss; while the writer of the chapter is like George Stephenson, toiling month after month to make the track along which you speed, in the face of difficulties and discouragements which you never think of. And so I say it may sometimes be somewhat easy and pleasant to write, but never so easy and pleasant as it is not to write. The odd thing, too, about the work of the pen is this: that it is often done best by the men who like it least and shrink from it most, and that it is often the most laborious writing along which the reader's mind glides most easily and pleasurably. It is not so in

other matters. As the general rule, no man does well
the work which he dislikes. No man will be a good
preacher who dislikes preaching. No man will be a
good anatomist who hates dissecting. Sir Charles
Napier, it must be confessed, was a great soldier, though
he hated fighting; and as for writing, some men have
been the best writers who hated writing, and who would
never have penned a line but under the pressure of
necessity. There is John Foster; what a great writer
he was: and yet his biography tells us, in his own words,
too, scores of times, how he shrunk away from the intense mental effort of composition; how he abhorred it
and dreaded it, though he did it so admirably well.
There is Coleridge: how that great mind ran to waste,
because Coleridge shrank from the painful labour of formal composition: and so *Christabel* must have remained
unfinished, save for the eloquent labours of that greatest,
wisest, most original, and least commonplace of men, Dr.
Martin Farquhar Tupper: and so, instead of volumes
of hoarded wisdom and wit, we have but the fading
remembrances of hours of marvellous talk. I do not by
any means intend to assert that there are not worse
things than work, even than very hard work; but I say
that work, as work, is a bad thing. It may once have
been otherwise, but the curse is in it now. We do it
because we must: it is our duty: we live by it; it is the
Creator's intention that we should; it makes us enjoy
leisure and recreation and rest; it stands between us and
the pure misery of idleness; it is dignified and honourable; it is the soil and the atmosphere in which grow
cheerfulness, hopefulness, health of body and mind.
But still, if we could get all these good ends without it,
we should be glad. We do not care for exertion for its

own sake. Even Mr. Kingsley does not love the north-east wind for itself, but because of the good things that come with it and from it. Work is not an end in itself. 'The end of work,' said Aristotle, 'is to enjoy leisure;' or, as *The Minstrel* hath it, 'the end and the reward of toil is rest.' I do not wish to draw from too sacred a source the confirmation of these summer-day fancies; but I think, as I write, of the descriptions which we find in a certain Volume of the happiness of another world. Has not many an over-wrought and wearied-out worker found comfort in an assurance of which I shall here speak no further, that 'There remaineth a rest to the people of God?'

And so, my reader, if it be true that nobody, any-where, would (in his sober senses) work if he could help it, how especially true is that great principle on this beautiful July day! It is truly a day on which to do nothing. I am here, far in the country, and when I this moment went to the window, and looked out upon a rich summer landscape, everything seemed asleep. The sky is sapphire-blue, without a cloud; the sun is pouring down a flood of splendour upon all things; there is not a breath stirring, hardly the twitter of a bird. All the air is filled with the fragrance of the young clover. The landscape is richly wooded; I never saw the trees more thickly covered with leaves, and now they are perfectly still. I am writing north of the Tweed, and the horizon is of blue hills, which some southrons would call mountains. The wheat-fields are beginning to have a little of the harvest-tinge, and they contrast beautifully with the deep green of the hedge-rows. The roses are almost over, but I can see plenty of honeysuckle in the hedges still, and a perfect blaze of it has covered one projecting branch of a

young oak. I am looking at a little well-shaven green
(I shall not call it a lawn, because it is not one); it has
not been mown for nearly a fortnight, and it is perfectly
white with daisies. Beyond, at a very short distance,
through the branches of many oaks, I can see a gable of
the church, and a few large gravestones shining white
among the green grass and leaves. I do not find all
these things any great temptation now, for I have got
interested in my work, and I like to write of them.
But I found it uncommonly hard to sit down this morning to my work. Indeed, I found it impossible, and thus
it is that at five o'clock P. M., I have got no further than
the present line. I had quite resolved that this morning
I would sit doggedly down to my essay, in which I have
really (though the reader may find it hard to believe it)
got something to say; but when I walked out after
breakfast, I felt that all nature was saying that this was
not a day for work. Come forth and look at me, seemed
the message breathed from her beautiful face. And then
I thought of Wordsworth's ballad, which sets out so
pleasing an excuse for idleness : —

> Books! 'tis a dull and endless strife,
> Come, hear the woodland linnet!
> How sweet his music! on my life
> There's more of wisdom in it.
>
> And hark! how blithe the throstle sings!
> He, too, is no mean preacher:
> Come forth into the light of things,
> Let Nature be your teacher.
>
> She has a world of ready wealth,
> Our minds and hearts to bless, —
> Spontaneous wisdom breathed by health,
> Truth breathed by cheerfulness.

One impulse from a vernal wood,
   May teach you more of man,
Of moral evil and of good,
   Than all the sages can!

Just at my gate, the man who keeps in order the roads
of the parish was hard at work. How pleasant, I thought,
to work amid the pure air and the sweet-smelling clover!
And how pleasant, too, to have work to do of such a nature that when you go to it every morning you can make
quite sure that, barring accident, you will accomplish a
certain amount before the sun shall set; while as for the
man whose work is that of the brain and the pen, he
never can be certain in the morning how much his day's
labour may amount to. He may sit down at his desk,
spread out his paper, have his ink in the right place, and
his favourite pen, and yet he may find that he cannot *get
on*, that thoughts will not come, that his mind is utterly
sterile, that he cannot see his way through his subject,
or that if he can produce anything at all it is poor miserable stuff, whose poorness no one knows better than
himself. And so, after hours of effort and discouragement, he may have to lay his work aside, having accomplished nothing, having made no progress at all — wearied, stupified, disheartened, thinking himself a mere
blockhead. Thus musing, I approached the roadman.
I inquired how his wife and children were. I asked
how he liked the new cottage he had lately moved into.
Well, he said, but it was far from his work: he had walked
eight miles and a half that morning to his work; he had
to walk the same distance home again in the evening after
labouring all day; and for this his wages were thirteen
shillings a-week, with a deduction for such days as he
might be unable to work. He did not mention all this

by way of complaint ; he was comfortably off, he said ;
he should be thankful he was so much better off than
many.   He had got a little pony lately very cheap,
which would carry himself and his tools to and from his
employment, and that would be very nice.   In all likelihood, my friendly reader, the roadman would not have
been so communicative to you ; but as for me, it is my
duty and my happiness to be the sympathizing friend of
every man, woman, and child in this parish, and it pleases
me much to believe that there is no one throughout its
little population who does not think of me and speak to
me as a friend.   I talked a little longer to the roadman
about parish affairs.   We mutually agreed in remarking the incongruous colours of a pair of ponies
which passed in a little phaeton, of which one was cream-
coloured and the other dapple-grey.   The phaeton came
from a friend's house a little way off, and I wondered if
it were going to the railway to bring some one who (I
knew) was expected ; for in such simple matters do we
simple country folk find something to maintain the interest of life.   I need not go on to describe what other
things I did ; how I looked with pleasure at a field of
oats and another of potatoes in which I am concerned,
and held several short conversations with passers-by ;
but the result of the whole was a conviction that, after
all, it was best to set to work at once, though well remembering how much by indoor work in the country
on such a day as this one is missing.   And the thought
of the roadman's seventeen miles of walking, in addition to his day's work, was something of a reproof and
a stimulus.   And thus, determined at least to make a
beginning, did I write this much *Concerning Work and
Play.*

I find a great want in all that is written on the subject of recreation. People tell me that I need recreation, that I cannot do without it, that mind and body alike demand it. I know all that, but they do not tell me how to recreate myself. They fight shy of all practical details. Now it is just these I want. All working men must have play ; but what sort of play can we have ? I envy schoolboys their facility of being amused, and of finding recreation which entirely changes the current of their thoughts. A boy flying his kite or whipping his top is pursued by no remembrance of the knotty line of Virgil which puzzled him a little while ago in school ; but when the grown-up man takes his sober afternoon walk — perhaps the only relaxation which he has during the day — he is thinking still of the book which he is writing and of the cares which he has left at home. Then, and all the worse for myself, I can feel no interest in flying a kite, or rigging and sailing a little ship, or making a mill-wheel and setting it going, or in marbles, or ball, or running races, or playing at leap-frog. And even if they did feel interest in athletic sports, the lungs and sinews of most educated men of middle age would forbid their joining in them. I need not therefore suggest the doubt which would probably be cast upon a man's sanity were he found eagerly knuckling down (how stiff it would soon make him), or wildly chasing the flying football, or making a rush at a friend and taking a flying leap over his head. Now what recreation, I want to know, is open to the middle-aged man of literary tastes? Shooting, coursing, fishing, says one ; but he does not care for shooting, or coursing, or fishing. Gardening, says another ; but he does not care for gardening. Watching ferns, caterpillars, frogs, and other 'common objects of the country ; '

well, but he lives in town, and if he did not, he does not
feel the least interest in ferns and caterpillars. Music is
suggested ; well, he has no great ear, and he may dwell
where he can have little or none of it. Society! pray
what is society ? No doubt the conversation of intelligent men and women is a most grateful and stimulating
recreation ; but is there any recreation in dreary dinner-
parties, where one listens to the twaddle of silly old gentlemen and emptier young ones, or in the hot-house atmosphere and crush of most evening parties? These
are not play; they are very hard work, and a treadmill
work producing no beneficial results, but rather provoca-
tive of all manner of ill-tempers. Then, no doubt, there
is most agreeable recreation for some people in the excitement of a polka or gallop and its attendant light and
cheerful talk, not to say flirtation ; but then our representative man has got beyond these things : these are for
young people — he is married now and sobered down ;
he probably was never the man to make himself eminently agreeable in such a scene, and he is less so now
than ever. Besides, if play be something from which
you are to return with renewed strength and interest to
work, I doubt whether the ball-room is the place where
it is to be found. Late hours, a feverish atmosphere,
and excessive exercise, tend to morning slumbers, head-
aches, crossness, and laziness. To find dancing which
answers the end of recreation, we must go to less fashionable places. I like the pictures which Goldsmith gives
us of the sunny summer evenings of France, where the
whole population of the village danced to his flute in the
shade ; and even the soured Childe Harold melted somewhat into sympathy with the Spanish peasants as they
twirled their castanets in the twilight. Southey's picture

is a pretty one, but its description sounds somewhat unreal :

> But peace was on the Cottage, and the fold
> From Court intrigue, from bickering faction far:
> Beneath the chestnut-tree love's tale was told,
> And to the tinkling of the light guitar,
> Sweet stooped the western sun, sweet rose the evening star!

Nor let it be fancied that such a scene cannot be
represented except in countries to which distance and
strangeness give their interest. This very season, on a
beautiful summer evening, I saw a happy party of eighty
country folk dancing upon a greener little bit of turf than
Goldsmith ever saw in France. And I wished such
things were more common ; though the grave Saxon
spirit, equal to the enjoyment of such gaiety now and
then, might perhaps flag under it did it come too often.
But on the occasion to which I refer, there was no lack
of innocent cheerfulness; the enjoyment seemed real ;
and though there were no castanets and no guitars, but
a fiddle for music and reels for dances, there were as
pretty faces and as graceful figures among the girls, I
warrant, as you would find from the Rhine to the
Pyrenees.

But, to resume the somewhat ravelled thread of our
discussion, — if a man has come to this, that he can feel no
interest in such recreations as those which we have mentioned, what is he to do ? And let it be remembered that
I am putting no fanciful case : be sorry, if you will, for the
man who from taste and habit cannot be easily amused ;
but remember that such is the lot of a very large proportion of the intellectual labourers of the race. And what
is such a man to do ? After using his eyes and exerting
his brain all the forenoon in reading and writing by way

8

of work, must he just use his eyes and exert his brain
all the evening in reading and writing by way of play?
Has it come to this, that he must find the only recreation that remains for him in the *Times*, the *Quarterly
Review*, and *Fraser's Magazine*? All these things are
indeed excellent in their way. They relax and interest
the mind: but then they wear out the eyes, they con-
tract the chest, and render the muscles flabby, they ruin
the ganglionic apparatus, they make the mind but unmake the body. Now that will not do. Does nothing
remain, in the way of play, but the afternoon walk or
drive: the vacant period between dinner and tea, when
no one works, notwithstanding Johnson's warning, that
he who resolves that he cannot work between dinner and
tea, will probably proceed to the conclusion that he cannot work between breakfast and dinner; a little quiet
gossip with your wife, a little romping with your children, if you have a wife and children; and then back
again to the weary books? Think of the elder Disraeli,
who looked at printed pages so long, that by and bye,
wherever he looked, he saw nothing but printed pages,
and then became blind. Think what poor specimens of
the human animal, physically, many of our noblest and
ablest men are. Do not men, by their beautiful, touching, and far-reaching thoughts, reach the heart and form
the mind of thousands, who could not run a hundred
yards without panting for breath, who could not jump
over a five-feet wall though a mad bull were after them,
who could not dig in the garden for ten minutes without
having their brain throbbing and their entire frame trembling, who could not carry in a sack of coals though they
should never see a fire again, who could never find a
day's employment as porters, labourers, grooms, or any-

thing but tailors? Educated and cultivated men, I tell
you that you make a terrible mistake; and a mistake
which, before the end of the twentieth century, will sadly
deteriorate the Anglo-Saxon race. You make your recreation purely mental. You give a little play to your
minds, after their day's work; but you give no play to
your eyes, to your brains, to your hearts, to your digestion, — in short to your bodies. And therefore you grow
weak, unmuscular, nervous, dyspeptic, near-sighted, out-
of-breath, neuralgic, pressure-on-the-brain, thin-haired
men. And in time, not only does all the train of evils
that follows your not providing proper recreation for
your physical nature, come miserably to affect your
spirits; but, besides that, it comes to jaundice and pervert and distort all your views of men and things. I
have heard of those who, though suffering almost ceaseless pain, could yet think hopefully of the prospects of
humanity, and take an unprejudiced view of some political question that appealed strongly to prejudice, and give
kindly sympathy and sound advice to a poor man who
came to seek advice in some little trouble which is great
to him. But I fear that in the majority of instances, the
human being whose liver is in a bad way, whose digestion is ruined, or even who is suffering from violent
toothache, is prone to snub the servants, to box the children's ears, to think that Britain is going to destruction,
and that the world is coming to an end.

It may be said, that the class of intellectual workers have their yearly holiday. August and September
in each year bring with them the 'Long Vacation.'
And it is well, indeed, that most men whose work is
brain-work have that blessed period of relief, wherein,
amid the Swiss snows, or the Highland heather, or out

upon the Mediterranean waves, they seek to re-invigorate the jaded body and mind, and to lay in a store of health and strength with which to face the winter work again. But this is not enough. A man might just as well say that he would eat in August or September all the food which is to support him through the year, as think in that time to take the whole year's recreation, the whole year's play, in one *bonne bouche*. Recreation must be a daily thing. Every day must have its play, as well as its work. There is much sound, practical sense in Sir Thomas More's *Utopia;* and nowhere sounder than where he tells us that in his model country he would have ' half the day allotted for work, and half for honest recreation.' Every day, bringing, as it does, work to every man who is worth his salt in this world, ought likewise to bring its play: play which will turn the thoughts into quite new and cheerful channels; which will recreate the body as well as the mind; and tell me, Great Father of Waters, to whom Rasselas appealed upon a question of equal difficulty, — or tell me, anybody else, what that play shall be! Practically, in the case of most educated men, of most intellectual workers, heavy reading and writing stand for work, and light reading and writing stand for play.

I can well imagine what a delightful thing it must be for a toil-worn barrister to throw briefs, and cases, and reports aside, and quitting the pestilential air of Westminster Hall, laden with odours from the Thames which are not the least like those of Araby the Blest, to set off to the Highlands for a few weeks among the moors. No schoolboy at holiday-time is lighter-hearted than he, as he settles down into his corner in that fearfully fast express train on the Great Northern Railway. And when he reaches his box in the North at last, what a fresh and happy sensation it must be to get up in the morning in that pure, unbreathed air, with the feeling that he has nothing to do, — nothing, at any rate, except what he chooses; and after the deliberately-eaten breakfast, to saunter forth with the delightful sense of leisure, — to know that he has time to breathe and think after the ceaseless hurry of the past months, — and to know that nothing will go wrong although he should sit down on the mossy parapet of the little one-arched bridge that spans the brawling mountain-stream, and there rest, and muse, and dream just as long as he likes. Two or three such men come to this neighbourhood yearly; and I enjoy the sight of them, they look so happy. Every little thing, if they indeed be genial, true, unstiffened men, is a source of interest to them. The total change makes them grow rapturous about matters which we, who are quite accustomed to them, take more coolly. I think, when I look at them, of the truthful lines of Gray:

> See the wretch, that long has tost,
>   On the thorny bed of pain,
> At length repair his vigour lost,
>   And breathe and walk again:
>
> The meanest flowret of the vale,
> The simplest note that swells the gale,
> The common sun, the air, the skies,
> To him are opening paradise.

Equidem invideo, a little. I feel somewhat vexed when I think how much more beautiful these pleasant scenes around me really are, than what, by any effort, I can make them seem to me. You hard-wrought town folk, when you come to rural regions, have the advantage of us leisurely country people.

But, much as that great Queen's Counsel enjoys his long vacation's play, you see it is not enough. Look how thin his hair is, how pale his cheeks are, how flesh-less those long fingers, how unmuscular those arms. What he needs, in addition to the autumn holiday, is some *bonâ fide* play every day of his life. What is his amusement when in town? Why, mainly it consists of going into society, where he gains nothing of elasticity and vigour, but merely injures his digestive organs. Why does he not rather have half an hour's lively bod-ily exercise, — rowing, or quoits, or tennis, or skating, or anything he may have taste for? And if it be foolish to take all the year's play at once, as so many intellectual workers think to do, much more foolish is it to keep all the play of life till the work is over: to toil and moil at business through all the better years of our time in this world, in the hope that at length we shall be able to retire from business, and make the evening of life all holiday, all play. In all likelihood the man who takes this course will never retire at all, except into an untimely grave; and if he should live to reach the long-coveted retreat, he will find that all play and no work makes life quite as wearisome and as little enjoy-able as all work and no play. *Ennui* will make him miserable; and body and mind, deprived of their wonted occupation, will soon break down. After very hard and long-continued work, there is indeed a pleasure in merely sitting still and doing nothing. But after the feeling of pure exhaustion is gone, *that* will not suffice. A boy enjoys play, but he is miserable in enforced idle-ness. In writing about retiring from the task-work of life, one naturally thinks of that letter to Wordsworth, in which Charles Lamb told what he felt when he was finally emancipated from his drudgery in the India House :

I came home FOR EVER on Tuesday week. The incomprehensibleness of my condition overwhelmed me. It was like passing from life into eternity. Every year to be as long as three; that is, to have three times as much real time — time that is my own — in it! I wandered about thinking I was happy, and feeling I was not. But that tumultuousness is passing off, and I begin to understand the nature of the gift. Holidays, even the annual month, were always uneasy joys, with their conscious fugitiveness, the craving after making the most of them. Now, when all is holiday, there are no holidays. I can sit at home, in rain or shine, without a restless impulse for walkings.

There are unhappy beings in the world, who secretly stand in fear of all play, on the hateful and wicked notion, which I believe some men regard as being of the essence of Christianity, though in truth it is its contradiction, that everything pleasant is sinful, — that God dislikes to see his creatures cheerful and happy. I think it is the author of *Friends in Council* who says something to the effect, that many people, infected with that Puritan falsehood, slink about creation, afraid to confess that they ever are enjoying themselves. It is a sad thing when such a belief is entertained by even grown-up men; but it stirs me to absolute fury when I know of it being impressed upon poor little children, to repress their natural gaiety of heart. Did you ever, my reader, read that dreary and preposterous book in which Thomas Clarkson sought to show that Quakerism is not inconsistent with common sense? Probably not; but perhaps you may have met with Jeffrey's review of it. Nothing short of a vehement kicking could relieve my feelings if I heard some sly, money-making old rascal impressing upon some merry children that

Stillness and quietness both of spirit and body are necessary, as far as they can be obtained. Hence, Quaker children are rebuked for all expressions of anger, as tending to raise those feelings which ought to be suppressed; a raising even of the voice beyond due bounds, is discouraged as leading to the disturbance of their minds. They are taught to rise in the morning in quietness; to go about their ordinary occupations with quietness; and with quietness to retire to their beds.

Can you think of more complete flying in the face of the purposes of the kind Creator? Is it not His manifest intention that childhood should be the time of merry laughter, of gaiety, and shouts, and noise? There is not a sadder sight than that of a little child prematurely subdued and ' quiet.' Let me know of any drab-coated humbug impressing such ideas on any child of mine ; and though from circumstances I cannot personally see him put under the pump, I know certain quarters in which it is only needful to drop a very faint hint, in order to have him first pumped upon, and then tarred and feathered.

But there is another class of mortals, who are free from the Puritan principle, and who have no objection to amusement for themselves, but who seem to have no notion that their inferiors and their servants ought ever to do anything but work. The reader will remember the fashionable governess in *The Old Curiosity Shop*, who insisted that only genteel children should ever be permitted to play. The well-known lines of Dr. Isaac Watts, —

> In books, or work, or healthful play,
> Let my first years be past,—

were applicable, she maintained, only to the children of families of the wealthier sort: while for poor children there must be a new reading, which she improvised as follows : —

In work, work, work. In work alway,
   Let my first years be past:
That I may give, for every day,
   Some good account at last.

And as for domestic servants, poor creatures, I fear
there is many a house in which there is no provision
whatever made for play for them. There can be no
drearier round of life than that to which their employers
destine them. From the moment they rise, hours before
any member of the family, to the moment when they
return to bed, it is one constant push of sordid labour, —
often in chambers to which air and light and cheerfulness
can never come. And if they ask a rare holiday, what a
fuss is made about it! Now, what is the result of all this?
Some poor solitary beings do actually sink into the spiritless drudges which such a life tends to make them: but
the greater number feel that they cannot live with all
work and no play; and as they cannot get play openly,
they get it secretly: they go out at night, when you, their
mistress, are asleep; or they bring in their friends at
those unreasonable hours: they get that amusement and
recreation on the sly, and with the sense that they are
doing wrong and deceiving, which they ought to be permitted to have openly and honestly: and thus you break
down their moral principle, you train them to cheat you,
you educate them into liars and thieves. Of course your
servants thus regard you as their natural enemy: it is
fair to take any advantage you can of a gaoler: you are
their task-imposer, their driver, their gaoler, — anything
but their friend; and if they can take advantage of you
in any way, they will. And serve you right.

I have known injudicious clergymen who did all they
could to discourage the games and sports of their parish-

ioncrs. They could not prevent them; but one thing they did, — they made them disreputable. They made sure that the poor man who ran in a sack, or climbed a greased pole, felt that thereby he was forfeiting his character, perhaps imperilling his salvation : and so he thought that having gone so far, he might go the full length : and thus he got drunk, got into a fight, thrashed his wife, smashed his crockery, and went to the lock-up. How much better it would have been had the clergyman sought to regulate these amusements; and since they *would* go on, try to make sure that they should go creditably and decently. Thus, poor folk might have been cheerful without having their conscience stinging them all the time : and let it be remembered, that if you pervert a man's moral sense (which you may quite readily do with the uneducated classes) into fancying that it is wicked to use the right hand or the right foot, while the man still goes on using the right hand and the right foot, you do him an irreparable mischief : you bring on a temper of moral recklessness ; and help him a considerable step towards the gallows. Since people must have amusement, and will have amusement; for any sake do not get them to think that amusement is wicked. You cannot keep them from finding recreation of some sort: you may drive them to find it at a lower level, and to partake of it soured by remorse, and by the wretched resolution that they will have it right or wrong. Instead of anathematizing all play, sympathize with it genially and heartily ; and say, with kind-hearted old Burton —

Let the world have their may-games, wakes, whitsunals; their dancings and concerts ; their puppet-shows, hobby-horses, tabors, bagpipes, balls, barley-breaks, and whatever sports and recreations please them best, provided they be followed with discretion.

Let it be here remarked, that recreation can be fully enjoyed only by the man who has some earnest occupation. The end of the work is to enjoy leisure; but to enjoy leisure you must have gone through work. Playtime must come after schooltime, otherwise it loses its savour. Play, after all, is a relative thing; it is not a thing which has an absolute existence. There is no such thing as play, except to the worker. It comes out by contrast. Put white upon white, and you can hardly see it: put white upon black and how plain it is. Light your lamp in the sunshine, and it is nothing: you must have darkness round it to make its presence felt. And besides this, a great part of the enjoyment of recreation consists in the feeling that we have earned it by previous hard work. One goes out for the afternoon walk with a light heart when one has done a good task since breakfast. It is one thing for a dawdling idler to set off to the Continent or to the Highlands, just because he is sick of everything around him; and quite another thing when a hard-wrought man, who is of some use in life, sets off, as gay as a lark, with the pleasant feeling that he has brought some worthy work to an end, on the self-same tour. And then a busy man finds a relish in simple recreations; while a man who has nothing to do, finds all things wearisome, and thinks that life is 'used up:' it takes something quite out of the way to tickle that indurated palate: you might as well think to prick the hide of a hippopotamus with a needle, as to excite the interest of that *blasé* being by any amusement which is not highly spiced with the cayenne of vice. And *that*, certainly, has a powerful effect. It was a glass of water the wicked old French woman was drinking when she said, 'Oh, that this were a sin, to give it a relish!'

So it is worth while to work, if it were only that we might enjoy play. Thus doth Mr. Heliogabalus, my next neighbour, who is a lazy man and an immense glutton, walk four miles every afternoon of his life. It is not that he hates exertion less, but that he loves dinner more; and the latter cannot be enjoyed unless the former is endured. And the man whose disposition is the idlest may be led to labour when he finds that labour is his only chance of finding any enjoyment in life. James Montgomery sums up much truth in a couple of lines in his *Pelican Island*, which run thus : —

> Labour, the symbol of man's punishment;
> Labour, the secret of man's happiness.

Why on earth do people think it fine to be idle and useless? Fancy a drone superciliously desiring a working bee to stand aside, and saying, 'out of the way, you miserable drudge; *I* never made a drop of honey in all my life!' I have observed too, that some silly people are ashamed that it should be known that they are so useful as they really are, and take pains to represent themselves as more helpless, ignorant, and incapable than the fact. I have heard a weak old lady boast that her grown-up daughters were quite unable to fold up their own dresses; and that as for ordering dinner they had not a notion of such a thing. This and many similar particulars were stated with no small exultation, and that by a person far from rich and equally far from aristocratic. 'What a silly old woman you are,' was my silent reflection; 'and if your daughters really are what you represent them, woe betide the poor man who shall marry one of the incapable young noodles.' Give me the man, I say, who can turn his hand to all things, and

who is not ashamed to confess that he can do so ; who
can preach a sermon, nail up a paling, prune a fruit tree,
make a waterwheel or a kite for his little boy, write an
article for *Fraser* or a leader for the *Times* or the *Spectator*. What a fine, genial, many-sided life did Sydney
Smith lead at his Yorkshire parish ! I should have
liked, I own, to have found in it more traces of the clergyman ; but perhaps the biographer thought it better not
to parade these. And in the regard of facing all difficulties with a cheerful heart, and nobly resolving to be useful and helpful in little matters as well as big, I think
that life was as good a sermon as ever was preached
from pulpit.

I have already said, in the course of this rambling discussion, that recreation must be such as shall turn the
thoughts into a new channel, otherwise it is no recreation
at all. And walking, which is the most usual physical
exercise, here completely fails. Walking has grown by
long habit a purely automatic act, demanding no attention : we think all the time we are walking ; Southey
even read while he took his daily walk. But Southey's
story is a fearful warning. It will do a clergyman no
good whatever to leave his desk and go forth for his *constitutional*, if he is still thinking of his sermon, and trying
to see his way through the treatment of his text. You
see in Gray's famous poem how little use is the mere
walk to the contemplative man, how thoroughly it falls
short of the end of play. You see how the hectic lad
who is supposed to have written the *Elegy* employed
himself when he wandered abroad :

> There, at the foot of yonder nodding beech,
> That wreaths its old fantastic roots so high,
> His listless length at noontide would he stretch,
> And pore upon the brook that babbles by.

Hard by yon wood, now smiling as in scorn,
Muttering his wayward fancies he would rove;
Now drooping, woful, wan, like one forlorn,
Or crazed with care, or crossed in hopeless love.

That was the fashion in which the poor fellow took his daily recreation and exercise! His mother no doubt packed him out to take a bracing walk; she ought to have set him to saw wood for the fire, or to dig in the garden, or to clean the door-handles if he had muscle for nothing more. These things would have distracted his thoughts from their grand flights, and prevented his mooning about in that listless manner. Of course while walking he was bothering away about the poetical trash he had in his desk at home; and so he knocked up his ganglionic functions, he encouraged tubercles on his lungs, and came to furnish matter for the 'hoary-headed swain's' narrative, the silly fellow!

Riding is better than walking, especially if you have a rather skittish steed, who compels you to attend to him on pain of being landed in the ditch, or sent, meteor-like, over the hedge. The elder Disraeli has preserved the memory of the diversions in which various hard thinkers found relaxation. Petavius, who wrote a deeply learned book, which I never saw, and which no one I ever saw ever heard of, twirled round his chair for five minutes every two hours that he was at work. Samuel Clark used to leap over the tables and chairs. It was a rule which Ignatius Loyola imposed on his followers, that after two hours of work, the mind should always be unbent by some recreation. Every one has heard of Paley's remarkable feats of rapid horsemanship. Hundreds of times did that great man fall off. The Sultan Mahomet, who conquered Greece, unbent his mind by carving wooden spoons. In all these things you see, kindly reader, that true recreation was aimed at : that is, entire change of thought and occupation. Izaak Walton, again, who sets forth so pleasantly the praise of angling as the ' Contemplative Man's Recreation,' wrongly thinks to recommend the gentle craft by telling us that the angler may think all the while he plies it. I do not care for angling; I never caught a minnow ; but still I joy in good old Izaak's pleasant pages, like thousands who do not care a pin for fishing, but who feel it like a cool retreat into green fields and trees to turn to his genial feeling and hearty pictures of quiet English scenery. He, however, had a vast opinion of the joys of angling in a pleasant country : only let him go quietly a-fishing : —

> And if contentment be a stranger then,
> I'll ne'er look for it, but in heaven, again.

And he repeats with much approval the sentiments of 'Jo. Davors, Esq.,' in whose lines we may see much more of scenery than of the actual fishing : —

> Let me live harmlessly; and near the brink
>   Of Trent or Avon have a dwelling-place,
> Where I may see my quill or cork down sink,
>   With eager bite of perch, or bleak, or dace :
> And on the world and my Creator think :
>   While some men strive ill-gotten goods to embrace;
> And others spend their time in base excess
> Of wine, or worse, in war and wantonness.
>
> Let them that list, these pastimes still pursue,
>   And on such pleasing fancies feed their fill;
> So I the fields and meadows green may view,
>   And daily by fresh rivers walk at will,
> Among the daisies and the violets blue,
>   Red hyacinth and yellow daffodil;
> Purple narcissus like the morning's rays,
> Pale gander-grass, and azure culver-keys.

All these, and many more of His creation,
  That made the heavens, the angler oft doth see;
Taking therein no little delectation,
  To think how strange, how wonderful they be!
Framing thereof an inward contemplation,
  To set his heart from other fancies free:
And whilst he looks on these with joyful eye,
His mind is rapt above the starry sky.

Who shall say that the *terza-rima* stanza was not written in English fluently and gracefully, before the days of Whistlecraft and *Don Juan?*

If thou desirest, reader, to find a catalogue of sports from which thou mayest select that which likes thee best, turn up Burton's *Anatomy of Melancholy,* or Joseph Strutt's *Sports and Pastimes of the People of England.* There mayest thou read of *Rural Exercises practised by Persons of Rank,* of *Rural Exercises Generally practised:* (note how ingeniously Strutt puts the case: he does not say practised by Snobs, or the Lower Orders, or the Mobocracy). Next are *Pastimes Exercised in Towns and Cities;* and finally, *Domestic Amusements,* and *Pastimes Appropriated to particular Seasons.* Were it not that my paper is verging to its close, I could surprise thee with a vast display of curious erudition; but I must content myself with having laid down the conditions which all true play must fulfil; and let every man choose the kind of play which hits his peculiar taste. There never has been in England any lack of sports in nominal existence: I heartily wish they were all (except the cruel ones of baiting and torturing animals) still kept up. The following lines are from a little book published in the reign of James I. : —

Man, I dare challenge thee to Throw the Sledge,
To Jump or Leape over ditch or hedge:

To Wrastle, play at Stooleball, or to Runne,
To Pitch the Barre, or to shoote off a Gunne:
To play at Loggetts, Nine Holes, or Ten Pinnes,
To try it out at Football by the shinnes:
At Ticktack, Irish Noddie, Maw, and Ruffe,
At Hot Cockles, Leapfrog, or Blindmanbuffe:
To drink half-pots, or deale at the whole canne,
To play at Base, or Pen and ynkhorne Sir Jan:
To daunce the Morris, play at Barley-breake,
At all exploytes a man can think or speak:
At Shove-Groate, Venterpoynt, or Crosse and Pile,
At Beshrow him that's last at yonder Style:
At leaping o'er a Midsommer-bon-fier,
Or at the Drawing Dun out of the Myer.

In most agricultural districts it is wonderful how little play there is in the life of the labouring class. Well may the agricultural labourer be called a 'working-man,' for truly he does little else than work. His eating and sleeping are cut down to the *minimum* that shall suffice to keep him in trim for working. And the consequence is, that when he does get a holiday, he does not know what to make of himself; and in too many cases he spends it in getting drunk. I know places where the working men have no idea of any play, of any recreation, except getting drunk. And if their overwrought wives, who must nurse five or six children, prepare the meals, tidy the house,—in fact, do the work which occupies three or four servants in the house of the poorest gentleman,—if the poor overwrought creatures can contrive to find a blink of leisure through their waking hours, they know how to make no nobler use of it than to gossip, rather ill-naturedly, about their neighbours' affairs, and especially to discuss the domestic arrangements of the squire and the parson. Working men and women too frequently have forgotten how to play. It is so long since they did it, and they have so little heart for it.

9

And God knows that the pressure of constant care, and
the wolf kept barely at arm's length from the door, do
leave little heart for it. O wealthy proprietors of land,
you who have so much in your power, try to infuse
something of joy and cheerfulness into the lot of your
humble neighbours! Read and ponder the essay and
the conversation on *Recreation*, which you will find in the
first volume of *Friends in Council*. And read again, I
trust for the hundredth time, the poem from which I
quote the lines which follow. Let me say here, that I
verily believe some of my readers will not know the
source whence I draw these lines. More is the shame:
but longer experience of life is giving me a deep conviction of the astonishing ignorance of my fellow-creatures.
I shall not tell them. They shall have the mortification
of asking their friends the question. Only let it be added,
that the poem where the passage stands, contains others
more sweet and touching by far, — so sweet and touching that in all the range of English poetry they have
never been surpassed.

> How often have I blest the coming day,
> When toil remitting, lent its turn to play;
> And all the village train, from labour free,
> Led up their sports beneath the spreading tree,
> While many a pastime circled in the shade,
> The young contending as the old surveyed;
> And many a gambol frolick'd o'er the ground,
> And sleights of art and feats of strength went round.
> And still, as each repeated pleasure tired,
> Succeeding sports the mirthful band inspired:
> The dancing pair that simply sought renown,
> By holding out to tire each other down, —
> The swain mistrustless of his smutted face,
> While secret laughter titter'd round the place, —
> The bashful virgin's sidelong looks of love,
> The matron's glance that would those looks reprove.
> These were thy charms, sweet village, sports like these,
> With sweet succession, taught even toil to please.

CHAPTER V.

CONCERNING COUNTRY HOUSES AND COUNTRY LIFE.

ONCE upon a time, I lived in the very heart of London : absolutely in Threadneedle-street. I lived in the house of a near relation, an opulent lawyer, who, after he had become a rich man, chose still to dwell in the locality where he had made his fortune. All around, for miles in every direction, there were nothing but piles of houses — streets and lanes of dingy brick houses everywhere. Not a vestige of nature could be seen, except in the sky above, in the stunted vegetation of a few little City gardens. and in the foul and discoloured river. The very surface of the earth, for yards in depth, was the work of generations that had lived and died centuries before amid the narrow lanes of the ancient city. There, for months together, I, a boy without youth, under the care of one who, though substantially kind, had not a vestige of sympathy with nature or with home affections, wearily counted the days which were to pass before the yearly visit to a home far away. I cannot by any words express the thirst and craving which I then felt for green fields and trees. The very name of *the country* was like music in my ear ; and when I heard any man say he was *going down to the country,* how I envied him ! It was not so bad in winter : though even then the clear frosty days called up many pictures of cheerful winter skies away from those weary streets ; — of boughs bending beneath the quiet snow ; — of the beautiful fretwork of the frost upon the hedges and the grass, and of its exhilarating crispness in the air ; — of the stretches of the frozen river, seen through the leafless boughs, covered with happy groups whose merry faces were like a good-natured defiance of the wintry weather. But when the spring revival began to make itself felt ; when the days began to lengthen, and the poor shrubs in the squares to bud, and when there was that accession of light during the day which is so cheerful after the winter gloom, then the longing for the country grew painfully strong, like the seaman's calenture, or the Swiss exile's yearning for his native hills. When I knew that the hawthorn hedges were white, and the fruit-trees laden with blossoms, how I longed to be among them ! I well remember the kindly feeling I bore to a dingy hostelry in a narrow lane off Cheapside, for the sake of its name. It was called *Blossom's Inn ;* and many a time I turned out of my way, and stood looking up at its sign, with eyes that saw a very different scene from the blackened walls. I remember how I used to rise at early morning, and take long walks in whatever direction I thought it possible that a glimpse of anything like the country could be seen: away up the New North-road there were some trees, and some little plots of grass. There was something at once pleasing and sad about those curious little gardens which still exist here and there in the heart of London, consisting generally of a plot of grass of a dozen yards in length and breadth, surrounded by a walk of yellow gravel, stared at on every side by the back windows of tall brick houses, and containing a few little trees, whose

leaves in spring look so strangely fresh against the smoke-
blackened branches. I do not wish to be egotistical; and
I describe all these feelings merely because I believe that
honestly to tell exactly what one has himself felt, is the
true way to describe the common feelings of most people
in like circumstances. I dare say that if any youth of
sixteen, pent up in Threadneedle-street now, should happen to read what I have written, he will understand it
all with a hearty sympathy which I shall not succeed in
exciting in the minds of many of my readers. But such
a one will know, thoroughly and completely, what pictures rise before the mind's eye of one pent up amid
miles of brick walls and stone pavements, at the mention
of the country, of trees, hedge-rows, fields, quiet lanes and
footpaths, and simple rustic people.

I wish to assure the man, shut up in a great city, that
he has compensations and advantages of which he probably does not think. The keenness of his relish for
country scenes, the intensity of his enjoyment of his occasional glimpses of them, counterbalance in a great degree the fact that his glimpses of them are but few. I
live in the country now, and have done so for several
years. It is a beautiful district of country too, and amid
a quiet and simple population; yet I must confess that
my youthful notion of rural bliss is a good deal abated.
'Use lessens marvel, it is said:' one cannot be always in
raptures about what one sees every hour of every day.
It is the man in populous cities pent, who knows the
value of green fields. It is your cockney (I mean your
educated Londoner) who reads *Bracebridge Hall* with
the keenest delight, and luxuriates in the thought of
country scenes, country houses, country life. He has
not come close enough to discern the flaws and blemishes

of the picture; and he has not learned by experience
that in whatever scenes led, human life is always much
the same thing. I have long since found that the country, in this nineteenth century, is by no means a scene
of Arcadian innocence;—that its apparent simplicity is
sometimes dogged stupidity;—that men lie and cheat in
the country just as much as in the town, and that the
country has even more of mischievous tittle-tattle;—
that sorrow and care and anxiety may quite well live in
Elizabethan cottages grown over with honeysuckle and
jasmine, and that very sad eyes may look forth from
windows round which roses twine. The poets (town
poets, no doubt) were drawing upon their imagination,
when they told how 'Virtue lives in Irwan's Vale,' and
how 'with peace and plenty there, lives the happy vil-
lager.' Virtue and religion are plants of difficult growth,
even in the country; and notwithstanding Cowper's exquisite poem, I am not sure that 'The calm retreat, the
silent shade, with prayer and praise agree,' better than
the closet into which the weary man may enter, in the
quiet evening, after the business and bustle of the town.
People may pace up and down a country lane, between
fragrant hedges of blossoming hawthorn, and tear their
neighbours' characters to very shreds. And the eye,
that is sharp to see the minutest object on the hillside
far away, may be blind to the beauty which is spread
over all the landscape. Nor is the country always in the
trim holiday dress which delights the summer wayfarer.
Country roads are not all nicely gravelled walks between
edges of clipped box, or through velvety turf, shaven by
weekly mowings. There are many days on which the
country looks, to any one without a most decided taste
for it, extremely bleak and drear. The roads are pud-

dles of mud, which will search its way through boots to
which art has supplied soles of two inches thickness.
The deciduous trees are shivering skeletons, bending before the howling blast. The sheep paddle about the
brown fields, eating turnips mingled with clay. Now,
for myself, I like all that: but a man from the town
would not. I positively enjoy the wet, blustering afternoon, with its raw wind, its driving sleet, its roads of
mud. How delightful the rapid 'constitutional' from
half-past two till half-past four, with the comfortable feeling that we have accomplished a good forenoon's work
at our desk (sermon or article, as the case may be), and
with the cheerful prospect of getting rid of all these
sloppy garments, and feeling so snug and clean ere we
sit down to dinner, when we shall hear the rain and wind
softened into music through the warm crimson drapery
of our windows; and then the evening of leisure amid
books and music, with the *placens uxor* on the other
easy-chair by the fireside, and the little children, scream-
ing with delight, tumbling about one's knees. So I like
even the gusty, rainy afternoon, for the sake of all that it
suggests to me. Nor will the true inhabitant of the
country forget the delight with which he has hailed a
gloomy, drizzling November day, when he has evergreen
shrubs to transplant. Have I not stood for hours, in a
state of active and sensible enjoyment, watching how the
hollies and yews and laurels gradually clothed some bare
spot or unsightly corner, rejoicing that the calm air and
ceaseless mizzle which made my attendants and myself
like soaked sponges, was life to these stout shoots and
these bright hearty green leaves! But a town man does
not understand all these things; and I have no doubt
that on one of these January days, when the entire dis-

tant prospect — hills, sky, trees, fields — might be faithfully depicted on canvas by different shades of Indian ink, he would see nothing in the prospect but gloom and desolation.

Then it is very picturesque to see the ploughman at work on a soft, mild winter day. It is a beautiful contrast, that light brown of the turned-over earth, and the fresh green of the remainder of the field; and what more pleasing than these lines of furrow, so beautifully straight and regular? But go up and walk by the ploughman's side, you man from town, and see how you like it. You will find it awfully dirty work. In a few minutes you will find it difficult to drag along your feet, laden with some pounds weight to each of adherent earth; and you will have formed some idea of the physical exertion, and the constant attention, which the ploughman needs, to keep his furrow straight and even, to retain the plough the right depth in the ground, and to manage his horses. Hard work for that poor fellow; and ill-paid work. No horse, mule, donkey, camel, or other beast of labour in the world, goes through so much exertion, in proportion to his strength, between sunrise and sunset, as does that rational being, all to earn the humblest shelter and the poorest fare that will maintain bare life. You walk beside him, and see how poorly he is dressed. His feet have been wet since six o'clock A.M., when he went half a mile from his cottage up to the stables of the farm to dress his horses: he has had a little tea and coarse bread, and nothing more, for his dinner at twelve o'clock (I speak from personal knowledge): he will have nothing more till his twelve (I have known it fifteen) hours of work are finished, when he will have his scanty supper: and while he is walking backwards and forwards all day,

his mind is not so engaged but that he has abundant time
to think of his little home anxieties, which are not little
to him, though they may be nothing, my reader, to you
— of the ailing wife at home, for whom the doctor orders
wine which he cannot buy, and of the children, poorly
fed, and barely clad, and hardly at all educated, born to
the same life of toil and penury as himself. I know
nothing about political economy : I have not understanding for it ; and I feel glad, when I think of the social
evils I see, that the responsibility of treating them rests
upon abler heads than mine. Neither do I know how
much truth there may be in the stories of which I hear
the echoes from afar, of the occasional privation and oppression of the manufacturing poor, against which, as it
seems to me, these unhappy strikes and trades unions
are their helpless and frantic appeal. But I can say,
from my own knowledge of the condition of our agricultural population, that sometimes men bearing the character of reputable farmers practise as great tyranny and
cruelty towards their labourers and cottars, under a pure
sky and amid beautiful scenery, as ever disgraced the
ugly and smoky factory-town, where such things seem
more in keeping with the locality.

Yet, though in a gloomy mood, one can easily make out
a long catalogue of country evils, — evils which I know
cannot be escaped in a fallen world, and among a sinful
race, — still I thank God that my lot is cast in the country. I know, indeed, that the town contains at once
the best and the worst of mankind. In the country,
we are, intellectually and morally, a sort of middling
species ; we do not present the extremes, either in good
or evil, which are to be found in the hot-house atmosphere of great cities. There is no reasoning with tastes,

as every one knows; but to some men there is, at every
season, an indescribable charm about a country life. I
like to know all about the people around me; and I do
not care though in return they know all, and more than
all, about me. I like the audible stillness in which one
lives on autumn days; the murmur of the wind through
trees even when leafless, and the brawl of the rivulet
even when swollen and brown. There is a constant
source of innocent pleasure and interest in little country
cares, in planting and tending trees and flowers, in sympathizing with one's horses and dogs,—even with pigs
and poultry. And although one may have lived beyond
middle age without the least idea that he had any taste
for such matters, it is amazing how soon he will find,
when he comes to call a country home his own, that the
taste has only been latent, kept down by circumstances,
and ready to spring into vigorous existence whenever
the repressing circumstances are removed. Men in whom
this is not so, are the exception to the universal rule.
Take the senior wrangler from his college, and put him
down in a pretty country parsonage; and in a few weeks
he will take kindly to training honeysuckle and climbing
roses. he will find scope for his mathematics in laying
out a flower-garden, and he will be all excitement in
planning and carrying out an evergreen shrubbery, a
primrose bank, a winding walk, a little stream with a
tiny waterfall, spanned by a rustic bridge. Proud he
will be of that piece of engineering, as ever was Robert
Stephenson when he had spanned the stormy Menai.
There is something in all this simple work that makes a
man kind-hearted: out-of-door occupation of this sort
gives one much more cheerful views of men and things,
and disposes one to sympathize heartily with the cottager

proud of his little rose-plots, and of his enormous gooseberry that attained to renown in the pages of the county newspaper. I do not say anything of the incalculable advantage to health which arises from this pleasant intermingling of mental and physical occupation in the case of the recluse scholar; nor of the animated rebound with which one lays down the pen or closes the volume, and hastens out to the total change of interest which is found in the open air; nor of the evening at mental work again, but with the lungs that play so freely, the head that feels so cool and clear, the hand so firm and ready, testifying that we have not forgotten the grand truth that to care for bodily health and condition is a Christian duty, bringing with its due discharge an immediate and sensible blessing. I am sure that the poor man who comes to ask a favour of his parish clergyman, has a far better chance of finding a kind and unhurried hearing, if he finds him of an afternoon superintending his labourers, rosy with healthful exercise, delighted with the good effect which has been produced by some little improvement — the deviation of a walk, the placing of an araucaria — than if he found the parson a bilious, dyspeptic, splenetic, gloomy, desponding, morose, misanthropic, horrible animal, with knitted brow and jarring nerves, lounging in his easy-chair before the fire, and afraid to go out into the fine clear air, for fear (unhappy wretch) of getting a sore throat or a bad cough. I remember to have read somewhere of an humble philanthropist who undertook the reformation of a number of juvenile thieves; and for that end employed them in a large garden somewhere near London, to raise vegetables and flowers for the market. There did the youthful prig concentrate his thoughts on the planting of cabbage, and find the unwonted de-

light of a day spent in innocent labour; there did the
area-sneak bud the rose and set the potato: and there,
as days passed on, under the gentle influence of vegetable
nature, did a healthier, happier, purer tone come over
the spiritual nature, even as a healthier blood came to
heart and veins. The philanthropist was a true philosopher. There is not a more elevating and purifying occupation than that of tending the plants of the earth. I
should never be afraid of finding a man revengeful, malignant, or cruel, whom I knew to be fond of his shrubs
and flowers. And I believe that in the mind of most
men of cultivation, there is some vague, undefined sense
that the country is the scene where human life attains its
happiest development. I believe that the great proportion of such men cherish the hope, perhaps a distant and
faint one, that at some time they shall possess a country
home where they may pass the last years tranquilly, far
from the tumult of cities. Many of those who cherish
such a hope will never realize it; and many more are
quite unsuited for enjoying a country life were it within
their reach. But all this is founded upon the instinctive
desire there is in human nature to possess some portion
of the earth's surface. You look with indescribable interest at an acre of ground which is your own. There is
something quite remarkable about your own trees. You
have a sense of property in the sunset over your own
hills. And there is a perpetual pleasure in the sight of
a fair landscape, seen from your own door. Do not believe people who say that all scenes soon become indifferent, through being constantly seen. An ugly street may
cease to be a vexation, when you get accustomed to it;
but a pleasant prospect becomes even more pleasant,
when the beauty which arises from your own associations

with it is added to that which is properly its own. No
doubt, you do grow weary of the landscape before your
windows, when you are spending a month at some place
of temporary sojourn, seaside or inland; but it is quite
different with that which surrounds your own home.
You do not try *that* by so exacting a standard. You
never think of calling your constant residence dull, though
it may be quiet to a degree which would make you think
a place insupportably dull, to which you were paying a
week's visit.

What an immense variety of human dwellings are
comprised within the general name of the Country
Home! We begin with such places as Chatsworth and
Belvoir, Arundel and Alnwick, Hamilton and Drum-
lanrig: houses standing far withdrawn within encircling
woods, approached by avenues of miles in length, which
debouch on public highways in districts of country quite
remote from one another; with acres of conservatory,
and scores of miles of walks; and shutting in their sacred
precincts by great park walls from the approach and the
view of an obtrusive world beyond. We think of the
old Edwardian Castle, weather-worn and grim, with
drawbridge and portcullis and moat and oak-roofed hall
and storied windows; of the huge, square, corniced,
many-chimnied, ugly building of the renaissance, which
never has anything to recommend its aspect except when
it gains a dignity from enormous size; then down through
the classes of manor-houses, abbeys, and halls, high-
gabled, oriel-windowed, turret-staired, long-corridored,
haunted-chambered, with their parks, greater or less,
their oaken clumps, their spreading horse-chestnuts, their
sunshiny glades, their startled deer; till we come to the
villa with a few acres of ground, such as Dean Swift

wished for himself, with its modest conservatory, its neat little shrubbery, its short carriage drive, its brougham or phaeton drawn by one stout horse. Then, upon the outskirts of the country town, we find a class of less ambitious dwellings, which yet struggle for the title of villa — cheap would-be Gothic houses, with overhanging eaves and latticed windows, standing in a half-acre plot of ground, which yet is large enough to give a new direction to the tradesman's thoughts, by giving him space to cultivate a few shrubs and flowers. Last comes the wayside cottage, sometimes neat and pretty, often cold, damp, and ugly ; sometimes gay with its little plot of flowers, sometimes odorous with its neighbouring dungheap ; the difference depending not half so much upon the income enjoyed by its tenant, as upon his having a tidy, active wife, and a kindly, improving, generous landlord.

And various as the varied dwellings, are the scenes amid which they stand. In rich English dales, in wild Highland glens, on the bank of quiet inland rivers, and on windy cliffs frowning over the ocean — there, and in a thousand other places, we have still the country home, with its peculiar characteristics. Thither comes the postman only once a day, always anxiously, often nervously expected : and thither the box of books, the magazines of last month, and the reviews of last quarter, sent from the Reading-club in the High-street of the town five miles off. How truly, by the way, has somebody or other stated that the next town and the railway station are always five miles away from every country house ! Thither the carrier, three times a week, brings the wicker-woven box of bread ; there does the managing housewife have her store-room, round whose shelves are arranged groceries of every sort and degree ; and there, at uncertain intervals, dies the home-fed sheep or pig, which yieldeth joints which are pronounced far superior to any which the butcher's shop ever supplied. There, sometimes, is found the cheerful, modest establishment, calculated rather within the income, with everything comfortable, neat, and even elegant; where family dinners may be enjoyed which afford real satisfaction to all, and win the approval of even the most refined *gourmet;* and there sometimes, especially when the mistress of the house is a fool, is found the unhappy scramble of the *ménage* that, with a thousand a year, aims at aping five thousand; where there is a French ladies'-maid of cracked reputation, and a lady who talks largely of 'what has she been accustomed to,' and 'what she regards herself as entitled to;' where every-day comfort is sacrificed to occasional attempts at showy entertainments, to which the neighbouring peer goes under the pressure of a most urgent invitation; where gooseberry champagne and very acid claret flow in hospitable profusion; and where dressed-up stable-boys and ploughmen dash wildly up against each other, as the uneasy banquet strains anxiously along.

Very incomplete would be any attempt at classifying the country homes of Britain, in which no mention should be made of the dwellings of the clergy. In this country, the parish priest is not isolated from all sympathy with the members of his flock, by an enforced celibacy; he is not only the spiritual guide of his parishioners, but he is in most instances the head of a family, the cultivator of the ground, the owner of horses, cows, sheep, pigs, and dogs. I do not deny that in theory, and once perhaps in a thousand times in practice, it is a finer thing that the clergyman should be one given exclusively to his sacred calling, standing apart from and elevated above the little prosaic cares of life, and 'having his conversation in Heaven.' It seems at first as if it better befitted one who has to be much exercised in sacred thoughts and duties — whose hands are to dispense the sacred emblems of Communion, and whose voice is to breathe direction and comfort into dying ears — to have nothing to do with such sublunary matters as seeing a cold bandage put upon a horse's foreleg, or arranging for the winter supply of hay, or considering as to laying in store of coals at the setting in of snowy weather. It jars somewhat upon our imagination of the even run of that holy calling, to think of the parson (like Sydney Smith) proudly producing his lemon-bag, or devising his patent Tantalus and his universal scratcher. But surely all this is a wrong view of things. Surely it is Platonism rather than Christianity to hold that there is anything necessarily debasing or materializing about the cares of daily life. All these cares take their character from the spirit with which we pass through them. The simple French monk, five hundred years since, who acted as cook to his brethren, indicated the clergyman's true path when he wrote, 'I put my little egg-cake on the fire for the sake of Christ;' and George Herbert, more gracefully, has shown how, as the eye may either look *on* glass, or look *through* it, we may look no farther than the daily task, or may look through it to something nobler beyond:

Teach me, my God and King,
In all things Thee to see:
And, what I do in anything,
To do it as for Thee.

A servant with this clause,
Makes drudgery divine:
Who sweeps a room, as for Thy laws,
Makes that, and the action, fine.

We have all in our mind some abstracted and idealized picture of what the country parsonage, as well as the country parson, should be : the latter, the clergyman and the gentleman : the former, the fit abode for him and his ; near the church, not too much retired from the public way, old and ivied, of course Gothic, with bay windows, fantastic gables, wreathed chimneys, and overhanging eaves ; with many evergreens, with ancient trees, with peaches ripening on the sunny garden wall, with an indescribable calm and peacefulness over the whole, deepened by the chime of the passing river, and the windy caw of the distant rookery ; such should the country parsonage be. But the best of anything is not the commonest of the class : and I can only add that I believe it would afford unmingled satisfaction to the tenant of rectory, vicarage, parsonage, deanery, or manse, if his dwelling were all that the writer would wish to see it.

It is pleasant to think over what we may call the poetry of country house-making, — the historical cases in which men have sought to idealize to the utmost the scene around them, and to live in a more ambitious or a humbler fairyland. Yet the instances that first occur to us do not encourage the belief that happiness is more certainly to be found in fairyland than in Manchester or in Siberia. One thinks of Beckford, the master of almost unlimited wealth, ' commanding his fairy-palace to glitter amid the orange groves, and aloes, and palms of Cintra : ' and after he had formed his paradise, wearying of it, and abandoning it, to move the gloomy moralizing of *Childe Harold*. One thinks of him, not yet content with his experience, spending twenty years upon the turrets and gardens of Fonthill, that ' cathedral turned into a toyshop ;' whose magnificence was yet but a faint and distant attempt to equal the picture drawn by the prodigal imagination of the author of *Vathek*. One thinks of Horace Walpole, amid the gim-crackery of Strawberry-hill; of Sir Walter Scott, building year by year that 'romance in stone and lime,' and idealizing the bleakest and ugliest portion of the banks of the Tweed, till the neglected Clartyhole became the charming but costly Abbotsford. One thinks of Shenstone, devoting his life to making a little paradise of the Leasowes, where, as Johnson tells us in his grand resounding prose, he set himself ' to point his prospects, to diversify his surface, to entangle his walks, and to wind his waters; which he did with such judgment and fancy as made his little domain the envy of the great and the admiration of the skilful ; a place to be visited by travellers and copied by designers.' Nor must we forget how the bitter little Pope, by the taste with which he laid out his five acres at Twickenham, did much to banish the stiff Dutch style, and to encourage the modern fashion of landscape-gardening in imitation of nature, which was so successfully carried out by the well-known Capability Brown. It is putting too extreme a case, when we pass to that which in our boyish days we all thought the perfection and delight of country residences, the island-cave of Robinson Crusoe : with its barricade of stakes which took root and grew into trees, and its impenetrable wilderness of wood, all planted by the exile's hand, which went down to the margin of the sea. It is coming nearer home, to pass to the French château ; the tower perched upon the rock above the Rhine ; and the German castle, which of course is somewhere in the Black Forest, frequented by robbers and haunted by ghosts. And we ascend to the sublime in human abodes, when we think of the magnificent Alhambra, looking down proudly upon Moorish Granada: that miracle of barbaric beauty, which Washington Irving has so finely described : with its countless courts and halls, its enchanted gateways, its graceful pillars of marble of different hues, and its fountains that once made cool music for the delight of Moslem prince and peer.

We pass, by an easy transition, to the literature of country-houses, of which there are two well-marked classes. We have the real and the ideal schools of the literature of country-houses and country life : or perhaps, as both are in a great degree ideal, we should rather call them the would-be real, and the avowedly romantic. We have the former charmingly exemplified in *Bracebridge Hall;* charmingly in the Spectator's account of Sir Roger de Coverley, amid his primitive tenantry ; with a little characteristic coarseness, in Swift's poem, beginning,

> I've often wished that I had clear,
> For life, six hundred pounds a year, —

which, by the way, is an imitation of that graceful Latin poet who delighted, so many centuries since, in his little Sabine farm. Then there are Miss Mitford's quiet, pleasing delineations of English country life ; many delightful touches of it in *Friends in Council* and its sequel ; and Samuel Rogers, though essentially a man of the town, has given a very complete picture of cottage life in his little poem, which thus sets out,

> Mine be a cot beside the hill;
> A beehive's hum shall soothe my ear:
> A willowy brook, that turns a mill,
> With many a fall, shall linger near.

We mention all these, not of course, as a thousandth part of what our literature contains of country-houses and life, but as a sample of that mode of treating these subjects which we have termed the would-be real : and as specimens of the avowedly romantic way of describing such things, we refer to Poe's gorgeous picture of the ' Domain of Arnheim,' where his affluent imagination has run riot, under the stimulus of fancied boundless wealth : and the same author's ' Landor's Cottage,' a scene of sweet simplicity, which is somewhat spoiled by just the smallest infusion of the theatrical. The writings of Poe, with all their extraordinary characteristics, are so little known in this country, that we dare say our readers will feel obliged to us for a short account of the former piece.

A certain man, named Ellison, suddenly came into the possession of a fortune of a hundred millions sterling. Poe, you see, being wretchedly poor, did not do things by halves. Ellison resolved that he would find occupation and happiness in making the finest place in the world ; and he made it. The approach to Arnheim was by the river. After intricate windings, pursued for some hours through wild chasms and rocks, the vessel suddenly entered a circular basin of water, of two hundred yards in diameter: this basin was surrounded by hills of considerable height : —

Their sides sloped from the water's edge at an angle of some forty-five degrees, and they were clothed from base to summit, not a perceptible point escaping, in a drapery of the most gorgeous flower-blossoms: scarcely a green leaf being visible among the sea of odorous and fluctuating colour. This basin was of great depth, but so transparent was the water that the bottom, which seemed to consist of a thick mass of small round alabaster pebbles, was distinctly visible by glimpses, — that is to say, whenever the eye could permit itself *not* to see, far down in the inverted heaven, the duplicate blooming of the hills. On these latter there were no trees, nor even shrubs of any size. * * * As the eye traced upwards the myriad-tinted slope, from its sharp junction with the water to its vague termination amid the folds of overhanging cloud, it became, indeed, difficult not to fancy a panoramic cataract of rubies, sapphires, opals, and golden onyxes, rolling silently out of the sky.

Here the visitor quits the vessel which has borne him so far, and enters a light canoe of ivory, which is wafted by unseen machinery : —

The canoe steadily proceeds, and the rocky gate of the vista is approached, so that its depths can be more distinctly seen. To the right arise a chain of lofty hills, rudely and luxuriantly wooded. It is observed, however, that the trait of exquisite *cleanness* where the bank dips into the water still prevails. There is not one token of the usual river *débris*. To the left, the character of the scene is softer and more obviously artificial. Here the bank slopes upward from the stream in a very gentle ascent, forming a broad sward of grass of a texture resembling nothing so much as velvet, and of a brilliancy of green which would bear comparison with the tint of the purest emerald. This plateau varies in breadth from ten to three hundred yards; reaching from the river bank to a wall, fifty feet high, which extends in an infinity of curves, but following the general direction of the river, until lost in the distance to the westward. This wall is of one continuous rock, and has been formed by cutting perpendicularly the once rugged precipice of the stream's southern bank; but no trace of the labour has been suffered to remain. The chiselled stone has the hue of ages, and is profusely hung and overspread with the ivy, the coral honeysuckle, the eglantine, and the clematis. * * * *

Floating gently onward, the voyager, after many short turns, finds his progress apparently barred by a gigantic gate, or rather door, of burnished gold, elaborately carved and fretted, and reflecting the direct rays of the now sinking sun with an effulgence that seems to wreathe the whole surrounding forest in flames. * * * The canoe approaches the gate. Its ponderous wings are slowly and musically unfolded. The boat glides between them, and commences a rapid descent into a vast amphitheatre entirely begirt with purple mountains, whose bases are laved by a gleaming river throughout the full extent of their circuit. Meanwhile the whole Paradise of Arnheim bursts upon the view. There is a gush of entrancing melody: there is an oppressive sense of strange sweet odour: there is a dream-like intermingling to the eye of tall, slender Eastern trees,—bosky shrubberies,—flocks of golden and crimson birds,—lily-fringed lakes,—meadows of violets, tulips, poppies, hyacinths, and tuberoses,—long intertangled lines of silver streamlets,—and, upspringing confusedly from amid all, a mass of semi-Gothic, semi-Saracenic architecture, sustaining itself as if by miracle in mid-air,—glittering in the red sunlight with a hundred oriels, minarets, and pinnacles; and seeming the phantom handiwork, conjointly, of the Sylphs, the Fairies, the Genii, and the Gnomes.*

This is certainly landscape-gardening on a grand scale : but the whole thing is a shade too immediately suggestive of the *Arabian Nights*. Why not, we are disposed to say, go the entire length of Aladdin's palace at once, and give us walls of alternate blocks of silver and gold ; gardens, whose trees bear fruits of diamond, emerald, ruby, and sapphire ; and a roc's egg hung up in the entrance-hall ? ; Fancy a man driving up in a post-chaise from the railway-station to a house like that ! Why, the only permissible way of arriving at its front-door would be on an enchanted horse, that has brought one from Bagdad through the air ; and instead of a footman in spruce livery coming out to take in one's portmanteau, I should look to be received by a porter with an elephant's head, or an afrit with bats' wings. I could not go up comfortably to my room to dress for dinner : and only fancy coming down to the drawing-room in a coat by Stulz and dress boots by Hoby ! Rather should we wreathe our brow with flowers, endue a purple robe, the gift of Noureddin, and perfume our handkerchief with odours which had formed part of the last freight of Sinbad the Sailor. If we made any remark, political or critical, which happened to be disagreeable to our host,

* *Works of Edgar Allan Poe.* Vol. I. pp. 400–403. American Edition.

of course he would immediately change us into an ape, and transport us a thousand leagues in a second to the Dry Mountains.

But to return to the sober daylight in which ordinary mortals live, and to the sort of country in which a man may live whose fortune is less than a hundred millions. we have abundance of the literature of the country in one shape or another: poetry and poetic prose which profess to depict country life, and books of detail which profess to instruct us how to manage country concerns. We breathe a clear, cool atmosphere for which we are the better, when we turn over the pages of *The Seasons: that* is a book which never will become stale. Cowper's poetry is redolent of the country: and though it is all nonsense to say that ' God made the country and man made the town,' yet *The Winter Walk at Noon* almost leads us to think so. You see the Cockney's fancy that the country is a paradise, always in holiday guise, in poor Keats's lines —

> O for a draught of vintage, that hath been
>   Cooled for a long age in the deep-delved earth;
> Tasting of Flora and the country green,
>   Dance, and Provençal song, and sun-burnt mirth!

And there are several books whose titles are sure to awaken pleasant thoughts in the mind of the lover of nature, who knows that, notwithstanding Dr. Johnson's axiom, one green field is not just like any other green field, and who prefers a country lane to Fleet-street. There is Mr. Jesse's *Country Life*, which is mainly occupied in describing, with a minute and kindly accuracy, the ways and doings of bird, beast, and insect; and thus calling forth a feeling of interest in all our humble fellow-creatures; for in the case of inferior animals the principle holds good, that all that is needed to make one like almost any of them is just to come to know them. And on this track one need do no more than name White's delightful *Natural History of Selborne*. There is Mr. William Howitt's *Boy's Country Book*, which sets out the sports and occupations of childhood and rural scenes, with a fulness of sympathy which makes us lament that its author should ever exchange these genial topics for the briars of polemical controversy. There is Mr. Willmott's *Summer Time in the Country;* a disappointing book; for notwithstanding the melody of its name, it is mainly a string of criticisms, good, bad, and indifferent: with a slight surrounding atmosphere, indeed, of country life; but most of the production might have been written in Threadneedle-street. There is a pleasant and well-informed little anonymous volume, called *The Flower Garden,* which contains the substance of two articles originally published in the *Quarterly Review;* and every one knows Bacon's *Essay of Gardens,* in which the writer gives the reins to his fancy, and pictures out a little paradise of thirty acres in extent, including in it some specimen of all schools of landscape gardening. Mrs. Loudon's various publications have done much to foster a taste for gardening among ladies. An exceedingly pleasing and genial book, called *The Manse Garden,* which has had a large circulation in Scotland, is intended to stimulate the Scottish clergy to neatness and taste in the arrangement of their gardens and glebes. A handsome work entitled *Rustic Adornments for Homes of Taste,* lately published, contains many practical instructions for the decoration of the country home. And an elegantly illustrated volume, which appeared a few months ago, is given to *Rhymes and Roundelays in*

Praise of a Country Life. Sir Joseph Paxton has not thought it unworthy of him to write a little tract, called *The Cottager's Calendar of Garden Operations*, the purpose of which is to show how much may be done in the most limited space in the way of growing vegetables for profit and flowers for ornament ; and in these days, when happily the social and sanitary elevation of the masses is beginning to attract something of the notice which it deserves, I trust that reformers will not forget the powerful influence of the garden, and a taste for gardening concerns, in elevating and purifying the working man's mind, and adding interest and beauty to the working man's home. And in truth, we shall never succeed in inducing working-men to spend their evenings at home rather than in the alehouse, till we have succeeded in rendering their own homes tidy, comfortable, and inviting to a degree that shall at least equal the neatly sanded floor and the well-scrubbed benches which they can enjoy for a few pence elsewhere.

If there be any among my readers who have it in view to build a country house, I strongly recommend them to have it done by Mr. George Gilbert Scott, whose pleasantly written book on *Secular and Domestic Architecture*, will be read with delight by many who are condemned to live in towns, or who must put up with such a country home as their means permit, but who can luxuriate in imagining what kind of a house they would have if they could have exactly such a house as they wish. Mr. Scott is an out and out supporter of Gothic architecture as the best style for every possible building, large or small, in town or country, from the nobleman's palace to the labourer's cottage, from a cathedral or a town-house to a barn or a pig-sty. But Mr. Scott gives a judicious view of Gothic architecture, as a style capable of unlimited expansion and adaptation, having in its nature the power to accommodate itself to every requirement of modern life and progress, and capable without surrendering its distinctive character, of modification, development, addition, and subtraction, to a degree which renders it the true architecture of the nineteenth century no less than of the thirteenth. It is doing Gothic architecture great injustice to speak of it as the mediæval architecture. Such a description vaguely suggests that it is a style especially suited to the requirements of life in the middle ages : and, by consequence, not well adapted to the exigencies of life at a period when life is very different from what it was in the middle ages. And the notion has been countenanced by the injudicious fashion in which houses were built at the beginning of the great reaction in favour of Gothic. When people grew wearied and disgusted at the ugly Grecian houses which disfigure so many fine old English parks, paltry and pitiful importations of a foreign style into a country which had an indigenous style incomparably superior in beauty, in comfort, in every requisite of the country house, the reaction ran into excess ; and instead of building Gothic *houses*. that is, instead of trying to produce buildings which should be noble and picturesque, and at the same time commodious and convenient to live in, architects built abbeys and castles; and in those cases where they did not produce specimens of mere confectioner's Gothic, they produced buildings utterly unsuited to the exigencies and conditions of modern English life, however beautiful they might be. Now, nothing could be a more flagrant violation of the *spirit* of Gothic, than this scrupulous conformity to the *letter* of Gothic. The

true Gothic architect must hold fitness and use in view
as his primary end ; and his skill is shown when upon
these he superinduces beauty. A fortified castle, with
moat and drawbridge, arrow-slits, and donjon-keep, was a
convenient and suitable building in an unsettled and
lawless age. It is a most inconvenient and unsuitable
building in England in the nineteenth century ; and
while we should prize and cherish the noble specimens
of the Edwardian Castle which we possess, for their
beauty and their associations, we ought to remember
that if the architects who built them were living now,
they would be the first to lay that style aside, as no
longer suitable ; and they would show the true Gothic
taste and spirit in devising dwellings as noble, as picturesque, as interesting, as thoroughly Gothic in character, but fitted for the present age, and the present age's
modes of life. It was not because the Edwardian Castle
was grand and beautiful, that the Edwardian architects
built it as they did ; they built it as they did because *that*
was the most suitable and convenient fashion ; and upon
fitness and use they engrafted grandeur and beauty.
And it is not by a slavish imitation of ancient details
and forms that we shall succeed in producing, at the
present day, what is justly entitled to be called Gothic
architecture. It is rather by a free development and
carrying out of old principles applied to new circumstances and requirements. And it is the glory of Gothic,
that you cannot make a new demand upon it for increased or altered accommodations and appliances, which
may not, in the hand of a worthy architect, be complied
with, not only without diminution of beauty, but even
with increase of beauty. It is beyond comparison the
most squeezable of all styles ; and, provided the squeez-

ing be effected by a master's hand, the style will look all the better for it.

There is a floating belief, entirely without reason, that Gothic is exclusively an ecclesiastical fashion of building. Many people fancy that Gothic architecture suits a church; but is desecrated, or at least becomes unsuitable, when applied to secular and domestic buildings. There can be no doubt, indeed, that to every person who possesses any taste, it is a self-evident axiom that Gothic is the true church architecture: but in the age during which the noblest Gothic churches were built, it was never fancied that churches must be built in one style, and secular buildings in a style essentially dissimilar. The belief which is entertained by the true lover of Gothic architecture is this: that Gothic is essentially the most beautiful architecture; that, properly treated, it is the most commodious architecture; and that, therefore, the Gothic is the style in which all buildings, sacred or secular, public or domestic, ought to be built; with such modifications in the style of each separate building as its special purpose and use shall suggest. It must be admitted, however, that Gothic architecture has one disadvantage as compared with that architecture which is exhibited in Baker-street, in the London suburban terraces, and in the Manchester cotton-mills. Gothic architecture costs more money; but, in judicious hands, not so very much more.

As to the capacity of Gothic architecture to accommodate itself to houses of all classes, let the reader ponder the following words:

It seems to be generally imagined that the merits of the Elizabethan style are most displayed in its grand baronial residences, such as Burleigh or Hatfield. I think quite the contrary. A style is best tested by reducing it to its humblest conditions; and the great glory of this style is, not that it produced gorgeous and costly mansions for the nobles — but that it produced beautifully simple, yet perfectly architectural, cottages for the poor; appropriate and comfortable farmhouses; and pleasant-looking residences for the smaller country-gentlemen, and for the inhabitants of country towns and villages.

Following up the same idea, Mr. Scott somewhere else says

What we want is a style which will stand this test — which will be pleasing in its most normal forms, yet be susceptible of every gradation of beauty, till it reach the noblest and most exalted objects to which art can aspire.

Let it be accepted as an indubitable axiom, that Gothic building is the best building for the town as well as for the country. But I am not called to enter upon that controversial ground; for we are dealing with country houses, in regard to which I believe there is no difference of opinion among people of taste and sense. The country house, as of course, must be Gothic. Tasteless blockheads will no doubt say that the Gothic house is all frippery and gingerbread (as indeed houses of confectioner's Gothic very often are): they will chuckle with delight whenever they hear that the rain has penetrated where the roof of a bay-window joins the wall, or through some ill-contrived gutter in the irregular roof of the house: they will maintain, in the face of fact, that Gothic windows will not admit sufficient light, and cannot exclude draughts: and they will praise the unpretending square-built house, ' with no nonsense about it.' Let us leave such tasteless people to the contemplation of the monstrosities they love : when the question is one of grace or beauty, *their* opinion is (as Coleridge used to say) 'neither here nor there.' Granting (which we do not grant) that Gothic architecture is out of place in the

town, and congenial and suitable in the country, I do not
know that we could pay to that style any higher tribute
than to say that it is the most seemly and suitable to be
placed in conjunction with the fairest scenes of nature.
I do not think we could say better of any work of man,
than that it bears with advantage to be set side by side
with the noblest works of God.   Yet, though a worthy
Gothic building looks beautiful anywhere, it has a special
charm in a sweet country landscape.   It seems just
what was wanted to render the scene perfect.   It is in
harmony with the trees and flowers and hills around, and
with the blue sky overhead.   It is a perpetual pleasure
to look at it.   I do not believe that any mortal can find
real enjoyment in standing and gazing at a huge square
house, with a great wagon roof, and with square holes
cut in a great level blank wall for windows.   It may
draw a certain grandeur from vast size : and it may possess fine accessories, — be shadowed by noble trees,
backed by wild or wooded hills, and *shaded off* into
the fields and lawns by courtly terraces ; but the big
square box is in itself ugly, and never can be anything but ugly.   But how long and delightedly one
can contemplate the worthy Gothic house of similar pretension — with its lights and shadows, its irregular sky-
line, its great mullioned bay-windows and its graceful
oriels perched aloft, its many gables, its wreathed chimneys, its towers and pinnacles, its hall and chapel boldly
shown on the external outline : — for the characteristic of
Gothic is, that it frankly exhibits construction, and makes
a beauty of the exhibition ; while the square-box architecture aims at concealing construction, — producing the
four walls, pierced with the regular rows of windows,
quite irrespective of internal requirements, and then con-

sidering how to fit in the requisite apartments, like the pieces of a child's dissected puzzle, into the square case made for them. Then Gothic admits, and indeed invites, the use of external colouring : and if *that* were only accomplished by the judicious employment of those bricks of different colours which have lately been brought to great perfection, the charm which the entire building possesses to please the eye is indefinitely increased. Only let it be remembered by every man who builds a Gothic country house, that it must be built with much taste and judgment. Gothic is an ambitious style ; and it is especially so in the present state of feeling in England with regard to it. We do not think of criticising a common square house. The taste is never called into play when we look at it. It is taken for granted, *à priori*, that it must be ugly. Not so with a Gothic house. There is a pretension about *that*. The Gothic house invites us to look at it ; and, of course, to form an opinion of it. And therefore, if it be ugly, it is offensively ugly. It aims high, and it must expect severity in case of failure. The square-box house comes forward humbly : it is a goose, and does not pretend to fly. And even a goose is respectable, while it keeps to its own line. But the ugly Gothic house is a goose that hath essayed the eagle's flight ; and if it come down ignominiously to the earth, it is deservedly laughed at. And so, let no man presume to build a country house without securing the services of a thoroughly good architect. And for myself I can say, that whenever I grow a rich man and build a Gothic house, the architect shall be Mr. Scott. Indeed a person of moderate means would be safe in seeking the advice of that accomplished gentleman : for he would, it is evident, take pains to render

even a very small house a pleasing picture. He holds
that a building of the smallest extent affords as decided
if not as abundant scope for fine taste and careful treatment, as the grandest baronial dwelling in Britain. A cottage may be quite as pretty and pleasing as a castle or a
palace could be in their more ambitious style.

Although Gothic architecture has an unlimited capacity of adapting itself to all circumstances and exigencies,
yet there is a freedom about a country site which suits
it bravely. In the country the architect is not ham-
pered by want of space : he is not tied to a street-line
beyond which he must not project, nor fettered by muni-
cipal regulations as to the height or sky-outline of his
building. He may spread over as much ground as he
pleases. And the only restrictions by which he is confined are thus set out by Mr. Scott, in terms which will
commend themselves to the common sense of all readers : —

" The grand principle of planning is, that every room should be in its
right position — both positively and relatively to each other — to the
approaches, views, and aspect ; and that this should be so effected as
not only to avoid disturbing architectural beauty, either within or
without, but to be in the highest degree conducive to it.

In treating of *Buildings in the Country,* Mr. Scott
gives us some account of his ideal of houses suited to all
ranks and degrees of men. Let us look at his picture of
what a villa ought to be : —

To begin, then, with the ordinary villa. Its characteristics should
be quiet cheerfulness and unpretending comfort; it should, both
within and without, be the very embodiment of innocent and simple
enjoyment. No foolish affectation of rusticity, but the reality of
everything which tends to the appreciation of country pleasures in
their more refined form. The external design should so unite itself
with the natural objects around, that they should appear necessary

to one another, and that neither could be very different without the other suffering. The architecture should be quiet and simple; the material that most suited to the neighbourhood — neither too formal and highly finished, nor yet too rustic. The interior should partake of the same general feeling. It should bear no resemblance to the formality of a town house; the rooms should be moderate in height, and not too rigidly regular in form; some of the ceilings should show their timbers wholly or in part; some of the windows should, if it suits the position, open out upon the garden or into conservatories. In most situations the house should spread wide rather than run up high; but circumstances may vary this.

I ask my readers' attention to the paragraph which follows; it contains sound social philosophy: —

In this as in other classes of house-building, the servants' apartments should be well cared for. They should be allowed a fair share in the enjoyments provided for their masters. I have seen houses replete with comfort and surrounded with beauty, where, when you once get into the servants' rooms, you might as well be in a prison. This is morally wrong; let us give our dependents a share in our pleasures, and they will serve us none the less efficiently for it.

Every one can see how pleasant and cheerful a home a villa would be which should successfully embody Mr. Scott's views of what a villa ought to be. Such a dwelling would be quite within the reach of all who possess such a measure of income as in this country now-a-days will suffice to provide those things which are the necessaries of life to people brought up as ladies and gentlemen. And with what heart and vigour a man would set himself to laying out the little piece of land around his house — to making walks, planting clumps of evergreens, and perhaps leading a little brooklet through his domain — if the house, seen from every point, were such as to be a perpetual feast to the eye and the taste! I heartily wish that the poorest clergyman in Britain had just such a parsonage as Mr. Scott has depicted, and the means of living in it without undue pinching and paring.

11

Then, leaving the villa, Mr. Scott points out with great taste and moderation what the cottage should be. Judiciously, he does not aim at too much. It serves no good end to represent the *beau ideal* cottage as a building so costly to erect and to maintain, that landlords of ordinary means get frightened at the mention of so expensive a toy. Cottages may be built so as to be very tasteful and pleasing, while yet the expense of their erection is so moderate that labourers tolerably well off can afford to pay such a rent for them as shall render their erection by no means an unprofitable investment of money. Not, indeed, that a landlord who feels his responsibility as he ought, will ever desire to screw a profit out of his cottagers; but it is well that it should be known that it need not entail any loss whatever to provide for the working class in the country, dwellings in which the requirements of comfort and decency shall be fulfilled. The merest touch from an artistic hand is often all that is needed to convert an ugly, though comfortable, cottage into a pretty and comfortable one. A cottage built of flint, dressed and reticulated with brick, with wood frames and mullions, and the gables of timber, will look exceedingly pleasing. Even of such inexpensive material as mud, thatched with reeds, a very pretty cottage may be built. The truth is, that nowhere is taste so much needed as in building with cheap materials. A good architect will produce a building which will form a pleasing picture, at as small a cost as it is possible to enclose a like space from the external air in the very ugliest way. Gracefulness of form adds nothing to the cost of material. And there is scope for the finest taste in disposing the very cheapest materials in the most effective and graceful fashion. I have seen a church (built, indeed, by a first-rate architect) which was a beautiful picture, both without and within, while yet it cost so little, that I should (if I were a betting man) be content to lay any odds that no mortal could produce a building which would protect an equal number of people from the weather for less money, though with unlimited licence as to ugliness.

The material *mud* is one's ideal of the very shabbiest material for building which is within human reach. *Hovel* is the word that naturally goes with *mud*. Yet Mr. Scott once built a large parsonage, which cost between two and three thousand pounds, of mud, thatched with reeds. Warmth was the end in view. I have no doubt the parsonage proved a most picturesque and quaint affair; and if I could find out where it is, I would go some distance to see it.

Having given us his idea of what a country villa and a country cottage ought to be, Mr. Scott proceeds to set out his ideal of the home of the nobleman or great landed proprietor : —

The proper expressions for a country mansion of the higher class —. the residence of a landed proprietor — beyond that degree of dignity suited to the condition of the owner, are perhaps, first, a friendly, unforbidding air, giving the idea of a kind of patriarchal hospitality; a look that seems to invite approach rather than repel it. Secondly, an air which appears to connect it with the history of the country, and a style which belongs to it. Thirdly, a character which harmonizes well with the surrounding scenery, and unites itself with it, as if not only were the best spot chosen for the house, and its natural beauties fostered and increased so as to render this the central focus, but further, that the house itself should seem to be the very thing which was necessary to give the last touch and finish to the scene — the object for which nature had prepared the site, and without which its charms would be incomplete.

It is not too much to say that a very great proportion

of the more ambitious dwellings of this country signally fail of coming up to these conditions, and serve only to disfigure the beautiful parks in which they stand. A huge Palladian house entirely lacks the genial, hearty, inviting look of the Elizabethan or Gothic house. Instead of having a look of that hospitality and welcome which we are proud to think of as especially English, the Palladian mansion is merely suggestive, as Mr. Scott remarks, of gamekeepers and park-rangers on the watch to turn all intruders out. Our author would have the architect who is entrusted with the building of a house of this class, retain in its design all that is practically useful and noble in the Elizabethan mansion — at the same time remembering that Elizabethan architecture is Gothic somewhat debased, and that its details, where faulty, should be set aside, and their place supplied by those of an earlier and purer period. Nor should it be forgotten that the purest and noblest Gothic is the most willing to bend itself to the requirements of altered circumstances : and it is therefore needful that the architect, in forming his plan, should hold it steadily in view that he is building a house which is to be inhabited by a nobleman or gentleman of the latter half of the nineteenth century ; and which must therefore be thoroughly suited to the demands of our own day, and our own day's modes and habits of thought and life. And the castle and the abbey, though both quite unfit to be taken as models out-and-out, may yet supply hints for noble and dignified details in the designing of a modern English home. Thus, borrowing ideas from all quarters, Mr. Scott would produce a noble dwelling — strictly Gothic in design — thoroughly English in its entire character — at once majestic and comfortable — at once dignified and inviting — with a mediæval nobility of aspect, and with the reality of every arrangement which our advanced civilization and increased refinement can require or suggest. As for lesser details, is there not something in the following passage which makes an architectural epicure's mouth water?

The chapel and corridors perhaps richly vaulted in stone — the hall nobly roofed with oak — the ceilings of the rooms either boldly showing their timbers, partially or throughout, or richly panelled with wood; or if plastered, treated genuinely and truthfully, without aping ideas borrowed from other materials: the floors of halls and passages paved with stone, tile, marble, enriched with incised or tessellated work, or a union of all; those of the leading apartments of polished oak and parqueterie (the rendering of mosaic into wood); rich wainscoting used where suitable, and the woodwork throughout honestly treated, and of character proportioned to its position, not neglecting the use of inlaying in the richer woods; marble liberally used in suitable positions, the plainer kinds inlaid and studiously contrasted with the richer; the coloured decorations, whether of walls or ceilings, or in stained glass, delicately and artistically treated, and of the highest art we can obtain, and everywhere proportioned to their position; historical and fresco painting freely used, and in a style at once suited to the architecture, and thoroughly free from what may be called mediaevalism, in the sense in which the term is misused to imply an antiquated, grotesque, or imperfect mode of drawing; all of these, and an infinity of other modes of ornamentation, are open to the architect in this class of building.

It is pleasant to read well-written descriptions of human dwellings in which art has done all it can do towards providing a pleasant and beautiful setting for human life. Such is Mr. Loudon's account of what he calls the *beau ideal English Villa*, in his *Cyclopædia of Rural Architecture*. Such is Mr. Scott's sketch of the *beau ideal* of a nobleman's house at the present day. The latter forms a pleasing companion picture to that long since drawn by the affluent imagination of Bacon. All who have a taste for such things will read it with great delight; nor

will it tend in the least degree to make the true lover of
the country envious or discontented. I can turn with
perfect satisfaction from that grand description to my
own little parsonage. There is a peculiar comfort and
interest about a little place, which vanishes with increasing magnitude and magnificence. And it is a law of all
healthy mind, that what is one's own has an attraction for
one's self far beyond that possessed by much finer things
which belong to another. A man with one little country
abode, may have more real delight in it, than a duke has
in his wide demesnes. Indeed, I heartily pity a duke
with half-a-score of noble houses. He can never have a
home feeling in any one of them. While the possessor
of a few acres knows every corner and every tree and
shrub in his little realm; and knows what is the aspect
of each upon every day of the year. I speak from experience. I am the possessor of twelve acres of mother
earth; and I know well what pleasure and interest are to
be found in the little affairs of that limited tract. My
study-window looks out upon a corner of the garden; a
blank wall faces it at a distance of five-and-twenty feet.
When I came here, I found that corner sown with potatoes, and that wall a dead expanse of stone and mortar.
But I resolved to make the most of my narrow view, and
so contrive that it should look cheerful at every season.
And now the corner is a little square of as soft and well-
shaven green turf as can be seen; through which snowdrops and crocuses peep in early spring; its surface is
broken by two clumps of evergreens, laurels, hollies,
cedars, yews, which look warm and pleasant all the
winter-time; and over one clump rises a standard rose of
ten feet in height, which, as I look up from my desk
through my window, shows like a crimson cloud in sum-

mer. The blank wall is blank no more, but beautiful
with climbing roses, honeysuckle, fuchsias, and variegated
ivy. What a pleasure it was to me, the making of this
little improvement ; and what a pleasure it is still every
time I look at it ! No one can sympathize justly with
the feeling till he tries something of the sort for himself.
And not merely is such occupation as that which I speak
of a most wholesome diversity from mental work. It has
many other advantages. It leads to a more intelligent
delight in the fairest works of the Creator ; and though
it might be hard to explain the logical steps of the process, it leads a man to a more kindly and sympathetic
feeling towards all his fellow men. Have not I, unfaith-
ful that I am, spent the forenoon in writing a very sharp
review of some foolish book ; and then, having gone out
to the garden for two or three hours, come in, thinking
that after all it would be cruel to give pain to the poor
fellow who wrote it ; and so proceeded to weed out everything severe, and give the entire article a rather compli-
mentary turn !

It is a vain fancy to try to sketch out the kind of life
which is to be led in the country house after we get it.
For almost every man gradually settles into a habitude
of being which is rather formed by circumstances than
adopted of purpose and by choice. Only let it be remembered, that pleasure disappears when it is sought as
an end. Happiness is a thing that is come upon incidentally, while we are looking for something else. The man
who would enjoy country life in a country home, must
have an earnest occupation besides the making and de-
lighting in his home, and the sweet scenes which surround it. If *that* be all he has to do, he will soon turn

weary, and find that life, and the interest of life, have stagnated and scummed over. The end of work is to enjoy leisure; but to enjoy leisure one must have performed work. It will not do to make the recreation of life the business of life. But I believe, that to the man who has a worthy occupation to fill up his busy hours, there is no purer or more happy recreation than may be found in the cares and interests of the country home.

CHAPTER VI.

CONCERNING TIDINESS:

BEING THOUGHTS UPON AN OVERLOOKED SOURCE OF HUMAN CONTENT.

AID Sydney Smith to a lady who asked him to recommend a remedy for low spirits, — Always have a cheerful, bright fire, a kettle simmering on the hob, and a paper of sugar-plums on the mantlepiece.

Modern grates, it is known, have no hobs; nor does it clearly appear for what purpose the kettle was recommended. If for the production of frequent cups of tea, I am not sure that the abundant use of that somewhat nervous and vaporous liquid is likely to conduce to an equable cheerfulness. And Sydney Smith, although he must have become well acquainted with whisky-toddy during his years in Edinburgh, would hardly have advised a lady to have recourse to alcoholic exhilaration, with its perilous tendencies and its subsequent depression. Sugar-plums, again, damage the teeth, and produce an effect the reverse of salutary upon a most important organ, whose condition directly affects the spirits. As for the bright fire, *there* the genial theologian was certainly right: for when we talk, as we naturally do, of a *cheerful* fire, we testify that long experience has proved that this peculiarly British institution tends to make people cheerful. But. without committing myself to any approval of the particular things recommended by Sydney Smith, I heartily assent to the principle which is implied in his advice to the nervous lady: to wit, that cheerfulness and content are to a great degree the result of outward and physical conditions; let me add, the result of very little things.

Time was, in which happiness was regarded as being perhaps too much a matter of one's outward lot. Such is the belief of a primitive age and an untutored race. Every one was to be happy, whatever his mental condition, who could but find admittance to Rasselas' *Happy Valley*. The popular belief that there might be a scene so fair that it would make blest any human being who should be allowed to dwell in it, is strongly shown in the name universally given to the spot which was inhabited by the parents of the race before evil was known. It was the *Garden of Delight:* and the name describes not the beauty of the scene itself, but the effect it would produce upon the mind of its tenants. The paradises of all rude nations are places which profess to make every one happy who enters them, quite apart from any consideration of the world which he might bear within his own breast. And the pleasures of these paradises are mainly addressed to sense. The gross Esquimaux went direct to eating and drinking: and so his heaven (if we may believe Dr. Johnson) is a place where 'oil is always fresh, and provisions always warm.' He could conceive nothing loftier than the absence of cold meat, and the presence of unlimited blubber. Quite as gross was the Paradise of the Moslem, with its black-eyed houris, and its musk-sealed wine: and the same principle, that the outward scene and circumstances in which a man is placed are able to make him perfectly and unfailingly happy, whatever he himself may be, is taken for granted in all we are told of the Scandinavian Valhalla, the Amenti of the old Egyptian, the Peruvian's Spirit-World, and the Red Man's Land of Souls. But the Christian Heaven, with deeper truth, is less a locality than a character : its happiness being a relation between the employments provided, and the mental condition of those who engage in them. It was a grand and a noble thing, too, when a Creed came forth, which utterly repudiated the notion of a Fortunate Island, into which, after any life you liked, you had only to smuggle yourself, and all was well. It was a grand thing, and an intensely practical thing, to point to an unseen world, which will make happy the man who is prepared for it, and who is fit for it; and no one else.

And, to come down to the enjoyments of daily life, the time was when happiness was too much made a thing of a quiet home, of a comfortable competence, of climbing roses and honeysuckle, of daisies and buttercups, of new milk and fresh eggs, of evening bells and mist stealing up from the river in the twilight, of warm firesides, and close-drawn curtains, and mellow lamps, and hissing urns, and cups of tea, and easy chairs, and old songs, and plenty of books, and laughing girls, and perhaps a gentle wife and a limited number of peculiarly well-behaved children. And indeed it cannot be denied that if these things, with health and a good conscience, do not necessarily make a man contented, they are very likely to do so. One cannot but sympathize with the spirit of snugness and comfort which breathes from Cowper's often-quoted lines, though there is something of a fallacy in them. Here they are again : they are pleasant to look at : —

Now stir the fire, and close the shutters fast,
Let fall the curtains, wheel the sofa round,
And while the bubbling and loud-hissing urn
Throws up a steamy column, and the cups
That cheer, but not inebriate, wait on each,
So let us welcome peaceful evening in.

I have said there is a fallacy in these lines. It is not that they state anything which is not quite correct, but that they contain a *suggestio falsi*. Although Cowper does not directly say so, you see he leaves on your mind the impression that if all these arrangements are made — the fire stirred, the curtains drawn, the sofa wheeled round, and so forth — you are quite sure to be extremely jolly, and to spend a remarkably pleasant evening. Now the fact is quite otherwise. You may have so much anxiety and care at your heart, as shall entirely neutralize the natural tendency of all these little bits of outward comfort; and no one knew that better than the poor poet himself. But that which Cowper does but insinuate, an unknown verse-writer boldly asserts: to wit, that outward conditions are able to make a man as happy as it is possible for man to be. He writes in the style which was common a couple of generations back: but he really makes a pleasant homely picture: —

The hearth was clean, the fire was clear,
  The kettle on for tea;
Palemon in his elbow-chair,
  As blest as man could be.

Clarinda, who his heart possessed,
  And was his new-made bride,
With head reclined upon his breast,
  Sat toying by his side.

Stretched at his feet, in happy state,
  A favourite dog was laid,

By whom a little sportive cat,
　In wanton humour played.

Clarinda's hand he gently pressed:
　She stole a silent kiss;
And, blushing, modestly confessed
　The fulness of her bliss.

Palemon, with a heart elate,
　Prayed to Almighty Jove,
That it might ever be his fate,
　Just so to live and love.

Be this eternity, he cried,
　And let no more be given;
Continue thus my loved fireside, —
　I ask no other heaven!

Poor fellow! It is very evident that he had not been married long. And it is charitable to attribute the wonderful extravagance of his sentiments to temporary excitement and obfuscation. But without saying anything of his concluding wish, which appears to border on the profane, we see in his verses the expression of the rude belief that, given certain outward circumstances, a man is sure to be happy.

Perhaps the pendulum has of late years swung rather too far in the opposite direction, and we have learned to make too little of external things. No doubt the true causes of happiness are *inter præcordia*. No doubt it touches us most closely, whether the world within the breast is bright or dark. No doubt content, happiness, our being's end and aim, call it what you will, is an inward thing, as was said long ago by the Latin poet, in words which old Lord Auchinleck (the father of Johnson's Boswell) inscribed high on the front of the mansion which he built amid the Scottish woods and rocks ' where Lugar flows : ' —

But then the question is, how to get the *animus æquus:* and I think that now-a-days there is with some a disposition to push the principle of

My mind to me a kingdom is,

too far. Happiness is indeed a mental condition, but we are not to forget that mental states are very strongly, very directly, and very regularly affected and produced by outward causes. In the vast majority of men outward circumstances are the great causes of inward feelings, and you can count almost as certainly upon making a man jolly by placing him in happy circumstances, as upon making a man wet by dipping him in water. And I believe a life which is too subjective is a morbid thing. It is not healthy nor desirable that the mind's shadow and sunshine should come too much from the mind itself. I believe that when this is so, it is generally the result of a weak physical constitution: and it goes along with a poor appetite and shaky nerves: and so I hail Sydney Smith's recommendation of sugar-plums, bright fires, and simmering kettles, as the recognition of the grand principle that mental moods are to a vast extent the result of outward conditions and of physical state. If Macbeth had asked Dr. Forbes Winslow the question —

Canst thou not minister to a mind diseased?

that eminent physician would instantly have replied, — 'Of course I can, by ministering to a body diseased.' No doubt such mental disease as Macbeth's is beyond the reach of opiate or purgative, and neither sin nor remorse can be cured by sugar-plums. But as for the little depressions and troubles of daily life, I believe that Sydney

Smith proposed to treat them soundly. Treat them physically. Treat them *ab extra.* Don't expect the mind to originate much good for itself. With commonplace people it is mainly dependent upon external influences. It is not a perennial fountain, but a tank which must be replenished from external springs. For myself, I never found my mind to be to me a kingdom. If a kingdom at all, it was a very sterile one, and a very unruly one. I have generally found myself, as my readers have no doubt sometimes done, a most wearisome and stupid companion. If any man wishes to know the consequence of being left to his own mental resources, let him shut himself up for a week, without books or writing materials or companions, in a chamber lighted from the roof. He will be very sick of himself before the week is over : he will (I speak of commonplace men) be in tolerably low spirits. The effect of solitary confinement, we know upon uneducated prisoners, is to drive them mad. And not only do outward circumstances mainly make and unmake our cheerfulness, but they affect our intellectual powers just as powerfully. They spur or they dull us. Till you enjoy, after long deprivation, the blessing of converse with a man of high intellect and cultivation, you do not know how much there is in you. Your powers are stimulated to produce thought of which you would not have believed yourself capable. And have not you felt, dear reader, when in the society of a blockhead, that you became a blockhead too ? Did you not feel your mind sensibly contracting, like a ball of india-rubber, when compressed by the dead weight of the surrounding atmosphere of stupidity ? But when you had a quiet evening with your friend Dr. Smith, or Mr. Jones, a brilliant talker, did he not make you talk too with (comparative) brilliancy? You found yourself saying much cleverer things than you had been able to say for months past. The machinery of your mind played fervidly; words came fittingly, and thoughts came crowding. The friction of two minds of a superior class, will educe from each much finer thought than either could have produced when alone.

And now, my friendly reader, the upshot of all this which I have been saying is, that I desire to recommend to you a certain overlooked and undervalued thing, which I believe to be a great source of content and a great keeper-off of depression. I desire to recommend something which I think ought to supplant Sydney Smith's kettle and sugar-plums, and which may co-exist nicely with his cheerful fire. And I beg the reader to remark what the end is towards which I am to prescribe a means. It is not *suprema felicitas :* it is quiet content. The happiness which we expect at middle age is a calm, homely thing. We don't want raptures : they weary us, they wear us out, they shatter us. We want quiet content; and above all, we want to be kept clear of over-anxiety and of causeless depression. As for such buoyancy as that of Sydney Smith himself, who tells us that when a man of forty he often longed to jump over the tables and chairs in pure glee and light-heartedness, — why, if nature has not given you *that*, you must just do without it. Art cannot give it you : it must come spontaneous if it come at all. But what a precious thing it is! Very truly did David Hume say, that for a man to be born with a fixed disposition always to look at the bright side of things, was a far happier thing than to be born to a fortune of ten thousand a year. But Hume was right, too, when he talked of *being born with* such a disposition. The hope-

ful, unanxious man, quite as truly as the poet, *nascitur*,
non fit. No training could ever have made the nervous,
shrinking, evil-foreboding Charlotte Brontë like the glee-
ful, boisterous, life-enjoying Christopher North. There
were not pounds enough in that little body to keep up a
spirit like that which dwelt in the Scotch Professor's
stalwart frame. And to indicate a royal road to constant
light-heartedness is what no man in his senses will pretend to do. But we may attain to something humbler.
Sober content is, I believe, within the reach of all who
have nothing graver to vex them than what James Montgomery the poet called the 'insect cares' of daily life.
There may be, of course, lots which are darkened over
by misfortunes so deep that to brighten *them* all human
skill would be unavailing. But ye who are commonplace
people, — commonplace in understanding, in feeling, in
circumstances; ye who are not very clever, not extraordinarily excitable, not extremely unlucky; ye who desire to be, day by day, equably content and even pass-
ably cheerful; listen to me while I recommend, in sub-
ordination of course to something too serious to discuss
upon this half-earnest page, the maintenance of a constant, pervading, active, all-reaching, energetic TIDI-
NESS!

No fire that ever blazed, no kettle that ever simmered,
no sugar-plums that ever corroded the teeth and soothed
to tranquil stupidity, could do half as much to maintain a
human being in a condition of moderate jollity and satisfaction, as a daily resolute carrying out of the resolution,
that everything about us, — our house, our wardrobe, our
books, our papers, our study-table, our garden-walks, our
carriage, our harness, our park-fences, our children, our
lamps, our gloves, yea, our walking-stick and our um-

brella, shall be in perfectly accurate order ; that is, shall be, to a hair's breadth, RIGHT !

If you, my reader, get up in the morning, as you are very likely to do in this age of late dinners, somewhat out of spirits, and feeling (as boys expressively phrase it), rather *down in the mouth*, you cannot tell why ; if you take your bath and dress, having still the feeling as if the day had come too soon, before you had gathered up heart to face it and its duties and troubles ; and if, on coming down stairs, you find your breakfast-parlour all in the highest degree snug and tidy, — the fire blazing brightly and warmly, the fire-irons accurately arranged, the hearth clean, the carpet swept, the chairs dusted, the breakfast equipage neatly arranged upon the snow-white cloth, — it is perfectly wonderful how all this will brighten you up. You will feel that you would be a growling humbug if you did not become thankful and content. ' Order is Heaven's first law : ' and there is a sensible pleasure attending the carrying of it faithfully out to the smallest things. Tidiness is nothing else than the carrying into the hundreds of little matters which meet us and touch us hour by hour, the same grand principle which directs the sublimest magnitudes and affairs of the universe. Tidiness is, in short, the being right in thousands of small concerns in which most men are slovenly satisfied to be wrong. And though a hair's breadth may make the difference between right and wrong, the difference between right and wrong is not a little difference. An untidy person is a person who is wrong, and is doing wrong, for several hours every day ; and though the wrong may not be grave enough to be indicated by a power so solemn as conscience (as the current through the Atlantic cable after it had been injured, though a magnetic current, was too faint to be indicated by the machines now in use), still, constant wrong-doing, in however slight a degree, cannot be without a jar of the entire moral nature. It cannot be without putting us out of harmony with the entire economy under which we live. And thus it is that the most particular old bachelor, or the most precise old maid, who insists upon everything about the house being in perfect order, is, in so far, co-operating with the great plan of Providence; and, like every one who does so, finds an innocent pleasure result from that unintended harmony. Tidiness is a great source of cheerfulness. It is cheering, I have said, even to come into one's breakfast room, and find it spotlessly tidy; but still more certainly will this cheerfulness come if the tidiness is the result of our own exertion.

And so I counsel you, my friend, if you are ever disheartened about some example which has been pressed upon you of the evil which there is in this world; if you get vexed and worried and depressed about some evil in the government of your country, or of your county, or of your parish; if you have done all you can to think how the evil may be remedied; and if you know that further brooding over the subject would only vex and sting and do no good; — if all this should ever be so, then I counsel you to have resort to the great refuge of Tidiness. Don't sit over your library fire, brooding and bothering; don't fly to sugar-plums, they will not avail. There is a corner of one of your fields that is grown up with nettles; there is a bit of wall or of palisade out of repair; there is a yard of the edging of a shrubbery walk where an overhanging laurel has killed the turf; there is a bed in the garden which is not so scrupulously tidy as it ought to be; there is a branch of a peach-tree that has

pulled out its fastenings to the wall, and that is flapping
about in the wind. Or there is a drawer of papers
which has for weeks been in great confusion; or a
division of your bookcase where the books might be better arranged. See to these things forthwith: the out-of-
door matters are the best. Get your man-servant — all
your people, if you have half-a-dozen — and go forth and
see things made tidy: and see that they are done thoroughly; work half done will not serve for our present
purpose. Let every nettle be cut down and carried off
from the neglected corner; then let the ground be dug
up and levelled, and sown with grass seed. If it rains,
so much the better: it will make the seed take root at
once. Let the wall or fence be made better than when
it was new; let a wheelbarrow-full of fresh green turf
be brought; let it be laid down in place of the decayed
edging; let it be cut accurately as a watch's machinery;
let the gravel beside it be raked and rolled: then put
your hands in your pockets and survey the effect with
delight. All this will occupy you, interest you, dirty
you, for a couple of hours, and you will come in again to
your library fireside quite hopeful and cheerful. The
worry and depression will be entirely gone; you will see
your course beautifully: you have sacrificed to the good
genius of Tidiness, and you are rewarded accordingly. I
am simply stating phenomena, my reader. I don't pretend to explain causes; but I hesitate not to assert, that
to put things *right*, and to know that things are put
right, has a wonderful effect in enlivening and cheering.
You cannot tell why it is so; but you come in a very different man from what you were when you went out. You
see things in quite another way. You wonder how you
could have plagued yourself so much before. We

all know that powerful effects are often produced upon
our minds by causes which have no logical connexion
with these effects. Change of scene helps people to get
over losses and disappointments, though not by any process of logic. If the fact that Anna Maria cruelly
jilted you, thus consigning you to your present state
of single misery, was good reason why you should be
snappish and sulky in Portland-place, is it not just as
good reason now, when, in the midst of a tag-rag procession you are walking into Chamouni after having climbed
Mont Blanc? The state of the facts remains precisely
as before. Anna Maria is married to Mr. Dunderhead,
the retired ironmonger with ten thousand a year. Nor
have any new arguments been suggested to you beyond
those which Smith good-naturedly addressed to you in
Lincoln's Inn-square, when you threatened to punch his
head. But you have been up Mont Blanc; you have
nearly fallen into a crevasse; your eyes are almost
burnt out of your head. You have looked over that sea
of mountains which no one that has seen will ever forget :
here is your alpen-stock, and you shall carry it home
with you as an ancient palmer his faded branch from the
Holy Land. And though all this has nothing earthly to
do with your disappointment, you feel that somehow all
this has tided you over it. You are quite content. You
don't grudge Anna Maria her ferruginous happiness.
You are extremely satisfied that things have turned out
as they did. The sale of nails, pots, and gridirons is a
legitimate and honourable branch of commercial enterprise. And Mr. Dunderhead, with all that money, must
be a worthy and able man.

I am writing, I need hardly say, for ordinary people

when I suggest Tidiness as a constant source of temperate satisfaction. Of course great and heroic men are above so prosaic a means of content. Such amiable characters as Roderick Dhu, in the Lady of the Lake, as Byron's Giaour and Lara, not to name Childe Harold, as the heroes of Locksley Hall and Maud, and Mr. Bailey's Festus, would no doubt receive my humble suggestions very much as Mynheer Van Dunk, who disposed of his two quarts of brandy daily, might be supposed to receive the advice to substitute for his favourite liquor an equal quantity of skimmed milk. And possibly Mr. Disraeli would not be content out of office, however orderly and tidy everything about his estate and his mansion might be. Yet it is upon record that a certain ancient emperor, who had ruled the greatest empire this world ever saw, found it a pleasant change to lay the sceptre and the crown aside, and, descending from the throne, to take to cultivating cabbages. And as he looked at the tidy rows and the bunchy heads, he declared that he had changed his condition for the better; that tidiness in a cabbage-garden could make a man happier than the imperial throne of the Roman Empire. It is well that it should be so, as in this world there are many more cabbage-gardens than imperial thrones; and tidiness is attainable by many by whom empire is not attainable.

A disposition towards energetic tidiness is a perennial source of quiet satisfaction. It always provides us with something to think of and to do: it affords scope for a little ingenuity and contrivance: it carries us out of ourselves: and prevents our leading an unhealthily subjective life. It gratifies the instinctive love of seeing things *right* which is in the healthy human being. And it is founded upon the philosophical fact, that there is a peculiar satisfaction in having a thing, great or small, which was wrong, put right. You have greater pleasure in such a thing, when it has been fairly set to rights, than if it never had been wrong. Had Brummell been a philosopher instead of a conceited and empty-pated coxcomb, I should at once have understood, when he talked of 'his favourite leg,' that he meant a leg which had been fractured, and then restored as good as ever. Is it a suggestion too grave for this place, that this principle of the peculiar interest and pleasure which are felt in an evil remedied, a spoiled thing mended, a wrong righted, may cast some light upon the Divine dealing with this world? It is fallen indeed, and evil: but it will be set right. And *then*, perhaps, it may seem better to its Almighty Maker than even on the First Day of Rest. And the human being who systematically keeps right, and sets right, all things, even the smallest, within his own little dominion, enjoys a pleasure which has a dignified foundation ; which is real, simple, innocent, and lasting. Never say that it is merely the fidgety particularity of an old bachelor which makes him impatient of suffering a weed or a withered leaf on his garden walk, a speck of dust on his library table, or a volume turned upside down on his shelves. He is testifying, perhaps unconsciously, to the grand, sublime, impassable difference between Right and Wrong. He is a humble combatant on the side of Right. He is maintaining a little outpost of the lines of that great army which is advancing with steady pace, conquering and to conquer. And if the quiet satisfaction he feels comes from an unexciting and simple source — why, it is just from such sources that the quiet content of daily life must come.

We cannot, from the make of our being, be always or be long in an excitement. Such things wear us and themselves out: and they cannot last. The really and substantially happy people of this world are always calm and quiet. In feverish youth, of course, young people get violently spoony, and are violently ambitious. *Then*, life is to be all romance. They are to live in a world over which there spreads a light such as never was on land or sea. They think that Thekla was right when she said, as one meaning that life, for her, was done, 'I have lived and loved!' Mistaken she! The solid work of life was then just beginning. She had just passed through the moral scarlet-fever; and the noblest, greatest, and happiest part of life was to come. And as for the dream of ambition, *that* soon passes away. A man learns to work, not to make himself a famous name, but to provide the wherewithal to pay his butcher's and his grocer's bills. Still, who does not look back on that time with interest! Was it indeed ourselves, now so sobered, grave, and matter-of-fact, whom we see as we look back?

Make me feel the wild pulsation that I felt before the strife,
When I heard my days before me, and the tumult of my life;

Yearning for the large excitement which the coming years would
    yield,
Eager-hearted as a boy when first he leaves his father's field,

And at night along the dusky highway near and nearer drawn,
Sees in heaven the light of London flaring like a dreary dawn.

But just what London proves to the eager-hearted boy, life proves to the man. He intended to be Lord Chancellor: he is glad by-and-bye to get made an Insolvent Commissioner. He intended to be a millionaire: he is glad, after some toiling years, to be able to pay his house-

rent and make the ends meet. He intended to startle
the quiet district of his birth, and make his mother's
heart proud with the story of his fame : he learns to be
glad if he does his home no discredit, and can now and
then send his sisters a ten-pound note : —

> So sleeps the pride of former days,
>   So glory's thrill is o'er:
> And hearts that once beat high for praise,
>   Now feel that pulse no more!

But though these excitements be gone, there still
remains to the middle-aged man the calm pleasure of
looking at the backs of the well-arranged volumes on his
book-shelves ; of seeing that his gravel-walks are nicely
raked, and his grass-plots smoothly mown ; of having his
carriage, his horses, and his harness in scrupulous order ;
the harness with the silver so very bright and the leather
so extremely black, and the horses with their coats so
shiny, their ribs so invisible, and all their corners so
round. Now, my reader, all these little things will appear little only to very unthinking people. From such
little things comes the quiet content of commonplace middle life, of matter-of-fact old age. I never admired or
liked anything about Lord Melbourne so much as that
which I shall now tell you in much better words than my
own : —

He went one night to a minor theatre, in company with two ladies
and a fashionable young fellow about town — a sort of man not easy
to be pleased.

The performance was dull and trashy enough, I daresay. The next
day Lord Melbourne called upon the ladies. The fashionable young
gentleman had been there before his lordship, and had been complaining of the dreadfully dull evening they had all passed. The ladies
mentioned this to Lord Melbourne. 'Not pleased! Not pleased!
Confound the man! Didn't he see the fishmongers' shops, and the

gas-lights flashing from the lobsters' backs, as we drove along? Wasn't that happiness enough for him?'

Lord Melbourne had then ceased to be Prime Minister, but you see he had not ceased to take pleasure in any little thing that could give it.*

Now, is not all this an admirable illustration of my great principle, that the tranquil enjoyment of life comes to be drawn a good deal from external sources, and a great deal more from very little things? An ex-Prime Minister thought that the sight of lobsters' backs shining in the gas-light, was quite enough to make a reasonable man content for one evening. But give me, say I, not the fleeting joy of the lobsters' backs, any more than Sydney Smith's sugar-plums, lazy satisfactions partaken in passiveness. Give me the perennial, calm, active, stimulating moral and intellectual content which comes of living amid hundreds of objects and events which are all scrupulously RIGHT; and thus, let us all (as Wordsworth would no doubt have written had I pressed the matter upon him)

> feed this mind of ours,
> In a wise TIDINESS!

I have long wished to write an essay on Tidiness; for it appears to me that the absence of this simple and humble quality is the cause of a considerable part of all the evil and suffering, physical and moral, which exist among ordinary folk in this world. Most of us, my readers, are little people; and so it is not surprising that our earthly comfort should be at the mercy of little things. But even if we were, as some of us probably think ourselves, very great and eminent people, not the less would our content be liable to be disturbed by very small mat-

* 'Friends in Council Abroad.' *Fraser's Magazine*, vol. liii. p. 2. (January, 1856.)

ters. A few gritty grains of sand finding their way amid
the polished shafts and axles of some great piece of machinery, will suffice to send a jar through it all ; and a
single drop of a corroding acid falling ceaselessly upon a
bright surface will speedily ruin its brightness. And in
the life of many men and women, the presence of that
physical and mental confusion and discomfort which
result from the absence of tidiness, is just that dropping
acid, those gritty particles. I do not know why it is
that by the constitution of this universe, evil has so much
more power than good to produce its effect and to propa-
gate its nature. One drop of foul will pollute a whole
cup of fair water ; but one drop of fair water has no
power to appreciably improve a cup of foul. Sharp
pain, present in a tooth or a toe, will make the whole
man miserable, though all the rest of his body be easy ;
but if all the rest of the body be suffering, an easy toe or
tooth will cause no perceptible alleviation. And so a
man with an easy income, with a pretty house in a
pleasant neighbourhood, with a good-tempered wife and
healthy children, may quite well have some little drop of
bitterness day by day infused into his cup, which will
take away the relish of it all. And this bitter drop, I
believe, in the lot of many men, is the constant existence
of a domestic muddle. . ,

And yet, practically important as I believe the subject
to be, still one rather shrinks from the formal discussion
of it. It is not a dignified matter to write about. The
name is naturally suggestive of a sour old maid, a precise
old bacheldor, a vinegar-faced schoolmistress, or at best
a plump and bustling house-maid. To some minds the
name is redolent of worry, fault-finding, and bother.
Every one can see that it is a fine thing to discuss the

laws and order of great things, — such as comets, plan-
ets, empires, and great cities; things, in short, with which
we have very little to do.   And why should law and order appear contemptible just where they touch ourselves?
Is it as the ocean, clear and clean in its distant depths,
grows foul and turbid just where it touches the shore?
That which we call law and order when affecting things
far away, becomes tidiness where it reaches us.   Yet it
is not a dignified topic for an essay.

This is a beautiful morning.   It is the morning of one of
the last days of September, but the trees, with the exception of some of the sycamores and limes, are as green
and thick-leaved as ever.   The dew lies thick upon the
grass, and the bright morning sun turns it to glancing
gems.   The threads of gossamer among the evergreen
leaves look like necklaces for Titania.   The crisp air,
just touched with frostiness, is exhilarating.   The dahlias
and hollyhocks are bright, but the frost will soon make
an end of the former.   The swept harvest-fields look
trim, and the outline of the distant hills shows sharp
against the blue sky.   Taking advantage of the moisture
on the grass, the gardener is busy mowing it.   Curious,
that though it sets people's teeth on edge to listen to the
sharpening of edge-tools in general, yet there is something that is extremely pleasing in the whetting of a
scythe.   It had better be a little way off.   But it is
suggestive of fresh, pleasant things; of dewy grass and
bracing morning air; of clumps of trees standing still in
the early mistiness; of 'milkmaids singing blythe.'   Let
us thank Milton for the last association: we did not get
it from daily life.   I never heard a milkmaid singing; in
this part of the country I don't think they do sing; and
I believe cows are invariably milked within doors.   But

now, how pleasant the trim look of that newly-mown lawn, so carefully swept and rolled ; there is not a dandelion in it at all, — no weed whatsoever. There are indeed abundant daisies, for though I am assured that daisies in a lawn are weeds, I never shall recognise them as such. To me they shall always be flowers, and welcome everywhere. Look too, at the well-defined outline of the grass against the gravel. I feel the joy of tidiness, and I gladly write in its praise.

Looking at this grass and gravel, I think of Mr. Tennyson. I remember a little poem of his which contains some description of his home. There, he tells us, the sunset falls

> All round a careless-ordered garden,
> Close by the ridge of a noble down.

I lament a defect in that illustrious man. Great is my reverence for the author of *Maud ;* great for the author of *Locksley Hall* and the *May Queen ;* greatest of all for the author of *In Memoriam :* but is it possible that the Laureate should be able to elaborate his verses to that last and most exquisite perfection, while thinking of weedy walks outside his windows, of unpruned shrubs, and fruit-trees fallen from the walls ? Must the thought be admitted to the mind, that Mr. Tennyson is not tidy ? I know not. I never saw his garden. Rather let me believe that these lines only show how tidy he is. Perhaps this garden would appear in perfect order to the visitor ; perhaps it seems ' careless-ordered ' only to his own sharp eye. Perhaps he discerns a weed here and there ; a blank of an inch length in a boxwood edging. Perhaps, like lesser men, he cannot get his servants to be as tidy as himself. No doubt such is the state of matters.

There are, indeed, many degrees in the scale of tidiness. It is a disposition that grows upon one, and sometimes becomes almost a bondage. Some great musical composer said, shortly before he died, that he was only then beginning to get an insight into the capabilities of his art; and I dare say a similar idea has occasionally occurred to most persons endowed with a very keen sense of order. In matters external, tidiness may go to the length of what we read of Brock, that Dutch paradise of scrubbing-brushes and new paint; in matters metaphysical, it may go the length of what John Foster tells us of himself, when his fastidious sense of the exact sequence of every shade of thought compelled him to make some thousands of corrections and improvements in revising a dozen printed pages of his own composition. Tidiness is in some measure a matter of natural temperament; there are human beings who never could by possibility sit down contentedly, as some can, in a chamber where everything is topsy-turvy, and who never could by possibility have their affairs, their accounts, their books and papers, in that inextricable confusion in which some people are quite satisfied to have theirs. There may, indeed, be such a thing as that a man shall be keenly alive to the presence or absence of order in his belongings, but at the same time so nerveless and washy that he cannot bestir himself and set things to rights; but as a general rule, the man who enjoys order and exactness will take care to have them about him. There are people who never go into a room but they see at a glance if any of its appointments are awry; and the impression is precisely that which a discordant note leaves on a musical ear. A friend of mine, not an ecclesiastical architect, never enters any church without de-

vising various alterations in it. The same person, when
he enters his library in the morning, cannot be easy until he has surveyed it minutely, and seen that everything
is right to a hair's breadth. Taught by long experience,
the servants have done their part, and all appears perfect already to the casual observer. Not so to his eye.
The hearth-rug needs a touch of the foot: the library-
table becomes a marvel of collocation. Inkstands, pen-
trays, letter-weighers, pamphlets, books, are marshalled
more accurately than Frederick the Great's grenadiers.
A chair out of its place, a corner of a crumb-cloth turned
up, and my friend could no more get on with his task of
composition than he could fly. I can hardly understand
how Dr. Johnson was able to write the *Rambler* and to
balance the periods of his sonorous prose while his books
were lying upstairs dog's-eared, battered, covered with
dust, strewed in heaps on the floor. But I do not wonder
that Sydney Smith could go through so much and so varied work, and do it all cheerfully, when I read how he
thought it no unworthy employment of the intellect
which slashed respectable humbug in the *Edinburgh Review*, to arrange that wonderful store-room in his rectory
at Foston, where every article of domestic consumption
was allotted its place by the genial, clear-headed, active-
minded man: where was the lemon-bag, where was the
soap of different prices (the cheapest placed in the wrap-
ings marked with the dearest price): where were salt,
pickles, hams, butter, cheese, onions, and medicines of
every degree, from the ' gentle jog ' of ordinary life to
the fearfully-named preparations reserved for extremity.
Of course it was only because the kind reviewer's wife
was a confirmed invalid that it became a man's duty to
intermeddle with such womanly household cares: let

masculine tidiness find its sphere out of doors, and feminine within. It is curious how some men, of whom we should not have expected it, had a strong tendency to a certain orderliness. Byron, for example, led a very irregular life, morally speaking; yet there was a curious tidiness about it too. He liked to spend certain hours of the forenoon daily in writing; then, always at the same hour, his horses came to the door; he rode along the same road to the same spot; there he daily fired his pistols, turned, and rode home again. He liked to fall into a kind of mill-horse round: there was an imperfectly developed tidiness about the man. And even Johnson himself, though he used to kick his books savagely about, and had his study floor littered with fragments of manuscript, showed hopeful symptom of what he might have been made, when he daily walked up Bolt-court, carefully placing his feet upon the self-same stones, in the self-same order.

Great men, to be sure, may do what they please, and if they choose to dress like beggars and to have their houses as frowsy as themselves, why, we must excuse it for the sake of all that we owe them. But Wesley was philosophically right when he insisted on the necessity, for ordinary men, of neatness and tidiness in dress; and we cannot help making a moral estimate of people from what we see of their conformity to the great law of rightness in little things. I cannot tolerate a harum-scarum fellow who never knows where to find anything he wants, whose boots and handkerchiefs and gloves are everywhere but where they are needed. And who would marry a slatternly girl, whose dress is frayed at the edges and whose fingers are through her gloves? The Latin poet wrote *Nulla fronti fides;* but I have consider-

able faith in a front-door. If when I go to the house of
a man of moderate means I find the steps scrupulously
clean, and the brass about the door shining like gold;
and if, when the door is opened by a perfectly neat servant (I don't suppose a footman), I find the hall trim as
it should be, the oilcloth shiny without being slippery,
the stair-carpet laid straight as an arrow, the brass rods
which hold it gleaming, I cannot but think that things
are going well in that house; that it is the home of
cheerfulness, hopefulness, and reasonable prosperity; that
the people in it speak truth and hate whiggery. Especially I respect the mistress of that house; and conclude
that she is doing her duty in that station in life to which
it has pleased God to call her.

But if tidiness be thus important everywhere, what
must it be in the dwellings of the poor? In these, so
far as my experience has gone, tidiness and morality are
always in direct proportion. You can see at once, when
you enter a poor man's cottage (always with your hat off,
my friend), how his circumstances are, and generally
how his character is. If the world is going against him;
if hard work and constant pinching will hardly get food
and clothing for the children, you see the fact in the
untidy house: the poor mistress of it has no heart for
that constant effort which is needful in the cottage to
keep things right; she has no heart for the constant
stitching which is needful to keep the poor little children's clothes on their backs. Many a time it has made
my heart sore to see, in the relaxation of wonted tidiness, the first indication that things are going amiss, that
hope is dying, that the poor struggling pair are feeling
that their heads are getting under water at last. Ah,
there is often a sad significance in the hearth no longer

so cleanly swept, in the handle wanting from the chest of drawers, in little Jamie's torn jacket, which a few stitches would mend, but which I remember torn for these ten days past! And remember, my reader, that to keep a poor man's cottage tidy his wife must always have spirit and heart to work. If *you* choose, when you feel unstrung by some depression, to sit all day by the fire, the house will be kept tidy by the servants without your interference. And indeed the inmates of a house of the better sort are putting things out of order from morning till night, and would leave the house in a sad mess if the servants were not constantly following in their wake and setting things to rights again. But if the labourer's wife, anxious and weak and sick at heart as she may rise from her poor bed, do not yet wash and dress the little children, they will not be either washed or dressed at all; if she do not kindle her fire, there will be no fire at all; if she do not prepare her husband's breakfast, he must go out to his hard work without any; if she do not make the beds and dust the chairs and tables and wash the linen, and do a host of other things, they will not be done at all. And then in the forenoon Mrs. Bouncer, the retired manufacturer's wife (Mr. Bouncer has just bought the estate), enters the cottage with an air of extreme condescension and patronage, and if everything about the cottage be not in tidy order, Mrs. Bouncer rebukes the poor down-hearted creature for laziness and neglect. I should like to choke Mrs. Bouncer for her heartless insolence. I think some of the hatefullest phases of human nature are exhibited in the visits paid by newly rich folk to the dwellings of the poor. You, Mrs. Bouncer, and people like you, have no more right to enter a poor man's house and insult his wife than that poor man has to enter your drawing-room and give you a piece of his mind upon matters in general and yourself in particular. We hear much now-a-days about the distinctive characteristics of ladies and gentlemen, as contrasted with those of people who are well-dressed and live in fine houses, but whom no house and no dress will ever make gentlemen and ladies. It seems to me that the very first and finest characteristic of all who are justly entitled to these names of honour, is a most delicate, scrupulous, chivalrous consideration for the feelings of the poor. Without *that* the cottage visitor will do no good to the cottager. If you, my lady friend, who are accustomed to visit the dwellings of the poor in your neighbourhood, convey by your entire demeanour the impression that you are, socially and intellectually, coming a great way down-stairs in order to make yourself agreeable and intelligible to the people you find there, you had better have stayed at home. You will irritate, you will rasp, you will embitter, you will excite a disposition to let fly at your head. You may sometimes gratify your vanity and folly by meeting with a servile and crawling adulation, but it is a hypocritical adulation that grovels in your presence and shakes the fist at you after the door has closed on your retreating steps. Don't fancy I am exaggerating: I describe nothing which I have not myself seen and known.

I like to think of the effect which tidiness has in equalizing the real content of the rich and poor. If even you, my reader, find it pleasant to go into the humblest little dwelling where perfect neatness reigns, think what pleasure the inmates (perhaps the solitary inmate) of that dwelling must have in daily maintaining that speckless tidiness, and living in the midst of it.

There is to me a perfect charm about a sanded floor, and about deal furniture scrubbed into the perfection of cleanliness. How nice the table and the chairs look; how inviting that solitary big arm-chair by the little fire! The fireplace indeed consists of two blocks of stone washed over with pipeclay, and connected by half a dozen bars of iron; but no register grate of polished steel ever pleased me better. God has made us so that there is a racy enjoyment, a delightful smack, about extreme simplicity co-existing with extreme tidiness. I don't mean to say that I should prefer that sanded floor and those chairs of deal to a Turkey carpet and carved oak or walnut; but I assert that there is a certain indefinable relish about the simpler furniture which the grander wants. In a handsome apartment you don't think of looking at the upholstery in detail; you remark whether the general effect be good or bad; but in the little cottage you look with separate enjoyment on each separate simple contrivance. Do you think that a rich man, sitting in his sumptuous library, all oak and morocco, glittering backs of splendid volumes, lounges and sofas of every degree, which he merely paid for, has half the enjoyment that Robinson Crusoe had when he looked round his cave with its rude shelves and bulkheads, its clumsy arm-chair and its rough pottery, all contrived and made by his own hands? Now the poor cottager has a good deal of the Robinson Crusoe enjoyment; something of the pleasure which Sandford and Merton felt when they had built and thatched their house and then sat within it, gravely proud and happy, whilst the pelting shower came down but could not reach them. When a man gets the length of considering the architectural character of his house, the imposing effect which the great entrance-hall will have upon visitors, the vista of drawing-room retiring within drawing-room, he loses the relish which accompanies the original idea of a house as a something which is to keep us snug and warm from wind and rain and cold. So if you gain something by having a grand house, you lose something too, and something which is the more constantly and sensibly felt — you lose the joy of simple tidiness ; and your life grows so artificial, that many days you never think of your dwelling at all, nor remember what it looks like.

I have not space to say anything of the importance of tidiness in the poor man's dwelling in a sanitary point of view. Untidiness *there* is the direct cause of disease and death. And it is the thing, too, which drives the husband and father to the ale-house. All this has been so often said, that it is needless to repeat it ; but there is another thing which is not so generally understood, and which deserves to be mentioned. Let me then say to all landed proprietors, it depends very much upon you whether the poor man's home shall be tidy or not. Give a poor man a decent cottage, and he has some heart to keep tidiness about the door, and his wife has some heart to maintain tidiness within. Many of the dwellings which the rich provide for the poor are such that the poor inmates must just sit down in despair, feeling that it is vain to try to be tidy, either without doors or within. If the cottage floor is of clay, which becomes a damp puddle in rainy weather ; if the roof be of very old thatch, full of insects, and open to the apartment below ; if you go *down* one or two steps below the level of the surrounding earth when you enter the house ; if there be no proper chimney, but merely a hole in the roof, to which the smoke seems not to find its way till it has visited every other nook; if swarms of parasitic vermin have established themselves beyond expulsion through fifty years of neglect and filth; if a dung-heap be by ancient usage established under the window;* then how can a poor overwrought man or woman (and energy and activity die out in the atmosphere of constant anxiety and care) find spirit to try to tidy a place like that? They do not know where to begin the hopeless task. A little encouragement will do wonders to develop a spirit of tidiness. The love of order and neatness, and the capacity of enjoying order and neatness, are latent in all human hearts. A man who has lived for a dozen years in a filthy hovel, without once making a resolute endeavour to amend it, will, when you put him down in a neat pretty cottage, astonish you by the spirit of tidiness he will exhibit. and his wife will astonish you as much. They feel that now there is some use in trying. There was none before. The good that is in most of us needs to be encouraged and fostered. In few human beings is tidiness, or any other virtue, so energetic that it will force its way in spite of extreme opposition. Anything good usually sets out with timid, weakly beginnings; and it may easily be crushed then. And the love of tidiness is crushed in many a poor man and woman by the kind of dwelling in which they are placed by their landlords. Let us thank God that better times are beginning; but times are still

---

* The writer describes nothing which he has not seen a hundred times. He has seen a cottage, the approach to which was a narrow passage, about two feet in breadth, cut through a large dung-heap, which rose more than a yard on either side of the narrow passage, and which was piled up to a fathom's height against the cottage wall. This was *not* in Ireland.

bad enough. I don't envy the man, commoner or peer, whom I see in his carriage-and-four, when I think how a score or two families of his fellow-creatures upon his property are living in places where he would not put his horses or his dogs. I am conservatively enough inclined; but I sometimes think I could join in a Chartist rising.

Experience has shown that healthy, cheerful, airy cottages for the poor, in which something like decency is possible, entail no pecuniary loss upon the philanthropic proprietor who builds them. But even if they did, it is his bounden duty to provide such dwellings. If he do not, he is disloyal to his country, an enemy to his race, a traitor to the God who entrusted him with so much. And surely, in the judgment of all whose opinion is worth a rush, it is a finer thing to have the cottages on a man's estate places fit for human habitation,— with the climbing-roses covering them, the little gravel-walk to the door, the little potato-plot cultivated at after-hours, with windows that can open and doors that can shut; with little children not pallid and lean, but plump and rosy (and fresh air has as much to do with that as abundant food has),— surely, I say, it is better a thousand times to have one's estate dotted with scenes such as *that*, than to have a dozen more paintings on one's walls, or a score of additional horses in one's stables.

And now, having said so much in praise of tidiness, let me conclude by remarking that it is possible to carry even this virtue to excess. It is foolish to keep houses merely to be cleaned, as some Dutch housewives are said to do. Nor is it fit to clip the graceful forms of Nature into unnatural trimness and formality, as Dutch

gardeners do.   Among ourselves, however, I am not
aware that there exists any tendency to either error: so
it is needless to argue against either.   The perfection of
Dutch tidiness is to be found, I have said, at Broek, a
few miles from Amsterdam.   Here is some account of it
from Washington Irving's ever-pleasing pen: —

What renders Broek so perfect an Elysium in the eyes of all true
Hollanders, is the matchless height to which the spirit of cleanliness
is carried there.   It amounts almost to a religion among the inhabitants, who pass the greater part of their time rubbing and scrubbing,
and painting and varnishing: each housewife vies with her neighbour in devotion to the scrubbing-brush, as zealous Catholics do in
their devotion to the Cross.

I alighted outside the village, for no horse or vehicle is permitted
to enter its precincts, lest it should cause defilement of the well-
scoured pavements.   Shaking the dust off my feet, then, I prepared
to enter, with due reverence and circumspection, this *sanctum sancto-
rum* of Dutch cleanliness.   I entered by a narrow street, paved with
yellow bricks, laid edgewise, and so clean that one might eat from
them.   Indeed, they were actually worn deep, not by the tread of
feet, but by the friction of the scrubbing-brush.

The houses were built of wood, and all appeared to have been
freshly painted, of green, yellow, and other bright colours.   They
were separated from each other by gardens and orchards, and stood
at some little distance from the street, with wide areas or courtyards,
paved in mosaic with variegated stones, polished by frequent rubbing.   The areas were divided from the streets by curiously wrought
railings or balustrades of iron, surmounted with brass and copper
balls, scoured into dazzling effulgence.   The very trunks of the trees
in front of the houses were by the same process made to look as if
they had been varnished.   The porches, doors, and window-frames of
the houses were of exotic woods, curiously carved, and polished like
costly furniture.   The front doors are never opened, except on chris-
tenings, marriages, and funerals; on all ordinary occasions, visitors
enter by the back-doors.   In former times, persons when admitted
had to put on slippers, but this Oriental ceremony is no longer insisted on.

We are assured by the same authority, that such is
the love of tidiness which prevails at Broek, that the

good people there can imagine no greater felicity than to
be ever surrounded by the very perfection of it.   And it
seems that the *prediger*, or preacher of the place, accom-
modates his doctrine to the views of his hearers ; and
in his weekly discourses, when he would describe that
Happy Place where, as I trust, my readers and I will
one day meet the quiet burghers of Broek, he strongly
insists that it is the very tidiest place in the universe : a
place where all things (I trust he says *within* as well as
around), are spotlessly pure and clean ; and where all
disorder, confusion, and dirt are done with for ever !. .

The End.

CHAPTER VII.

HOW I MUSED IN THE RAILWAY TRAIN:

BEING THOUGHTS ON RISING BY CANDLELIGHT; ON NERVOUS FEARS; AND ON VAPOURING.

NOT entirely awake, I am standing on the platform of a large railway terminus in a certain great city, at 7.20 A.M., on a foggy morning early in January. I am about to set out on a journey of a hundred miles by the 7.30 train, which is a slow one, stopping at all the stations. I am alone; for more than human would that friendship be which would bring out mortal man to see one off at such an hour in winter. It is a dreamy sort of scene; I can hardly feel that it substantially exists. Who has not sometimes, on a still autumn afternoon, suddenly stopped on a path winding through sere, motionless woods, and felt within himself, Now, I can hardly believe in all this? You talk of the difficulty of realizing the unseen and spiritual: is it not sometimes, in certain mental moods, and in certain aspects of external nature, quite as difficult to feel the substantial existence of things which we can see and touch? Extreme stillness and loneliness, perhaps, are the usual conditions of this peculiar feeling. Sometimes most men have thought to themselves that it would be well for them if they could but have the evidence of sense to assure them of certain great realities

which while we live in this world we never can touch or
see ; but I think that many readers will agree with me
when I say, that very often the evidence of sense comes
no nearer to producing the solid conviction of reality than
does that widely different evidence on which we believe
the existence of all that is not material. You have climbed,
alone, on an autumn day, to the top of a great hill; a
river runs at its base unheard ; a champaign country
spreads beyond the river ; cornfields swept and bare ;
hedge-rows dusky green against the yellow ground ; a
little farmhouse here and there, over which the smoke
stagnates in the breezeless air. It is heather that you
are standing on. And as you stand there alone, and look
away over that scene, you have felt as though sense, and
the convictions of sense, were partially paralysed : you
have been aware that you could not *feel* that the landscape before you was solid reality. I am not talking to
blockheads, who never thought or felt anything particu-
larly ; of course *they* could not understand my meaning.
But as for you, thoughtful reader, have you not sometimes, in such a scene, thought to yourself, not without a
certain startled pleasure, — Now, I realize it no more
substantially that there spreads a landscape beyond that
river, than that there spreads a country beyond the
grave !

There are many curious moods of mind, of which you
will find no mention in books of metaphysics. The
writers of works of mental philosophy keep by the bread
and butter of the world of mind. And every one who
knows by personal experience how great a part of the
actual phases of thought and feeling lies beyond the
reach of logical explanation, and can hardly be fixed and
represented by any words, will rejoice when he meets

with any account of intellectual moods which he himself
has often known, but which are not to be classified or
explained.   And people are shy about talking of such
things.   I felt indebted to a friend, a man of high talent
and cultivation, whom I met on the street of a large city
on a snowy winter day.   The streets were covered with
unmelted snow ; so were the housetops ; how black and
dirty the walls looked, contrasting with the snow.   Great
flakes were falling thickly, and making a curtain which
at a few yards' distance shut out all objects more effectually than the thickest fog.   ' It is a day,' said my friend,
' I don't believe in ; ' and then he went away.   And I
know he would not believe in the day, and he would not
feel that he was in a world of reality, till he had escaped
from the eerie scene out of doors, and sat down by his
library fire.   But has not the mood found a more
beautiful description in Coleridge's tragedy of *Remorse ?*
Opium, no doubt, may have increased such phases of
mind in his case ; but they are well known by numbers
who never tasted opium : —

> On a rude rock,
> A rock, methought, fast by a grove of firs,
> Whose thready leaves to the low-breathing gale,
> Made a soft sound most like the distant ocean,
> I staid, as though the hour of death were passed,
> And I were sitting in the world of spirits —
> For all things seemed unreal.

And there can be no doubt that the long vaulted vistas
through a pine wood, the motionless trunks, dark and
ghostly, and the surgy swell of the wind through the
spines, are conditions very likely to bring on, if you are
alone, this particular mental state.

But to return to the railway station which suggested

all this; it is a dreamy scene, and I look at it with sleepy
eyes. There are not many people going by the train,
though it is a long one. Daylight is an hour or more
distant yet; and the directors, either with the design of
producing picturesque lights and shadows in their shed,
or with the design of economizing gas, have resorted to
the expedient of lighting only every second lamp.
There are no lamps, too, in the carriages ; and the blank
abysses seen through the open doors remind one of the
cells in some feudal dungeon. A little child would assuredly howl if it were brought to this place this morning. Away in the gloom, at the end of the train, the
sombre engine that is to take us is hissing furiously, and
throwing a lurid glare upon the ground underneath it.
Nobody's wits have fully arrived. The clerk who gave
me my ticket was yawning tremendously ; the porters on
the platform are yawning; the guard, who is standing
two yards off, looking very neat and trimly dressed
through the gloom, is yawning; the stoker who was
shovelling coke into the engine fire was yawning awfully
as he did so. We are away through the fog, through
the mist, over the black country which is slowly turning
gray in the morning twilight. I have with me various
newspapers ; but for an hour and more it will be impossible to see to read them. Two fellow-travellers, whose
forms I dimly trace, I hear expressing indignation that
the railway company give no lamps in the carriages. I
lean back and try to think.

It is most depressing and miserable work, getting up
by candlelight. It is impossible to shave comfortably ;
it is impossible to have a satisfactory bath ; it is impossible to find anything you want. Sleep, says Sancho
Panza, covers a man all over like a mantle of comfort ;

but rising before daylight envelopes the entire being in petty misery. An indescribable vacuity makes itself felt in the epigastric regions, and a leaden heaviness weighs upon heart and spirits. It must be a considerable item in the hard lot of domestic servants, to have to get up through all the winter months in the cold dark house: let us be thankful to them through whose humble labours and self-denial we find the cheerful fire blazing in the tidy breakfast parlour when we find our way down-stairs. That same apartment looked cheerless enough when the housemaid entered it two hours ago. It is sad when you are lying in bed of a morning, lazily conscious of that circling amplitude of comfort, to hear the chilly cry of the poor sweep outside; or the tread of the factory hands shivering by in their thin garments towards the great cotton mill, glaring spectral out of its many windows, but at least with a cosy suggestion of warmth and light. Think of the baker, too, who rose in the dark of midnight that those hot rolls might appear on your breakfast table; and of the printer, intelligent, active, accurate to a degree that you careless folk who put no points in your letters have little idea of, whose labours have given you that damp sheet which in a little will feel so crisp and firm after it has been duly dried, and which will tell you all that is going on over all the world, down to the opera which closed at twelve, and the Parliamentary debate which was not over till half-past four. It is good occasionally to rise at five on a December morning, that you may feel how much you are indebted to some who do so for your sake all the winter through. No doubt they get accustomed to it: but so may you by doing it always. A great many people, living easy lives, have no idea of the discomfort of rising by candlelight. Probably they hardly ever did it: when they did it, they had a blazing fire and abundant light to dress by; and even with these advantages, which essentially change the nature of the enterprise, they have not done it for very long. What an aggregate of misery is the result of that inveterate usage in the University of Glasgow, that the early lectures begin at 7.30 A.M. from November till May! How utterly miserable the dark, dirty streets look. as the unhappy student splashes through mud and smoke to the black archway that admits to those groves of Academe! And what a blear-eyed, unwashed, unshaven, blinking, ill-natured, wretched set it is that fills the benches of the lecture-room! The design of the authorities in maintaining that early hour has been much misunderstood. Philosophers have taught that the professors, in bringing out their unhappy students at that period, had it in view to turn to use an hour of the day which otherwise would have been wasted in bed, and thus set free an hour at a better season of the day. Another school of metaphysicians, among whom may be reckoned the eminent authors, Brown, Jones, and Robinson, have maintained with considerable force of argument that the authorities of the University, eager to advance those under their charge in health, wealth, and wisdom, have resorted to an observance which has for many ages been regarded as conducive to that end. Others, again, the most eminent among whom is Smith, have taken up the ground that the professors have fixed on the early hour for no reason in particular; but that, as the classes must meet at some hour of each day, they might just as well meet at that hour as at any other. All these theories are erroneous. There is more in the system than meets the eye. It originated in Roman Catholic days;

and something of the philosophy of the stoic and of the faith of the anchorite is involved in it. Grim lessons of endurance; dark hints of penance; extensive disgust at matters in general, and a disposition to punch the head of humanity; are mystically connected with the lectures at 7.30 A.M. in winter. It is quite different in summer, when everything is bright and inviting; if you are up and forth by five or six o'clock any morning then, you feel ashamed as you look at the drawn blinds and the closed shutters of the house in the broad daylight. There is something curious in the contrast between the stillness and shut-up look of a country-house in the early summer morning, and the blaze of light, the dew sparkling life-like on the grass, the birds singing, and all nature plainly awake though man is asleep. You feel that at 7.30 in June, Nature intends you to be astir; but believe it, ye learned doctors of Glasgow College, at 7.30 in December, her intention is quite the reverse. And if you fly in Nature's face, and persist in getting up at unseasonable hours, she will take it out of you by making you horribly uncomfortable.

There is, indeed, one fashion in which rising by candle-light, under the most uncomfortable circumstances, may turn to a source of positive enjoyment. And the more dreary and wretched you feel, as you wearily drag yourself out of bed into the searching cold, the greater will that peculiar enjoyment be. Have you not, my reader, learned by your own experience that the machinery of the human mind and heart may be *worked backwards,* just as a steam-engine is reversed, so that a result may be produced which is exactly the opposite of the normal one? The fundamental principle on which the working of the human constitution, as regards pleasure and pain, goes, may be stated in the following formula, which will not appear a truism except to those who have not brains to understand it —

THE MORE JOLLY YOU ARE, THE JOLLIER YOU ARE.

But by reversing the poles, or by working the machine backwards, many human beings, such as Indian fakirs, mediæval monks and hermits, Simeon Stylites, very early risers, very hard students, Childe Harold, men who fall in love and then go off to Australia without telling the young woman, and the like, bring themselves to this : — that their fundamental principle, as regards pleasure and pain, takes the following form —

THE MORE MISERABLE YOU ARE, THE JOLLIER YOU ARE.

Don't you know that all *that* is true? A man may bring himself to this point, that it shall be to him a positive satisfaction to think how much he is denying himself, and how much he is taking out of himself. And all this satisfaction may be felt quite irrespective of any worthy end to be attained by all this pain, toil, endurance, self-denial. I believe indeed that the taste for suffering as a source of enjoyment is an acquired taste ; it takes some time to bring any human being to it. It is not natural, in the obvious meaning of the word ; but assuredly it is natural in the sense that it founds on something which is of the essence of human nature. You must penetrate through the upper stratum of the heart, so to speak — that stratum which finds enjoyment in enjoyment — and then you reach to a deeper *sensorium*, one whose sensibility is as keen, one whose sensibility is longer in getting dulled — that *sensorium* which finds enjoyment in endurance. Nor have many years to pass over us before we come to feel that this peculiar sensibility

14

has been in some measure developed. If you, my friend, are now a man, it is probable (alas! not certain) that you were once a boy. Perhaps you were a clever boy; perhaps you were at the head of your class; perhaps you were a hardworking boy. And now tell me, when on a fine summer evening you heard the shouts and merriment of your companions in the playground, while you were toiling away with your lexicon and your Livy, or turning a passage from Shakspeare into Greek iambics (a hardly-acquired accomplishment, which has proved so useful in after life), did you not feel a certain satisfaction — it was rather a sad one, but still a satisfaction — as you thought how pleasant it would be to be out in the beautiful sunshine, and yet felt resolved that out you would not go! Well for you if your father and mother set themselves stoutly against this dangerous feeling; well for you if you never overheard them relating with pride to their acquaintances what a laborious, self-denying, wonderful boy thou wast! For the sad satisfaction which has been described is the self-same feeling which makes the poor Hindoo swing himself on a large hook stuck through his skin, and the fakir pleased when he finds that his arm, stretched out for twenty years, cannot now be drawn back. It is precisely the feeling which led the saints of the middle ages to starve themselves till their palate grew insensible to the taste of food, or to flagellate themselves as badly as Legree did Uncle Tom, or to refrain wholly from the use of soap and water for forty years. It is a most dangerous thing to indulge in, this enjoyment arising from the principle of the greatest jollity from the greatest suffering; for although we ought to feel thankful that God has so ordered things, that in a world where little that is good can be done except by painful exertion and resolute self-denial, a certain satisfaction is linked even with that exertion and self-denial in themselves, apart from the good results to which they lead; it seems to me that we have no right to add needless bitterness to life that our morbid spirit may draw from it a morbid enjoyment. No doubt self-denial, and struggle against our nature for the right, is a noble thing: but I think that in the present day there is a tendency unduly to exalt both work and self-denial, as though these things were excellent in themselves apart from any excellent ends which follow from them. Work merely as work is not a good thing: it is a good thing because of the excellent things that come with it and of it. And so with self-denial, whether it appear in swinging on a hook or in rising at five on a winter morning. It is a noble thing if it is to do some good; but very many people appear to think it a noble thing in itself, though it do no good whatever. The man deserves canonization who swings on a hook to save his country; but the man is affected with a morbid reversal of the constitution of human nature who swings on a hook because he finds a strange satisfaction in doing something which is terribly painful and abhorrent. The true nobility of labour and self-denial is reflected back on them from a noble end: there is nothing fine in accumulating suffering upon ourselves merely because we hate it, but feel a certain secondary pleasure in resolutely submitting to what primarily we hate. There is nothing fine in going into a monastery merely because you would much rather stay out. There is nothing fine in going off to America, and never asking a woman to be your wife, merely because you are very fond of her, and know that all this will be a fearful trial to go through. You will be in truth ridiculous, though you may fancy yourself sublime, when you are sitting at the door of your log-hut away in backwoods lonely as those loved by Daniel Boone, and sadly priding yourself on the terrible sacrifice you have made. That sacrifice would have been grand if it had been your solemn duty to make it; it is silly, and it is selfish, if it be made for mere self-denial's sake.

Now a great many people do not remember this. David Copperfield was pleased in thinking that he was taking so much out of himself. He was pleased in think-ing so, even though no earthly good came of his doing all that. His kind aunt was ruined, and he was deter-mined that he would deny himself in every way that he might not be a burden upon her; and so when he was walking to any place he walked at a furious pace, and was glad to find himself growing fagged and out of breath, because surely it must be a good thing to feel so jaded and miserable. It was self-sacrifice; it was self-denial. And if to walk at five miles and a half an hour had had any tendency to restore his aunt's little fortune, it could not have been praised too much; and the less David liked it, the more praise it would have deserved. And I venture to think that a good deal of the present talk about muscular Christianity is based upon this error. I do not know that exertion of the muscles, as such, is necessarily a good or an essentially Christian thing. It is good because it promotes health of body and of mind; but you find many books which appear to teach that it is a fine thing in itself to leap a horse over a five-barred gate, or to crumple up a silver jug, or to thrash a prize-fighter. It is very well to thrash the prize-fighter if it becomes necessary, but surely it would be better to es-cape the necessity of thrashing the prize-fighter. Certain of the poems of Longfellow, much admired and quoted

by young ladies, are instinct with the mischievous notion
that self-denial for mere self-denial's sake is a grand, heroic, and religious thing. The *Psalm of Life* is extremely vague, and somewhat unintelligible. It is philosophically false to say that

> Not enjoyment, and not sorrow,
> Is our destined end or way.

For, rightly understood, happiness not only *is* our aim,
but is plainly intended to be such by our Creator. He
made us to be happy : the whole bearing of revealed
religion is to make us happy. Of course, the man who
grasps at selfish enjoyment turns his back on happiness.
Self-sacrifice and exertion, where needful, are the way to
happiness ; and the main thing which we know of the
Christian Heaven is, that it is a state of happiness. But
Longfellow, talking in that fashion (no doubt sitting in a
large easy chair by a warm fire in a snug study when he
did so), wants to convey the utterly false notion, that
there is something fine in doing what is disagreeable,
merely for the sake of doing it. Now, that notion is
Bhuddism, but it is not Christianity. Christianity says
to us, Suffer, labour, endure up to martyrdom, when duty
calls you ; but never fancy that there is anything noble
in throwing yourself in martyrdom's way. ' Thou shalt
not tempt the Lord thy God.' And as for Longfellow's
conception of the fellow who went up the Alps, bellowing
out *Excelsior*, it is nothing better than childish. Any
one whose mind is matured enough to discern that Childe
-Harold was a humbug, will see that the lad was a fool.
What on earth was he to do when he got to the top of
the Alps ? The poet does not even pretend to answer
that question. He never pretends that the lad whose

brow was sad, and his eye like a faulchion, &c., had anything useful or excellent to accomplish when he reached
the mountain-top at last.   Longfellow wishes us to understand that it was a noble thing to push onward and
upward through the snow, merely because it is a very
difficult and dangerous thing.   He wishes us to understand that it was a noble thing to turn away from warm
household fires to spectral glaciers, and to resist the invitations of the maiden, who, if the lad was a stranger in
those parts, as seems to be implied, must have been a
remarkably free and easy style of young lady — merely
because average human nature would have liked extremely to get out of the storm to the bright fireside, and
to have had a quiet chat with the maiden.   I don't mean
to say that about ten years ago I did not think that
Excelsior was a wonderful poem, setting out a true and
noble principle.   A young person is captivated with the
notion of self-sacrifice, with or without a reason for it;
but self-sacrifice, uncalled for and useless, is stark folly.
It was very good of Curtius to jump into the large hole
in the Forum ; no doubt he saved the Senate great expense in filling it up, though probably it would have been
easier to do so than to carry the Liverpool and Manchester Railway through Chatmoss.   And we cannot think,
even yet, of Leonidas and his three hundred at Ther-
mopylæ, without some stir of heart ; but would not the
gallant Lacedæmonians have been silly and not heroic,
had not their self-sacrifice served a great end, by gaining
for their countrymen certain precious days ? Even Dickens, though not much of a philosopher, is more philosophic than Longfellow.   He wrote a little book one
Christmas time, *The Battle of Life*, whose plot turns entirely upon an extraordinary act of self-sacrifice ; and

which contains many sentences which sound like the cant
of the day. Witness the following : —

> It is a world on which the sun never rises, but it looks upon a
> thousand bloodless battles, that are some set-off against the miseries
> and wickedness of battle-fields.
>
> There are victories gained every day, in struggling hearts, to which
> these fields of battle are as nothing.

But although the book contains such sentences, which
seem to teach that struggle and self-conquest are noble
in themselves, apart from their aim or their necessity,
the lesson taught by the entire story is the true and just
one, that there is no nobler thing than self-sacrifice and
self-conquest, when they are right, when they are needful,
when a noble end is to be gained by them. As some
dramatist or other says —

> That's truly great! What think ye, 'twas set up
> The Greek and Roman names in such a lustre,
> But doing right, in stern despite of nature!
> Shutting their ears 'gainst all her little cries,
> When great, august, and godlike virtue called!

The author, you see, very justly remarks that you are
not called to fly in the face of danger, unless when there
is good reason for it. And therefore, my friend, don't
get up at seven o'clock on a winter morning, if you can
possibly help it. If virtue calls, it will indeed be noble
to rise by candlelight; but not otherwise. If you are the
engine-driver of an early train, if you are a factory-hand,
if you are a Glasgow student of philosophy, get up at an
unseasonable period, and accept the writer's sympathy
and admiration. Poor fellow, you cannot help it ! But
if you are a Glasgow professor, I have no veneration for
that needless act of self-denial. *You* need not get up so
early unless you like. *You* do the thing of your free

choice.   And *your* heroism is only that of the Brahmin who swings on the hook, when nobody asks him to do so.

Having mused in this fashion, I look out of the carriage window.   The morning is breaking, cold and dismal.   There is a thick white mist.   We are flying on, across gray fields, by spectral houses and trees, showing indistinct through the uncertain light.   It is light enough to read, by making an effort.   I draw from my pocket a letter, which came late last night: it is from a friend, who is an eminent Editor.   I do not choose to remember the name of the periodical which he conducts.   I have had time to do no more than glance over it; and I have not yet arrived at its full meaning.   I feel as Tony Lumpkin felt, who never had the least difficulty in reading the outside of his letters, but who found it very hard work to decipher the inside.   The circumstance was the more annoying, he justly observed, inasmuch as the inside of a letter generally contains the cream of the correspondence.

When I receive a letter from my friend the Editor, I am able, by an intense application of attention for a few minutes, to make out its general drift and meaning.   The difficulty in the way of grasping the entire sense does not arise from any obscurity of style, but wholly from the remarkable nature of the penmanship.   And after gaining the general bearing of the document, I am well aware that there are many recesses and nooks of meaning which will not be reached but after repeated perusals.   What appeared at first a flourish of the pen may gradually assume the form of an important clause of a sentence, materially modifying its force.   What appears at present a blot may turn out to be anything whatever; what at present looks like No may prove to have stood for Yes.

I think sympathetically of the worthy father of Dr.
Chalmers. When he received his weekly or fortnightly
letter from his distinguished son, he carefully locked it
up. By the time a little store had accumulated, his son
came to pay him a visit; and then he broke all the seals,
and got the writer of the letters to read them. I read
my letter over; several shades of thought break upon me,
of whose existence in it I was previously unaware. That
handwriting is like *In Memoriam*. Read it for the twentieth time, and you will find something new in it. I fold
the letter up; and I begin to think of a matter concerning which I have thought a good deal of late.

Surely, I think to myself, there is a respect in which the
more refined and cultivated portion of the human race in
Britain is suffering a rapid deterioration, and getting into
a morbid state. I mean in the matter of nervous irritability or excitability. Surely people are far more *nervous*
now than they used to be some generations back. The
mental cultivation and the mental wear which we have to
go through, tends to make that strange and inexplicable
portion of our physical constitution a very great deal too
sensitive for the work and trial of daily life. A few days
ago I drove a friend who had been paying us a visit
over to our railway-station. He is a man of fifty, a
remarkably able and accomplished man. Before the
train started the guard came round to look at the tickets.
My friend could not find his; he searched his pockets
everywhere, and although the entire evil consequence,
had the ticket not turned up, could not possibly have
been more than the payment a second time of four or
five shillings, he got into a nervous tremor painful to see.
He shook from head to foot; his hand trembled so that
he could not prosecute his search rightly, and finally he

found the missing ticket in a pocket which he had already searched half a dozen times. Now contrast the condition of this highly-civilized man, thrown into a painful flurry and confusion at the demand of a railway ticket, with the impassive coolness of a savage, who would not move a muscle if you hacked him in pieces. Is it not a dear price we pay for our superior cultivation, this morbid sensitiveness which makes us so keenly alive to influences which are painful and distressing? I have known very highly educated people who were positively trembling with anxiety and undefined fear every day before the post came in. Yet they had no reason to anticipate bad news; they could conjure up indeed a hundred gloomy forebodings of evil, but no one knew better than themselves how vain and weak were their fears. Surely the knights of old must have been quite different. They had great stalwart bodies, and no minds to speak of. They had no doubt a high sense of honour — not a very enlightened sense — but their purely intellectual nature was hardly developed at all. They never read anything. There were not many knights or squires like Fitz Eustace, who

> Much had pored
> Upon a huge romantic tome,
> In the hall window of his home,
> Imprinted at the antique dome
> Of Caxton or De Worde.

They never speculated upon any abstract subject : and although in their long rides from place to place they might have had time for thinking, I suppose their attention was engrossed by the necessity of having a sharp look-out around them for the appearance of a foe. And we all know that *that* kind of sharpness — the hunter's sharpness, the guerilla's sharpness — may coexist with the densest stupidity in all matters beyond the little range that is familiar. The aboriginal Australian can trace friend or foe with the keenness almost of brute instinct: so can the Red Indian, so can the Wild Bushman; yet the intellectual and moral nature in all these races is not very many degrees above the elephant or the shepherd's dog. And stupidity is a great preservative against nervous excitability or anxiety. A dull man cannot think of the thousand sad possibilities which the quicker mind sees are brooding over human life. Nor does this friendly stupidity only dull the understanding; it gives *inertia*, immobility, to the emotional nature. Compare a pure thoroughbred horse with a huge heavy cart-horse without a trace of breeding. The thoroughbred is a beautiful creature indeed: but look at the startled eye, look at the quick ears, look at the blood coursing through those great veins so close to the surface, look how tremblingly alive the creature is to any sudden sight or sound. Why, there you have got the perfection of equine nature, but you have paid for it just the same price that you pay for the perfection of human nature — what a *nervous* creature you have there! Then look at the cart-horse. It is clumsy in shape, ungraceful in movement, rough in skin, dull of eye; in short, it is a great ugly brute. But what a placid equanimity there is about it! How composed, how immovable it looks, standing with its head hanging down, and its eyes half-closed. It is a low type of its race no doubt, but it enjoys the blessing which is enjoyed by the dull, stupid, unrefined woman or man; it is not nervous. Let something fall with a whack, *it* does not start as if it had been shot. Throw a little pebble at its flank, it turns round tranquilly to see what is the matter. Why, the thoroughbred would have been over that hedge at much less provocation.

The morbid nervousness of the present day appears in several ways. It brings a man sometimes to that startled state that the sudden opening of a door, the clash of the falling fire-irons, or any little accident, puts him in a flutter. How nervous the late Sir Robert Peel must have been when, a few weeks before his death, he went to the Zoölogical Gardens, and when a monkey suddenly sprang upon his arm, the great and worthy man fainted! Another phase of nervousness is when a man is brought to that state that the least noise, or cross-occurrence, seems to jar through the entire nervous system — to upset him, as we say; when he cannot command his mental powers except in perfect stillness, or in the chamber and at the writing-table to which he is accustomed; when, in short, he gets fidgety, easily worried, full of whims and fancies which must be indulged and considered, or he is quite out of sorts. Another phase of the same morbid condition is, when a human being is always oppressed with vague undefined fears that things are going wrong; that his income will not meet the demands upon it, that his child's lungs are affected, that his mental powers are leaving him — a state of feeling which shades rapidly off into positive insanity. Indeed, when matters remain long in any of the fashions which have been described, I suppose the natural termination must be disease of the heart, or a shock of paralysis, or insanity in the form either of mania or idiocy. Numbers of commonplace people who could feel very acutely, but who could not tell what they felt, have been worried into fatal heart-disease by prolonged anxiety and misery. Every one knows how paralysis laid its hand upon Sir

Walter Scott, always great, lastly heroic. Protract-
ed anxiety how to make the ends meet, with a large
family and an uncertain income, drove Southey's first
wife into the lunatic asylum : and there is hardly a more
touching story than that of her fears and forebodings
through nervous year after year. Not less sad was the
end of her overwrought husband, in blank vacuity ; nor
the like end of Thomas Moore. And perhaps the saddest instance of the result of an overdriven nervous
system, in recent days, was the end of that rugged,
honest, wonderful genius, Hugh Miller.

Is it a reaction, a desperate rally against something
that is felt to be a powerful invader, that makes it so
much a point of honour with Englishmen at this day to
retain, or appear to retain, a perfect immobility under all
circumstances? It is pretty and interesting for a lady,
at all events for a young lady, to exhibit her nervous
tremors ; a man sternly represses the exhibition of these.
Stoic philosophy centuries since, and modern refinement
in its last polish of manner, alike recognise the Red
Indian's principle, that there is something manly, something fine, in the repression of human feeling. Here is
a respect in which the extreme of civilization and the
extreme of barbarism closely approach one another.
The Red Indian really did not care for anything ; the
modern fine gentleman, the youthful exquisite, though
really pretty nervous, wishes to convey by his entire
deportment the impression, that he does not care for anything. A man is to exhibit no strong emotion. It is
unmanly. If he is glad, he must not look it. If he
loses a great deal more money than he can afford on the
Derby, he must take it coolly. Everything is to be
taken coolly : and some indurated folk no doubt are truly
as cool as they look. Let me have nothing to do with

such. *Nil admirari* is not a good maxim for a man.
The coolest individual who occurs to me at this moment
is Mephistopheles in Goethe's *Faust*. *He* was not a
pleasant character. That coolness is not human. It is
essentially Satanic. But in many people in modern days
the apparent coolness covers a most painful nervousness.
Indeed, as a general rule, whenever any one does anything which is (socially speaking,) outrageously daring,
it is because he is nervous; and struggling with the feeling, and striving to conceal the fact. A speaker who is
too forward, who is jauntily free and easy, is certainly
very nervous. And though I have said that perfect
coolness in all circumstances is not amiable or desirable,
still one cannot look but with interest, if not with sympathy, at Campbell's fine description of the Red Indian :

> He said, —and strained unto his heart the boy:
> Far differently, the mute Oneyda took
> His calumet of peace and cup of joy:
> As monumental bronze unchanged his look;
> A soul that pity touched, but never shook;
> Trained from his tree-rocked cradle to his bier
> The fierce extremes of good and ill to brook
> Impassive, — fearing but the shame of fear, —
> A Stoic of the woods, — a man without a tear!

The writings of Mr. Dickens furnish me with a companion picture adapted to modern times. I confess that,
upon reflection, I doubt whether a considerable portion of
the interest of Outalissi's peculiar manner may not be
derived from distance in time and space. Indian immobility and stoical philosophy are not sublime in the servants' hall of modern society : —

'I don't know anything,' said Britain, with a leaden eye and an
immovable visage. 'I don't care for anything. I don't make out
anything. I don't believe anything. And I don't want anything.' *

* *The Battle of Life; Christmas Books.* p. 169.

Nervous people should live in large towns. The houses are so big and afford such impervious shadow, that the nervous man, very little when compared with them, does not feel himself pushed into painful prominence. It is a comfort, too, to see many other people going about. It carries the nervous man out of himself. It reminds him that multitudes more have their cares as well as he. It dispels the uncomfortable feeling which grows on such people in the country, that everybody is thinking and talking of them, — to see numbers of men and women, all quite occupied with their own concerns, and evidently never thinking of them at all.

I have known one of these shrinking and evil-foreboding persons say, that he could not have lived in the country (as he did), had not the district where his home was been very thickly wooded with large trees. It was a comfort to a man who wished to shrink out of sight and get quietly by, when the road along which he was walking wound into a thick wood. The trees were so big and so old, and they seemed to make a shelter from the outer world. In walking over a vast bare level down, a man is the most conspicuous figure in the landscape. There is nothing taller than himself, and he can be seen from miles away. Now, to be pushed into notice — to be made a conspicuous figure — is intensely painful to the nervous man. You and I, my reader, no doubt think such a state of feeling morbid, but it is probably a state to which circumstances might bring most people. And we can quite well understand that when pressed by care, sorrow, or fear, there is something friendly in the shade of trees — in anything that dims the light, and hides from public view. You remember the poor fellow (a very silly fellow indeed, but very silly fellows can suffer), who asked Little Dorrit to marry him, and met a decided though a kind refusal. He lived somewhere over in Southwark, in a street of poor houses, which had little back-greens, but of course no trees in them. But the poor fellow felt the instinctive longing of the stricken heart for shadow; and so, when his mother hung out the clothes from the wash on ropes crossing and re-crossing the little green, he used to go out and sit amid the flapping sheets, and say that 'he felt it *like groves!*' Was not that a testimony to the friendly congeniality of trees to the sad or timorous human being? And when Cowper wearied to get away from a turbulent world to some quiet retreat, he did not wish that that retreat should be in an open country. No, he says —

> Oh, for a lodge in some vast wilderness,
> Some boundless *contiguity of shade*,
> Where rumour of oppression and deceit,
> Of unsuccessful or successful war,
> Might never reach me more!

To the same effect did the same shrinking poet express himself in lines equally familiar : —

> I was a stricken deer that left the herd
> Long since: with many an arrow deep infixed
> My panting side was charged, when I withdrew
> To seek a tranquil death in *distant shades*.

I suppose that if some heavy blow had fallen upon any of us, we should not choose the open field or the bare hillside as the place to which we should go to think about it. We should rather choose some low-lying, sheltered, shaded spot. Great sorrow does not parade itself. It wishes to get out of sight.

As to the question how this nervousness may be got rid of, it is difficult to know what to think. It is in great

measure a physical condition, and not under the control
of the will. Some people would treat it physically —
send the nervous man to the water cure, — put him in
training like a prize-fighter or a pedestrian, and the like.
These are excellent things; still I have greater confidence in mental remedies. Give the evil-foreboding man
plenty to do; push him out of his quiet course of life into
the turmoil which he shrinks away from, and the turmoil
will lose its fears. Work is the healthy atmosphere for
a human being. The soul of man is a machine with this
great peculiarity about it, — that we cannot stop it from
motion when we will. Perhaps *that* is a defect. Many
a man, through a weary sleepless night, has longed for
the power to push some lever or catch into the swift-
running engine that was whirring away within him, and
bring it to a stand. However, it cannot be. And as the
machine *will* go on, we must provide it with grist to
grind, we must give it work to do, or it will knock itself
in pieces; or if not *that*, then get all warped and twisted,
so that it never shall go without creaking, and straining,
and trembling. And so, if you find a man or woman,
young or old, vexed with ceaseless fears, worried with
all kinds of odd ideas, doubts upon religious matters and
the like, don't argue with them; *that* is not the treatment
that is necessary in the meantime. There is something
else to be done first. It would do no good to blister a
horse's legs till the previous inflammation has gone down.
It will do no good to present the soundest views to a nervous, idle man. Set him to hard work. Give him lots
to do. And then that invisible machine, which has been
turning off misery and delusion, will begin to turn off
content and sound views of all things. After two or
three weeks of this healthful treatment you may proceed

15

to argue with your friend. In all likelihood you will find that argument will not be necessary. He has arrived at truth and sense already. There is a wonderfully close connexion between work and sound views ; between doing and knowing. It is in life as it is in religion : ' If any man will do His will, he shall know of the doctrine whether it be of God.'

Looking out now, I see it has grown quite light, though the day is gloomy, and will be so to its close. The train is speeding round the base of a great hill. Far below us a narrow little river is dashing on, all in foam. Its sound is faintly heard at this height. I said to myself, by way of winding up my musing upon nervousness : After all, is not this painful fact just an over-degree of that which makes us living beings? Is it not just *life* too sensitively present in every atom of even the dull flesh? There is that gray rock which we are passing ; how still and immovable *it* is ! All the stoicism of Greece, all the impassiveness of the mute Oneyda, all the indifference of the *pococurante* Englishman, how far they fall short of that sublime stillness ! But it is still because it is senseless. It looks as if it felt nothing, because it really feels nothing. I compare it with Lord Derby before he gets up to make a great speech ; fidgeting on his seat ; watching every movement and word of the man he is going to smash ; his wonderfully ready mind working with a whirr like wheel-work revolving unseen through its speed ; *living intensely,* in fact, in every fibre of his frame. Well, *that* is the finer thing, after all. The big cart-horse, already thought of, is something midway between the Premier and the granite. The stupid blockhead is cooler than the Premier, indeed ; but he is not so cool as the granite. If coolness be so fine a thing, of course the per-

fection of coolness must be the finest thing ; and *that* we
find in the lifeless rock.   What is life but that which
makes us more sensitive than the rock : what is the highest type of life but that which makes us most sensitive ?
It is better to be the warm, trembling, foreboding human
being, than to be Ben Nevis, knowing nothing, feeling
nothing, fearing nothing, cold and lifeless.

It is natural enough to pass from thinking of one
human weakness to thinking of another : and certain
remarks of a fellow-traveller, not addressed to me, suggest the inveterate tendency to vapouring and big talking
which dwells in many men and women.   Who is there
who desires to appear to his fellow-creatures precisely
what he is ?   I have known such people and admired
them, for they are comparatively few.   Why does Mr.
Smith, when some hundreds of miles from home, talk of
his *place in the country*?   In the etymological sense of
the words it certainly is a place in the country, for it is a
seedy one-storied cottage without a tree near it, standing
bleakly on a hillside.   But *a place in the country* suggests to the mind long avenues, great shrubberies, extensive greenhouses, fine conservatories, lots of horses, abundance of servants ; and *that* is the picture which Mr.
Smith desires to call up before the mind's eye of those
whom he addresses.   When Mr. Robinson talks with
dignity about the political discussions which take place
in his *Servants' Hall*, the impression conveyed is that
Robinson has a vast establishment of domestics.   A
vision rises of ancient retainers, of a dignified house-
keeper, of a bishop-like butler, of Jeamses without number, of unstinted October.   A man of strong imagination
may even think of huntsmen, falconers, couriers — of a

grand baronial *menage*, in fact. You would not think
that Robinson's establishment consists of a cook, a house-
maid, and a stable-boy. Very well for the fellow too;
but why will he vapour? When Mr. Jones told me the
other day that something or other happened to him when
he was going out 'to *the stables* to look at *the horses*,' I
naturally thought, as one fond of horseflesh, that it would
be a fine sight to see Jones's *stables*, as he called them.
I thought of three handsome carriage-horses sixteen
hands high, a pair of pretty ponies for his wife to drive,
some hunters, beauties to look at and tremendous fellows
to go. The words used might even have justified the
supposition of two or three racehorses, and several lads
with remarkably long jackets walking about the yard. I
was filled with fury when I learned that Jones's *horses*
consisted of a large brougham-horse, broken-winded, and
a spavined pony. I have known a man who had a
couple of moorland farms habitually talk of his *estate*.
One of the commonest and weakest ways of vapouring is
by introducing into your conversation, very familiarly,
the names of people of rank whom you know nothing
earthly about. 'How sad it is,' said Mrs. Jenkins to me
the other day, 'about the duchess being so ill! Poor
dear thing! *We are all in such great distress about her!*'
'*We all*' meant, of course, the landed aristocracy of the
district, of which Mrs. Jenkins had lately become a member, Jenkins having retired from the hardware line and
bought a small tract of quagmire. Some time ago a
man told me that he had been down to Oatmealshire to
see his *tenantry*. Of course he was not aware that I
knew that he was the owner of just one farm. 'This is
my parish we have entered,' said a youth of clerical appearance to me in a railway carriage. In one sense it

was; but he would not have said so had he been aware that I knew he was the curate, not the rector. 'How can Brown and his wife get on?' a certain person observed to me; 'they cannot possibly live: they will starve. Think of people getting married with not more than *eight or nine hundred a year!*' How dignified the man thought he looked as he made the remark! It was a fine thing to represent that he could not understand how human beings could do what he was well aware was done by multitudes of wiser people than himself. 'It is a cheap horse that of Wiggins's,' remarked Mr. Figgins; 'it did not cost more than seventy or eighty pounds.' Poor silly Figgins fancies that all who hear him will conclude that his own broken-kneed hack (bought for £25) cost at least £150. Oh, silly folk who talk big, and then think you are adding to your importance. don't you know that you are merely making fools of yourselves? In nine cases out of ten the person to whom you are relating your exaggerated story knows what the precise fact is. He is too polite to contradict you and to tell you the truth, but rely on it he *knows* it. No one believes the vapouring story told by another man; no, not even the man who fancies that his own vapouring story is believed. Every one who knows anything of the world knows how, by an accompanying process of mental arithmetic, to make the deductions from the big story told, which will bring it down to something near the truth. Frequently has my friend Mr. Snooks told me of the crushing retort by which he shut up Jeffrey upon a memorable occasion. I can honestly declare that I never gave credence to a syllable of what he said. Repeatedly has my friend Mr. Longbow told me of his remarkable adventure in the Bay of Biscay, when a whale very nearly swallowed

him. Never once did I fail to listen with every mark of
implicit belief to my friend's narrative, but do you think
I believed it? And more than once has Mrs. O'Calla-
ghan assured me that the hothouses on her fawther's
esteet were three miles in length, and that each cluster
of grapes grown on that favoured spot weighed above a
hundred weight. With profound respect I gave ear to
all she said; but, gentle daughter of Erin, did you think
I was as soft as I seemed? You may just as well tell
the truth at once, ye big talkers, for everybody will know
it, at any rate.

It is a sad pity when parents, by a long course of big
talking and silly pretension, bring up their children with
ideas of their own importance which make them appear
ridiculous, and which are rudely dissipated on their entering into life. The mother of poor Lollipop, when he
went to Cambridge, told me that his genius was such that
he was sure to be Senior Wrangler. And possibly he
might have been if he had not been plucked.

It is peculiarly irritating to be obliged to listen to a
vapouring person pouring out a string of silly exaggerated stories, all tending to show how great the vapouring
person is. Politeness forbids your stating that you don't
believe them. I have sometimes derived comfort under
such an infliction from making a memorandum, mentally,
and then, like Captain Cuttle, 'making a note' on the
earliest opportunity. By taking this course, instead of
being irritated by each successive stretch, you are rather
gratified by the number and the enormity of them. I
hereby give notice to all ladies and gentlemen whose
conscience tells them that they are accustomed to vapour,
that it is not improbable that I have in my possession a
written list of remarkable statements made by them. It

is possible that they would look rather blue if they were permitted to see it.

Let me add, that it is not always vapouring to talk of one's self, even in terms which imply a compliment. It was not vapouring when Lord Tenterden, being Lord Chief Justice of England, standing by Canterbury Cathedral with his son by his side, pointed to a little barber's shop, and said to the boy, ' I never feel proud except when I remember that in that shop your grandfather shaved for a penny!' It was not vapouring when Burke wrote, ' I was not rocked, and swaddled, and dandled into a legislator: *Nitor in adversum* is the motto for a man like me !' It was not vapouring when Milton wrote that he had in himself a conviction that ' by labour and intent study, which he took to be his portion in this life, he might leave to after ages something so written as that men should not easily let it die.' Nor was it vapouring, but a pleasing touch of nature, when the King of Siam begged our ambassador to assure Queen Victoria that a letter which he sent to her, in the English language, was composed and written entirely by himself. It is not vapouring, kindly reader, when upon your return home after two or three days' absence, your little son, aged four years, climbs upon your knee, and begs you to ask his mother if he has not been a very good boy when you were away ; nor when he shows you, with great pride, the medal which he has won a few years later. It is not vapouring when the gallant man who heroically jeoparded life and limb for the women's and children's sake at Lucknow, wears the Victoria Cross over his brave heart. Nor is it a piece of national vapouring, though it is, sure enough, an appeal to proud remembrances, when England preserves religiously the stout old *Victory*, and points strangers to the spot where Nelson fell and died.

But a shrieking whistle yells in my ear : my musings are suddenly pulled up. The hundred miles are traversed : the train is slackening its speed. It was half-past seven when we started : it is now about half-past eleven. We draw alongside the platform : *there* are faces I know. I see a black head over the palisade : *that* is my horse. It would be vapouring to say that my *carriage* awaits me ; for though it has four wheels, it is drawn by no more than four legs. Drag out a portmanteau from under the seat, exchange a cap for a hat, open the door, jump out, bundle away home. And then, perhaps, I may tell some unknown friends who have the patience to read my essays, *How I mused in the railway train.*

CHAPTER VIII.

CONCERNING THE MORAL INFLUENCES OF THE DWELLING.

WHEN the great Emperor Napoleon was packed off to Elba, he had, as was usual with him, a sharp eye to theatrical effect. Indeed that distinguished man, during the period of his great elevation as well as of his great downfall, was subject, in a degree almost unexampled, to the tyranny of a principle which in the case of commonplace people finds expression in the representative inquiry, 'What will Mrs. Grundy say?' Whenever Napoleon was about to do anything particular, or was actually doing anything particular, he was always thinking to himself, 'What will Mrs. Grundy say?' Of course *his* Mrs. Grundy was a much bigger and much more important individual than *your* Mrs. Grundy, my reader. *Your* Mrs. Grundy is the ill-natured, tattling old tabby who lives round the corner, and whose window you feel as much afraid to pass as if it were a battery commanding the pavement, and as if the ugly old woman's baleful eyes were so many Lancaster guns. Or perhaps your Mrs. Grundy is the goodnatured friend (as described by Mr. Sheridan) who is always ready to tell you of anything he has heard to your disadvantage, but who would not

for the world repeat to you any kind or pleasant remark,
lest the vanity thereby fostered should injuriously affect
your moral development. But Napoleon's Mrs. Grundy
consisted of Great Britain and Ireland, Russia, Prussia,
Austria, Italy, Spain, Denmark, Sweden, Norway, Switz-
erland, the United States; in brief, to Napoleon, Mrs.
Grundy meant Europe, Asia, Africa, and America. And
really, when a man is asking himself what the whole
civilized world will think and say about what he is
doing, and when he feels quite sure that it will think and
say *something*, it is excusable if in what he does he has
an eye to what Mrs. Grundy will think and say.

Accordingly, when the great Emperor was forced to
exchange the imperial throne of France for the sover-
eignty of that little speck in the Mediterranean, his first
and most engrossing reflection on his journey to Elba
was, what will Mrs. Grundy say? And many thoughts
not very pleasant to an ambitious man of unphilosophical
temperament, would be suggested by the question. He
would naturally think, Mrs. Grundy will be chuckling
over my downfall. Mrs. Grundy will be saying that I,
and all my aspirations and hopes, have been fearfully
smashed. Mrs. Grundy will be saying, that it serves me
right for my impudence. Mrs. Grundy will be saying
(kindly) that it will do me a great deal of good. Amiable and benevolent old lady! Mrs. Grundy will be
saying that I am now going away to my exile in very low
spirits, feeling very bitter, very much disappointed, very
thoroughly humbled, — going away (only Napoleon had
not read Swift) in the extremity of impotent fury to
'die in a rage, like a poisoned rat in a hole.' Mrs.
Grundy will be saying that when I get to Elba finally, I
shall lead a poor life there; kicking about the dogs and

cats, swearing at the servants, whacking the horses
viciously, perhaps even throwing plates at the attendants'
heads. Such, the Emperor would think, will be the sayings of Mrs. Grundy. And the Emperor, not a man of
resigned or philosophical temper, would know that in all
this Mrs. Grundy would be nearly right. But at all
events, says Napoleon to himself, she shall not have the
satisfaction of thinking that she is so. I shall mortify
Mrs. Grundy by making her think that I am perfectly
jolly. I shall get her to believe that all this humiliation
which she has heaped upon me is impotent to touch me
where I can really feel. She shall think that she has
not found the raw. And so, when Napoleon settled at-
Elba — stamped upon his coin, engraven upon his silver
plate, emblazoned on his carriage panels, written upon
his very china and crockery, — there blazed forth in Mrs.
Grundy's view the defiant words, *Ubicunque felix!*

Now, had Mrs. Grundy had much philosophic insight
into human conduct and motives, she would have known
that her purpose of humiliation and embitterment was attained, and that all her ill-set sayings had proved right. It
was because in Elba the great exile was a bitterly disappointed man, that he so ostentatiously paraded before
the world the assurance that he was ' happy anywhere.'
It was because he thought so much of Mrs. Grundy, and
attached so much importance to what she might say, that
he hung out this flag of defiance. If he had really been
as happy and as independent of outward circumstances as
he said he was, he would not have taken the trouble to
say so. Had Napoleon said nothing about himself, but
begun to grow cabbages and train flowers, and grow fat
and rosy, we should not have needed the motto. But if
any man, Emperor or not, trumpet forth on the house-

tops that he is *ubicunque felix;* and if we find him walking moodily by the sea-shore, with a knitted brow and absent air, and a very poor appetite, why, my reader, the
answer to his statement may be conveyed, inarticulately,
by a low and prolonged whistle; or articulately, by an
advice to address that statement to the marines.

If there be a thing which I detest, it is a diffuse and
rambling style.   Let any writer always treat his subject
in a manner terse and severely logical.   My own model
is Tacitus, and the earlier writings of Bacon.   Let a man
say in a straightforward way what he has got to say; and
the more briefly the better.   And above all, young writer,
avoid that fashion which is set by the leading articles of
the *Times,* of beginning your observations upon a subject
with something which to the ordinary mind appears to
have nothing earthly to do with it.   By carefully carrying out the advices here tendered to you, you may ultimately, after several years of practice, attain to a limited success as an obscure third-rate essayist.

Napoleon, then (to resume our argument after this little *excursus*), paraded before the world the declaration
that it did not matter to him where he might be; he
would be 'happy anywhere.'   What tremendous nonsense he talked!   Why, setting aside altogether such
great causes of difference as an unhealthy climate, stupid
society or no society at all, usefulness or uselessness, honour or degradation,— I do not hesitate to say that the
scenery amid which a man lives, and the house in which
he lives, have a vast deal to do with making him what he
is.   The same man (to use an expression which is only
seemingly Hibernian) is an entirely different man when
put in a different place.   Life is in itself a neutral thing,
colourless and tasteless; it takes its colour and its fla-

vour from the scenes amid which we lead it. It is like
water, which external influences may make the dirtiest or
cleanest, the bitterest or sweetest, of all things. Life, character, feeling, are things very greatly dependent on external influences. In a larger sense than the common saying
is usually understood, we are 'the creatures of circumstances.' Only very stolid people are not affected by the
scenes in which they live. I do not mean to say that an
appreciable difference will be produced on a man's character by varied *classes* of scenery ; that is, that the same man
will be appreciably different, morally, according as you
place him for days on a rocky, stormy coast ; on a level
sandy shore ; inland in a fertile wooded country ; inland
among bleak wild hills ; among Scotch firs with their long
bare poles ; horse-chestnuts blazing with their June blossoms ; or thick full laurels, and yews, and hollies, thick to the
ground, and shutting an external world out. I do not mean
to say that ordinary people will feel any appreciable varia-
tion of the moral and spiritual atmosphere, traceable for
its cause to such variety of scene. A man must be fash-
ioned of very delicate clay, he must have a nervous system very sensitive, morbidly sensitive perhaps, if such
things as these very decidedly determine what he
shall be, morally and intellectually, for the time. Yet
no doubt such matters have upon many human beings a real effect. If you live in a country house into
whose grounds you enter through a battlemented gateway
under a lofty arch ; if the great leaves of the massive oak
and iron gate are swung back to admit you, as you pass
from the road outside to the sequestered pleasance within,
where the grass, the gravel, the evergreens, the flowers,
the winding paths, the little pond, the noisy little brook
that passes beneath the rustic bridge, are all cut off from

the outer world by a tall battlemented wall, too tall for
leaping or looking over, — I think that, at first at least,
you will have a different feeling all day, you will be a
different man all day, for that arched gateway and that
battlemented wall.   You will not feel as if you had come
in by a common five-bar gate, painted green, hung from
freestone pillars five or six feet high, and shaded with
laurels.   It is wonderful what an effect is produced
upon many minds by even a single external circumstance such as that; nor can I admit that there is anything morbid in the mind which is affected by such things.
A very little thing, a solitary outward fact, may, by the
influence of associations not necessarily personal, become
idealized into something whose flavour reaches, like salt
in cookery, perceptibly through all life. 'You may laugh
as you please,' says one of the most thoughtful and delightful of English essayists, 'but life seems somewhat
insupportable to me without a pond — a squarish pond,
not over clean.' You and I do not know, my readers,
what early recollections may have made such a little
piece of water something whose presence shall appreciably affect the genial philosopher's feeling day by day,
and hour by hour. The savour of its presence (I don't
speak materially) may reach everywhere. And if there
be anything which that writer is *not*, he is not morbid;
and he is not fanciful in the sense in which a fanciful person means a chronicler of morbid impressions. And we
all remember the little child in Wordsworth's poem, who
persisted in expressing a decided preference for one
place in the country above another which appeared likely
to have greater attractions; and who, when pressed for
his reasons, did, after much reflection, fix upon a single
fact as the cause of his preference: —

> At Kilve there was no weathercock;
> And that's the reason why.

No one can tell how that weathercock may have obtruded itself upon the little man's dreams, or how thoroughly its presence may have permeated all his life. I know a little child, three years and a half old, whose entire life for many weeks appeared embittered by the presence of a dinner-bell upon the hall-table of her home. She could not be induced to go near it; she trembled with terror when she heard it rung: it fulfilled for her the part of Mr. Thackeray's famous skeleton. And I am very sure that we have all of us dinner-bells and weathercocks which haunt and worry us, and squarish ponds which give a savour to our life. And for any ordinary mortal to say that he is *ubicunque felix* is pure nonsense. Napoleon found it was nonsense even at Elba; and at St. Helena he found it yet more distinctly. No man can say truly that he is the same wherever he goes. That sublime elevation above outward circumstances is not attainable by beings all of whom are half, and a great many of whom are a good deal more than half, material. We are all moral chameleons; and we take the color of the objects among which we are placed.

Here am I this morning, writing on busily. I am all alone in a quiet little study. The prevailing colour around me is green — the chairs, tables, couches, bookcases, are all of oak, rich in colour, and growing dark through age, but green predominates: window-curtains, table-covers, carpet, rug, covers of chairs and couches, are green. I look through the window, which is some distance off, right before me. The window is set in a frame of green leaves: it looks out on a quiet corner of the garden. There is a wall not far off green with ivy and other climbing plants ; there is a bright little bit of turf like emerald, and a clump of evergreens varying in shade. Over the wall I see a round green hill. crowned by oaks which autumn has not begun to make sere. How quiet everything is! I am in a comparatively remote part of the house, and there is no sound of household life ; no pattering of little feet ; no voices of servants in discussion less logical and calm than might be desired. The timepiece above the fire-place ticks audibly ; the fire looks sleepy ; and I know that I may sit here all day if I please, no one interrupting me. No man worth speaking of will spend his ordinary day in idleness ; but it is pleasant to think that one may divide one's time and portion out one's day at one's own will and pleasure. Such a mode of life is still possible in this country : we do not all as yet need to live in a ceaseless hurry. ever drive, driving on till the worn-out machine breaks down. By and bye this life of unfeverish industry, and of work whose results are tangible only to people of cultivation, will no doubt cease ; and it will tend materially to hasten that consummation when the views of the *Times* are carried out. and all the country clergy are required to keep a diary like a rural policeman, showing how each hour of their time is spent, and open to the inspection of their employers. Now, in a quiet scene like this, where there is not even the little noise of a village near, though I can hear the murmur of a pretty large river. must not the ordinary human being be a very different being from what he would be were he sitting in some gas-lighted counting-house in Manchester, turning over large vellum-bound volumes, adding long rows of figures. talking on sales and prices to a hundred and fifty people in the course of the day. looking out through the window upon a foggy atmosphere, a muddy pavement, a crowded street, huge drays lumbering by with their great horses, with a general impression of noise, hurry, smoke, dirt, confusion, and no rest or peace? It would be an interesting thing for some one equal to the task to go over Addison's papers in the *Spectator*, and try to make out the shade of difference in them which might be conceived as resulting from the influences of the place where they were severally written. It is generally understood that the well-known letters by which Addison distinguished his essays referred to the places where they were composed; the letters in the CLIO indicating Chelsea, London, Islington, and the Office. Did the sensitive, shy genius feel that in the production dated from each scene there would be some trace of what Yankees call the surroundings amid which it was produced? No doubt a mind like Addison's, impassive as he was, would turn off very different material according to the conditions in which the machine was working. As for Dick Steele, probably it made very little difference to him where he was: at the coffeehouse table, with noise and bustle all about him, he would write as quietly as though he had been quietly at home. *He* was indurated by long usage; the hide of a hippopotamus is not sensitive to gentle influences which would be felt by your soft hand, my fair friend. But in the case of ordinary educated men there is no greater fallacy than that suggested by that vile old subject for Latin themes, that *cœlum, non animum mutant, qui trans mare currunt.* Ordinary people, in changing the *cœlum*, undergo a great change of the *animus* too. A judicious man would be extremely afraid of marrying any girl in England, and forthwith taking her out to India with him; for it would

16

be quite certain that she would be a very different person *there* from what she had been *here ;* and how different and in what mode altered and varied only experience could show. So one might marry one woman in Yorkshire, and live with quite another at Boggley-wollah : and in marriage it is at least desirable to know what it is you are getting. Every one knows people who are quite different people according as they are in town or country. I know a man — an exceedingly clever and learned man — who in town is sharp, severe, hasty, a very little bitter, and just a shade ill-tempered, who on going to the country becomes instantly genial, frank, playful, kind, and jolly : you would not know him for the same man if his face and form changed only half as much as his intellectual and moral nature. Many men, when they go to the country, just as they put off frock coats and stiff stocks, and put on loose shooting suits, big thick shoes, a loose soft handkerchief round their neck ; just as they pitch away the vile hard hat of city propriety that pinches, cramps, and cuts the hapless head, and replace it by the light yielding wideawake ; do mentally pass through a like process of relief : their whole spiritual being is looser, freer, less tied up. Such changes as that from town to country must, I should think, be felt by all educated people, and make an appreciable difference in the moral condition of all educated people. Few men would feel the same amid the purple moors round Haworth, and amid the soft English scenery that you see from Richmond Hill. Some individuals, indeed, whose mind is not merely torpid, may carry the same *animus* with them wherever they go ; but their *animus* must be a very bad one. Mr. Scrooge, before his change of nature, was no doubt quite independent of external circumstances, and would no doubt have thought it proof of great weakness had he not been so. Nor was it a being of an amiable character in whose mouth Milton has put the words, ' No matter where, so *I* be still the same!' And even in *his* mouth the sentiment was rather vapouring than true. But a dull, heavy, prosaic, miserly, cantankerous, cynical, suspicious, bitter old rascal would probably be much the same anywhere. Such a man's nature is indurated against all the influences of scenery, as much as the granite rock against sunshine and showers.

I dare say there are few people who do not unconsciously admit the principle of which so much has been said. Few people can look at a pretty tasteful villa, all gables, turrets, bay windows, twisted chimneys, verandahs, and balconies, set in a pleasant little expanse of shrubbery, with some fine forest-trees, a green bit of open lawn, and some winding walks through clumps of evergreens, without tacitly concluding that the people who live there must lead a very different life from that which is led in a dull smoky street, and a blackened, gardenless, grassless, treeless house in town; very different even from the life of the people in the tasteless square stuccoed box, with a stiff gravel walk going up to its door, a few hundred yards off. If you are having a day's sail in a steamer, along a pretty coast dotted with pleasant villages, you cannot repress some notion that the human beings whom you see loitering about there upon the rocks, in that pure air and genial idleness, are beings of a different order from those around you. You feel that to set foot on that pier, and to mingle with that throng, would carry you away a thousand miles in a moment; and make you as different from what you are as though you had suddenly dropt from

the sky into that quiet voluptuous valley of Typee,
where Hermann Melville was so perfectly happy till he
discovered that all the kindness of the natives was intended to make him the fatter and more palatable
against that festival at which he was to be eaten.   And
no wonder that he felt comfortable, if that happy valley
was indeed what he assures us it was :

> There were no cares, griefs, troubles, or vexations, in all Typee.
> There were none of those thousand sources of irritation that the
> ingenuity of civilized man has created to mar his own felicity.
> There were no foreclosures of mortgages, no protested notes, no bills
> payable, no debts of honour, in Typee; no unreasonable tailors or
> shoemakers perversely bent on being paid, no duns of any descrip-
> tion, no assault and battery attorneys to foment discord, backing
> their clients up to a quarrel, and then knocking their heads together;
> no poor relations everlastingly occupying the spare bedchamber, and
> diminishing the elbowroom at the family-table; no destitute widows,
> with their children starving on the cold charities of the world; no
> beggars, no debtors' prisons, no proud and hard-hearted nabobs in
> Typee; or, to sum up all in one word,—no Money!   That root of all
> evil was not to be found in the valley.
>
> In this secluded abode of happiness there were no cross old women,
> no cruel step-dames, no withered spinsters, no love-sick maidens, no
> sour old bachelors, no inattentive husbands, no melancholy young
> men, no blubbering youngsters, and no squalling brats.   All was
> mirth, fun, and high good humour.

It is pleasant to read such a description.   It is like
being carried suddenly from the Royal Exchange on a
crowded afternoon, to a grassy, shady bank by the side
of a country river.   Probably most of us have travelled by railway through a wild country; and when
we stopped at some remote station among the hills,
have wondered how the people there live, and thought
how different their life must be from ours.   Nor is it a
mere fancy that takes possession of us when we look at
the pretty Elizabethan dwelling, the thought of which

carried us all the way to the South Pacific. If people
are calm enough to be susceptible of external impressions, life really *is* very different there. I do not say it
is necessarily happier; but it is very different. Habit,
indeed, equalizes the practical enjoyment of all lots, excepting only those of extreme suffering and degradation. Whatever level you get to in the scale of advantage, you soon get so accustomed to it that you do not
mind much about it. When I used to study metaphysical philosophy, I remember that it appeared to me that
this thought supplies by far the most serious of all
objections to the doctrine (as taught by nature) of the
Divine benevolence. It is a graver objection than the
existence of positive evil. *That* may be conceived to
be in some way inevitable; but why should it be that to
get a thing instantly diminishes its value to half? I
can think of a reason why; and a good reason too: but
it is not drawn from the domain of philosophy. A poor
fellow, toiling wearily along the dusty road, thinks how
happy that man must be who is just now passing him,
leaning back upon the cushions of that luxurious carriage, swept along by that pair of smoking thoroughbreds. Of course the poor fellow is mistaken. The
man in the carriage is no happier than he. And, indeed, I can say conscientiously that the very saddest,
most peevish, most irritable, and most discontented faces
I have ever seen, I have seen looking out of extremely
handsome carriage-windows. Luxury destroys real enjoyment. There is more real enjoyment in riding in a
wheelbarrow than in driving in a carriage and four.
Who does not remember the keen relish of the rapid
run in the wheelbarrow of early youth, bumping and
rolling about, and finally turning a corner at full speed

and upsetting? Who does not remember the delight of
the little springless carriage that threatened to dislocate
and grind down the bones? But it is indeed much to
be lamented, that merely to get near the possession of
any coveted thing instantly changes the entire look of it :
it may still appear very good and desirable : but the
romance is gone. When Mr. John Campbell, Student
of Theology in St. Mary's College, St. Andrews, N. B.,
was working away at his Hebrew, or drilling the lads to
whom he acted as tutor, and living sparingly on a few
pounds a year, he would no doubt have thought it a
tremendous thing if he had been told that he would yet
be a peer — that he would be, first Lord Chief Justice
and then Lord High Chancellor of England — and that
he would, upon more than one great occasion, preside
over the assembled aristocracy of Britain. But as he
got on step by step the gradation took off the force of
contrast : each successive step appeared natural enough,
no doubt : and now, when he is fairly at the top of the
tree, if that most amiable and able Judge should ever
wish to realize his elevation, I suppose he can do so only
by recurring in thought to the links of St. Andrews, and
to the days when he drilled his pupils in Latin and
Greek. Student of Divinity, newspaper reporter, utter
barrister, King's Counsel, Solicitor-General, Member for
Edinburgh, Attorney-General, Baron Campbell of St.
Andrews, Chief Justice of England, Lord Chancellor of
Great Britain — each successive point was natural
enough when won, though the end made a great change
from the Manse of Cupar. And when another Scotch
clergyman's son, from a parish adjoining that of Lord
Campbell's father, also went up to London about the
same time, a poor struggling artist, he and all his family

would doubtless have thought it a grand elevation,
had they been told that he was to become one of the
most distinguished members of the Royal Academy.
There is something intensely affecting in the letters which
the minister of Cults (it was a very poor living) sent to
his boy in London, saying that he could, by pinching,
send him, if needful, four or five pounds. But before
Sir David became the great man he grew, old Mr. Wil-
kie was in his grave: 'his son came to honour, and he
knew it not.' No doubt it was better as it was; but if
you or I, kindly reader, had had the ordering of things,
the worthy man should have lived to see what would
have gladdened his simple heart at last.

Still, making every deduction for the levelling result of
getting used to things, a great deal of the enjoyment of
life, high or low, depends on the scenery amid which one
dwells, and the house in which one lives — I mean the
house regarded even in a merely æsthetic point of view.
It needs no argument to prove that if one's abode is subject to the grosser physical disadvantages of smoky
chimneys, damp walls, neighbouring bogs, incurable
draughts, rattling windows, unfitting doors, and the like,
the result upon the temper and the views of the man
thus afflicted will not be a pleasing one. A constant succession of little contemptible worries tends to foster a
querulous, grumbling disposition, which renders a human
being disagreeable to himself and intolerable to his
friends. Real, great misfortunes and trials may serve to
ennoble the character; but ever-recurring petty annoyances produce a littleness and irritability of mind. And
while great misfortune at once engages our sympathy,
petty annoyances ill borne make the sufferer a laughing-
stock. There is something dignified in Napoleon smashed

at Waterloo: there is nothing fine about Napoleon at St.
Helena, swearing at his ill-made soup, and cursing up
and down stairs at his insufficient allowance of clean
shirts.   But I am not now talking of abodes pressed by
physical inconveniences.   It is somewhat of a truism to
say a man cannot be comfortable when he is uncomfortable: and *that* is the sum of what is to be said on that
head.   I mean now that one's home, æsthetically regarded,
has much influence upon our enjoyment of life.   It is a
great matter towards making the best of this world (and
possibly, too, of the next), that our dwelling shall be a
pretty one, a pleasant one, and placed amid pleasant
scenes.   It is a constant pleasure to live in such a home;
and it is a still greater pleasure to make it.   I do not
think I have ever seen happier people, or people who
appeared more thoroughly enviable, than people who
have been building a pretty residence in the country.
Of course they must be building it for themselves to
have the full satisfaction of it; also it must not be too
large; and finally, it must not be bigger nor grander than
they can afford.   The last-named point is essential.   A
duke inherits his castle — he did not build it; and it is
too large and splendid for the peculiar feeling which I
am describing.   It has its own peculiar charms: the charm
of vastness of dwelling and domain; the charm of hoary
age and historic memories, and of connexion with
departed ancestors, and of associations which the millions of the *parvenu* cannot buy.   But it lacks the
especial charm which Scott felt when he was building
Abbotsford; and which lesser men feel when sitting on a
stone on a summer morning, and watching the walls going
up, listening to the clinking of the chisel, planning out
the few acres of ground, and idealizing the life which is

to be led there; seeing with half-closed eyes that muddy
wheel-cut expanse all green and trim; and little Jamie
running about the walk which will be there in after-days;
and little Lucy diligently planting weeds in the corner
where her garden will be. Here, surely, we think, the
last days or years may peacefully go by; and here may
we, though somewhat scarred in the battle of life, and
somewhat worn with its cares, find a quiet haven at last.
To me it is always pleasant reading when I fall in with
books about planning and building such homes as these.
At the mention of the *Cottage*, and even of the *Villa*
(though I don't like that latter word, it sounds vulgar and
cockneyfied and affected; but I fear we must accept it,
for there is no other which conveys the idea of the
modest yet elegant country-house for people of refinement, but not of great means), there rises up before the
mind's-eye, as if by an enchanter's wand, a whole life of
quiet enjoyment. Surely, life in the cottage or the
country-house might be made a very pleasing, pure, and
happy thing. In that unbreathed air, amid those beautiful scenes, surrounded by the gentle processes and teach-
ings of nature, it is but that outward nature and human
life should, on some fair summer day, be wrought into
a happy conformity; and we should need no other
heaven. Take the outward creation at her best, and for
all the thorns and thistles of the Fall, *she* would do yet!

I find a great pleasure in reading books of practical
architecture: and I have lately found out one by an
American architect, one Mr. Calvert Vaux, which carries one into fresh fields. It is a large handsome volume,
luxurious in the size of its type, and admirable for the
excellence of its abundant illustrations. I have more to
say of its contents by-and-bye, and shall here say only,

that to read such a book with pleasure, the reader must
have some little imagination and a good deal of sympathy, so as not to rest on mere architects' designs and
builders' specifications, but to picture out and enter into
the quiet life which these suggest. Everything depends
upon *that*. Therein lies the salt of such a book. The
enjoyment of all things beyond eating and drinking arises
out of our idealizing them. Do you think that a child
who will spend an hour delightedly in galloping round
the garden on his horse, which horse is a stick, regards
that stick as the mere bit of wood? No: that stick is to
him instinct with imaginings of a pony's pattering feet
and shaggy mane, and erect little ears. It is not so long
since the writer was accustomed to ride on horseback in
that inexpensive fashion, but what he can remember all
that the stick was; and remember too how sometimes
fancy would flag, the idealizing power would break down,
and from being a horse the stick became merely a stick,
a dull, wearisome, stupid thing. And of what little
things imagination, thus elevating and enchanting them,
can make how much! You remember the poor little
solitary girl, in the wretched kitchen of Sally Brass, in
the *Old Curiosity Shop*. Never was there life more
bare of anything like enjoyment than the life which that
poor creature led. Think, you folk who grumble at
your lot, of a life whose features are sketched by such
lines as a dark cellar, utter solitude, black beetles, cold
potatoes, cuffs and kicks. Yet the idealizing power
could convey some faint tinge of enjoyment even into the
cellar of House of Brass. The poor little thing, when
she made the acquaintance of Mr. Richard Swiveller,
inquired of him had he ever tasted orange-peel wine.
How was it made, he asked. The recipe was simple:

take a tumbler of cold water, put a little bit of orange-peel into it, and the beverage is ready for use. It has not much taste, added the little solitary, unless you *make believe very much.* Sound and deep little philosopher! We must apply the same prescription to life, and all by which life is surrounded. You are not to accept them as bare prosaic facts : you must make believe very much. Scott made believe very much at Abbotsford ; we all make believe very much at Christmas-time. Likewise at sight of the first snowdrop in springs after we have begun to grow old ; also when hawthorn blossoms and lilacs come again. And what a bare, cold, savourless life is sketched by the memorable lines which set before us the entire character of a man who could not make believe : —

In vain, through every changing year,
Did nature lead him as before ;
A primrose by a river's brim,
A yellow primrose was to him, —
And it was nothing more!

Let me recommend to the man with a taste for such subjects, Mr. Sanderson's *Rural Architecture,* a neat little manual of a hundred pages, with a number of drawings and ground-plans of labourers' cottages, pretty little villas, village schools, and farm-steadings. And any reader may call it his upon payment of one shilling. To the man who has learned to make believe, there will be more than a shilling's worth of enjoyment in the frontispiece, which is a plain but pretty Gothic cottage, surrounded with trees, a little retired from the road, which is reached through a neat rustic gateway, and with the spire of a village church two hundred yards off, peeping through trees and backed by quiet fields rising into hills

of no more than English height. A footpath winds
through the field towards the clump of wood in which
stands the church. The book is a sensible and well-informed one. Its author tells us, but not till the seven-
tieth page of his hundred, that he is 'simply desirous of
having an agreeable half-hour's chat with the reader,
who may take a fancy to indulge in the instructive pastime of building his own house, and who does not please
to appear thoroughly ignorant of the matter he is about.'

Mr. Sanderson appears from his book to have but a
poor opinion of human nature. He is by no means a
'confidence-man.' The book is full of cautions as to
the necessity of closely watching work-people lest they
should cheat you, and do their work in a dishonest and
insufficient manner. I lament to say that my own little
experience leads me to think that these cautions are by no
means unnecessary. I do not think that builders and
carpenters are as bad as horsedealers, whose word no
man in his senses should regard as of the worth of a pin ;
but it is extremely advisable to keep a sharp eye upon
them while their work is progressing. Work improperly
done, or done with insufficient materials, will certainly
cause much expense and annoyance at a future day ; still,
the constantly-recurring statements as to the likelihood of
fraud, leave on one's mind an uncomfortable impression.
Our race is not in a sound state. But perhaps it is too
severe to judge that a decent-looking and well-to-do individual is a dishonest man, merely because he will at any
time tell a lie to make a little money by it.

There is a satisfaction in finding confirmation of one's
own views in the writings of other men ; and so I
quote with pleasure the following from Dr. Southwood
Smith : —

A clean, fresh, and well-ordered house exercises over its inmates a moral, no less than a physical influence, and has a direct tendency to make the members of the family sober, peaceable, and considerate of the feelings and happiness of each other; nor is it difficult to trace a connexion between habitual feelings of this sort and the formation of habits of respect for property, for the laws in general, and even for those higher duties and obligations the observance of which no laws can enforce. Whereas, a filthy, squalid, unwholesome dwelling, in which none of the decencies common to society — even in the lowest stage of civilization — are or can be observed, tends to make every dweller in such a hovel regardless of the feelings and happiness of each other, selfish, and sensual. And the connexion is obvious between the constant indulgence of appetites and passions of this class, and the formation of habits of idleness, dishonesty, debauchery, and violence.

There is something very touching in a description in *Household Words* of the moral results of wretched dwellings, such as those in parts of Bethnal-green, in the eastern region of London. Misery and anxiety have here crushed energy out; the people are honest, but they are palsied by despair : —

The people of this district are not criminal. A lady might walk unharmed at midnight through their wretched lanes. Crime demands a certain degree of energy; but if there were ever any harm in these well-disposed people, it has been tamed out of them by sheer want. They have been sinking for years. Ten years ago, or less, the men were politicians; now, they have sunk below that stage of discontent. They are generally very still and hopeless; cherishing each other; tender not only towards their own kin, but towards their neighbours; and they are subdued by sorrow to a manner strangely resembling the quiet and refined tone of the most polished circles.

Very true to nature! How well one can understand the state of mind of a poor man quite crushed and spirit-broken : poisoned by ceaseless anxiety ; with no heart to do anything ; many a time wishing that he might but creep into a quiet grave ; and meanwhile trying to shrink out of sight and slip by unnoticed ! Despair nerves for a little while, but constant care saps, and poisons, and palsies. Nor does it do so in Bethnal-green alone, or only in dwellings which are undrained and unventilated, and which cannot exclude rain and cold. Elsewhere, as many of my readers have perhaps learned for themselves, it has shattered many a nervous system, unstrung many a once vigorous mind, crushed down many a once hopeful spirit, and aged many a man who should have been young by his years.

I suppose it is now coming to be acknowledged by all men of sense, that it is a Christian duty to care for our fellow-creatures' bodies as well as for their souls; and that it is hateful cant and hypocrisy to pray for the removal of diseases which God by the revelations of Nature has taught us may be averted by the use of physical means, while these means have not been faithfully employed. When cholera or typhus comes, let us whitewash blackened walls, flush obstructed sewers, clear away intermural pigsties, abolish cesspools, admit abundant air and light, and supply unstinted water:—and having done all we can, let us then pray for God's blessing upon what we have done, and for His protection from the plague which by these means we are seeking to hold away from us. Prayers and pains must go together alike in the physical and in the spiritual world. And I think it is now coming to be acknowledged by most rational beings, that houses ought to be pretty as well as healthy; and that houses, even of the humblest class, *may* be pretty as well as healthy. By the Creator's kind arrangement, beauty and use go together; the prettiest house will be the healthiest, the most convenient, and the most comfortable. And I am persuaded that great moral results follow from people's houses being pretty as well as healthy. Every one understands at once that a wretched hovel, dirty, ruinous, stifling, bug-infested, dunghill surrounded, will destroy any latent love of neatness and orderliness in a poor man ; will destroy the love of home, that preservative against temptation which ranks next after religion in the heart, and send the poor man to the public-house, with all its ruinous temptations. But probably it is less remembered than it ought to be, that the home of poor man or well-to-do man ought to be pleasing and inviting, as well as healthy. If not, he will not and cannot have the feeling towards it that it is desirable he should have. And all this is not less to be sought after in the case of people who are so well off that though their home afford no gratification of taste, and even lack the comfort which does not necessarily come with mere abundance, they are not likely to seek refuge at the ale-house, or to take to sottish or immoral courses of any kind. It makes an educated man domestic, it makes him a lover of neatness and accuracy, it makes him gentle and amiable (I mean in all but very extreme cases), to give him a pretty home. I wish it were generally understood that it does not of necessity cost a shilling more to build a pretty house of a certain size, than to build a hideous one yielding the like accommodation. Taste costs nothing. If you have a given quantity of building materials to arrange in order, it is just as easy and just as cheap to arrange them in a tasteful and graceful order and collocation, as in a tasteless, irritating, offensive, and disgusting one. Elaborate ornament, of course, costs dear : but it does not need elaborate ornament to make a pleasing house which every man of taste will feel enjoyment in looking at. Simple gracefulness is all that is essentially needful in cottage and villa architecture. And in this æsthetic age, when there is a general demand for greater beauty in all physical appliances; when we are getting rid of the vile old willow-pattern, when bedroom crockery must be of graceful form and embellishment, when grates and fenders, chairs and couches, window curtains and carpets, oilcloth for lobby floors and paper for covering walls, must all be designed in conformity with the dictates of an elevated taste, — it is not too much to hope that the day will come when every human dwelling that shall be built shall be so built and so placed that it shall form a picture pleasant to all men to look at. It is not necessary to say that this implies a considerable change from the state of matters at present existing in most districts of this country. And I trust it is equally unnecessary to say what school of domestic architecture must predominate if the day we wish for is ever to come. I trust that all my readers (excepting of course the one impracticable man in each hundred, who always thinks differently from everybody else, and always thinks wrong) will agree with me in holding it as an axiom needing no argument to support it, that every building which ranks under the class of villa or cottage, must, if intended to be tasteful or pleasing, be built in some variety of that grand school which is commonly styled the GOTHIC.

I know quite well that there are many persons in this world who would scout the idea that there is any necessity or any use for people who are not rich, to make any provision for their ideal life, for their taste for the beautiful. I can picture to myself some utilitarian old hunks, sharp-nosed, shrivelled-faced, with contracted brow, narrow intellect, and no feeling or taste at all, who would be

ready (so far as he was able) to ridicule my assertion
that it is desirable and possible to provide something to
gratify taste and to elevate and refine feeling, in the aspect and arrangement of even the humblest human dwellings. Beauty, some donkeys think, is the right and
inheritance of the wealthy alone ; food to eat, clothes to
wear, a roof to shelter from the weather, are all that
working men should pretend to. And indeed, if the secret belief of such dull grovellers were told, it would be
that all people with less than a good many hundreds a
year are stepping out of their sphere and encroaching on
the demesne of their betters, when they aim at making
their dwelling such that it shall please the cultivated eye
as well as keep off wind and wet. Such mortals cannot
understand or sympathize with the gratification arising
from the contemplation of objects which are graceful and
beautiful; and they think that if there be such a gratification at all, it is a piece of impudence in a poor man to
aim at it. It is, they consider, a luxury to which he has
no right; it is as though a ploughman should think to
have champagne on his simple dinner-table. I verily
believe that there are numbers of wealthy men, especially in the ranks of those who have made their own
wealth, and who receive little education in youth, who
think that the supply of animal necessities is all that any
mortal (but themselves, perhaps) can need. I have
known of such a man, who said with amazement of a
youth whose health and life premature care was sap-
ping. ' He is well-fed, and well-dressed, and well-lodged,
and what the capital D more can the fellow want?'
Why, if he had been a horse or a pig, he would have
wanted nothing more ; but the possession of a rational
soul brings with it pressing wants which are not of a ma-

17

terial nature, which are not to be supplied by material
things, and which are not felt by pigs and horses. And
the craving for surrounding objects of grace and beauty
is one of these ; and it cannot be killed out but by many
years of sordid money-making, or racking anxiety, or
grinding want. The man whose whole being is given
to finding food and raiment and sleep, is but a somewhat
more intelligent horse. We have something besides a
body, whose needs must be supplied ; or if not supplied,
then crushed out, and we be brought thus nearer to the
condition of being mere soulless bodies. Mr. Vaux has
some just remarks on the importance of a pleasant home
to the young. It is indeed a wretched thing when,
whether from selfish heedlessness or mistaken principle,
the cravings of youthful imagination and feeling are systematically ignored, and life toned down to the last and
most prosaic level. Says Mr. Vaux —

It is not for ourselves alone, but for the sake of our children, that
we should love to build our homes, whether they be villas, cottages,
or log-houses, beautifully and well. The young people are mostly at
home : it is their storehouse for amusement, their opportunity for
relaxation, their main resource; and thus they are exposed to its influence for good or evil unceasingly : their pliable, susceptible minds
take in its whole expression with the fullest possible force, and with
unerring accuracy. It is only by degrees that the young hungry
soul, born and bred in a hard, unlovely home, accepts the coarse fate
to which not the poverty but the indifference of its parents condemns
it. It is many many years before the irrepressible longing becomes
utterly hopeless : perhaps it is never crushed out entirely ; but it is
so stupified by slow degrees into despairing stagnation, if a perpet-
ually recurring blank surrounds it, that it often seems to die, and to
make no sign : the meagre, joyless, torpid home atmosphere in which
it is forced to vegetate absolutely starves it out ; and thus the good
intention that the all-wise Creator had in view, when instilling a
desire for the beautiful into the life of the infant, is painfully frustrated. It is frequently from this cause, and from this alone, that an
impulsive, high-spirited, light-hearted boy will dwindle by degrees

into a sharp, shrewd, narrow-minded, and selfish youth; from thence again into a prudent, hard, and horny manhood; and at last into a covetous, unloving, and unloved old age. The single explanation is all-sufficient: he never had a pleasant home.*

I trust my readers will conclude from this brief specimen of Mr. Vaux's quality, that if he be as thoroughly *up* in the practice of pleasant rural architecture as he is in the philosophy of it, he will be a very agreeable architect indeed. And, in truth, he is so, and his book is a very pleasant one. It is a handsome royal octavo volume of above three hundred pages; it is prodigally illustrated with excellent wood-engravings, which show the man who intends building a country-house an abundance of engaging examples from which to choose one. Nor are we shown merely a number of taking views in perspective; we have likewise the ground-plan of each floor, showing the size and height of each chamber; and further we are furnished with a careful calculation of the probable expense of each cottage or villa. Nor does Mr. Vaux's care extend only to the house proper: he shows some good designs for rustic gateways and fences, and some pretty plans for laying out and planting the piece of shrubbery and lawn which surrounds the abode. America, every one knows, is a country where a man must *push* if he wishes to get on; he must not be held back by any false modesty; and Mr. Vaux's book is not free from the suspicion of being a kind of advertisement of its author, who is described on the title-page as ' Calvert Vaux, Architect, late Downing and Vaux, of Newburgh, on the Hudson.' Then, on an otherwise blank page at the end of the volume, we find in large capitals the significant inscription, which renders it impossible for any one

---

* *Villas and Cottages*, pp. 115, 116.

who reads the book to say that he does not know where
to find Mr. Vaux when he wants him : —

> '*Calvert Vaux, Architect,*
>   *Appleton's Building,*
>   *348, Broadway.*'

American architecture appears to stand in sad need of
improvement. Mr. Vaux tells us, no doubt very truly,
that 'ugly buildings are the almost invariable rule.' In
that land of measureless forests there is a building material common, which is little used now in Britain — to
wit, wood. Still, wood will furnish the material for very
graceful and picturesque houses, even when in the rude
form of logs; and the true blight of housebuilding in
America was less the poverty and the hurry of the early
colonists, than their puritan hatred and contempt of art,
and of everything beautiful. Further, the democratic
spirit could not tolerate the notion of anything being suffered to flourish which, as was wrongly thought, was to
minister to the delight of only a select few.

American houses are for the most part square boxes,
with no character at all. They are generally painted ·
white, with bright green blinds : the effect is staring and
ugly. In America, a perfectly straight line is esteemed
the line of beauty, and a cube the most graceful of forms.
Two large gridirons, laid across one another, exhibit the
ground-plan of the large towns. Two smaller gridirons
represent the villages. Mr. Vaux is strong for the use
of graceful curves, and for laying out roads with some regard to the formation of the ground, and the natural
features of interest. But a man of taste must meet
many mortifications in a country where the following
barbarity could be perpetrated : —

In a case that recently occurred near a country town at some distance from New York, a road was run through a very beautiful estate, one agreeable feature of which was a pretty though small pond, that, even in the dryest seasons, was always full of water, and would have formed an agreeable adjunct to a country seat. A single straight pencil line on the plan doubtless marked out the direction of the road; and as this line happened to go straight through the pond, straight through the pond was the road accordingly carried, the owner of the estate personally superintending the operation, and thus spoiling his sheet of water, diminishing the value of his lands, and incurring expense by the cost of filling-in without any advantage whatever; for a winding road so laid out as to skirt the pond would have been far more attractive and agreeable than the harsh, straight line that is now scored like a railway track clear though the undulating surface of the property; and such barbarisms are of constant occurrence.

No doubt they are, and they are of frequent recurrence nearer home. I have known places where, if you are anxious to get a body of men to make any improvement upon a church or school-house, it is necessary that you should support your plan solely by considerations of utility. Even to suggest the increase of beauty which would result would be quite certain to knock the entire scheme on the head.

Some features of American house-building follow from the country and climate. Such are the verandahs, and the hooded-windows which form part of the design of every villa and every cottage represented in Mr. Vaux's book. The climate makes these desirable, and even essential. Such, too, is the abundance of houses built of wood, several designs for such houses being of considerable pretension. And only a hurried and hasty people, with little notion of building for posterity, would accept the statement, that in building with brick, eight inches thick are quite enough for the walls of any country-house, however large. The very slightest brick walls run up in England are, I believe, at least twelve inches thick. The

materials for roofing are very different from those to
which we are accustomed.   Slates are little used, having
to be brought from England; tin is not uncommon.
Thick canvas is thought to make a good roof when the
surface is not great ; zinc is a good deal employed; but
the favourite roofing material is shingle, which makes a
roof pleasing to American eyes.

It is agreeably varied in surface, and assumes by age a soft
pleasant, neutral tint that harmonizes with any colour that may be
used in the building.

I am not much captivated by Mr. Vaux's description
of the representative American drawing-room, which, it
appears, is entitled the *best parlour :* —

The walls are hardfinished white, the woodwork is white, and a
white marble mantlepiece is fitted over a fireplace which is never
used.   The floor is covered with a carpet of excellent quality, and of
a large and decidedly sprawling pattern, made up of scrolls and flowers in gay and vivid colours.   A round table with a cloth on it, and a
thin layer of books in smart bindings, occupies the centre of the room,
and furnishes about accommodation enough for one rather small person to sit and write a note at.   A gilt mirror finds a place between
the windows.   A sofa occupies irrevocably a well-defined space
against the wall, but it is just too short to lie down on, and too high
and slippery with its spring convex seat to sit on with any comfort.
It is also cleverly managed that points or knobs (of course ornamen-
tal and french-polished) shall occur at all those places towards which
a wearied head would naturally tend, if leaning back to snatch a few
moments' repose from fatigue.   There is also a row of black walnut
chairs, with horse-hair (!) seats, all ranged against the white wall.
A console-table, too, under the mirror, with a white marble top and
thin gilt brackets.   I think there is a piano.   There is certainly a tri-
angular stand for knickknacks, china, &c., and this, with some chimney ornaments, completes the furniture, which is all arranged according to stiff, immutable law.   The windows and venetian blinds are
tightly closed, the door is tightly shut, and the best room is in consequence always ready — for what?   For daily use?   Oh, no; it is in

every way too good for that. For weekly use? Not even for that; but for *company* use. And thus the choice room, with the pretty view, is sacrificed to keep up a conventional show of finery which pleases no one, and is a great, though unacknowledged, bore to the proprietors.

I am not sure that we in this country have much right to laugh at the folly which maintains such chilly and comfortless apartments. Even so uninhabited and useless is many a drawing-room which I could name on this side of the Atlantic. What an embodiment of all that is stiff, repellent, and uneasy, are the drawing-rooms of most widow ladies of limited means! My space does not permit another extract from Mr. Vaux, in which he explains his ideal of the way in which a cottage parlour should be arranged and furnished. Very pleasantly he sketches an unpretending picture, in which snugness and elegance, the *utile* and the *dulce*, are happily and inexpensively combined. But even here Mr. Vaux feels himself pulled up by a vision of a hard-headed and close-fisted old Yankee, listening with indignation, and bursting out with 'This will never do!'

We talk about houses, my friend; we look at houses; but how little the stranger knows of what they are! Search from cellar to garret some old country house, in which successive generations of boys and girls have grown up, but be sure that the least part of it is that which you can see, and not the most accurate inventory that ever was drawn up by appraiser will include half its belongings. There are old memories crowding about every corner of that home unknown to us: and to minds and hearts far away in India and Australia everything about it is sublimed, saddened, transfigured into something different from what it is to you and me. You know for yourself, my reader, whether there be not something not present elsewhere about the window where you sat when a child and learned your lessons, the table once surrounded by many merry young faces which will not surround it again in this world, the fireside where your father sat, the chamber where your sister died. Very little indeed can sense do towards showing us the Home; or towards showing us any scene which has been associated with human life and feeling and embalmed in human memories. The same few hundred yards along the seashore, which are nothing to one man but so much ribbed sea-sand and so much murmuring water, may be to another something to quicken the heart's beating and bring the blood to the cheek. The same green path through the spring-clad trees, with the primroses growing beneath them, which lives in one memory year after year with its fresh vividness undiminished, may be in another merely a vague recollection, recalled with difficulty or not at all.

> Each in his hidden sphere of joy or woe,
>   Our hermit spirits dwell and range apart;
> Our eyes see all around in gloom or glow,—
>   Hues of their own, fresh borrowed from the heart.

CHAPTER IX.

CONCERNING HURRY AND LEISURE.

OH what a blessing it is to have time to breathe, and think, and look around one! I mean, of course, that all this is a blessing to the man who has been overdriven: who has been living for many days in a breathless hurry, pushing and driving on, trying to get through his work, yet never seeing the end of it, not knowing to what task he ought to turn first, so many are pressing upon him altogether. Some folk, I am informed, like to live in a fever of excitement, and in a ceaseless crowd of occupations: but such folk form the minority of the race. Most human beings will agree in the assertion that it is a horrible feeling to be in a hurry. It wastes the tissues of the body; it fevers the fine mechanism of the brain; it renders it impossible for one to enjoy the scenes of nature. Trees, fields, sunsets, rivers, breezes, and the like, must all be enjoyed at leisure, if enjoyed at all. There is not the slightest use in a man's paying a hurried visit to the country. He may as well go there blindfold, as go in a hurry. He will never see the country. He will have a perception, no doubt, of hedgerows and grass, of green lanes and silent cottages, perhaps of great hills and rocks, of various items which go towards making the country; but the country itself he will never see.

That feverish atmosphere which he carries with him will distort and transform even individual objects; but it will utterly exclude the view of the whole. A circling London fog could not do so more completely. For quiet is the great characteristic and the great charm of country scenes; and you cannot see or feel quiet when you are not quiet yourself. A man flying through this peaceful valley in an express train at the rate of fifty miles an hour might just as reasonably fancy that to us, its inhabitants, the trees and hedges seem always dancing, rushing, and circling about, as they seem to him in looking from the window of the flying carriage; as imagine that, when he comes for a day or two's visit, he sees these landscapes as they are in themselves, and as they look to their ordinary inhabitants. The quick pulse of London keeps with him: he cannot, for a long time, feel sensibly an influence so little startling, as faintly flavoured, as that of our simple country life. We have all beheld some country scenes, pleasing, but not very striking, while driving hastily to catch a train for which we feared we should be late; and afterwards, when we came to know them well, how different they looked!

I have been in a hurry. I have been tremendously busy. I have got through an amazing amount of work in the last few weeks, as I ascertain by looking over the recent pages of my diary. You can never be sure whether you have been working hard or not, except by consulting your diary. Sometimes you have an oppressed and worn-out feeling of having been overdriven, of having done a vast deal during many days past; when lo! you turn to the uncompromising record, you test the accuracy of your feeling by that unimpeachable standard; and you find that, after all, you have accomplished very little. The discovery is mortifying, but it does you good ; and besides other results, it enables you to see how very idle and useless people, who keep no diary, may easily bring themselves to believe that they are among the hardest-wrought of mortals. They know they feel weary; they know they have been in a bustle and worry ; they think they have been in it much longer than is the fact. For it is curious how readily we believe that any strongly-felt state of mind or outward condition — strongly felt at the present moment — has been lasting for a very long time. You have been in very low spirits : you fancy now that you have been so for a great portion of your life, or at any rate for weeks past : you turn to your diary, — why, eight-and-forty hours ago you were as merry as a cricket during the pleasant drive with Smith, or the cheerful evening that you spent with Snarling. I can well imagine that when some heavy misfortune befalls a man, he soon begins to feel as if it had befallen him a long, long time ago : he can hardly remember days which were not darkened by it : it seems to have been the condition of his being almost since his birth. And so, if you have been toiling very hard for three days — your pen in your hand almost from morning to night perhaps — rely upon it that at the end of those days, save for the uncompromising diary that keeps you right, you would have in your mind a general impression that you had been labouring desperately for a very long period — for many days, for several weeks, for a month or two. After heavy rain has fallen for four or five days, all persons who do not keep diaries invariably think that it has rained for a fortnight. If keen frost lasts in winter for a fortnight, all persons without diaries have a vague belief that there has been frost for a month or six weeks.

You resolve to read Mr. Wordy's valuable *History of the Entire Human Race throughout the whole of Time* (I take for granted you are a young person) : you go at it every evening for a week. At the end of that period you have a vague uneasy impression, that you have been soaked in a sea of platitudes, or weighed down by an incubus of words, for about a hundred years. For even such is life.

Every human being, then, who is desirous of knowing for certain whether he is doing much work or little, ought to preserve a record of what he does. And such a record, I believe, will in most cases serve to humble him who keeps it, and to spur on to more and harder work. It will seldom flatter vanity, or encourage a tendency to rest on the oars, as though enough had been done. You must have laboured very hard and very constantly indeed, if it looks much in black and white. And how much work may be expressed by a very few words in the diary! Think of Elihu Burrit's 'forged fourteen hours, then Hebrew Bible three hours.' Think of Sir Walter's short memorial of his eight pages before breakfast, — and what large and closely written pages they were! And how much stretch of such minds as they have got — how many quick and laborious processes of the mental machinery — are briefly embalmed in the diaries of humbler and smaller men, in such entries as ' after breakfast, walk in garden with children for ten minutes ; then Sermon on 10 pp. ; working hard from 10 till 1 P.M. ; then left off with bad headache, and very weary?' The truth is, you can't represent work by any record of it. As yet, there is no way known of photographing the mind's exertion, and thus preserving an accurate memorial of it. You might as well expect to find in such a general phase as a *stormy sea* the delineation of the countless shapes and transformations of the waves throughout several hours in several miles of ocean, as think to see in Sir Walter Scott's *eight pages before breakfast* an adequate representation of the hard, varied, wearing-out work that went to turn them off. And so it is, that the diary which records the work of a very hard-wrought man, may very likely appear to careless, unsympathizing readers, to express not such a very laborious life after all. Who has not felt this, in reading the biography of that amiable, able, indefatigable, and over-wrought man, Dr. Kitto? He worked himself to death by labour at his desk: but only the reader who has learned by personal experience to feel for him, is likely to see how he did it.

But besides such reasons as these, there are strong arguments why every man should keep a diary. I cannot imagine how many reflective men do not. How narrow and small a thing their actual life must be! They live merely in the present; and the present is only a shifting point, a constantly progressing mathematical line, which parts the future from the past. If a man keeps no diary, the path crumbles away behind him as his feet leave it; and days gone by are little more than a blank, broken by a few distorted shadows. His life is all confined within the limits of to-day. Who does not know how imperfect a thing memory is? It not merely forgets; it misleads. Things in memory do not merely fade away, preserving as they fade their own lineaments so long as they can be seen: they change their aspect, they change their place, they turn to something quite different from the fact. In the picture of the past, which memory unaided by any written record sets before us, the perspective is entirely wrong. How capriciously some events seem quite recent, which the diary shows are really far away; and how unaccountably many things look far away, which in truth are not left many weeks behind us! A man might almost as well not have lived at all as entirely forget that he has lived, and entirely forget what he did on those departed days. But I think that almost every person would feel a great interest in looking back, day by day, upon what he did and thought upon that day twelvemonths, that day three or five years. The trouble of writing the diary is very small. A few lines, a few words, written at the time, suffice, when you look at them, to bring all (what Yankees call) the *surroundings* of that season before you. Many little things come up again which you know quite well you never would have thought of again but for your glance at those words, and still which you feel you would be sorry to have forgotten. There must be a richness about the life of a person who keeps a diary, unknown to other men. And a million more little links and ties must bind him to the members of his family circle, and to all among whom he lives. Life, to him, looking back, is not a bare line, stringing together his personal identity; it is surrounded, intertwined, entangled, with thousands and thousands of slight incidents, which give it beauty, kindliness, reality. Some folk's life is like an oak walking-stick, straight and varnished; useful, but hard and bare. Other men's life (and such may yours and mine, kindly reader, ever be), is like that oak when it was not a stick but a branch, and waved, leaf-enveloped, and with lots of little twigs growing out of it, upon the summer tree. And yet more precious than the power of the diary to call up again a host of little circumstances and facts, is its power to bring back the indescribable but keenly-felt atmosphere of those departed

days. The old time comes over you. It is not merely
a collection, an aggregate of facts, that comes back; it is
something far more excellent than *that* : it is the soul of
days long ago; it is the dear *Auld lang syne* itself!
The perfume of hawthorn-hedges faded is there; the
breath of breezes that fanned our gray hair when it
made sunny curls, often smoothed down by hands that
are gone; the sunshine on the grass where these old fingers made daisy chains; and snatches of music, compared with which anything you hear at the Opera is
extremely poor. Therefore keep your diary, my friend.
Begin at ten years old, if you have not yet attained that
age. It will be a curious link between the altered seasons of your life; there will be something very touching
about even the changes which will pass upon your handwriting. You will look back at it occasionally, and shed
several tears of which you have not the least reason to
be ashamed. No doubt when you look back, you will
find many very silly things in it; well, you did not think
them silly at the time; and possibly you may be humbler,
wiser, and more sympathetic, for the fact that your diary
will convince you (if you are a sensible person now),
that probably you yourself, a few years or a great many
years since, were the greatest fool you ever knew. Possibly at some future time you may look back with similar feelings on your present self: so you will see that it
is very fit that meanwhile you should avoid self-confi-
dence and cultivate humility; that you should not be
bumptious in any way; and that you should bear, with
great patience and kindliness, the follies of the young.
Therefore, my reader, write up your diary daily. You
may do so at either of two times: 1st. After breakfast,
whenever you sit down to your work, and before you be-

gin your work ; 2nd. After you have done your indoors
work, which ought not to be later than two P.M., and
before you go out to your external duties. Some good
men, as Dr. Arnold, have in addition to this brought up
their history to the present period before retiring for the
night. This is a good plan; it preserves the record of
the day as it appears to us in two different moods : the
record is therefore more likely to be a true one, uncol-
oured by any temporary mental state. Write down
briefly what you have been doing. Never mind that
the events are very little. Of course they must be ; but
you remember what Pope said of little things. State
what work you did. Record the progress of matters in
the garden. Mention where you took your walk, or
ride, or drive. State anything particular concerning the
horses, cows, dogs, and pigs. Preserve some memorial
of the progress of the children. Relate the occasions on
which you made a kite or a water-wheel for any of them ;
also the stories you told them, and the hymns you heard
them repeat. You may preserve some mention of their
more remarkable and old-fashioned sayings. *Forsitan et
olim hæc meminisse jurabit :* all these things may bring
back more plainly a little life when it has ceased ; and
set before you a rosy little face and a curly little head
when they have mouldered into clay. Or if you go, as
you would rather have it, before them, why, when one of
your boys is Archbishop of Canterbury and the other
Lord Chancellor, they may turn over the faded leaves,
and be the better for reading those early records, and
not impossibly think some kindly thoughts of their governor who is far away. Record when the first snowdrop
came, and the earliest primrose. Of course you will
mention the books you read, and those (if any) which

you write. Preserve some memorial, in short, of everything that interests you and yours; and look back each
day, after you have written the few lines of your little
chronicle, to see what you were about that day the preceding year. No one who in this simple spirit keeps a
diary, can possibly be a bad, unfeeling, or cruel man.
No scapegrace or blackguard could keep a diary such as
that which has been described. I am not forgetting that
various blackguards, and extremely dirty ones, *have* kept
diaries, but they have been diaries to match their own
character. Even in reading Byron's diary, you can see
that he was not so much a very bad fellow, as a very
silly fellow, who thought it a grand thing to be esteemed
very bad. When, by the way, will the day come when
young men will cease to regard it as the perfection of
youthful humanity to be a reckless, swaggering fellow,
who never knows how much money he has or spends,
who darkly hints that he has done many wicked
things which he never did, who makes it a boast that
he never reads anything, and thus who affects to be even
a more ignorant numskull than he actually is? When
will young men cease to be ashamed of doing right,
and to boast of doing wrong (which they never did)?
'Thank God,' said poor Milksop to me the other day,
'although I have done a great many bad things, I never
did, &c. &c. &c.' The silly fellow fancied that I should
think a vast deal of one who had gone through so much,
and sown such a large crop of wild oats. I looked at
him with much pity. Ah! thought I to myself, there
are fellows who actually do the things you absurdly pretend to have done; but if you had been one of those I
should not have shaken hands with you five minutes
since. With great difficulty did I refrain from patting

18

his empty head, and saying, 'Oh, poor Milksop, you are a tremendous fool!'

It is indeed to be admitted that by keeping a diary you are providing what is quite sure in days to come to be an occasional cause of sadness. Probably it will never conduce to cheerfulness to look back over those leaves. Well, you will be much the better for being sad occasionally. There are other things in this life than to put things in a ludicrous light, and laugh at them. *That*, too, is excellent in its time and place: but even Douglas Jerrold sickened of the forced fun of *Punch*, and thought this world had better ends than jesting. Don't let your diary fall behind: write it up day by day: or you will shrink from going back to it and continuing it, as Sir Walter Scott tells us he did. You will feel a double unhappiness in thinking you are neglecting something you ought to do, and in knowing that to repair your omission demands an exertion attended with especial pain and sorrow. Avoid at all events *that* discomfort of diary-keeping, by scrupulous regularity: there are others which you cannot avoid, if you keep a diary at all, and occasionally look back upon it. It must tend to make thoughtful people sad, to be reminded of things concerning which we feel that we cannot think of them; that they have gone wrong, and cannot now be set right: that the evil is irremediable, and must just remain, and fret and worry whenever thought of; and life go on under that condition. It is like making up one's mind to live on under some incurable disease, not to be alleviated, not to be remedied, only if possible to be forgotten. Ordinary people have all some of these things: tangles in their life and affairs that cannot be unravelled and must be left alone: sorrowful things which they think cannot be helped. I think it highly inexpedient to give way to such a feeling; it ought to be resisted as far as it possibly can. The very worst thing that you can do with a skeleton is to lock the closet door upon it, and try to think no more of it. No: open the door: let in air and light: bring the skeleton out, and sort it manfully up: perhaps it may prove to be only the skeleton of a cat, or even no skeleton at all. There is many a house, and many a family, in which there is a skeleton, which is made the distressing nightmare it is, mainly by trying to ignore it. There is some fretting disagreement, some painful estrangement, made a thousand times worse by ill-judged endeavours to go on just as if it were not there. If you wish to get rid of it, you must recognise its existence, and treat it with frankness, and seek manfully to set it right. It is wonderful how few evils are remediless, if you fairly face them, and honestly try to remove them. Therefore, I say it earnestly, don't lock your skeleton-chamber door. If the skeleton *be* there, I defy you to forget that it is. And even if it could bring you present quiet, it is no healthful draught, the water of Lethe. Drugged rest is unrefreshful, and has painful dreams. And further; don't let your diary turn to a small skeleton, as it is sure to do if it has fallen much into arrear. There will be a peculiar soreness in thinking that it is in arrear; yet you will shrink painfully from the idea of taking to it again and bringing it up. Better to begin a fresh volume. There is one thing to be especially avoided. Do not on any account, upon some evening when you are pensive, down-hearted, and alone, go to the old volumes, and turn over the yellow pages with their faded ink. Never recur to volumes telling the story of years long

ago, except at very cheerful times in very hopeful
moods : — unless, indeed, you desire to feel, as did Sir
Walter, the connexion between the clauses of the scrip-
tural statement, that *Ahithophel set his house in order
and hanged himself.* In that setting in order, what old,
buried associations rise up again : what sudden pangs
shoot through the heart, what a weight comes down upon
it, as we open drawers long locked, and come upon the
relics of our early selves, and schemes and hopes ! Well,
your old diary, of even five or ten years since (especially if you have as yet hardly reached middle age), is
like a repertory in which the essence of all sad things
is preserved. Bad as is the drawer or the shelf which
holds the letters sent you from home when you were a
schoolboy ; sharp as is the sight of that lock of hair of
your brother, whose grave is baked by the suns of Hin-
dostan ; riling (not to say more) as is the view of that
faded ribbon or those withered flowers which you still
keep, though Jessie has long since married Mr. Beest,
who has ten thousand a-year : they are not so bad, so
sharp, so riling, as is the old diary, wherein the spirit of
many disappointments, toils, partings, and cares, is dis-
tilled and preserved. So don't look too frequently into
your old diaries, or they will make you glum. Don't
let them be your usual reading. It is a poor use of the
past, to let its remembrances unfit you for the duties of
the present.

I have been in a hurry, I have said ; but I am not so
now. Probably the intelligent reader of the preceding
pages may surmise as much. I am enjoying three days
of delightful leisure. I did nothing yesterday : I am
doing nothing to-day : I shall do nothing to-morrow.
This is June : let me feel that it is so. When in a

hurry, you do not realize that a month, more especially a summer month, has come, till it is gone. June: let it be repeated: the *leafy month of June*, to use the strong expression of Mr. Coleridge. Let me hear you immediately quote the verse, my young lady reader, in which that expression is to be found. Of course you can repeat it. It is now very warm, and beautifully bright. I am sitting on a velvety lawn, a hundred yards from the door of a considerable country house, not my personal property. Under the shadow of a large sycamore is this iron chair; and this little table, on which the paper looks quite green from the reflection of the leaves. There is a very little breeze. Just a foot from my hand, a twig with very large leaves is moving slowly and gently to and fro. There, the great serrated leaf has brushed the pen. The sunshine is sleeping (the word is not an affected one, but simply expresses the phenomenon) upon the bright green grass, and upon the dense masses of foliage which are a little way off on every side. Away on the left, there is a well-grown horse-chestnut tree, blazing with blossoms. In the little recesses where the turf makes bays of verdure going into the thicket, the grass is nearly as white with daisies as if it were covered with snow, or had several table-cloths spread out upon it to dry. Blue and green, I am given to understand, form an incongruous combination in female dress; but how beautiful the little patches of sapphire sky, seen through the green leaves! Keats was quite right; any one who is really fond of nature must be very far gone indeed, when he or she, like poor Isabella with her pot of basil, 'forgets the blue above the trees.' I am specially noticing a whole host of little appearances and relations among the natural objects within view, which no man in a hurry

would ever observe ; yet which are certainly meant to be
observed, and worth observing. I don't mean to say that
a beautiful thing in nature is lost because no human
being sees it : I have not so vain an idea of the importance of our race. I do not think that that blue sky,
with its beautiful fleecy clouds, was spread out there just
as a scene at a theatre is spread out, simply to be looked
at by us ; and that the intention of its Maker is baulked
if it be not. Still, among a host of other uses, which
we do not know, it cannot be questioned that one end of
the scenes of nature, and of the capacity of noting and
enjoying them which is implanted in our being, is, that
they should be noted and enjoyed by human minds and
hearts. It is now 11.30 A.M., and I have nothing to do
that need take me far from this spot till dinner, which
will be just seven hours hereafter. It requires an unin-
terrupted view of at least four or five hours ahead, to
give the true sense of leisure. If you know you have
some particular engagement in two hours, or even three
or four, the feeling you have is not that of leisure. On
the contrary you feel that you must push on vigorously
with whatever you may be about ; there is no time to sit
down and muse. Two hours are a very short time. It
is to be admitted that much less than half of that period
is very long, when you are listening to a sermon ; and
the man who wishes his life to appear as long as possible
can never more effectually compass his end than by
going very frequently to hear preachers of that numerous class whose discourses are always sensible and in
good taste, and also sickeningly dull and tiresome. Half
an hour under the instruction of such good men has
oftentimes appeared like about four hours. But for quiet
folk, living in the country, and who have never held the

office of attorney-general or secretary of state, two hours
form quite too short a vista to permit of sitting down to
begin any serious work, such as writing a sermon or an
article. Two hours will not afford elbow-room. One is
cramped in it. Give me a clear prospect of five or six;
so shall I begin an essay. It is quite evident that Hazlitt was a man of the town, accustomed to live in a hurry,
and to fancy short blinks of unoccupation to be leisure, —
even as a man long dwelling in American woods might
think a little open glade quite an extensive clearing. He
begins his essay on *Living to One's-self*, by saying that
being in the country he has a fine opportunity of writing
on that long contemplated subject, and of writing at
leisure, because he has *three hours good before him*, not
to mention a partridge getting ready for his supper. Ah,
not enough! Very well for the fast-going high-pressure
London mind; but quite insufficient for the deliberate,
slow-running country one, that has to overcome a great
inertia. How many good ideas, or at least ideas which
he thinks good, will occur to the rustic writer; and be
cast aside when he reflects that he has but two hours to
sit at his task, and that therefore he has not a moment to
spare for collateral matters, but must keep to the even
thread of his story or his argument! A man who has
four miles to walk within an hour, has little time to stop
and look at the view on either hand; and no time at
all for scrambling over the hedge to gather some wild
flowers. But now I rejoice in the feeling of an unlimited
horizon before me, in the regard of time. Various new
books are lying on the grass; and on the top of the
heap, a certain number of that trenchant and brilliant
periodical, the *Saturday Review*. This is delightful!
It is jolly! And let us always be glad, if through

training or idiosyncrasy we have come to this, my reader,
that whenever you and I enjoy this tranquil feeling of
content, there mingles with it a deep sense of gratitude.
I should be very sorry to-day, if I did not know Whom to
thank for all this. I like the simple, natural piety, which
has given to various seats, at the top of various steep
hills in Scotland, the homely name of *Rest and be thankful!* I trust I am now doing both these things. O ye
men who have never been overworked and overdriven,
never kept for weeks on a constant strain and in a
feverish hurry, you don't know what you miss! Sweet
and delicious as cool water is to the man parched with
thirst, is leisure to the man just extricated from breathless hurry! And nauseous as is that same water to the
man whose thirst has been completely quenched, is
leisure to the man whose life is nothing but leisure.

Let me pick up that number of the *Saturday Review*,
and turn to the article which is entitled *Smith's Drag.**
That article treats of a certain essay which the present
writer once contributed to a certain monthly magazine; †
and it sets out the desultory fashion in which his compositions wander about. I have read the article with great
amusement and pleasure. In the main it is perfectly
just. Does not the avowal say something for the writer's
good-humour? Not frequently does the reviewed acknowledge that he was quite rightly pitched into. Let
me, however, say to the very clever and smart author of
Smith's Drag, that he is to some extent mistaken in his
theory as to my system of essay writing. It is not entirely true that I begin my essays with irrelevant descrip-

---

* June 4th, 1859, pp. 677-8.
† 'Concerning Man and his Dwelling-place.' — *Fraser's Magazine*,
June, 1859, pp. 645-661.

tions of scenery, horses, and the like, merely because
when reviewing a book of heavy metaphysics, I know
nothing about my subject, and care nothing about it, and
have nothing to say about it : and so am glad to get over
a page or two of my production without *bonâ fide* going
at my subject. Such a consideration, no doubt, is not
without its weight ; and besides this, holding that every
way of discussing all things whatsoever is good except
the tiresome, I think that even Smith's Drag serves a
useful end if it pulls one a little way through a heavy
discussion ; as the short inclined plane set Mr. Henson's
aerial machine off with a good start, without which it
could not fly. But there is more than this in the case.
The writer holds by a grand principle. The writer's
great reason for saying something of the scenery amid
which he is writing, is, that he believes that it materially
affects the thought produced, and ought to be taken in
connexion with it. You would not give a just idea of a
country house by giving us an architect's elevation of its
façade, and showing nothing of the hills by which it is
backed, and the trees and shrubbery by which it is surrounded. So, too, with thought. We think in time and
space ; and unless you are a very great man, writing a
book like Butler's *Analogy*, the outward scenes amid
which you write will colour all your abstract thought.
Most people hate abstract thought. Give it in a setting
of scene and circumstances, and *then* ordinary folk will
accept it. Set a number of essays in a story, however
slight ; and hundreds will read them who would never
have looked twice at the bare essays. Human interest
and a sense of reality are thus communicated. When
any one says to me, ' I think thus and thus of some
abstract topic,' I like to say to him, ' Tell me where you

thought it, how you thought it, what you were looking at when you thought it, and to whom you talked about it.' I deny that in essays what is wanted is results. Give me processes. Show me how the results are arrived at. In some cases, doubtless, this is inexpedient. You would not enjoy your dinner if you inquired too minutely into the previous history of its component elements, before it appeared upon your table. You might not care for one of Goldsmith's or Sheridan's pleasantries, if you traced too curiously the steps by which it was licked into shape. Not so with the essay. And by exhibiting the making of his essay, as well as the essay itself when made, the essayist is enabled to preserve and exhibit many thoughts, which he could turn to no account did he exhibit only his conclusions. It is a grand idea to represent two or three friends as discussing a subject. For who that has ever written upon abstract subjects, or conversed upon them, but knows that very often what seem capital ideas occur to him, which he has not had time to write down or to utter before he sees an answer to them, before he discovers that they are unsound. Now, to the essayist writing straightforward these thoughts are lost; he cannot exhibit them. It will not do to write them, and then add that now he sees they are wrong. Here, then, is the great use — *one* great use — of the Ellesmere and Dunsford, who shall hold friendly council with the essayist. They, understood to be talking off-hand, can state all these interesting and striking, though unsound views; and then the more deliberate Milverton can show that they are wrong. And the three friends combined do but represent the phases of thought and feeling in a single individual: for who does not know that every reflective man is, at the very fewest, 'three gentlemen at once?'

Let me say for myself, that it seems to me that no small part of the charm which there is about the *Friends in Council* and the *Companions of My Solitude* arises from the use of the two expedients ; of exhibiting processes as well as results, of showing how views are formed as well as the views themselves ; and also of setting the whole abstract part of the work in a framework of scenes and circumstances. All this makes one feel a life-like reality in the entire picture presented, and enables one to open the leaves with a home-like and friendly sympathy. Do not fancy, my brilliant reviewer, that I pretend to write like that thoughtful and graceful author, so rich in wisdom, in wit, in pathos, in kindly feeling. All I say is, that I have learned from him the grand principle, that abstract thought, for ordinary readers, must gain reality and interest from a setting of time and place.

There is the green branch of the tree, waving about. The breeze is a little stronger, but still the air is perfectly warm. Let me be leisurely ; I feel a little hurried with writing that last paragraph ; I wrote it too quickly. To write a paragraph too quickly, putting in too much pressure of steam, will materially accelerate the pulse. *That* is an end greatly to be avoided. Who shall write hastily of leisure ! Fancy Izaak Walton going out fishing, and constantly looking at his watch every five minutes, for fear of not catching the express train in half an hour ! It would be indeed a grievous inconsistency. The old gentleman might better have stayed at home.

It is all very well to be occasionally, for two or three days, or even for a fortnight, in a hurry. Every earnest man, with work to do, will find that occasionally there comes a pressure of it ; there comes a crowd of

things which must be done quickly if they are done at
all; and the condition thus induced is hurry. I am
aware, of course, that there is a distinction between
haste and hurry — hurry adding to rapidity the element
of painful confusion; but in the case of ordinary people,
haste generally implies hurry. And it will never do to
become involved in a mode of life which implies a constant breathless pushing on. It must be a horrible
thing to go through life in a hurry. It is highly expedient for all, it is absolutely necessary for most men,
that they should have occasional leisure. Many enjoyments — perhaps all the tranquil and enduring enjoyments of life — cannot be felt except in leisure. And
the best products of the human mind and heart can be
brought forth only in leisure. Little does he know of
the calm, unexciting, unwearying, lasting satisfaction of
life, who has never known what it is to place the leisurely hand in the idle pocket, and to saunter to and fro.
Mind, I utterly despise the idler — the loafer, as Yankees term him, who never does anything — whose idle
hands are always in his idle pockets, and who is always
sauntering to and fro. Leisure, be it remembered, is
the intermission of labour: it is the blink of idleness in
the life of a hard-working man. It is only in the case
of such a man that leisure is dignified, commendable, or
enjoyable. But to him it is all these, and more. Let
us not be ever driving on. The machinery, physical
and mental, will not stand it. It is fit that one should
occasionally sit down on a grassy bank, and look list-
lessly, for a long time, at the daisies around, and watch
the patches of bright-blue sky through green leaves
overhead. It is right to rest on a large stone by the
margin of a river; to rest there on a summer day for a

long time, and to watch the lapse of the water as it passes away, and to listen to its silvery ripple over the pebbles. Who but a blockhead will think you idle? Of course blockheads may; but you and I, my reader, do not care a rush for the opinion of blockheads. It is fit that a man should have time to chase his little children about the green, to make a kite and occasionally fly it, to rig a ship and occasionally sail it, for the happiness of those little folk. There is nothing unbecoming in making your Newfoundland dog go into the water to bring out sticks, nor in teaching a lesser dog to stand on his hinder legs. No doubt Goldsmith was combining leisure with work when Reynolds one day visited him; but it was leisure that aided the work. The painter entered the poet's room unnoticed. The poet was seated at his desk, with his pen in his hand, and with his paper before him; but he had turned away from *The Travel-ler*, and with uplifted hand was looking towards a corner of the room, where a little dog sat with difficulty on his haunches, with imploring eyes. Reynolds looked over the poet's shoulder, and read a couplet whose ink was still wet: —

> By sports like these are all their cares beguiled;
> The sports of children satisfy the child.

Surely, my friend, you will never again read that couplet, so simply and felicitously expressed, without remembering the circumstances in which it was written. Who should know better than Goldsmith what simple pleasures 'satisfy the child?'

It is fit that a busy man should occasionally be able to stand for a quarter of an hour by the drag of his friend Smith; and walk round the horses, and smooth down their fore-legs, and pull their ears, and drink in their general aspect, and enjoy the rich colour of their bay coats gleaming in the sunshine ; and minutely and critically inspect the drag, its painting, its cushions, its fur robes, its steps, its spokes, its silver caps, its lamps, its entire expression. These are enjoyments that last, and that cannot be had save in leisure. They are calm and innocent; they do not at all quicken the pulse, or fever the brain ; it is a good sign of a man if he feels them as enjoyments : it shows that he has not indurated his moral palate by appliances highly spiced with the cayenne of excitement, all of which border on vice, and most of which imply it.

Let it be remembered, in the praise of leisure, that only in leisure will the human mind yield many of its best products. Calm views, sound thoughts, healthful feelings, do not originate in a hurry or a fever. I do not forget the wild geniuses who wrote some of the finest English tragedies — men like Christopher Marlowe, Ford, Massinger, Dekker, and Otway. No doubt *they* lived in a whirl of wild excitement, yet they turned off many fine and immortal thoughts. But their thought was essentially morbid, and their feeling hectic : all their views of life and things were unsound. And the beauty with which their writings are flushed all over, is like the beauty that dwells in the brow too transparent, the check too rosy, and the eye too bright, of a fair girl dying of decline. It is entirely a hot-house thing, and away from the bracing atmosphere of reality and truth. Its sweetness palls, its beauty frightens : its fierce passion and its wild despair are the things in which it is at home. I do not believe the stories which are told about Jeffrey scribbling off his articles while dressing for a ball, or after returning from one at four in the morning: the fact is, nothing good for much was ever produced in that jaunty, hasty fashion. which is suggested by such a phrase as *scribbled off*. Good ideas flash in a moment on the mind: but they are very crude then; and they must be mellowed and matured by time and in leisure. It is pure nonsense to say that the *Poetry of the Anti-jacobin* was produced by a lot of young men sitting over their wine, very much excited, and talking very loud, and two or three at a time. Some happy impromptu hits may have been elicited by that mental friction; but, rely upon it, the *Needy Knife-Grinder,* and the song whose chorus is *Niversity of Gottingen,* were composed when their author was entirely alone, and had plenty of time for thinking. Brougham is an exception to all rules: he certainly did write his *Discourse of Natural Theology* while rent asunder by all the multifarious engagements of a Lord Chancellor; but, after all, a great deal that Brougham has done exhibits merely the smartness of a sort of intellectual legerdemain; and that celebrated *Discourse,* so far as I remember it, is remarkably poor stuff. I am now talking not of great geniuses, but of ordinary men of education, when I maintain that to the labourer whose work is mental, and especially to the man whose work it is to write, leisure is a pure necessary of intellectual existence. There must be long seasons of quiescence between the occasional efforts of production. An electric eel cannot always be giving off shocks. The shock is powerful, but short, and then long time is needful to rally for another. A field, however good its soil, will not grow wheat year after year. Such a crop exhausts the soil: it is a strain to produce it; and after it the field must lie fallow for a while, — it must have leisure, in

short.   So is it with the mind.   Who does not know that
various literary electric eels, by repeating their shocks
too frequently, have come at last to give off an electric
result which is but the faintest and washiest echo of the
thrilling and startling ones of earlier days? *Festus* was
a strong and unmistakeable shock; *The Angel World*
was much weaker; *The Mystic* was extremely weak; and
The Age was twaddle.   Why did the author let himself
down in such a fashion?   The writer of *Festus* was a
grand, mysterious image in many youthful minds : dark,
wonderful, not quite comprehensible.   The writer of
The Age is a smart but silly little fellow, whom we could
readily slap upon the back and tell him he had rather
made a fool of himself.   And who does not feel how
weak the successive shocks of Mr. Thackeray and Mr.
Dickens are growing?   The former, especially, strikes
out nothing new.   Anything good in his recent productions is just the old thing, with the colours a good deal
washed out, and with salt which has lost its savour.   Poor
stuff comes of constantly cutting and cropping.   The potatoes of the mind grow small; the intellectual wheat
comes to have no ears; the moral turnips are infected
with the finger and toe disease.   The mind is a reservoir
which can be emptied in a much shorter time than it is
possible to fill it.   It fills through an infinity of little tubes,
many so small as to act by capillary attraction.   But in
writing a book, or even an article, it empties as through a
twelve-inch pipe.   It is to me quite wonderful that most of
the sermons one hears are so good as they are, considering the unintermittent stream in which most preachers are
compelled to produce them.   I have sometimes thought,
in listening to the discourse of a really thoughtful and
able clergyman — If you, my friend, had to write a ser-

mon once a month instead of once a week, how very
admirable it would be!

Some stupid people are afraid of confessing that they
ever have leisure. They wish to palm off upon the
human race the delusion that they, the stupid people,
are always hard at work. They are afraid of being
thought idle unless they maintain this fiction. I have
known clergymen who would not on any account take
any recreation in their own parishes, lest they should
be deemed lazy. They would not fish, they would not
ride, they would not garden, they would never be seen
leaning upon a gate, and far less carving their name
upon a tree. What absurd folly! They might just as
well have pretended that they did without sleep, or
without food, as without leisure. You cannot always
drive the machine at its full speed. I know, indeed,
that the machine may be so driven for two or three
years at the beginning of a man's professional life; and
that it is possible for a man to go on for such a period
with hardly any appreciable leisure at all. But it
knocks up the machine: it wears it out: and after an
attack or two of nervous fever, we learn what we should
have known from the beginning, that a far larger
amount of tangible work will be accomplished by regular exertion of moderate degree and continuance, than
by going ahead in the feverish and unrestful fashion in
which really earnest men are so ready to begin their
task. It seems, indeed, to be the rule rather than the
exception, that clergymen should break down in strength
and spirits in about three years after entering the
church. Some die: but happily a larger number get
well again, and for the remainder of their days work at

19

a more reasonable rate. As for the sermons written in that feverish stage of life, what crude and extravagant things they are : stirring and striking, perhaps, but hectic and forced, and entirely devoid of the repose, reality, and daylight feeling of actual life and fact. Yet how many good, injudicious people, are ever ready to expect of the new curate or rector an amount of work which man cannot do ; and to express their disappointment if that work is not done ! It is so very easy to map out a task which you are not to do yourself : and you feel so little wearied by the toils of other men ! As for you, my young friend, beginning your parochial life, don't be ill-pleased with the kindly-meant advice of one who speaks from the experience of a good many years, and who has himself known all that you feel, and foolishly done all that you are now disposed to do. Consider for how many hours of the day you can labour, without injury to body or mind : labour faithfully for those hours, and for no more. Never mind about what may be said by Miss Limejuice and Mr. Snarling. They will find fault at any rate ; and you will mind less about their fault-finding, if you have an unimpaired digestion, and unaffected lungs, and an unenlarged heart. Don't pretend that you are always working : it would be a sin against God and Nature if you were. Say frankly, There is a certain amount of work that I *can* do ; and *that* I *will* do : but I *must* have my hours of leisure. I must have them for the sake of my parishioners as well as for my own ; for leisure is an essential part of that mental discipline which will enable my mind to grow and turn off sound instruction for their benefit. Leisure is a necessary part of true life ; and if I am to live at all, I must have it. Surely it is a thousand times better

candidly and manfully to take up *that* ground, than to
take recreation on the sly, as though you were ashamed
of being found out in it, and to disguise your leisure as
though it were a sin. I heartily despise the clergyman
who reads *Adam Bede* secretly in his study, and when
any one comes in, pops the volume into his waste-paper
basket. An innocent thing is wrong to you if you think
it wrong, remember. I am sorry for the man who is
quite ashamed if any one finds him chasing his little children about the green before his house, or standing looking at a bank of primroses or a bed of violets, or a high
wall covered with ivy. Don't give in to that feeling for
one second. You are doing right in doing all that ; and
no one but an ignorant, stupid, malicious, little-minded,
vulgar, contemptible blockhead will think you are doing
wrong. On a sunny day, you are not idle if you sit
down and look for an hour at the ivied wall, or at an
apple-tree in blossom, or at the river gliding by. You
are not idle if you walk about your garden, noticing the
progress and enjoying the beauty and fragrance of each
individual rose-tree on such a charming June day as
this. You are not idle if you sit down upon a garden
seat, and take your little boy upon your knee, and talk
with him about the many little matters which give
interest to his little life. You are doing something
which may help to establish a bond between you closer
than that of blood ; and the estranging interests of after
years may need it all. And you do not know, even as
regards the work (if of composition) at which you are
busy, what good ideas and impulses may come of the
quiet time of looking at the ivy, or the blossoms, or the
stream, or your child's sunny curls. Such things often
start thoughts which might seem a hundred miles away

from them. That they do so, is a fact to which the
experience of numbers of busy and thoughtful men can
testify. Various thick skulls may think the statement
mystical and incomprehensible : for the sake of such let
me confirm it by high authority. Is it not curious, by
the way, that in talking to some men and women, if you
state a view a little beyond their mark, you will find
them doubting and disbelieving it so long as they regard
it as resting upon your own authority ; but if you can
quote anything that sounds like it from any printed
book, or even newspaper, no matter how little worthy
the author of the article or book may be, you will find
the view received with respect, if not with credence?
The mere fact of its having been printed, gives any
opinion whatsoever much weight with some folk. And
your opinion is esteemed as if of greater value, if you
can only show that any human being agreed with you in
entertaining it. So, my friend, if Mr. Snarling thinks it
a delusion that you may gain some thoughts and feelings
of value, in the passive contemplation of nature, inform
him that the following lines were written by one Wordsworth, a stamp-distributor in Cumberland, regarded by
many competent judges as a very wise man : —

> Why, William, on that old grey stone,
>   Thus for the length of half a day,
> Why, William, sit you thus alone,
>   And dream your time away?
>
> One morning thus, by Esthwaite lake,
>   When life was sweet, I knew not why,
> To me my good friend Matthew spake,
>   And thus I made reply:
>
> The eye, — it cannot choose but see;
>   We cannot bid the ear be still:

Our bodies feel, where'er they be,
  Against or with our will.

Nor less I deem that there are Powers,
  Which of themselves our minds impress;
That we can feed this mind of ours,
  In a wise passiveness.

Think you, 'mid all this mighty sum,
  Of things for ever speaking,
That nothing of itself will come,
  But we must still be seeking?

Then ask not wherefore, here, alone,
  Conversing as I may,
I sit upon this old grey stone,
  And dream my time away!

Such an opinion is sound and just. Not that I believe
that instead of sending a lad to Eton and Oxford, it
would be expedient to make him sit down on a grey
stone, by the side of any lake or river, and wait till
wisdom came to him through the gentle teaching of
nature. The instruction to be thus obtained must be
supplementary to a good education, college and professional, obtained in the usual way; and it must be
sought in intervals of leisure, intercalated in a busy and
energetic life. But thus intervening, and coming to sup-
plement other training, I believe it will serve ends of the
most valuable kind, and elicit from the mind the very
best material which is there to be elicited. Some people
say they work best under pressure: De Quincey, in a
recent volume, declares that the conviction that he *must*
produce a certain amount of writing in a limited time
has often seemed to open new cells in his brain, rich in
excellent thought; and I have known preachers (very
poor ones) declare that their best sermons were written

after dinner on Saturday. As for the sermons, the best were bad; as for De Quincey, he is a wonderful man. Let us have elbow room, say I, when we have to write anything! Let there be plenty of time, as well as plenty of space. Who could write if cramped up in that chamber of torture, called *Little Ease*, in which a man could neither sit, stand, nor lie, but in a constrained fashion? And just as bad is it to be cramped up into three days, when to stretch one's self demands at least six. Do you think Wordsworth could have written against time? Or that *In Memoriam* was penned in a hurry?

Said Miss Limejuice, I saw Mr. Swetter, the new rector, to-day. Ah! she added, with a malicious smile, I fear he is growing idle already, though he has not been in the parish six months. I saw him, at a quarter before two precisely, standing at his gate with his hands in his pockets. I observed that he looked for three minutes over the gate into the clover field he has got. And then Smith drove up in his drag, and stopped and got out; and he and the rector entered into conversation, evidently about the horses, for I saw Mr. Swetter walk round them several times, and rub down their fore-legs. Now *I* think he should have been busy writing his sermon, or visiting his sick. Such, let me assure the incredulous reader, are the words which I have myself heard Miss Limejuice, and her mother, old Mrs. Snarling Limejuice, utter more than once or twice. Knowing the rector well, and knowing how he portions out his day, let me explain to those candid individuals the state of facts. At ten o'clock precisely, having previously gone to the stable and walked round the garden, Mr. Swetter sat down at his desk in his study and worked hard till one. At two he is to ride up the parish to see various sick persons among the cottagers. But from one to two he has laid his work aside, and tried to banish all thought of his work. During that period he has been running about the green with his little boy, and even rolling upon the grass; and he has likewise strung together a number of daisies on a thread, which you might have seen round little Charlie's neck if you had looked sharply. He has been unbending his mind, you see, and enjoying leisure after his work. It is entirely true that he did look into the clover field and enjoy the fragrance of it, which you probably regard as a piece of sinful self-indulgence. And his friend coming up, it is likewise certain that he examined his horses (a new pair), with much interest and minuteness. Let me add, that only contemptible humbugs will think the less of him for all this. The days are past in which the ideal clergyman was an emaciated eremite, who hardly knew a cow from a horse, and was quite incapable of sympathizing with his humbler parishioners in their little country cares. And some little knowledge as to horses and cows, not to mention potatoes and turnips, is a most valuable attainment to the country parson. If his parishioners find that he is entirely ignorant of those matters which they understand best, they will not unnaturally draw the conclusion that he knows nothing. While if they find that he is fairly acquainted with those things which they themselves understand, they will conclude that he knows everything. Helplessness and ignorance appear contemptible to simple folk, though the helplessness should appear in the lack of power to manage a horse, and the ignorance in a man's not knowing the way in which potatoes are planted. To you, Miss Limejuice, let me further say a word as to your parish clergyman. Mr. Swetter, you probably do not know, was Senior Wrangler at Cambridge. He chose his present mode of life, not merely because he felt a special leaning to the sacred profession, though he did feel that strongly ; but also because he saw that in the Church, and in the care of a quiet rural parish, he might hope to combine the faithful discharge of his duty with the enjoyment of leisure for thought ; he might be of use in his generation without being engaged to that degree that, like some great barristers, he should grow a stranger to his children. He concluded that it is one great happiness of a country parson's life, that he may work hard without working feverishly ; he may do his duty, yet not bring on an early paralytic stroke. Swetter might, if he had liked, have gone in for the Great Seal ; the man who was second to him will probably get it; but he did not choose. Do you not remember how Baron Alderson, who might well have aspired at being a Chief Justice or a Lord Chancellor, fairly decided that the prize was not worth the cost, and was content to turn aside from the worry of the bar into the comparative leisure of a puisne judgeship ? It was not worth his while, he rightly considered, to run the risk of working himself to death, or to live for years in a breathless hurry. No doubt the man who thus judges must be content to see others seize the great prizes of human affairs. Hot and trembling hands, for the most part, grasp these. And how many work breathlessly, and give up the tranquil enjoyment of life, yet never grasp them after all !

There is no period at which the feeling of leisure is a more delightful one, than during breakfast and after breakfast on a beautiful summer morning in the country.

It is a slavish and painful thing to know that instantly
you rise from the breakfast-table you must take to your
work. And in that case your mind will be fretting and
worrying away all the time that the hurried meal lasts.
But it is delightful to be able to breakfast leisurely ; to
read over your letters twice ; to skim the *Times,* just to
see if there is anything particular in it (the serious reading of it being deferred till later in the day) ; and then
to go out and saunter about the garden, taking an interest in whatever operations may be going on there ; to
walk down to the little bridge and sit on the parapet,
and look over at the water foaming through below ; to
give your dogs a swim ; to sketch out the rudimentary
outline of a kite, to be completed in the evening ; to stick
up, amid shrieks of excitement and delight, a new coloured picture in the nursery ; to go out to the stable and
look about there ; — and to do all this with the sense
that there is no neglect, that you can easily overtake your
day's work notwithstanding. For this end the country
human being should breakfast early; not later than nine
o'clock. Breakfast will be over by half-past nine ; and
the half hour till ten is as much as it is safe to give to
leisure, without running the risk of dissipating the mind
too much for steady application to work. After ten one
does not feel comfortable in idling about, on a common
working-day. You feel that you ought to be at your
task ; and he who would enjoy country leisure must beware of fretting the fine mechanism of his moral percep-
tions by doing anything which he thinks even in the least
degree wrong.

And here, after thinking of the preliminary half hour
of leisure before you sit down to your work, let me advise that when you fairly go at your work, if of composi-

tion, you should go at it leisurely. I do not mean that
you should work with half a will, with a wandering attention, with a mind running away upon something else.
What I mean is, that you should beware of flying at
your task, and keeping at it, with such a stretch, that
every fibre in your body and your mind is on the strain,
is tense and tightened up; so that when you stop, after
your two or three hours at it, you feel quite shattered and
exhausted. A great many men, especially those of a
nervous and sanguine temperament, write at too high a
pressure. They have a hundred and twenty pounds on
the square inch. Every nerve is like the string of Robin
Hood's bow. All this does no good. It does not appreciably affect the quality of the article manufactured, nor
does it much accelerate the rate of production. But it
wears a man out awfully. It sucks him like an orange.
It leaves him a discharged Leyden jar, a torpedo entirely used up. You have got to walk ten miles. You
do it at the rate of four miles an hour. You accomplish
the distance in two hours and a half; and you come in,
not extremely done up. But another day, with the same
walk before you, you put on extra steam, and walk at
four and a half miles an hour, perhaps at five. (*Mem.:*
People who say they walk six miles an hour are talking
nonsense. It cannot be done, unless by a trained pedestrian.) You are on a painful stretch all the journey:
you save, after all, a very few minutes; and you get to
your journey's end entirely knocked up. Like an over-
driven horse, you are off your feed; and you can do
nothing useful all the evening. I am well aware that the
good advice contained in this paragraph will not have the
least effect on those who read it. *Fungar inani munere.*
I know how little all this goes for with an individual

now not far away. And, indeed, no one can say that because two men have produced the same result in work accomplished, therefore they have gone through the same amount of exertion. Nor am I now thinking of the vast differences between men in point of intellectual power. I am content to suppose that they shall be, intellectually, precisely on a level: yet one shall go at his work with a painful, heavy strain; and another shall get through his lightly, airily, as if it were pastime. One shall leave off fresh and buoyant; the other, jaded, languid, aching all over. And in this respect, it is probable that if your natural constitution is not such as to enable you to work hard, yet leisurely, there is no use in advising you to take things easily. Ah, my poor friend, you cannot! But at least you may restrict yourself from going at any task on end, and keeping yourself ever on the fret until it is fairly finished. Set yourself a fitting task for each day; and on no account exceed it. There are men who have a morbid eagerness to get through any work on which they are engaged. They would almost wish to go right on through all the toils of life and be done with them; and then, like Alexander, 'sit down and rest.' The prospect of anything yet to do, appears to render the enjoyment of present repose impossible. There can be no more unhealthful state of mind. The day will never come when we shall have got through our work: and well for us that it never will. Why disturb the quiet of to-night, by thinking of the toils of to-morrow? There is deep wisdom, and accurate knowledge of human nature, in the advice, given by the Soundest and Kindest of all advisers, and applicable in a hundred cases, to 'Take no thought for the morrow.'

It appears to me, that in these days of hurried life, a

great and valuable end is served by a class of things
which all men of late have taken to abusing, — to wit,
the extensive class of dull, heavy, uninteresting, good,
sensible, pious sermons. They afford many educated men
almost their only intervals of waking leisure. You are
in a cool, quiet, solemn place: the sermon is going forward : you have a general impression that you are listening to many good advices and important doctrines, and
the entire result upon your mind is beneficial; and at the
same time there is nothing in the least striking or startling to destroy the sense of leisure, or to painfully arouse
the attention and quicken the pulse. Neither is there a
syllable that can jar on the most fastidious taste. All
points and corners of thought are rounded off. The entire composition is in the highest degree gentlemanly,
scholarly, correct; but you feel that it is quite impossible
to attend to it. And you do not attend to it; but at the
same time, you do not quite turn your attention to anything else. Now, you remember how a dying father,
once upon a time, besought his prodigal son to spend an
hour daily in solitary thought: and what a beneficial
result followed. The dull sermon may serve an end as
desirable. In church you are alone, in the sense of being
isolated from all companions, or from the possibility of
holding communication with anybody; and the wearisome sermon, if utterly useless otherwise, is useful in
giving a man time to think, in circumstances which will
generally dispose him to think seriously. There is a
restful feeling, too, for which you are the better. It is a
fine thing to feel that church is a place where, if even for
two hours only, you are quite free from worldly business
and cares. You know that all these are waiting for you
outside: but at least you are free from their actual endur-

ance here. I am persuaded, and I am happy to entertain
the persuasion, that men are often much the better for
being present during the preaching of sermons to which
they pay very little attention. Only some such belief as
this could make one think, without much sorrow, of the
thousands of discourses which are preached every Sunday over Britain, and of the class of ears and memories
to which they are given. You see that country congregation coming out of that ivy-covered church in that
beautiful churchyard. Look at their faces, the ploughmen, the dairy-maids, the drain-diggers, the stable-boys:
what could *they* do towards taking in the gist of that well-
reasoned, scholarly, elegant piece of composition which
has occupied the last half-hour? Why, they could not
understand a sentence of it. Yet it has done them good.
The general effect is wholesome. They have got a little
push, they have felt themselves floating on a gentle
current, going in the right direction. Only enthusiastic
young divines expect the mass of their congregation to
do all they exhort them to do. You must advise a man
to do a thing a hundred times, probably, before you can
get him to do it once. You know that a breeze, blowing
at thirty-five miles an hour, does very well if it carries a
large ship along in its own direction at the rate of eight.
And even so, the practice of your hearers, though truly
influenced by what you say to them, lags tremendously
behind the rate of your preaching. Be content, my
friend, if you can maintain a movement, sure though
slow, in the right way. And don't get angry with your
rural flock on Sundays, if you often see on their blank
faces, while you are preaching, the evidence that they
are not taking in a word you say. And don't be entirely
discouraged. You may be doing them good for all that.

And if you do good at all, you know better than to grumble, though you may not be doing it in the fashion that you would like best. I have known men, accustomed to sit quiet, pensive, half-attentive, under the sermons of an easy-going but orthodox preacher, who felt quite indignant when they went to a church where their attention was kept on the stretch all the time the sermon lasted, whether they would or no. They felt that this intrusive interest about the discourse, compelling them to attend, was of the nature of an assault, and of an unjustifiable infraction of the liberty of the subject. Their feeling was, 'What earthly right has that man to make us listen to his sermon, without getting our consent ? We go to church to rest : and lo ! he compels us to listen !'

I do not forget, musing in the shade this beautiful summer day, that there may be cases in which leisure is very much to be avoided. To some men, constant occupation is a thing that stands between them and utter wretchedness. You remember the poor man, whose story is so touchingly told by Borrow in *The Romany Rye*, who lost his wife, his children, all his friends, by a rapid succession of strokes ; and who declared that he would have gone mad if he had not resolutely set himself to the study of the Chinese language. Only constant labour of mind could 'keep the misery out of his head.' And years afterwards, if he paused from toil for even a few hours, the misery returned. The poor fisherman in *The Antiquary* was wrong in his philosophy, when Mr. Oldbuck found him, with trembling hands, trying to repair his battered boat the day after his son was buried. 'It's weel wi' you gentles,' he said, 'that can sit in the house wi' handkerchers at your cen, when ye lose a freend ; but the like o' us maun to our wark again, if our hearts were beating as hard as my hammer!' We love the kindly sympathy that made Sir Walter write the words: but bitter as may be the effort with which the poor man takes to his heartless task again, surely he will all the sooner get over his sorrow. And it is with gentles, who can 'sit in the house' as long as they like, that the great grief longest lingers. There is a wonderful efficacy in enforced work to tide one over every sort of trial. I saw not long since a number of pictures, admirably sketched, which had been sent to his family in England by an emigrant son in Canada, and which represented scenes in daily life there among the remote settlers. And I was very much struck with the sad expression which the faces of the emigrants always wore, whenever they were represented in repose or inaction. I felt sure that those pensive faces set forth a sorrowful fact. Lying on a great bluff, looking down upon a lovely river; or seated at the tent-door on a Sunday, when his task was laid apart; — however the backwoodsman was depicted, if not in energetic action, there was always a very sad look upon the rough face. And it was a peculiar sadness — not like that which human beings would feel amid the scenes and friends of their youth: a look pensive, distant, full of remembrance, devoid of hope. You glanced at it, and you thought of Lord Eglintoun's truthful lines : —

> From the lone shieling on the misty island,
>   Mountains divide us, and a world of seas:
> But still the blood is strong, the heart is Highland,
>   And we in dreams behold the Hebrides:
> Fair these broad meads, these hoary woods are grand,—
> But we are exiles from our fathers' land!

And you felt that much leisure will not suit *there*. Therefore, you stout backwoodsman, go at the huge for-

est-tree : rain upon it the blows of your axe, as long as
you can stand ; watch the fragments as they fly ; and
jump briskly out of the way as the reeling giant falls : —
for all this brisk exertion will stand between you and
remembrances that would unman you.　There is nothing
very philosophical in the plan, to ' dance sad thoughts
away,' which I remember as the chorus of some Cana-
dian song.　I doubt whether that peculiar specific will
do much good.　But you may *work* sad thoughts away ;
you may crowd morbid feelings out of your mind by
stout daylight toils ; and remember that sad remembrances, too long indulged, tend strongly to the maudlin.
Even Werter was little better than a fool ; and a contemptible fool was Mr. Augustus Moddle.

How many of man's best works take for granted that
the majority of cultivated persons, capable of enjoying
them, shall have leisure in which to do so.　The architect, the artist, the landscape-gardener, the poet, spend
their pains in producing that which can never touch the
hurried man.　I really feel that I act unkindly by the
man who did that elaborate picking-out in the painting of a railway carriage, if I rush upon the platform at
the last moment, pitch in my luggage, sit down and take
to the *Times*, without ever having noticed whether the
colour of the carriage is brown or blue.　There seems a
dumb pleading eloquence about even the accurate diag-
onal arrangement of the little woollen tufts in the morocco cushions, and the interlaced network above one's
head, where umbrellas go, as though they said, ' We are
made thus neatly to be looked at, but we cannot make
you look at us unless you choose ; and half the people
who come into the carriage are so hurried that they

never notice us.' And when I have seen a fine church-
spire, rich in graceful ornament, rising up by the side of
a city street, where hurried crowds are always passing
by, not one in a thousand ever casting a glance at the
beautiful object, I have thought, Now surely you are not
doing what your designer intended! When he spent so
much of time, and thought, and pains in planning and exe-
cuting all those beauties of detail, surely he intended
them to be looked at; and not merely looked at in their
general effect, but followed and traced into their lesser
graces. But he wrongly fancied that men would have
time for that; he forgot that, except on the solitary artistic visitor, all he has done would be lost, through the
nineteenth century's want of leisure. And you, architect
of Melrose, when you designed that exquisite tracery,
and decorated so perfectly that flying buttress, were you
content to do so for the pleasure of knowing you did your
work thoroughly and well; or did you count on its producing on the minds of men in after ages an impression
which a prevailing hurry has prevented from being produced, save perhaps in one case in a thousand? And
you, old monk, who spent half your life in writing and
illuminating that magnificent Missal; was your work its
own reward in the pleasure its execution gave you; or
did you actually fancy that mortal man would have time
or patience — leisure, in short — to examine in detail all
that you have done, and that interested you so much, and
kept you eagerly engaged for so many hours together, on
days the world has left four hundred years behind? I
declare it touches me to look at that laborious appeal to
men with countless hours to spare: men, in short, hardly
now to be found in Britain. No doubt, all this is the old
story: for how great a part of the higher and finer hu-

20

man work is done in the hope that it will produce an
effect which it never will produce, and attract the interest of those who will never notice it! Still, the ancient
missal-writer pleased himself with the thought of the admiration of skilled observers in days to come; and so the
fancy served its purpose.

Thus, at intervals through that bright summer day,
did the writer muse at leisure in the shade; and note
down the thoughts (such as they are) which you have
here at length in this essay. The sun was still warm
and cheerful when he quitted the lawn; but somehow,
looking back upon that day, the colours of the scene are
paler than the fact, and the sunbeams feel comparatively
chill. For memory cannot bring back things freshly as
they lived, but only their faded images. Faces in the
distant past look wan; voices sound thin and distant; the
landscape round is uncertain and shadowy. Do you not
feel somehow, when you look back on ages forty centuries ago, as if people then spoke in whispers and lived in
twilight?

CHAPTER VIII.

CONCERNING THE WORRIES OF LIFE, AND HOW TO MEET THEM.

BUT now to my proper task. I have certain suggestions to offer *Concerning the Worries of Life, and How to Meet them.* I am quite aware that the reader of a metaphysical turn, after he has read my essay, may be disposed to find fault with its title. The plan which is to be advocated for the treatment of the *Worries of Life,* can only in a modified sense be described as *Meeting them.* You cannot be said to face a thing on which you turn your back. You cannot accurately be described as meeting a man whom you walk away from. You do not, in strictness, regard a thing in any mode or fashion, which you do not regard at all. But, after intense reflection, I could devise no title that set out my subject so well as the present: and so here it is. Perfection is not generally attainable in human doings. It is enough, if things are so, that they *will do.* No doubt this is no excuse for not making them as good as one can. But the fact is, as you get older, you seldom have time to write down any plausible excuse, before you see a crushing answer to it. The man who has thought longest, comes back to the point at which the man stands who has hardly thought at all. He feels, more deeply year by year, the truth of the grand axiom, that *Much may be said on Both Sides.*

Now, my reader, you shall have, in a very brief space, the essence of my Theory as to the treatment of Human Worry.

Let us picture to ourselves a man, living in a pleasant home, in the midst of a beautiful country. Pleasing scenes are all around him, wherever he can look. There are evergreens and grass : fields and hedgerows : hills and streams; in the distance, the sea ; and somewhat nearer, the smoke of a little country town. Now, what would you think of this man, if he utterly refused to look at the cheerful and beautiful prospects which everywhere invite his eye ; and spent the whole day gazing intently at the dunghill, and hanging over the pigsty ? And all this though his taste were not so peculiar as to lead him to take any pleasure in the contemplation of the pigsty or the dunghill ; all this, though he had a more than ordinary dislike to contemplate pigsties or dunghills ? No doubt, you would say the man is a monomaniac.

And yet, my reader, don't you know (possibly from your own experience) that in the moral world many men and women do a thing precisely analogous, without ever being suspected of insanity ? Don't you know that multitudes of human beings turn away from the many blessings of their lot, and dwell and brood upon its worries ? Don't you know that multitudes persistently look away from the numerous pleasant things they might contemplate, and look fixedly and almost constantly at painful and disagreeable things ? You sit down, my friend, in your snug library, beside the evening fire. The blast without is hardly heard through the drawn curtains. Your wife is there, and your two grown-up daughters.

You feel thankful that after the bustle of the day, you have this quiet retreat where you may rest, and refit yourself for another day with its bustle. But the conversation goes on. Nothing is talked of but the failings of the servants and the idleness and impudence of your boys; unless indeed it be the supercilious bow with which Mrs. Snooks that afternoon passed your wife, and the fact that the pleasant dinner-party at which you assisted the evening before at Mr. Smith's, has been ascertained to have been one of a second-chop character, his more honoured guests having dined on the previous day. Every petty disagreeable in your lot, in short, is brought out, turned ingeniously in every possible light, and aggravated and exaggerated to the highest degree. The natural and necessary result follows. An hour, or less, of this discipline brings all parties to a sulky and snappish frame of mind. And instead of the cheerful and thankful mood in which you were disposed to be when you sat down, you find that your whole moral nature is jarred and out of gear. And your wife, your daughters, and yourself, pass into moody, sullen silence, over your books — books which you are not likely for this evening to much appreciate or enjoy. Now, I put it to every sensible reader, whether there be not a great deal too much of this kind of thing. Are there not families that never spend a quiet evening together, without embittering it by raking up every unpleasant subject in their lot and history? There are folk who, both in their own case and that of others, seem to find a strange satisfaction in sticking the thorn in the hand farther in: even in twisting the dagger in the heart. Their lot has its innumerable blessings, but they will not look at these. Let the view around in a hundred directions be ever so charming, they cannot be got to turn their mental view in one of these. They persist in keeping nose and eyes at the moral pigsty.

Oh, what a blessing it would be if we human beings could turn away our mind's eye at will, as we can our physical! As we can turn away from an ugly view in the material world, and look at a pleasing one; if we could but do the like in the world of mind! As you turn your back on a dunghill, or a foul stagnant ditch: if you could so turn your back on your servants' errors, on your children's faults, on the times when you made a fool of yourself, on the occasions when sad disappointment came your way, — in short, upon those prospects which are painful to look back upon! You go to bed, I may assume, every evening. How often, my friend, have you tossed about there, hour after hour, sleepless and fevered, stung by care, sorrow, worry: as your memory persisted in bringing up again a thousand circumstances which you could wish for ever forgot: as each sad hour and sad fact came up and stuck its little sting into your heart! I do not suppose that you have led a specially wicked life; I do not write for blackguards; I suppose your life has been innocent on the whole, and your lot prosperous: — I assume no more than the average of petty vexations, mortifications, and worries. You remember how that noble man, Sir Charles Napier, tells us in his *Diary*, that sometimes, when irritated by having discovered some more than usually infamous job or neglect, or stung by a keener than ordinary sense of the rascally injustice which pursued him through life, he tossed about all night in a half-frantic state, shouting, praying, and blaspheming. Now, whether you be a great man or a little man, when you lay your head on your thorny pillow, have you not longed oftentimes for the power of resolutely turning the mind's eye in another direction than that which it was so miserable a thing for you to contemplate? We all know, of course, how some, when the mind grew into that persistent habit of looking in only one direction, of harbouring only one wretched thought, which is of the essence of madness, have thought, as they could not turn away the mind's eye at will, to blind-fold the mind (so to speak) altogether: to make sure that it should see nothing at all. By opium, by strong drink, men have endeavoured to reduce the mind to pure stupefaction, as their sole chance of peace. And you know too, kindly reader, that even such means have sometimes failed of their sorrowful purpose; and that men have madly flung off the burden of this life, as though thus they could fling off the burden of self and of remembrance.

I have said that it would be an unspeakable blessing if we could as easily turn the eyes away from a moral as from a physical pigsty; and in my belief we may, to a great degree, train ourselves to such a habit. You see, from what I have just said, that I do not think the thing is always or entirely to be done. The only way to forget a thing is to cease to feel any interest in it; and we cannot cheat ourselves into the belief that we feel no interest in a thing which we intensely desire to forget. But though the painful thing do not, at our will, quite die away into nothing, still we may habituate ourselves to look away from it. Only time can make our vexations and worries fade into nothing, though we are looking at them: even as only distance in space can make the pigsty disappear, if we retire from it still looking in its direction. But we may turn our back on the pigsty, and so cease to behold it though it be close at hand. And in like manner, we may get our mind so under control, that in ordinary cases it will answer the rein. We may acquire, by long-continued effort, the power to turn our back upon the worry — that is, in unmetaphoric language, to think of something else.

I have often occasion to converse with poor people about their little worries, their cares and trials; and from the ingenious way in which they put them, so as to make them look their very worst, it is sometimes easy to see that the poor man or woman has been brooding for long hours over the painful thing, turning it in all different ways, till the thing has been got into that precise point of view in which it looks its very ugliest. It is like one of those gutta-percha heads, squeezed into its most hideous grin. And I have thought, how long this poor soul must have persisted in looking at nothing but this dreary prospect before finding out so accurately the spot whence it looks most dreary. I might mention one or two amusing instances; but I do not think it would be fair to give the facts, and I could not invent any parallel cases unless by being myself painfully worried. And we all know that, apart from other reasons, it is impolitic to look too long at a disagreeable object, for this reason — that all subjects, pleasing or painful, greaten on our view if we look at them long. They grow much bigger. You can hardly write a sermon (writing it as carefully and well as you can) without being persuaded before you have done with it, that the doctrine or duty you are seeking to enforce is one of the very highest possible importance. You feel this incomparably more strongly when you have finished your discourse than you did when you began it. So with an essay or an article. Half in jest, you choose your subject; half earnestly, you sketched out your plan; but as you carefully write it out, it begins to grow upon you that it would be well for the human race would it but listen to your advice and act upon it. It is so also with our worries, so with all the ills of our lot, so especially with any treachery or injustice with which we may have been treated. You may brood over a little worry till, like the prophet's cloud, it passes from being of the size of a man's hand into something that blackens all the sky, from the horizon to the zenith. You may dwell upon the cruelty and treachery with which you have been used, till the thought of them stings you almost to madness. Who but must feel for the abandoned wife, treated unquestionably with scandalous barbarity, who broods over her wrongs till she can think of nothing else, and can hardly speak or write without attacking her unworthy husband? You may, in a moral sense, look at the pigsty or the open sewer till, wherever you look, you shall see nothing save open sewers and pigsties. You may dwell so long on your own care and sorrow, that you shall see only care and sorrow everywhere. Now, don't give in to that if you can help it.

Some one has used you ill — cheated you, misrepresented you. An ugly old woman, partially deaf, and with a remarkably husky voice, has come to your house without any invitation, and notwithstanding the most frigid reception which civility will permit, persists in staying for ten days. You overhear Mr. Snarling informing a stranger that your essays in *Fraser* are mainly characterized by conceit and ill-nature (Mr. Snarling, put on the cap). Your wife and you enter a drawing-room to make a forenoon visit. Miss Limejuice is staying at the house.

Your friend, Mr. Smith, drove you down in his drag, which is a remarkably handsome turn-out. And entering the drawing-room somewhat faster than was expected, you surprise Miss Limejuice, still with a malignant grin on her extraordinarily ugly countenance, telegraphing across the room to the lady of the house to come and look at the carriage. In an instant the malignant grin is exchanged for a fawning smile, but not so quickly but that you saw the malignant grin. A man has gone to law with you about a point which appears to you perfectly clear. Now, don't sit down and think over and over again these petty provocations. Exclude them from your mind. Most of them are really too contemptible to be thought of. The noble machinery of your mind, though you be only a commonplace good-hearted mortal, was made for something better than to grind that wretched grist. And as for greater injuries, don't think of them more than you can help. You will make yourself miserable. You will think the man who cheated or misrepresented you an incarnate demon, while probably he is in the main not so bad, though possessed of an unhappy disposition to tell lies to the prejudice of his acquaintance. Remember that if you could see his conduct, and your own conduct, from his point of view, you might see that there is much to be said even for him. No matter how wrong a man is, he may be able to persuade himself into the honest belief that he is in the right. You may kill an apostle, and think you are doing God service. You may vilify a curate, who is more popular than yourself; and in the process of vilification, you may quote much Scripture and shed many tears. Very, very few offenders see their offence in the precise light in which you do while you condemn it. So resolve that in any complicated case, in

which misapprehension is possible ; in all cases in which
you cannot convict a man of direct falsehood ; you shall
give him credit for honesty of intention. And as to all
these petty offences which have been named — as to most
petty mortifications and disappointments — why, turn
your back on them. Turn away from the contemplation
of Mr. Snarling's criticism as you would turn away from
a little stagnant puddle to look at fairer sights. Look in
the opposite direction from all Miss Limejuice's doings
and sayings, as you would look in the opposite direction
from the sole untidy corner of the garden, where the rotten pea-sticks are. As for the graver sorrow, try and
think of it no more. Learn its lesson indeed ; God sent
it to teach you something and to train you somehow ; but
then try and think of it no more.

But there are mortals who are always raking up
unpleasant subjects, because they have a real delight in
them. Like the morbid anatomist, they would rather
look at a diseased body than a healthy one. Well, in the
case of their own lot, let such be indulged. At first,
when you find them every time you see them, beginning
again the tedious story of all their discomforts and worries, you are disposed to pity them, tedious and uninteresting though the story of their slights and grievances
be. Do not throw away pity upon such. They are not
suitable objects of charity. They have a real though
perverted enjoyment in going over that weary narration.
It makes them happy to tell at length how miserable they
are. They would rather look at the pigsty than not.
Let them. It is all quite right. But unhappily such
people, not content themselves to contemplate pigsties,
generally are anxious to get their acquaintances to contemplate *their* pigsties too ; and as their acquaintances, in

most instances, would rather look at a clover-field than a
pigsty, such people become companions of the most disagreeable sort. As you are sitting on a fine summer evening on the grass before your door, tranquil, content, full
of thankful enjoyment, they are fond (so to speak) of suddenly bringing in a scavenger's cart, and placing it before
you, where it will blot out all the pleasant prospect.
They will not let you forget the silly thing you said or
did, the painful passage in your life on which you wish
to shut down the leaf for ever. They are always prob-
ing the half-healed wound, sticking the knife into the
sensitive place. If the view in a hundred directions is
beautiful, they will, by instant affinity and necessity of
nature, beg you to look at the dunghill, and place the
dunghill before you for that purpose. I believe there are
many able, sensitive men, who never had a fair chance
in life. Their powers have been crippled, their views
embittered, their whole nature soured, by a constant discipline of petty whips and scourges, and little pricking
needles, applied (in some cases through pure stolidity
and coarseness of nature) by an ill-mated wife. It is
only by flying from their own fireside that they can
escape the unceasing gadfly, with its petty, irritating,
never-ending sting. They live in an atmosphere of pigsty. They cannot lift their eyes but some ugly, petty,
contemptible wrong is sure to be crammed upon their
aching gaze. And it must be a very sweet and noble
nature that years of this training will not embitter. It
must be a very great mind that years of this training will
fail to render inconceivably petty and little. Oh! woful
and miserable to meet a man of fifty or sixty, an educated
man, who in this world of great interests and solemn anticipations, can find no subjects to talk of but the neglect

of his wealthy neighbour, the extortionate price he is
charged for sugar, the carelessness of his man-servant,
the flirtations of his maid-servants, the stiffness of Lord
Dunderhead when he lately met that empty-pated peer.
In what a petty world such a man lives! Under what
a low sky he walks: how muggy the atmosphere he
breathes!

You remember Mr. Croaker, in Goldsmith's *Goodnatured Man*. Whenever he saw a number of people cheerful and happy, he always contrived to throw a chill and
damp over the circle by wishing, with a ghastly air, that
they might all be as well that day six months. I have
known many Croakers. I have known men who, if they
saw a young fellow quite happy in his lot and his work,
hopeful and hearty, would instantly try to suggest something that might make him unhappy; that might pull
him down to a congenial gloom. I have known persons
who, if they had looked upon a gay circle of sweet, lively
girls, rosy and smiling, would have enjoyed extremely to
have (in a moral sense) suddenly brought into that fair
circle a hearse and a coffin. And I have been filled with
fiery indignation, when I knew that such persons, really
acting from malignant spite and bitterness to see others
happy, would probably have claimed to be acting from
religious motives, and doing a Christian duty. The very
foundation, and primary axiom, in some men's religious
belief, is, that Almighty God is spitefully angry to see
His creatures happy. Oh what a wicked, mischievous
lie! God is love. And we know it on the highest of
all authorities, that the very first and grandest duty He
claims of His creatures, is to love Him with heart and
soul and strength and mind; not to shrink before Him,
like whipped slaves before a capricious, sulky tyrant; but

to love Him and trust to Him as loving children might gather at the kindest parent's knee. I am content to look at a pigsty when needful: God intends that we should oftentimes look at such in the moral world; but God intends that we should look at clover-fields and fragrant flowers whenever we can do so without a dereliction of duty. I am quite sure that when the Blessed Redeemer went to the marriage at Cana of Galilee, he did not think it his duty to cast a gloom and a damp over the festive company there. Do not misunderstand me, my spiteful acquaintance. There is a time to mourn, as well as a time to dance; and in this life we shall have quite enough of the former time, without seeking for supererogatory woes. I am not afraid, myself, to look upon the recent grave; I would train my children to sit upon the daisied mound, pensive, but not afraid, as I told them that Christianity has turned the *sepulchrum* into the κοιμητήριον, — the *burying-place* into the *sleeping-place;* as I told them how the Christian dead do but sleep for the Great Awaking. But I should not think it right to break in upon their innocent cheer by rushing in and telling them that their coffin would soon be coming, and that their grave was waiting in the churchyard. There are times enough and events enough which will tell them that. Don't let us have Mr. Croaker. And don't let us fancy that by making ourselves miserable, we are doing something pleasing to God. It is not His purpose that we should look at pigsties when we can honestly help it. No doubt, the erroneous belief that God wishes that we should, runs through all religions. India, Persia, Arabia, have known it, no less than Rome, England, Scotland; the fakir, the eremite, the monk, the Covenanter, have erred together here. The Church of England, and

the Church of Scotland, are no more free from the tendency to it, than the Church of Rome; and the grim
Puritan, who thought it sinful to smile, was just as far
wrong as the starved monastic and the fleshless Brahmin.
Every now and then, I preach a sermon against this
notion; not that people now-a-days will actually scourge
and starve themselves; but that they carry with them an
inveterate belief that it would be a fine thing if they
did. Here is the conclusion of the last sermon; various
friendly readers of *Fraser* have sent me fancy specimens
of bits of my discourses; let them compare their notion
of them with the fact:—

It shows how all men, everywhere, have been pressed by a common sense of guilt against God, which they thought to expiate by
self-inflicted punishment. But we, my friends, know better than *that*.
Jesus died for us; Jesus suffered for us; *His* sufferings took away our
sins, our own sufferings, how great soever, never could; Christ's
sacrifice was all-sufficient; and any penance on our part is just as
needless as it would be unavailing. Take, then, brethren, without a
scruple or a misgiving, the innocent enjoyment of life. Let your
heart beat, gladly and thankfully, by your quiet fireside; and never
dream that there is anything of sinful self-indulgence in that pure
delight with which you watch your children's sports, and hear their
prattle. Look out upon green spring fields and blossoms, upon summer woods and streams; gladden in the bright sunshine, as well as
muse in the softening twilight; and never fancy that though these
things cheer you amid the many cares of life, you are falling short of
the ideal sketched by that kindly Teacher of self-denial who said, ' If
any man will come after me, let him deny himself, and take up his
cross daily!'

Having relieved my feelings by thus stating my resolute protest against what I think one of the most mischievous and wicked errors I ever knew, I proceed to
say that although I think nothing can be more foolish
than to be always looking at moral pigsties, still the principle cannot be laid down without some restriction. You

may, by indulging the disposition to look away from unpleasant prospects, bring your mind to a morbid state:
you may become so over-sensitive, that you shall shrink
away from the very thought of injustice, cruelty, or suffering. I do not suppose selfishness. I am not talking
to selfish, heartless persons, who can look on with entire
composure at suffering of any sort, provided it do not
touch themselves. I am quite content that such should
endure all that may befal them, and more. The heart of
some men is like an extremely tough beef-steak, which
needs an immense deal of beating before it will grow tender. The analogy does not hold entirely; for I believe
the very toughest steak may be beaten till it grows tender; or at least the beating will not make it tougher.
Whereas the human heart is such, that while in generous
natures it learns, by suffering, to feel for the suffering of
others, in selfish and sordid natures it becomes only the
more selfish and self-contained the more it is called to
feel. But I am not speaking to selfish persons. I am
thinking of generous, sensitive human beings, to whom
the contemplation of injustice and cruelty and falsehood
is as painful when these are pressing upon others, as
when they are pressing upon themselves. I am thinking
of men and women who feel their hearts quicken and
their cheeks flush when they read the stupid and unjust
verdicts of occasional (must I say frequent?) juries; and
the preposterous decisions of London police magistrates
now and then. To such, I well believe, the daily reading of the law report in the *Times* is a painful worry; it
sets before one so sad a picture of human sin and folly;
and it shows so strongly that human laws labour most
vainly to redress the greater part of the evils that press
on human life. You remember how once Byron, at Ven-

ice, durst not open the *Quarterly Review;* and sent it away after it had been several days in his house, ignorant even whether it contained any notice of him. Of course this was a purely selfish shrinking; the poet knew that his nature would so wince under the dreaded attack, that he was afraid even to ascertain whether there were any attack at all. Have not you, my reader, from a morbid though more generous sensitiveness, sometimes shrunk from opening the newspaper which day by day reported some iniquitous court-martial, some scandalous trial in the Ecclesiastical Court, revealing human depravity in its foulest manifestation, and setting out and pressing upon your view evils which were practically remediless? And so, thinking of such things, I wish to qualify my great principle, that in the moral world it is wise and right to turn your back upon the pigsty, where practicable. I have thought of two limitations of this principle. The first limitation is this; that however painful it may be to look at unpleasant things, we ought fairly to face them so long as there is any hope of remedying them. The second limitation is this; that however painful it may be to look at unpleasant things, we ought not to train ourselves, by constantly refusing to look at them, to a morbidly shrinking habit of mind. Such a habit, by indulgence, will grow upon us to that degree, that it will unfit us for the rude wear of life. And the moral nature, grown sensitive as the mimosa, will serve as a conductor to convey many a wretched and debilitating pang to the heart.

Let us think of these two limitations of my theory as to the fashion in which the worries of life should be met.

Though it is wise, generally speaking, to look away from painful sights, it is not wise or right to do so while,

by facing them, we may hope to mend them. It is not
good, like a certain priest and Levite of ancient times,
to turn our back on the poor man lying half dead by the
way-side; while it is still possible for a Good Samaritan
to pour in oil and wine. However unpleasing the sight,
however painful the effort, let us look fairly at the worry
in our lot, till we have done our best to put it right.
It is not the act of wisdom, it is the doing of indolence,
selfishness, and cowardice, to turn our back on that
which we may remedy or even alleviate by facing it.
It is only when no good can come of brooding over the
pigsty that I counsel the reader persistently to turn away
from it. Many men try to forget some family vexation, some neglected duty, some social or political grievance, when they ought manfully to look full at it, to see
it in its true dimensions and colours, and to try to mend
matters. They cannot truly forget the painful fact.
Even when it is not distinctly remembered, a vague,
dull, unhappy sense of something amiss will go with
them everywhere — all the more unhappy because conscience will tell them they are doing wrong. It is so in
small matters as well as great. Your bookcase is all in
confusion; the papers in your drawers have got into a
sad mess. It is easier, you think, to shut the doors, to
lock the drawers, to go away and think of something
else, than manfully to face the pigsty and sort it up.
Possibly you may do so. If you are a nerveless, cow-
ardly being, you will; but you will not be comfortable
though you have turned your back on the pigsty: a
gnawing consciousness of the pigsty's existence will go
with you wherever you go. Say your affairs have become embarrassed; you are living beyond your means;
you are afraid to add up your accounts and ascertain

how you stand. Ah, my friend, many a poor man well knows the feeling! Don't give in to it. Fairly face the fact: know the worst. Many a starving widow and orphan, many a pinched family reduced from opulence to sordid shifts, have suffered because the dead father would not while he lived face the truth in regard to his means and affairs! Let not that selfish being quote my essay in support of the course he takes. However complicated and miserable the state of the facts may be — though the pigsty should be like the Augean stable — look fairly at it; see it in its length and breadth; cut off your dinner-parties, sell your horses, kick out the fellows who make a hotel of your house and an ordinary of your table; bring your establishment to what your means can reach, to what will leave enough to insure your life. Don't let your miserable children have to think bitterly of you in your grave. And another respect in which you ought to carry out the same resolute purpose to look the pigsty full in the face is, in regard to your religious views and belief. Don't turn your back upon your doctrinal doubts and difficulties. Go up to them and examine them. Perhaps the ghastly object which looks to you in the twilight like a sheeted ghost, may prove to be no more than a tablecloth hanging upon a hedge; but if you were to pass it distantly without ascertaining what it is, you might carry the shuddering belief that you had seen a disembodied spirit all your days. Some people (very wrongly, as I think) would have you turn the key upon your sceptical difficulties, and look away from the pigsty altogether. From a stupid though prevalent delusion as to the meaning of *Faith*, they have a vague impression that the less ground you have for your belief, and the more

objections you stoutly refuse to see, the more faith you
have got. It is a poor theory, that of some worthy
divines; it amounts to just this: Christianity is true,
and it is proved true by evidence; but for any sake don't
examine the evidence, for the more you examine it the
less likely you are to believe it. I say, No! Let us
see your difficulties and objections; only to define them
will cut them down to half their present vague, misty
dimensions. I am not afraid of them; for though, after
all is said, they continue to be difficulties, I shall show
you that difficulties a hundredfold greater stand in the
way of the contrary belief; and it is just by weighing
opposing difficulties that you can in this world come to
any belief, scientific, historical, moral, political. Let me
say here that I heartily despise the man who professes
a vague scepticism on the strength of difficulties which
he has never taken the pains fairly to measure. It is
hypocritical pretence when a man professes at the same
instant to turn his back upon a prospect, and to be
guided by what he discerns in that prospect. But there
are men who would like to combine black with white,
yes with no. There are men who are always anxious
to combine the contradictory enterprises, *How to do a
thing* and *How at the same time not to do it.*

In brief, my limitation is this: Do not refuse to
admit distressing thoughts, if any good is to come of
admitting them; do not turn your back on the ugly
prospect, so long as there is a hope of mending it; don't
be like the wrecked sailor, who drinks himself into insensibility, while a hope of rescue remains; don't refuse
to worry yourself by thinking what is to become of your
children after you are gone, if there be still time to
devise some means of providing for them. Look fairly

at the blackest view, and go at it bravely if there be the
faintest chance of making it brighter.

And, in truth, a great many bad things prove to be
not so bad when you fairly look at them. The day
seems horribly rainy and stormy when you look out of
your library-window ; but you wrap up and go out resolutely for a walk, and the day is not so bad. By the
time your brisk five miles are finished, you think it
rather a fine breezy day, healthful though boisterous.
All remediable evils are made a great deal worse by
turning your back on them. The skeleton in the closet
rattles its bare bones abominably, when you lock the
closet-door. Your disorderly drawer of letters and papers
was a bugbear for weeks, because you put off sorting it
and tried to forget it. It made you unhappy — vaguely
uneasy, as all neglected duties do ; yet you thought the
trouble of putting it right would be so great that you would
rather bear the little gnawing uneasiness. At length
you could stand it no more. You determined some day
to go at your task and do it. You did it. It was done
speedily ; it was done easily. You felt a blessed sense
of relief, and you wondered that you had made such a
painful worry of a thing so simple. By the make of
the universe every duty deferred grows in bulk and
weight and painful pressure.

It may here be said that when a worry cannot be
forgotten, and yet cannot be mended, it is a good thing
to try to define it. Measure its exact size. That is
sure to make it look smaller. I have great confidence
in the power of the pen to give most people clearer
ideas than they would have without it. You have a
vague sense that in your lot there is a vast number of
worries and annoyances. Just sit down, take a large

sheet of paper and a pen, and write out a list of all
your annoyances and worries. You will be surprised
to find how few they are, and how small they look.
And if on another sheet of paper you make a list of
all the blessings you enjoy, I believe that in most
cases you will see reason to feel heartily ashamed
of your previous state of discontent. Even should the
catalogue of worries not be a brief one, still the killing
thing — the vague sense of indefinite magnitude and
number — will be gone. Almost all numbers diminish
by accurately counting them. A clergyman may honestly believe that there are five hundred people in his
church; but unless he be a person accustomed accurately to estimate numbers, you will find on counting
that his congregation does not exceed two hundred and
fifty. When the Chartist petition was presented to Parliament some years ago, it was said to bear the signa-
tures of five or six millions of people. It looked such
an immense mass that possibly its promoters were honest in promulgating that belief. But the names were
counted, and they amounted to no more than a million
and a half. So, thoughtful reader, who fancy yourself
torn by a howling pack of worries, count them. You
will find them much fewer than you had thought; and
the only way to satisfactorily count them is by making a
list of them in writing.

　Yet here there is a difficulty too. The purpose for
which I advise you to make such a list, is to assure
yourself that your worries are really not so very many
or so very great. But there is hardly any means in this
world which may not be worked to the opposite of the
contemplated end. And by writing out and dwelling on
the list of your worries, you may make them worse.

You may diminish their number, but increase their intensity. You may set out the relations and tendencies of the vexations under which you suffer, of the ill usage of which you complain, till you whip yourself up to a point of violent indignation. In reading the life of Sir Charles Napier, I think one often sees cause to lament that the great man so chronicled and dwelt upon the petty injustices which he met with from petty men. And when a poor governess writes the story of her indignities, recording them with painful accuracy, and putting them in the most unpleasing light, one feels that it would have been better had she not taken up the pen. But indeed these are instances coming under the general principle set out some time since, that irremediable worries are for the most part better forgotten.

So much for the first limitation of my theory for the treatment of worries. The second, you remember, is, that we ought not to give in to the impulse to turn our back upon the ugly prospect to such a degree that any painful sight or thought shall be felt like a mortal stab. You may come to that point of morbid sensitiveness. And I believe that the greatest evil of an extremely retired country life is, that it tends to bring one to that painfully shrinking state. You may be afraid to read the *Times*, for the suffering caused you by the contemplation of the irremediable sin and misery of which you read the daily record there. You may come to wish that you could creep away into some quiet corner, where the uproar of human guilt and wretchedness should never be heard again. You may come to sympathize heartily with the weary aspiration of the Psalmist, 'Oh that I had wings like a dove: then would I flee away and be at rest!' Sometimes as you stand in your sta-

ble, smoothing down your horse's neck, you may think
how quiet and silent a place it is, how free from worry,
and wish you had never to go out of the stall.   Or when
you have been for two or three days ill in bed, the days
going on and going down so strangely, **you** may have
thought that you would stay there for the remainder of
your life ; that you could not muster resolution to set
yourself again to the daily worry.   You people who cannot understand the state of feeling which I am trying to
describe, be thankful for it : but do not doubt that such
a state of feeling exists in many minds.

Let me confess, for myself, that for several years past
I have been afraid to read a good novel.   It is intensely
painful to contemplate and realize to one's mind the
state of matters set out in most writings of the class.
Apart from the question of not caring for that order of
thought (and to me dissertation is much more interesting
than narrative), don't you shrink from the sight of struggling virtue and triumphant vice, of cruelty, oppression,
and successful falsehood ?   Give us the story that has
no exciting action ; that moves along without incident
transcending the experience of ordinary human beings ;
that shows us quiet, simple, innocent modes of life,
free from the intrusion of the stormy and wicked world
around.   Don't you begin, as you grow older, to sympathize with that feeling of the poet Beattie, which when
younger you laughed at, that Shakspeare's admixture of
the grotesque in his serious plays was absolutely necessary
to prevent the tragic part from producing an effect too
painful for endurance ?   The poet maintained that Shakspeare was aiming to save those who might witness his
plays from a ' disordered head or a broken heart.'   You
see there, doubtless, the working of a morbid nervous

system ; but there is a substratum of truth. Once upon a time, when a man was worried by the evils of his lot, he could hope to escape from them by getting into the world of fiction. But now much fiction is such that you are worse there than ever. I do not think of the grand, romantic, and tremendously melodramatic incidents which one sometimes finds ; these do not greatly pain us, because we feel both characters and incidents to be so thoroughly unreal. I do not mind a bit when the hero of *Monte Christo* is flung into the sea in a sack from a cliff some hundreds of feet high ; that pains one no more than the straits and misfortunes of *Munchausen.* The wearing thing is to be carried into homely scenes, and shown life-like characters, bearing and struggling with the worries of life we know so well. We are reminded, only too vividly, of the hard strife of reduced gentility to keep up appearances, of the aging, life-wearing battle with constant care. It is as much wear of heart to look into that picture truthfully set before us by a man or woman of genius, as to look at the sad reality of this world of struggle, privation, and failure. It was just the sight of these that we wished to escape, and lo ! there they are again. So one shrinks from the sympathetic reading of a story too truthfully sad. I once read *Vanity Fair.* I would not read it again on any account, any more than one would willingly go through the delirium of a fever, or revive distinctly the circumstances of the occasion on which one acted like a fool. The story was admirable, incomparable ; but it was too sadly true. We see quite enough of that sort of thing in actual life : let us not have it again when we seek relief from the realities of actual life. Once you get into a sunshiny atmosphere when you began to read a work of fiction; or if the light was lurid, it was manifestly the glare of some preparation of sulphur in a scene-shifter's hand. But now, you are often in a doleful grey from the beginning of a story to its end.

It is a great blessing when a man's nature or training is such that he is able to turn away entirely from his work when he desists from actual working, and to shut his eyes to the contemplation of any painful thing when its contemplation ceases to be necessary or useful. There is much in this of native idiosyncrasy, but a good deal may be done by discipline. You may to a certain extent acquire the power to throw off from the mind the burden that is weighing upon it, at all times except the moment during which the burden has actually to be borne. I envy the man who stops his work and instantly forgets it till it is time to begin again. I envy the man who can lay down his pen while writing on some subject that demands all his mental stretch, and go out for a walk, and yet not through all his walk be wrestling with his subject still. Oh! if we could lay down the mind's load as we can lay down the body's! If the mind could sit down and rest for a breathing space, as the body can in climbing a hill! If, as we decidedly stop walking when we cease to walk, we could cease thinking when we intend to cease to think! It was doubtless a great secret of the work which Napoleon did with so little apparent wear, that he could fall asleep whenever he chose. Yet even he could not at will look away from the pigsty: no doubt one suddenly pressed itself upon his view on that day when he was sitting alone at dinner, and in a moment sprang up with a furious execration, and kicked over the table, smash-

ing his plates as drunken Scotch weavers sometimes do.
Let us do our best to right the wrong; but when we
have done our best, and go to something else, let us
quite forget the wrong: it will do no good to remember
it now. It is long-continued wear that kills. We can
do and bear a vast deal if we have blinks of intermission of bearing and doing. But the mind of some men
is on the stretch from the moment they begin a task till
they end it. Slightly and rapidly as you may run over
this essay, it was never half-an-hour out of the writer's
waking thoughts from the writing of the first line to the
writing of the last. I have known those who when busied
with any work, legal, literary, theological, parochial, domestic, hardly ever consciously ceased from it; but were,
as Mr. Bailey has expressed it, 'about it, lashing at it day
and night.' The swell continued though the wind had
gone down; the wheels spun round though the steam
was shut off. Let me say here (I say it for myself), that
apart entirely from any consideration of the religious
sanctions which hallow a certain day of the seven, it
appears to me that its value is literally and really inestimable to the overworked and worried man, if it be
kept sacred, not merely from worldly work, but from the
intrusion of worldly cares and thoughts. The thing can
be done, my friend. As the last hour of Saturday
strikes, the burden may fall from the mind: the pack of
worries may be whipped off; and you may feel that
you have entered on a purer, freer, happier life, which
will last for four-and-twenty hours. I am a Scotchman,
and a Scotch clergyman, and I hold views regarding
the Sunday with which I know that some of my most
esteemed readers do not sympathize; but I believe, for
myself, that a strict resolution to preserve the Lord's day

sacred (in no Puritanical sense), would lengthen many a valuable life; would preserve the spring of many a noble mind; would hold off in some cases the approaches of imbecility or insanity.

I do not forget, in urging the expediency of training the mind to turn away from worries which it will do no good to continue to look at, that anything evil or painful has a peculiar power to attract and compel attention to it. A little bad thing bulks larger on the mind's view than a big good thing. It persistently pushes its ugly face upon our notice. You cannot forget that you have bad tooth-ache, though it be only one little nerve that is in torment, and all the rest of the body is at ease. And some little deformity of person, some little worry in your domestic arrangements, keeps always intruding itself, and defying you to forget or overlook it. If the pigsty already referred to be placed in the middle of the pretty lawn before your door, it will blot out all the landscape: you will see nothing save the pigsty. Evil has the advantage of good in many ways. It not merely detracts from good: it neutralizes it all. I think it is Paley who says that the evils of life supply no just argument against the divine benevolence; inasmuch as when weighed against the blessings of life, the latter turn the scale. It is as if you gave a man five hundred a-year, and then took away from him one hundred: this would amount virtually to giving him a clear four hundred a-year. It always struck me that the case put is not analogous to the fact. The four hundred a-year left would lose no part of their marketable value when the one hundred was taken away. The fact is rather as if you gave a man a large jug of pure water, and then cast into it a few drops of black-

draught. That little infusion of senna would render the
entire water nauseous. No doubt there might be fifty
times as much pure water as vile senna: but the vile
senna would spoil the whole. Even such is the influence
of evil in this system of things. It does not simply
diminish the quantity of good to be enjoyed: to a great
degree it destroys the enjoyment of the whole of the good.
Good carries weight in the race with evil. It has not a
fair start, nor a fair field. Don't you know, reader, that
it needs careful, constant training to give a child a good
education; and possibly you may not succeed in giving
the good education after all: while no care at all suffices
to give a bad education; and a bad education is generally
successful. So in the physical world. No field runs to
wheat. If a farmer wants a crop of good grain, he must
work hard to get it. But he has only to neglect his field
and do nothing, and he will have weeds enough. The
whole system of things in this world tends in favour of evil
rather than of good. But happily, my friend, we know
the reason why. And we know that a day is coming
which will set these things right.

I trust I have made sufficiently plain the precise error
against which this essay is directed. The thing with
which I find fault is that querulous, discontented, unhappy disposition which sits down and broods over disa-
greeables and worries: not with the view of mending
them, nor of bracing the moral nature by the sight of
them: but simply for the sake of harping upon that tedious string;—of making yourself miserable, and making
all who come near you miserable too. There are people
into whose houses you cannot go, without being sickened
by the long catalogue of all their slights and worries. It is
a wretched and contemptible thing to be always hawking

about one's griefs, in the hope of exciting commiseration. Let people be assured that their best friends will grow wearied of hearing of their worries: let people be assured that the pity which is accorded them will be in most cases mingled with something of contempt. There are men and women who have a wonderful scent for a grievance. If you are showing them your garden, and there be one untidy corner, they will go straight to that, and point it out with mournful elation, and forget all the rest of the trim expanse. If there be one mortifying circumstance in an otherwise successful and happy lot, they will be always reminding you of that. You write a book. Twenty favourable reviews of it appear, and two unfavourable : Mr. Snarling arrives after breakfast, sure as fate, with the two unfavourable reviews in his pocket. You are cheerful and contented with your lot and your house : Mr. Snarling never misses an opportunity of pointing out to you the dulness of your situation, the inconvenience of your dwelling, the inferiority of the place you hold in life to what you might *à priori* have anticipated. You are quite light-hearted when Mr. Snarling enters ; but when he goes, you cannot help feeling a good deal depressed. The blackest side of things has been pressed on your notice during his stay. I do not think this is entirely the result of malice. It is ignorance of the right way to face little worries. The man has got a habit of looking only at the dunghill. Would that he could learn better sense !

Let me here remark a certain confusion which exists in the minds of many. I have known persons who prided themselves on their ability to inflict pain on others. They thought it a proof of power. And no doubt to scarify a man as Luther and Milton did, as Croker, Lockhart, and Macaulay did, is a proof of power. But sometimes people inflict pain on others simply by making themselves disgusting; and to do this is no proof of power. No doubt you may severely pain a refined and cultivated man or woman by revolting vulgarity of language and manner. You may, Mrs. Bouncer, embitter your poor governess's life by your coarse, petty tyranny; and you may infuriate your servants by talking at them before strangers at table. But let me remind you that there is a dignified and an undignified way of inflicting pain. There are what may be called the Active and the Passive ways. You may inflict annoyance as a viper does; or you may inflict annoyance as a dunghill does. Some men (sharp critics belong to this class) are like the viper. They actively give pain. You are afraid of *them*. Others, again, are like a dunghill. They are merely passively offensive. You are disgusted at these. Now the viperish man may perhaps be proud of his power of stinging: but the dunghill man has no reason earthly to be proud of his power of stinking. It is just that he is an offensive object, and men would rather get out of his way. Yet I have heard a blockhead boast how he had driven away a refined gentleman from a certain club. No doubt he did. The gentleman could never go there without the blockhead offensively revolting him. The blockhead told the story with pride. Other blockheads listened, and expressed their admiration of his cleverness. I looked in the blockhead's face, and inwardly said, Oh you human dunghill! Think of a filthy sewer boasting, ' Ah, I can drive most people away from *me!* '

To the dunghill class many men belong. Such, generally, are those who will never heartily say anything pleasant; but who are always ready to drop hints of what

they think will be disagreeable for you to hear. Such
are the men who will walk round your garden, when you
show it to them in the innocent pride of your heart : and
after having accomplished the circuit, will shrug their
shoulders, snuff the air, and say nothing. Such are the
men who will call upon an old gentleman, and incidentally
mention that they were present the other Sunday when
his son preached his first sermon, but say no kindly word
as to the figure made by the youthful divine. Such are
the men who, when you show them your fine new church,
will walk round it hurriedly, say carelessly, ' Very nice ; '
and begin to talk earnestly upon topics not connected
with ecclesiastical architecture. And such, as a general
rule, are all the envious race, who will never cordially
praise anything done by others, and who turn green with
envy and jealousy if they even hear others speak of a
third party in words of cordial praise. Such men are for
the most part under-bred, and always of third or fourth-
rate talent. A really able man heartily speaks well of
the talent that rivals or eclipses his own. He does so
through the necessity of a noble and magnanimous nature.
And a gentleman will generally do as much, through the
influence of a training which makes the best of the best
features in the character of man. It warms one's heart
to hear a great and illustrious author speak of a young
one who is struggling up the slope. But it is a sorry
thing to hear Mr. Snarling upon the same subject.

I have sometimes wondered whether what is commonly
called *coolness* in human beings is the result of a remarkable power of looking away from things which it is not
thought desirable to see ; or of a still more remarkable
power of looking at disagreeable things and not minding.

You remember somewhere in the *Life of Sir Walter Scott*, we are told of a certain joyous dinner-party at his house in Castle-street. Of all the gay party there was none so gay as a certain West Country baronet. Yet in his pocket he had a letter containing a challenge which he had accepted; and next morning early he was off to the duel in which he was killed. Now, there must have been a woful worry gnawing at the clever man's heart, you would say. How did he take it so coolly? Did he really forget for the time the risk that lay before him? Or did he look fairly at it, yet not care? He was a kind-hearted man as well as a brave one: surely he must have been able, through the jovial evening, to look quite away from the possibility of a distracted widow, and young children left fatherless. Sometimes this coolness appears in base and sordid forms: it is then the result of obtuseness of nature, — of pure lack of discernment and feeling. People thus qualified are able with entire composure to do things which others could not do to save their lives. Such are the people who constitute a class which is an insufferable nuisance of civilized society, — the class of uninvited and unwelcome guests. I am thinking of people who will without any invitation push themselves and their baggage into the house of a man who is almost a stranger to them; and in spite of the studied presentation of the cold shoulder, and in spite of every civil hint that their presence is most unwelcome, make themselves quite at home for so long as it suits them to remain. I have heard of people who would come, to the number of three or four, to the house of a poor gentleman to whom every shilling was a consideration; and without invitation remain for four, six, ten weeks at a stretch. I have heard of people who would not only

22

come uninvited to stay at a small house, but bring with
them some ugly individual whom its host had never seen :
and possibly a mangy dog in addition. And such folk
will with great freedom drink the wine, little used by that
plain household, and hospitably press the ugly individual
to drink it freely too. I declare there is something that
approaches the sublime in the intensity of such folk's
stolidity. They *will not* see that they are not wanted.
They jauntily make themselves quite at home. If they
get so many weeks' board and lodging, they don't care
how unpleasantly it is given. They will write for your
carriage to meet them at the railway station, as if they
were ordering a hackney-coach. This subject, however,
is too large to be taken up here : it must have an entire
essay to itself. But probably my reader will agree with
me in thinking that people may possess in an excessive
degree the valuable power of looking away from what
they don't wish to see.

And yet — and yet — do you not feel that it is merely
by turning our mind's eye away from many thoughts
which are only too intrusive, that you can hope to enjoy
much peace or quiet in such a world as this ? How could
you feel any relish for the comforts of your own cheerful
lot if you did not forget the wretchedness, anxiety, and
want which enter into the pinched and poverty-stricken
lot of others ? You do not like, when you lay yourself
down at night on your quiet bed, to think of the poor
wretch in the condemned cell of the town five miles off,
who will meet his violent death to-morrow in the dismal
drizzling dawn. Some, I verily believe, will not sympathize with the feeling. There are persons, I believe, who
could go on quite comfortably with their dinner with a

starving beggar standing outside the window and watching each morsel they ate with famished eyes. Perhaps there are some who would enjoy their dinner all the better; and to that class would belong (if indeed he be not a pure, dense, unmitigated, unimprovable blockhead, who did not understand or feel the force of what he said) that man who lately preached a sermon in which he stated that a great part of the happiness of heaven would consist in looking down complacently on the torments of hell, and enjoying the contrast! What an idea must that man have had of the vile, heartless selfishness of a soul in bliss! No. For myself, though holding humbly all that the Church believes and the Bible teaches, I say that if there be a mystery hard of explanation, it is how the happy spirit can be happy even *There*, though missing from its side those who in this life were dearest. You remember the sublime prayer of Aquinas — a prayer for Satan himself. You remember the gush of kindliness which made Burns express a like sorrow even for the dark Father of Evil: 'I'm wae to think upon your den, Even for your sake!' No. The day *may* come when it will not grieve us to contemplate misery which is intolerable and irremediable; but this will be because we shall then have gained such clear and right views of all things, that we shall see things as they appear to God, and then doubtless see that all He does is right. But we may be well assured that it will not be the selfish satisfaction of contrasting our own happiness with that misery which will enable us to contemplate it with complacency: it will be a humble submission of our own will to the One Will that is always wise and right. Yet you remember, reader, how one of the profoundest and acutest of living theologians is fain to have recourse, in the case of this saddest of all sad thoughts, to the same relief which I have counselled for life's little worries — oh how little when we think of this! Archbishop Whately, in treating of this great difficulty, suggests the idea that in a higher state the soul may have the power of as decidedly turning the thoughts away from a painful subject as we now have of turning the eyes away from a disagreeable sight.

I thought of these things this afternoon in a gay and stirring scene. It was a frozen lake of considerable extent, lying in a beautiful valley, at the foot of a majestic hill. The lake was covered with people, all in a state of high enjoyment: scores of skaters were flying about, and there was a roaring of curling-stones like the distant thunder that was heard by Rip van Winkle. The sky was blue and sunshiny; the air crisp and clear; the cliffs, slopes, and fields around were fair with untrodden snow; but still one could not quite exclude the recollection that this brisk frost, so bracing and exhilarating to us, is the cause of great suffering to multitudes. The frost causes most outdoor work to cease. No building, no fieldwork, can go forward, and so the frost cuts off the bread from many hungry mouths; and fireless rooms and thin garments are no defence against this bitter chill. Well, you would never be cheerful at all but for the blessed gift of occasional forgetfulness! Those who have seen things too accurately as they are, have always been sorrowful even when unsoured men. Here, you man (one of six or seven eager parties with chairs and gimlets), put on my skates. Don't bore that hole in the heel of the boot too deep; you may penetrate to something more sensitive than leather. Screw in; buckle the straps, but not too tight: and now we are on our feet,

with the delightful sense of freedom to fly about in any
direction with almost the smooth swiftness of a bird.
Come, my friend, let us be off round the lake, with long
strokes, steadily, and not too fast. We may not be quite
like Sidney's Arcadian shepherd-boy, piping as if he
never would grow old; yet let us be like kindly skaters.
forgetting, in the exhilarating exercise that quickens the
pulse and flushes the cheek, that there are such things as
evil and worry in this world!

CHAPTER V.

CONCERNING GIVING UP AND COMING DOWN.

NOT so very much depends upon a beginning after all. The inexperienced writer racks his brain for something striking to set out with. He is anxious to make a good impression at first. He fancies that unless you hook your reader by your first sentence, your reader will break away; making up his mind that what you have got to say is not worth the reading. Now it cannot be doubted that a preacher, who is desirous of keeping his congregation in that dead silence and fixedness of attention which one sometimes sees in church, must, as a general rule, produce that audible hush by his first sentence if he is to produce it at all. If people in church are permitted for even one minute at the beginning of the sermon to settle themselves, bodily and mentally, into the attitude of inattention, and of thinking of something other than the preacher's words the preacher will hardly catch them up again. He will hardly, by any amount of earnestness, eloquence, pointedness, or oddity, gain that universal and sympathetic interest of which he flung away his chance by some long, involved, indirect, and dull sentence at starting. But the writer is not tried by so exacting a standard. Most readers will glance over the first few pages of a book before throwing it aside as stupid. The writer may

overcome the evil effect of a first sentence, or even a
first paragraph, which may have been awkward, ugly,
dull — yea silly. I could name several very popular
works which set out in a most unpromising way. I par-
ticularly dislike the first sentence of *Adam Bede*, but it is
redeemed by hundreds of noble ones. It is not certain
that the express train which is to devour the four hundred miles between London and Edinburgh in ten hours,
shall run its first hundred yards much faster than the
lagging parliamentary. There can be no question that
the man whom all first visitants of the House of Commons
are most eager to see and hear is Mr. Disraeli. He is
the lord of debate ; not unrivalled perhaps, but certainly
unsurpassed. Yet everybody knows he made a very
poor beginning. In short, my reader, if something that
is really good is to follow, a bad outset may be excused.

One readily believes what one wishes to believe ; and
I wish to hold by this principle. For I have accumulated many thoughts *Concerning Giving Up and Coming
Down;* and I have got them lying upon this table, noted
down on six long slips of paper. I vainly fancy that I
have certain true and useful things to say ; but I have
experienced extraordinary difficulty in deciding how I
should begin to say them. I have sat this morning by the
fireside for an hour, looking intently at the glowing coals ;
but though I could think of many things to say about the
middle of my essay, I could think of nothing satisfactory with which to begin it. But comfort came as the
thought gradually developed itself, that it really mat-
tered very little how the essay might be begun, provided
it went on ; and, above all, ended. A dull beginning will
probably be excused to the essayist more readily than to
the writer whose sole purpose is to amuse. The essayist

pleases himself with the belief that his readers are by
several degrees more intelligent and thoughtful than the
ordinary readers of ordinary novels; and that many of
them, if they find thoughts which are just and practical,
will regard as a secondary matter the order in which
these thoughts come. The sheep's head of northern
cookery has not, at the first glance, an attractive aspect:
nor is the nutriment it affords very symmetrically arranged: but still, as Dr. John Brown has beautifully
remarked, it supplies a deal of *fine confused feeding*. I
look at my six pieces of paper, closely written over in a
very small hand. They seem to me as the sheep's head.
There is feeling *there*, albeit somewhat confused. It
matters not much where we shall begin. Come, my
friendly reader, and partake of the homely fare.

The great lesson which the wise and true man is
learning through life, is, how to COME DOWN without
GIVING UP. Reckless and foolish people confuse these
two things. It is far easier to give up than to come
down, it is far less repugnant to our natural self-conceit.
It befits much better our natural laziness. It enables us
to fancy ourselves heroic, when in truth we are vain,
slothful, and fretful. I have not words to express my
belief on this matter so strongly as I feel it. Oh! I venerate the man who with a heart unsoured has come
down, and come down far, but who never will give up!

I fancy my reader wondering at my excitement, and
doubtful of my meaning. Let me explain my terms.
What is meant by giving up: what by coming down?

By coming down I understand *this:* Learning from
the many mortifications, disappointments, and rebuffs
which we must all meet as we go on through life, to
think more humbly of ourselves, intellectually, morally,

socially, physically, æsthetically: yet, while thinking thus humbly of ourselves and our powers, to resolve that we shall continue to do our very best: and all this with a kindly heart and a contented mind. Such is my ideal of true and Christian coming down: and I regard as a true hero the man who does it rightly. It is a noble thing for a man to say to himself, 'I am not at all what I had vainly fancied myself: my mark is far, very far lower than I thought it had been: I had fancied myself a great genius, but I find I am only a man of decent ability: I had fancied myself a man of great weight in the county, but I find I have very little influence indeed: I had fancied that my stature was six feet four, but I find that I am only five feet two: I had fancied that in such a competition I never could be beaten, but in truth I have been sadly beaten: I had fancied [suffer me, reader, the solemn allusion] that my Master had entrusted me with ten talents, but I find I have no more than one. But I will accept the humble level which is mine by right, and with God's help I will do my very best there. I will not kick dogs nor curse servants: I will not try to detract from the standing of men who are cleverer, more eminent, or taller than myself: I will heartily wish them well. I will not grow soured, moping, and misanthropic. I know I am beaten and disappointed, but I will hold on manfully still, and never give up!' Such, kindly reader, is Christian coming down!

And what is giving up? Of course, you understand my meaning now. Giving up means that when you are beaten and disappointed, and made to understand that your mark is lower than you had fancied, you will throw down your arms in despair, and resolve that you will try no more. As for you, brave man, if you don't get all you

want, you are resolved you shall have nothing. If you
are not accepted as the cleverest and greatest man, you
are resolved you shall be no man at all. And while the
other is Christian coming down, *this* is un-Christian, foolish, and wicked giving up. No doubt, it is an extremely
natural thing. It is the first and readiest impulse of the
undisciplined heart. It is in human nature to say, ' If I
don't have all the pudding, I shall have none.' The
grand way of expressing the same sentiment is, *Aut Cæsar aut nullus.* Of course, the Latin words stir the youthful heart. You sympathize with them, I know, my reader
under five-and-twenty. You will see through them some
day. They are just the heroic way of saying, I shall
give up, but I never shall come down! They state a
sentiment for babies, boys, and girls, not for reasonable
women and men. For babies, I say. Let me relate a
parable. Yesterday I went into a cottage, where a child
of two years old sat upon his mother's knee. The little
man had in his hand a large slice of bread and butter
which his mother had just given him. By words not intelligible to me, he conveyed to his mother the fact that
he desired that jam should be spread upon the slice of
bread and butter. But his mother informed him that
bread and butter must suffice, without the further luxury.
The young human being (how thoroughly human) considered for a moment; and then dashed the bread and
butter to the further end of the room. There it was: *Aut
Cæsar aut nullus!* The baby would give up, but it
would not come down! Alexander the Great, look at
yourself! Marius among the ruins of Carthage, what do
you think you look like here? By the time the youthful
reader comes to understand that Byron's dark, mysterious
heroes, however brilliantly set forth, are in conception

simply childish ; by the time he is able to appreciate
Philip Van Artevelde (I mean Mr. Henry Taylor's noble tragedy) ; he will discern that various things which
look heroic at the first glance, will not *work* in the long
run. And that practical principle is irrational which will
not work. And that sentiment which is irrational is not
heroic. The truly heroic thing to say, as well as the rational thing, is this : If I don't get all the pudding, I shall
be content if I get what I deserve, or what God sends.
If I am not *Cæsar*, there is no need that I should be
nullus : I shall be content to be the highly respectable
Mr. Smith. Though I am not equal to Shakspeare, I
may write a good play. Though inferior to Bishop Wil-
berforce, I shall yet do my best to be a good preacher.
It is a fine thing, a noble thing, as it appears to me, for a
man to be content to labour hard and do his utmost,
though well aware that the result will be no more than
decent mediocrity, after all. It is a finer thing, and more
truly heroic, to do your very best and only be second-rate,
than even to resolve, like the man in the *Iliad*, —

" 'Αἰὲν ἀριστένειν, καὶ ὑπείροχον ἔμμεναι ἄλλων."

There is a strain put upon the moral nature in contentedly
and perseveringly doing this, greater than is put upon the
intellectual by the successful effort to be best. And what
would become of the world if all men went upon Homer's
principle ; and rather than come down from its sublime
elevation, would fling down their tools and give up?
Shall I, because I cannot preach like Mr. Melvill, cease
to write sermons ? Or shall I, because I cannot counsel
and charm like the author of *Friends in Council*, cease to
write essays ? You may rely upon it I shall not. I do
not forget who said, in words of praise concerning one

who had done what was absolutely but very little, 'She
hath done what she could!' And what would become of
me and my essays, if the reader, turning to them from
the pages of Hazlitt or Charles Lamb, should say, 'I
shall not come down; and if I find I have to do so I shall
give up?' What if the reader refused to accept the plain
bread and butter which I can furnish, unless it should be
accompanied by that jam which I am not able to add?

Giving up, then, is the doing of mortified self-conceit,
of sulky pettishness, of impatience, of recklessness, of desperation. It says virtually to the great Disposer of
events, 'Every thing in this world must go exactly as I
wish it, or I shall sit down and die.' It is of the nature
of a moral strike. But coming down generally means
coming to juster and sounder views of one's self and one's
own importance and usefulness; and if you come down
gracefully, genially, and Christianly you work on diligently and cheerfully at that lower level. No doubt, to
come down is a tremendous trial; it is a sore mortification. But trials and mortifications, my reader, are useful
things for you and me. The hasty man, when obliged to
come down, is ready to conclude that he may as well give
up. In some matters it is a harder thing to go the one
mile and stop at the end of it, than to go the twain. It
is much more difficult to stop decidedly half-way down a
very steep descent, than to go all the way. If you are
beaten in some competition, it is much easier to resolve
recklessly that you will never try again, than to set manfully to work, with humble views of yourself, and try
once more. Wisdom comes down: folly gives up. Wisdom, I say, comes down: for I think there can be little
doubt that most men, in order to think rightly of themselves, must come to think much more humbly of them-

selves than they are naturally disposed to do. Few men estimate themselves too lowly. Even people who lack confidence in themselves are not without a great measure of latent self-esteem ; and, indeed, it is natural enough that men should rate themselves too high, till experience compels them to come down. I am talking of even sensible and worthy men. They know they have worked hard ; they know that what they have done has cost them great pains ; they look with instinctive partiality at the results they have accomplished ; they are sure these results are good, and they do not know *how* good till they learn by comparative trial. But when the comparative trial comes, there are few who do not meet their match — few who do not find it needful to come down. Perhaps even Shakspeare felt he must come down a little when he looked into one or two of Christopher Marlowe's plays. Clever boys at school, and clever lads at college, naturally think their own little circle of the cleverest boys or lads to contain some of the cleverest fellows in the world. They know how well they can do many things, and how hard they have worked to do them so well. Of course, they will have to come down, after longer experience of life. It is not that the set who ranked first among their young companions are not clever fellows ; but the world is wide and its population is big, and they will fall in with cleverer fellows still. It is not that the head boy does not write Greek iambics well, but it will go hard but somewhere he will find some one who will write them better. They are rare exceptions in the race of mankind who, however good they may be, and however admirably they may do some one thing, will not some day meet their match — meet their superior, and so have painfully to come down. And, so far as my own experience has

gone. I have found that the very, very few, who never meet
a taking down, who are first at school, then first at college,
then first in life, seem by God's appointment to have
been so happily framed that they could do without it;
that to think justly of themselves they did not need to
come down; that their modesty and humility equalled
their merit; and that (though not unconscious of their
powers and their success) they remained, amid the in-
cense of applause which would have intoxicated others,
unaffected, genial, and unspoiled.

People who lead a quiet country life amid their own
belongings, seeing little of those of bigger men, insensibly
form so excessive an estimate of their personal possessions as lays them open to the risk of many disagreeable
takings down. You, solitary scholar in the country parsonage, have lived for six months among your books till
you have come to fancy them quite a great library. But
you pay a visit to some wealthy man of literary tastes.
You see his fine editions, his gorgeous bindings, his
carved oak book-cases; and when you return home you
will have to contend with a temptation to be disgusted
with your own little collection of books. Now, if you
are a wise man, you will come down, but you wont give
up; you will admit to yourself that your library is not
quite what you had grown to think it, but you will hold
that it is a fair library after all. When you go and see
the grand acres of evergreens at some fine country house,
do not return mortified at the prospect of your own little
shrubbery which looked so fine in the morning before
you set out. When you have beheld Mr. Smith's fine
thoroughbreds, resist the impulse to whack your own
poor steed. Rather pat the poor thing's neck: gracefully
come down. It was a fine thing, Cato, banished from

Rome, yet having his little senate at Utica. He had
been compelled to come down, indeed, but he clung to
the dear old institution ; he would not give up. I have
enjoyed the spectacle of a lady, brought up in a noble
baronial dwelling, living in a pretty little parsonage, and
quite pleased and happy there ; not sulking, not fretting,
not talking like an idiot of ' what she had been accustomed to,' but heartily reconciling herself to simpler
things — coming down, in short, but never dreaming of
giving up. So have I esteemed the clergyman like Sydney Smith, who had commanded the attention of crowded
congregations of educated folk, of gentlemen and gentle-
women, yet who works faithfully and cheerfully in a
rural parish, and prepares his sermons diligently, with
the honest desire to make them interesting and instructive to a handful of simple country people. Of course,
he knows that he has come down, but he does not dream
of giving up.

There is in human nature a curious tendency to think
that if you are obliged to fall, or if you have fallen, a
good deal, you may just as well go all the way ; and it
would be hard to reckon the amount of misery and ruin
which have resulted from this mistaken fancy, that if you
have come down, you may give up at once. A poor
man, possibly under some temptation that does not come
once in ten years, gets tipsy ; walking along in that state
he meets the parish clergyman ; the clergyman's eye rests
on him in sorrow and reproach. The poor man is heartily ashamed ; he is brought to a point at which he may
turn the right way or the wrong way. He has not read
this essay, and he takes the wrong. He thinks he has
been so bad, he cannot be worse. He goes home and
thrashes his wife ; he ceases attending church ; he takes

his children from school : he begins to go to destruction.
All this founds on his erroneously imagining that you
cannot come down without giving up. But I believe that,
in truth, as the general rule, the fatal and shameful deed
on which a man must look back in bitterness, and sorrow
all his life, was done *after* the point at which he grew
reckless.   It was *because* he had given up that he took
the final desperate step ; he did not give up because he
had taken it.   The man did a really desperate deed because he thought wrongly that he had done a desperate
deed already, and could not now be any worse ; and sad
as are intellectual and social coming down, and likely to
result in giving up as these are, they are not half so sad
nor half so perilous as moral coming down.   It must indeed be a miserable thing for man or woman to feel that
they have done something which will shame all after life
— something which will never let them hold up their
head again, something which will make them (to use the
expressive language of Scripture) ‘go softly all their
days.’   Well, let such come down ; let them learn to be
humble and penitent ; but for any sake don’t let them
give up !   *That* is the great Tempter’s last and worst
suggestion.   *His* suggestion to the fallen man or woman
is, You are now so bad that you cannot be worse — you
had better give up at once ; and Judas listened to it and
went and hanged himself ; and the poor Magdalen, fallen
far, but with a deep abyss beneath her yet, steals at midnight, to the dark arch and the dark river, with the bitter
desperate resolution of Hood’s exquisite poem, ‘ Anywhere, anywhere, out of the world !’   I remember an
amusing exemplification of the natural tendency to think
that having come down you must give up, in a play in
which I once saw Keeley, in my play-going days.   He

fancied that he had (unintentionally) killed a man: his horror was extreme. Soon after, by another mischance, he killed (as he is led to believe) another man: his horror is redoubled; but now there mingles with it a reckless desperation. Having done such dreadful things, he concludes that he cannot be worse, whatever he may do. Having come so far down, he thinks he may as well give up; and so the little fat man exclaims, with a fiendish laugh, 'Now I think I had better kill somebody else!' Ah, how true to nature! The plump desperado was at the moment beyond remembering that the sound view of the case was, that if he had done so much mischief it was the more incumbent on him to do no more. The poor lad in a counting-house who wellnigh breaks his mother's heart by taking a little money not his own, need not break it outright by going entirely to ruin. Rather gather yourself up from your fall. Though the sky-scraping spars are gone, we may rig a jury mast:—

'And from the wreck, far scattered o'er the rocks,
  Build us a little bark of hope once more.'

We are being taught all through life to come down in our anticipations, our self-estimation, our ambition. We aim high at first. Children expect to be kings, or at least to be always eating plum pudding and drinking cream. Clever boys expect to be great and famous men. They come gradually to soberer views and hopes. Our vanity and self-love and romance are cut in upon day by day: step by step we come down, but, if we are wise, we never give up. We hold on steadfastly still; we try to do our best. The painful discipline begins early. The other day I was at our sewing-school. A very little girl came up with great pride to show me her work. It was very

23

badly done, poor little thing. I tried to put the fact as
kindly as possible; but of course I was obliged to say that
the sewing was not quite so good as she would be able to
do some day. I saw the eyes fill and the lips quiver:
there were mortification and disappointment in the little
heart. I saw the temptation to be petted, to throw the
work aside — to give up. But better thoughts prevailed.
She felt she must come down. She went away silently
to her place and patiently tried to do better. Ah, thought
I to myself, there is a lesson for *you*.

Let me now think of intellectual giving up and coming down.

I do not suppose that a thorough blockhead can ever
know the pain of intellectual coming down. From his
first schooldays he has been made to understand that he
is a blockhead, and he does not think of entering himself to run against clever men. A large dray-horse is
saved the mortification of being beaten for the Derby;
for he does not propose to run for the Derby. The
pain of intellectual coming down is felt by the really
clever man, who is made to feel that he is not so clever
as he had imagined; that whereas he had fancied himself a first-class man, he is no more than a third-class
one; or that, even though he be a man of good ability,
and capable of doing his own work well, there are
others who can do it much better than he. You would
not like, my clever reader, to be told that not much is
expected of you; that no one supposes that you can
write, ride, walk, or leap like Smith. There was something that touched one in that letter which Mr. R. H.
Horne wrote to the *Times*, explaining how he was going
away to Australia because his poetry was neglected and
unappreciated. What slow, painful years of coming

down the poet must have gone through before he thus
resolved to give up. I never read *Orion;* and living
among simple people, I never knew any one who had
read the work. It may be a work of great genius. But
the poet insisted on giving up when, perhaps, the right
thing for him was to have come down. Perhaps he
over-estimated himself and his poetry; perhaps it met
all the notice it deserved.

The poet stated, in his published letter, that his writings had been most favourably received by high-class
critics; but he was going away because the public
treated him with entire neglect. Nobody read him, or
cared for him, or talked about him. 'And what did
the learned world say to your paradoxes?' asked good
Dr. Primrose; but his son's reply was, 'The learned
world said nothing at all to my paradoxes.' Such appears to have been the case with Mr. Horne; and so he
grew misanthropic, and shook from his feet the dust of
Britain. He gave up, in short; but he refused to come
down. And no doubt it is easier to go off to the wilderness at once than to conclude that you are only a middling man after having long regarded yourself as a great
genius. It must be a sad thing for an actor who came
out as a new Kean, to gradually make up his mind that
he is just a respectable, painstaking person, who never
will draw crowds and take the town by storm. Many
struggles must the poor barrister know before he comes
down from trying for the great seal, and aims at being
a police magistrate. So with the painter; and you
remember how poor Haydon refused to come down,
and desperately gave up. It cannot be denied that, to
the man of real talent, it is a most painful trial to intellectually come down; and that trial is attended with a

strong temptation to give up. Really clever men not
unfrequently have a quite preposterous estimate of their
own abilities; and many takings down are needful to
drive them out of *that*. And men who are essentially
middling men intellectually, sometimes have first-class
ambition along with third-rate powers; and these coming
together make a most ill-matched pair of legs, which
bear a human being very awkwardly along his path in
life, and expose him to numberless mortifications. It is
hard to feel any deep sympathy for such men, though
their sufferings must be great. And, unhappily, such
men, when compelled to come down, not unfrequently
attempt by malicious arts to pull down to their own level
those to whose level they are unable to rise. I have
sometimes fancied one could almost see the venomous
vapours coming visibly from the mouth of a malignant,
commonplace, ambitious man, when talking of one more
able and more successful than himself.

Possibly social coming down is even more painful
than intellectual. It is very sad to see, as we sometimes do, the father of a family die, and his children in
consequence lose their grade in society. I do not mean,
merely to have to move to a smaller house, and put
down their carriage; for all *that* may be while social
position remains unchanged. I mean, drop out of the
acquaintance of their father's friends; fall into the society of coarse, inferior people; be addressed on a footing
of equality by persons with whom they have no feelings
or thoughts in common; be compelled to sordid shifts
and menial work and frowsy chambers. Threadbare
carpets and rickety chairs often indicate privation as
extreme as shoeless feet and a coat out at elbows. We
might probably smile at people who felt the painfulness

of coming down, because obliged to pass from one set to another in the society of some little country town, where the second circle is not unfrequently (to a stranger's view) very superior to the first in appearance, manners, and means. But there is one line which it must cost a parent real anguish to make up his mind that his children are to fall below after having been brought up above it: I mean the one essentially impassable line of society — the line which parts the educated, well-bred gentleman from the man who is not such. There is something terrible about *that* giving up. And how such as have ever known it, cling to the upper side of the line of demarcation. We have all seen how people work and pinch and screw to maintain a decent appearance before the world, while things were bare and scanty enough at home. And it is an honest and commendable pride that makes the poor widow, of small means but with the training and feeling of a lady, determine never to give up the notion that her daughters shall be ladies too. It need not be said that such a determination is not at all inconsistent with the most stringent economy or the most resolute industry on her own or her girls' part. I did not sympathize with a letter which S. G. O. lately published in the *Times*, in which he urged that people with no more than three hundred a-year, should at once resolve to send their daughters out as menial servants, instead of fighting for the position of ladies for them. I thought, and I think, that *that* letter showed less than its author's usual genial feeling, less than his usual sound sense. Kind and judicious men will probably believe that a good man's or woman's resistance to social coming down, and especially to social giving up, is deserving of all respect and sympathy. A poor clergyman, or a poor military man, may have no more than three hundred a-year; but I heartily venerate his endeavours to preserve his girls from the society of the servants' hall and the delicate attentions of Jeames. The world may yet think differently, and manual or menial work may be recognized as not involving social giving up; but meanwhile the step is a vast one, between the poorest governess and the plumpest housemaid.

A painful form of social coming down falls to the lot of many women when they get married. I suppose young girls generally have in their mind a glorified ideal of the husband whom they are to find; wonderfully handsome, wonderfully clever, very kind and affectionate, probably very rich and famous. Sad pressure must be put upon a worthy woman's heart before she can resolve to give up all romantic fancies, and marry purely for money. There must be sad pressure before a young girl can so far come down as to resolve to marry some man who is an old and ugly fool. Yet how many do! No doubt, reader, you have sometimes seen couples who were paired, but not matched; a beautiful young creature tied to a foul old satyr. Was not your reflection, as you looked at the poor wife's face, 'Ah! how wretchedly you must have come down.' And even when the husband is really a good old man, you cannot but think how different he is from the fair ideal of a girl's first fancy. Before making up her mind to such a partner as that, the young woman had a good deal to give up. And probably men, if of an imaginative turn, have, when they get married, to come down a good deal too. I do not suppose any thing about the clever man's wife but what is very good; but surely, she is not always the sympathetic, admiring companion of his early visions. Think of the great author, walking in the summer fields, and saying to his wife, as he looked at the frisking lambs, that they seemed so innocent and happy that he did not wonder that in all ages the lamb has been taken as the emblem of happiness and innocence. Think of the revulsion in his mind when the thoughtful lady replied, after some reflection, 'Yes, lamb is very nice, especially with mint sauce!' The great man had no doubt already come down very much in his expectation of finding in his wife a sympathetic companion; but after *that*, he would probably give up altogether. Still, it is possibly less painful for a clever man to find, as years go on, and life sobers into the prosaic, that he must come down sadly in his ideas of the happiness of wedded life, than it is for such a man fairly to give up before marriage, making up his mind that in *that* matter, as in most others, men must be content with what they can get, though it be very inferior to what they could wish. I feel a great disgust for what may be called sentimentality; in practical life sentimental people, and people who talk sentimentally, are invariably fools; still it appears to me that there is sober truth in the following lines, which I remember to have read somewhere or other, though the truth be somewhat sickly and sentimentally expressed: —

'And as the dove, to far Palmyra flying,
　From where her native founts of Antioch gleam
Weary, exhausted, longing, panting, sighing,
　Lights sadly at the desert's bitter stream;

'So many a soul, o'er life's drear desert faring, —
　Love's pure, congenial spring unfound, unquaffed, —
Suffers, recoils, then, thirsty and despairing
　Of what it would, descends and sips the nearest draught.'

Most people find it painful to come down in the matter of growing old. Most men and women cling, as long as may be, to the belief that they are still quite young, or at least not so very old. Let us respect the clinging to youth: there seems to me much that is good in it. It is an unconscious testimony to the depth and universality of the conviction that, as time goes on, we are leaving behind us the more guileless, innocent, and impressionable season of our life. We feel little sympathy, indeed, for the silly old woman who affects the airs and graces of a girl of seventeen: who makes her daughters attire themselves like children when they are quite grown up; and who renders herself ridiculous in low dresses and a capless head when her head is half bald and her shoulders like an uncooked plucked fowl. *That* is downright offensive and revolting. And to see such an individual surrounded by a circle of young lads to whom she is talking in a buoyant and flirting manner, is as melancholy an exhibition of human folly as can anywhere be seen. But it is quite a different thing when man or woman, thoughtful, earnest, and pious, sits down and muses at the sight of the first gray hairs. Here is the slight shadow, we think, of a certain great event which is to come; here is the earliest touch of a chill hand which must prevail at length. Here is manifest decay; we have begun to die. And no worthy human being will pretend that this is other than a very solemn thought. And we look back as well as forward: how short a time since we were little children, and kind hands smoothed down the locks now growing scanty and gray! You cannot recognize in the glass, when you see the careworn, anxious face, the smooth features of the careless child. You feel you must come down; you

are young no more! Yet you know by what shifts
people seek in this respect to avoid coming down. We
postpone, year after year, the point at which people
cease to be young. We are pleased when we find people talking of men above thirty as young men. Once,
indeed, Sir Robert Peel spoke of Lord Derby at forty-
five as a man in "the buoyancy of youth." Many men
of five-and-forty would feel a secret elation as they read
the words thus employed. The present writer wants a
good deal yet of being half-way; yet he remembers
how much obliged he felt to Mr. Dickens for describing
Tom Pinch, in *Martin Chuzzlewit* (in an advertisement
to be put in the *Times*), as 'a respectable young man,
aged thirty-five.' You remember how Sir Bulwer Lytton, as he has himself grown older, has made the heroes
of his novels grow older *pari passu*. Many years ago
his romantic heroes were lads of twenty; *now* they are
always sentimental men of fifty. And in all this we
can trace a natural conviction of the intellect, as well
as the natural disinclination in any respect to come down.
For youth, with all its folly, is by common consent regarded as a better thing than age, with all its experience : and thus to grow old is regarded as coming down.
And there is something very touching, something to be
respected and sympathized with by all people in the
vigour of life, in the fashion in which men who have
come down so far as to admit that they have grown old,
refuse to give up by admitting that they are past their
work ; and, indeed, persist in maintaining, after fifty
years in the church or thirty on the bench, that they
are as strong as ever. Let us reverence the old man.
Let us help him in his determination not to give up.
Let us lighten his burden when we can do so, and then

give him credit for bearing it all himself. If there be
one respect in which it is especially interesting and
respectable when a man refuses to give up at any price,
and indeed is most unwilling to come down, it is in
regard of useful, honest labor in the service of God and
man. Sometimes the unwillingness to come down in
any degree is amusing, and almost provoking. I remember once, coming down a long flight of steps from
a railway station, I saw a venerable dignitary of the
church, who had served it for more than sixty years,
coming down with difficulty, and clinging to the railing.
Now, what I ought to have done was, to remain out of
his view, and see that he got safely down without making him aware that I was watching him. But I hastily
went up to him and begged him to take my arm, as the
stair was so slippery and steep. I think I see the indignation of the good man's look. 'I assure you,' he
replied, 'my friend, I am quite as able to walk down
the steps alone as you are!'

Apart from the more dignified regrets which accompany
the coming down of growing old, there are petty mortifications which vain people will feel as they are obliged to
come down in their views as to their personal appearance.
As a man's hair falls off, as he grows unwieldily stout, as
he comes to blow like a porpoise in ascending a hill, as
his voice cracks when he tries to sing, he is obliged step
by step to come down. I heartily despise the contemptible creature who refuses to come down when nature bids
him : who dyes his hair and his moustache, rouges his
face, wears stays, and pads out his chest. Yet more disgusting is the made-up old reprobate when, padded, rouged,
and dyed, as already said, he mingles in a circle of fast
young men, and disgusts even them by the foul pruriency

of his talk. Kick him out, muscular Christian! Tell
him what you think of him, and see how the despicable
wretch will cower! But while this refusing to come
gracefully down as to physical aspect with advancing
time is thoroughly abominable, let it be remembered that
even in this matter the judicious man will not give up,
though he will come down. Don't grow slovenly and
careless as you grow old. Be scrupulously neat and tidy
in dress. It is a pleasant sight — pleasant like the trimly
raked field of autumn — the speckless, trim, white neck-
clothed, well-dressed old man.

That we may wisely come down, we need frequently
to be reminded that we ought to do so. We need, in fact,
a good many takings down as we go on through life, or we
should all become insufferable. I speak of ordinary men.
The old vanity keeps growing up ; and like the grass of
a lawn, it needs to be often mown down ; and however
frequently and closely it is mown, there will always (as
with the lawn) be quite enough of it. You meet with
some wholesome, mortifying lesson ; you feel you must
come down ; and you do. You think humbly and reasonably of yourself for a while. But the grass is growing
again : your self-estimation is getting up again ; you are
beginning to think yourself very clever, great, and eminent, when some rude shock undeceives you. You are
roughly compelled to think of yourself more meekly.
You find that in the general judgment you are no great
author, artist, actor, cricket-player, shot, essay writer,
preacher. You are so mortified that you think you may
at once give up ; but, after deliberating, you resolve that
you will only come down.

Great men have no doubt given up ; but it was either
in some time of morbid depression, or when it was really

unavoidable that they should do so. Pitt gave up when on his dying-bed he heard of several great victories of the First Napoleon; and, crying out with his blackening lips, '*Roll up the map of Europe*,' turned his face to the wall and never spoke more. Sir Robert Peel gave up, when he tendered to the queen his final resignation of office. When the queen asked him if there was nothing he could wish her to do in testimony of her regard for him, his answer was — '*Only that your majesty would never call me to your counsels again !*' What a giving up for that ambitious man ! Notwithstanding what has already been said in this essay, I am not, on reflection, sure that Marius had given up, or even come down, when he sat, in his lowest depression of fortune, amid the ruins of Carthage. Gelimer had finally given up when he was carried as a captive in the Roman triumph, looking with a smile upon all the pomp of the grand procession, and often exclaiming, '*Vanity, vanity: all is vanity !*' But Diocletian, busy among his cabbages, interested and content though the purple had been flung aside, had neither given up nor come down. Nor had Charles V. done either in that beautiful retreat which Mr. Stirling has so gracefully described. There was no coming down *there*, in the loss of self-estimation; there was no giving up, in the bitter and despairing sense, when the greatest monarch of the great sixteenth century, in his greatest eminence, calmly laid down the cares of royalty, that in his last days he might enjoy quiet, and have space in which to prepare for the other world. It was only that '*the royal eagle would rest his weary wings.*'

But we have all known very small men who were always ready to give up, rather than that their silly vanity should be mortified by any degree of coming down. We

have all known cases highly analogous to that of the little child who threw away his bread and butter, because
he could not have jelly too. I dare say, my reader, you
may have seen a man who if he were not allowed to be
the first man in some little company, the only talker, the
only singer, the only philosopher, or the only jack-pud-
ding, would give up, and sit entirely silent. In his own
small way, he must be *aut Cæsar aut nullus*. A rival
talker, singer, or mountebank, turns him pale with envy
and wrath. Of course, all this founds on extreme pettiness of character, co-existing with inordinate vanity
and silliness. And it is an offence which is its own severe punishment. The petty sin whips itself with a stinging scourge of pack-thread.

I have sometimes thought that it is a remarkable thing,
how very quickly human beings can quite give up. An
entire revolution may pass in a few hours, perhaps in a few
minutes, upon our whole estimate of things. I should
judge that a soldier, charging some perilous position in a
delirium of excitement, and fancying military glory the
sublimest thing in life; if he suddenly be disabled by
some ghastly wound, and is borne away to the rear deadly
sick, fevered, and wrung with agony, would give up
many notions which he had cherished before. But I have
been especially struck by witnessing how fast men can
resign themselves to the last and largest giving up : how
quickly they can make up their mind that they are dying,
and that all will be over in two or three hours. A man
stricken with cholera at morning, and gone before night,
has not the feeling that his death is sudden. When
eternity comes very near, this world and all its concerns
are speedily discerned as little more than shadows. We
give up quickly, and with little effort, all those things and

fancies and opinions to which we clung very closely in
health and life. The dying man feels that to him these
are not. A Christian man, busy in the morning at his
usual work, and smitten down at midday by some fatal
disease or accident, could be quite resigned to die at
evening. He may have had a hundred plans in his mind
at daybreak: but it would cost him little effort to give
them all up. And but for the dear ones he must
leave behind, a very short time would suffice to resign
a pious man to the *Nunc dimittis*. We grow accustomed, wonderfully fast, to the most new and surprising
things.

But returning to matters less solemn, let me sum up
what has been said so far, by repeating my grand principle, that in most cases the wise and good man will come
down, but never give up. The heroic thing to say is this:
Things are bad, but they may be worse; and with God's
blessing I shall try to make them better. Who does not
know that by resolute adherence to this principle, many
battles have been won after they had been lost? Don't the
French say that the English have conquered on many
fields because they did not know when they had been
beaten; in short, because they would never give up?
Pluck is a great quality. Let us respect it everywhere;
at least, wherever enlisted on the side of right. Ugly is
the bull-dog, and indeed blackguard-looking: but I admire one thing about it: it will never give up. And
splendid success has often come at length to the man who
fought on through failure, hoping against hope. Mr.
Disraeli might well have given up after his first speech
in the House of Commons: many men would never have
opened their lips there again. I declare I feel something
sublime in that defiant *The day will come when you will*

be glad to hear me, when we read it by the light of
after events. Of course, only extraordinary success
could justify the words. They might have been the
vapouring of a conceited fool. Galileo, compelled to
appear to come down, did not give up: *Still it moves.*
The great nonconformist preacher, Robert Hall, fairly
broke down in his first attempt to preach ; but he did not
give up. Mr. Tennyson might have given up, had he
been disheartened by the sharp reviews of his earliest volume. George Stephenson might also have given up, when
his railway and his locomotive were laughed out of the
parliamentary committee. Mr. Thackeray might have
given up, when the publishers refused to have anything to
do with *Vanity Fair.* The first articles of men who have
become most successful periodical writers, have been
consigned to the Balaam-box. Possibly this was in some
measure the cause of their success. It taught them to
take more pains. It was a taking down. It showed
them that their task was not so easy : if they would succeed, they must do their very best. And if they had
stamina to resolve that though taken down they would
not give up, the early disappointment was an excellent
discipline. I have known students at college whose success in carrying off honors was unexampled, who in their
first one or two competitions were ignominiously beaten.
Some would have given up. They only came down :
then they went at their work with a will; and never
were beaten more.

The man who is most likely to give up, is the man
who foolishly refuses to come down. Every human
being (excepting men like Shakspeare) must do either
the one thing or the other at many points in their life:
and the latter is the safer thing, and will save from the

former. It is the milder form of that suffering which
follows disappointment and mortification. It is to the
other as cow-pox to small-pox: by submitting to pass
through many comings down, you will escape the sad
misery of many givings up. Yet even vaccination, when
it takes full effect, though much less serious than small-
pox, is a painful and disagreeable thing : and in like manner, coming down in any way, socially, intellectually,
physically, morally, is an infliction so painful, that men
have devised various arts by which to escape coming
down at all. The great way to escape intellectual coming down, is to hold that men will not do you justice;
that the reviewers have conspired against you ; that the
anonymous assassins of the press stab you out of malignity and envy; that you are an unappreciated genius;
and that if your powers were only known, you would be
universally recognized as a very great man. When you
preach, the people fall asleep: but *that* is because the
people are stupid, not because your sermons are dull.
When you send an article to a magazine, it is rejected:
that is not because the article is bad, but because the
editor is a fool. You write a book, and nobody reads it ;
it is because the book is carelessly printed, and the publisher devoid of energy. You paint a picture, and everybody laughs at it ; it is because the taste of the age is low.
You write a prize essay, and don't get the prize; it is because the judges had an objection to sound doctrine. And
indeed there have been great men to whom their own age
did injustice; and you may be one of these. It is highly
probable that you are not. It is highly probable that
your mark is gauged pretty fairly ; no doubt it is lower
than you think right : but it is best to come down to it.
It is but a foolish world, and it will not last long ; and

there are things more excellent than even to be a very
clever man, and to be recognized as such. It is curious
how men soothe themselves and avoid coming down, or
mitigate the pain of doing so, by secretly cherishing the
belief that in some one little respect they are different
from, and higher than, all the rest of their kind. And it
is wonderful how such a reflection has power to break
one's fall, so to speak. You don't much mind being only
a commonplace man in all other respects, if only there
be one respect in which you can fondly believe you are
superior to everybody else. A very little thing will suffice. A man is taller than anybody else in the town or
parish; he has longer hair; he can walk faster; he is
the first person who ever crossed the new bridge; when
the queen passed near she bowed to him individually;
he was the earliest in the neighbourhood who got the
perforated postage stamps; he has the swiftest horse in
the district; he has the largest cabbages; he has the old-
est watch: one Smith spells his name as no other Smith
was ever known to do. It is quite wonderful how far it
is possible for men to find reason for cherishing in their
heart a deep-seated belief, that in something or other
they stand on a higher platform than all the remainder
of mankind. Few men live, who do not imagine that in
some respect they stand alone in the world, or stand first.
I have seen people quite proud of the unexampled disease under which they were suffering. It was none of
the common maladies that the people round about suffered from. I have known a country woman boast,
with undisguised elation, that the doctor had more difficulty in pulling out her tooth, than he ever before had in
the case of mortal man. There is not a little country
parish in Britain, but its population are persuaded that in

24

several respects and for several reasons, it is quite the
most important in the empire.

There is an expedient not uncommonly employed by
men to lessen their mortification when obliged to come
down, which may possibly be effectual as a salve to
wounded vanity, but which is in the last degree miserable and contemptible. It consists in endeavouring to
bring everybody else down along with you. A man is
unpopular as a preacher; he endeavours to disseminate
the notion that the clergyman of the next parish is unpopular too, and that the current reports about his
church being overcrowded, are gross exaggerations.
A man has a very small practice as a physician; he
assures an inquiring stranger that Dr. Mimpson, who
(everybody says) makes fourteen thousand a-year, does
not really make fourteen hundred. A man's horses are
always lame; he tells you malignantly that he knows
privately, that the fine pair which Smith drives in his
drag, are very groggy, and require to be shod with
leather. Now I do not mean to assert that there is any
essential malignity in a man's feeling comfort, when
obliged to come down himself, in the reflection that other
men have had to come down too; and that after coming
down he still stands on the same level with multitudes
more. It is a natural thing to find a certain degree of
consolation in such reflections. Notwithstanding what
Milton says to the contrary, there is no doubt at all that
'fellowship in pain' does 'divide smart.' If you were
the only bald man in the world, or the only lame man, or
the only man who had lost several teeth, you would find
it much harder to resign your mind to your condition; in
brief, to come down to it. There is real and substantial
mitigation of all human ills and mortifications in the sight

of others as badly off. To fall on the ice along with twenty more is no great matter, unless indeed the physical suffering be great. To be guillotined as one of fifty is not nearly so bad as to go all alone. To be beaten in a competition along with half a dozen very clever fellows mitigates your mortification. The poor fellow, plucked for his degree, is a little cheered up when he goes out for a walk with three other men who have been plucked along with him. Napoleon, standing before a picture in which Alexander the Great was a figure, evinced a pleasing touch of nature when he said repeatedly, ' Alexander was smaller than me ; much smaller.' The thing which I condemn is not that the man who has come down should look around with pleasure on his brethren in misfortune, but that the man who has come down should seek to pull down to his own level those whom in his secret soul he knows stand on a higher. What I condemn is envious and malignant detraction, with its train of wilful misrepresentation, sly innuendoes, depreciating shrugs and nods. I hate to hear a man speaking in terms of faint praise of another who has outstripped him in their common profession, saying that he is ' rather a clever lad,' that he ' really has some talent,' that he is ' not wholly devoid of power,' that he ' has done better than could be expected,' and the like. Very contemptible is a method of depreciation which I have often witnessed. It consists in asserting that Mr. A., whom everybody knows for a very ordinary man, is far superior to Mr. B., whom you are commending as a man of superior parts. I remember a certain public meeting. Dr. C. made a most brilliant and stirring speech ; Dr. D. followed in a very dull one ; Mr. E. next made a decent one. After the meeting was over, the envious E. thought to take down C., and cover his own coming down, by walking up to D., and in a very marked manner, in the presence of C., congratulating D. on having made the speech of the evening. Oh, that we could all learn to acknowledge with frankness and heartiness the merit that overtops us! Don't let us try to pull it down. Read with pleasure the essay which you feel is far better than you could have written: listen with improvement to the sermon which you feel is far better than you could have preached. I think envy is a distant feeling. In a true heart it cannot live when you have come to know the envied man well. It is in our nature to like the man that surpassed us when we come to know him. Perhaps it is impossible to look at merit or success in our own peculiar line without making an involuntary comparison between these and our own. Perhaps it is natural to fancy that our great doings have hardly, as yet, met the appreciation they deserved. But I do not believe that it is natural, except in men of very bad natures, to cherish any other feeling than a kindly one towards the man whose powers are so superior to ours, that with hardly an apparent effort he beats us, far as Eclipse beat his compeers, in the especial walk of our own tastes and talents, when we have done our most laborious and our best.

It is oftentimes a real kindness to assure a man, though not quite truly, that he is not coming down. It may tend to keep him from giving up. Very transparent deceptions sometimes suffice to deceive us. You remember how Dr. Johnson, when he was breaking up in the last weeks of his long life, felt very indignant at any one who told him that in health and strength he was coming down. Once, when the good man was tottering on the verge of the grave, a new acquaintance said to him, ' Ah, doctor,

I see the glow of health returning to your cheek:' whereupon Johnson grasped his hand warmly, and said, 'God bless you: you are the kindest friend I ever had!' If you, benevolent reader, wish to do a kindness, and to elicit a grateful feeling, go and tell a man who is growing bald that his hair is getting thicker: tell a man of seventy that he is every day looking younger: tell a man who can now walk but at a slow pace that he walks uncommonly fast: tell a middle-aged lady whose voice is cracking, that it is always growing finer: tell a cottager who is proud of his garden, about the middle of October, that his garden is looking more blooming than in June: tell the poor artisan, the skilled workman, who has been driven by want of work to take to breaking stones for the road (which in the Scotch mind holds the place which sweeping a crossing holds in the English) that you are pleased to see he has got nice light work for these winter days; and if you be the parish clergyman, stop for a few minutes and talk cheerfully to him: if you passed that poor down-hearted fellow to-day with only a slight recognition, he would certainly fancy (with the ingenious self-torment of fallen fortunes) that you did it because he has been obliged so sadly to come down. But if you want to prove yourself devoid of the instinctive benevolence of the gentleman, you will walk up to the man with a look of mingled grief and astonishment, and say, 'O, John, I am sorry to see you have come to this!' I have seen the like done. I have known people who, not from malignity, but from pure stolidity and coarseness of nature, would insist on impressing on the man's mind how far he had come down. Gelimer at Rome (or Constantinople, I forget which) did not feel his fall more than the decent Scotch carpenter or mason busy at his

heap of stones by the roadside. And who, that had
either heart or head, but would rather try to keep him up,
than to take him further down? It is the delicate discernment of these things that marks the gentleman and
the gentlewoman. Such instinctively shrink from saying
or doing a thing that will pain the feelings of another: if
they say or do anything of the kind, it is not because
they don't know what they are about. While vulgar
people go through life, unintentionally and ignorantly
sticking pins into more sensitive natures at every turn.
You, my friend, accidentally meet an old school companion. You think him a low looking fellow as could well be
seen. But you say to him kindly that you are happy to
see him looking so well. He replies to you, with a con-
founded candour, ' I cannot say *that* of you ; you are looking very old and careworn.' The boor did not mean to
say anything disagreeable. It was pure want of discernment. It was simply that he is not a gentleman, and
never can now be made one. ' Your daughter, poor
thing, is getting hardly any partners,' said a vulgar rich
woman to an old lady in a ball-room : ' it is really very
bad of the young men.' The vulgar rich woman fancied
she was making a kind and sympathetic remark. It is
to be recorded that sometimes such remarks have their
origin not in ignorance but in intentional malignity. Mr.
Snarling, of this neighbourhood, deals in such. He sees
a man looking cheerful after dinner, and laughing heartily. Mr. Snarling exclaims, ' Bless me, how flushed you
are getting! Did any of your relations die of apo-
plexy?' If you should cough in the unhappy wretch's
presence, he will ask, with an anxious look, if there is
consumption in your family. And he will receive your
negative answer with an ominous shake of his head. ' I

am sorry to hear.' says Mr. Snarling, the week after your
new horse comes home, 'I am sorry to hear about that
animal proving such a bad bargain. I was sure the dealer
would cheat you.' 'It was very sad indeed,' says Mr.
Snarling, 'that you could not get that parish which you
wanted.' He shakes his head, and kindly adds, 'Especially, as you were so very anxious to get it.' 'I read the
December number of *Fraser*' (in which you have an article), says the fellow, 'and of all the contemptible rub-
bish that ever was printed, *that* was decidedly the worst.'
You cannot refrain from the retort, 'Yes, it was very
stupid of the editor to refuse that article you sent him: it
would have raised the character of the magazine.' Snarling's face grows blue: he was not aware that you knew
so much. Never mind poor Snarling: he punishes himself very severely. Only a man who is very unhappy
himself will go about doing all he can to make others unhappy. And gradually Snarling is understood, and then
Snarling is shunned.

I trust that none of my readers have in them anything
of the snarling spirit; but I doubt not that even the
best-natured of them have occasionally met with human
beings who were blown up with vanity and conceit to a
degree so thoroughly intolerable, that it would have been
felt as an unspeakable privilege to be permitted (so to
speak) to stick a skewer into the great inflated wind-bag,
and to take the individual several pegs down. It is fit and
pleasing that a man in any walk of life should magnify his
office, and be pleased with his own proficiency in its duties. One likes to see that. The man will be the happier, and will go through his work the better. But the
irritating thing is to find a human being who will talk of
nothing whatsoever except himself, and his own doings
and importance; who plainly shows that he feels not the

least interest in any other topic of discourse; and who is
ever trying to bring back the conversation to number one.
I have at this moment in my mind's eye a man, a woman,
and a lad, in each of whom conceit appears to a degree
which I never saw paralleled elsewhere. When you look
at or listen to any one of them, the analogy to the blown-
up bladder instantly suggests itself. They are very much
alike in several respects. They are not ill-natured: though
very commonplace, they are not utter blockheads: their
great characteristic is self-complacency so stolid that it
never will see reason to come down; and so pachy-
dermatous that it will be unaware of any gentle effort to take it down. There is a beautiful equanimity about the thorough dunce. He is so completely
stupid, that he never for an instant suspects that he is
stupid at all. He never feels any necessity to intellectually come down. A clever man has many fears that
his powers are but small, but your entire booby knows no
such fear. The clever man can appreciate, when done
by another, that which he could not have done himself:
and he is able to make many comparisons which take him
down. But there are men, who could read a sermon of
their own, and then a sermon by the bishop of Oxford,
and see no great difference between the two.

And now, kindly reader, we have arrived at the end of
the six long slips of paper, and this essay approaches its
close. Let me say, before laying down the pen, that it is
for commonplace people I write, when I advise those who
look at these pages to come down intellectually to the
mark fixed for them by their fellow-creatures — to believe
that they are estimated pretty fairly, and appreciated
much as they deserve. You and I, my friend, may possibly have fancied, once upon a time, that we were great
and remarkable men; but many takings down have

taught us to think soberly, and we know better now. We shall never do anything very extraordinary: our biography will not be written after we are gone. So be it. *Fiat Voluntas Tua!* We are quite content to come down genially. It does not matter much that we never shall startle the world with the echoes of our fame. Let us rank ourselves with ' Nature's unambitious underwood, and flowers that prosper in the shade.' But, of course, there are great geniuses who ought not thus to come down — men who, though lightly esteemed by those around them, will some day take their place, by the consent of all enlightened judges, among the most illustrious of human kind. The very powers which are yet to make you famous, may tend to make the ignorant folk around you regard you as a crackbrained fool. You remember the beautiful fairy tale of the ugly duckling. The poor little thing was laughed at, pecked, and persecuted, because it was so different from the remainder of the brood, till it fled away in despair. But it was unappreciated, just because it was too good; for it grew up at length, and *then* met universal admiration: the ugly duckling was a beautiful swan ! Even so that great man John Foster, preaching among a petty dissenting sect fifty years since, was set down as ' a perfect fool.' But intelligent men have fixed *his* mark now. It was because he was a swan that the quacking tribe thought him such an ugly duck. *You* may be such another. The chance is, indeed, ten thousand to one that you are not. Still, if you have the fixed consciousness of the divine gift within you, do not be false to your nature. Resolutely refuse to come down — only be assured, my friend, that should such be your resolution, you will have to resist many temptations to give up !

CHAPTER XII.

CONCERNING THE DIGNITY OF DULNESS.

IF any man wishes to write with vigour and decision upon one side of any debated question, it is highly expedient that he should write before he has thought much or long upon the debated question. For calmly to look at a subject in all its bearings, and dispassionately to weigh that which may be said *pro* and *con.*, is destructive of that unhesitating conviction which takes its side and keeps it without a misgiving whether it be the right side, and which discerns in all that can be said by others, and in all that is suggested by one's own mind, only something to confirm the conclusion already arrived at. It must be often a very painful thing to have what may be termed *a judicial mind* — that is, a mind so entirely free from bias of its own, that in forming its opinion upon any subject, it is decided simply by the merits of the case as set before it; for the arguments on either side are sometimes all but exactly balanced. Yet it may be necessary to say yes to the one side and no to the other; it may be impossible to make a compromise — i. e., to say to both sides at once both yes and no. And if great issues depend upon the conclusion come to, a conscientious man may undergo an indescribable distraction and anguish before he concludes what to believe or to do. If a man be lord-

chancellor, or general commanding an army in action,
there must often be a keen misery in the incapacity to
decide which of two competing courses has most to say
for itself. Oh, that every question could be answered
rightly by either yes or no ! Oh, that one side in every
quarrel, in every debate, were decidedly right, and the
other decidedly wrong ! Or, if *that* cannot be, the next
blessing that is to be desired by a human being who
wishes to be of use where God has put him in this world,
is, the gift of vigorous and intelligent one-sidedness ; for
in practice conflicting views are often so nearly balanced,
and the loss of time and energy caused by indecision is
so great, that it is better to adopt the wrong view resolutely, and act upon it unhesitatingly, than to adopt the
right view dubiously, and take the right path falteringly,
and often looking back. And one feels somehow as if
there were something degrading in indecision ; something
manly and dignified in a vigorous will, provided that vigorous will be barely clear of the charge of blind, uncal-
culating obstinacy. For the spiritual is unquestionably a
higher thing than the material, the living is better than
the inert, the man than the machine. But the judicial
mind approaches to the nature of a machine. It seems
to lack the power of originating action ; to be determined
entirely by foreign forces. It is simply a very delicate
pair of scales. In one scale you put all that can be said
on one side, in the other scale you put all that can be
said on the other side, and the beam passively follows the
greater weight. Of course, the analogy between the
physical and the spiritual is never perfect. The scales
which weigh argument differ in various respects from the
scales which weigh sugar or tea. The material weighing-
machine accepts its weights at the value marked upon

them, while the spiritual weighing-machine has the additional anguish of deciding whether the argument put into it shall be esteemed as an ounce, a pound, or a ton.

All this which has been said has been keenly felt by the writer in thinking of the subject of the present essay. I am sorry now that I did not begin to write it sooner. I could then have taken my side without a scruple, and have expressed an opinion which would have been resolute if not perfectly right. Various facts which came within my observation impressed upon me the fact that, in the judgment of very many people, there is a dignity about dulness. Various considerations suggested themselves as tending to prove that it is absurd to regard dulness as a dignified thing ; and the business of the essay was designed to be, first to state and illustrate the common view, and next, to show that the common view is absurd. But who is there that does not know how in most instances, if it strikes you on a first glance that the majority of mankind hold and act upon a belief that is absurd, longer thought shakes your confident opinion, and ultimately you land in the conviction that the majority of mankind are quite right ? The length of time requisite to reach those second thoughts which are proverbially best, varies much. It seems to require a lifetime (at least for men of warm heart and quick brain) to arrive at calm. enduring sense in the complications of political and social science.

In the mellow autumn of his days, the man who started as a republican, communist, and atheist, has settled (never again to be moved) into liberal conservatism and unpretending Christianity. It requires two or three years (reckoning from the first inoculation with the poison) to return to common sense in metaphysics. For myself, it cost a week of constant thought to reach my present wit-stand, which may be briefly expressed as follows. Although many men carry their belief in the dignity of dulness to an unjustifiable excess, yet there is no small amount of sense in the doctrine of the dignity of dulness. Thus, in the lengthening light of various April evenings, did the writer muse ; thus, while looking at many crocuses, yellow in the sun of several April mornings. Why is it, thought I, that dulness is dignified? Why is it, that to write a book which no mortal can read, because it is so heavy and uninteresting, is a more dignified thing than to write a book so pleasing and attractive that it shall be read (not as work, but as play) by thousands? Why is it that any article, essay, or treatise, which handles a grave subject and propounds grave truth, only in an interesting and readable style, is at once marked with the black cross of contempt, by being referred to the class of *light literature*, and spoken of as flimsy, flashy, slight, and the like ; while a treatise on the self-same subject, setting out the self-same views, only in a ponderous, wearisome, unreadable, and (in brief) *dull* fashion, is regarded as a composition solid, substantial, and eminently respectable? Is it not hard, that by many stupid people a sermon is esteemed as deep, massive, theological, solid, simply because it is such that they find they cannot for their lives attend to it ; and another sermon is held as flimsy, superficial, flashy, light, simply because it attracts or compels their attention? And I saw that the doctrine of the dignity of dulness, as held by commonplace people, is at the first glance mischievous and absurd, and apparently invented by stupid men for their encouragement in their stupidity. But gradually the thought developed itself, that rapidity of movement is inconsis-

tent with dignity. Dignity is essentially a slow thing.
Agility of mind, no less than of body, befits it not. Rapid
processes of thought, quick turns of feeling — a host of
the little arts and characteristics which give interest to
composition — have too much of the nimble and mercu-
rial about them. A harlequin in ceaseless motion is undignified ; a chief justice, sitting very still on the bench
and scarcely moving, save his hands and head, is tolerably dignified ; the king of Siam at a state pageant, sitting
in a gallery in a sumptuous dress, and so immovable,
even to his eyes, that foreign ambassadors have doubted
whether he were not a wax figure, is very dignified ; but
the most dignified of all in the belief of millions of people
of extraordinary stupidity was the Hindoo deity Brahm,
who through innumerable ages remained in absolute quiescence, never stirring, and never doing anything whatever. So here, I thought, is the key of the mystery.
There is a general prepossession that slowness has more
dignity than agility ; and a particular application of this
general prepossession leads to a common belief, sometimes
grossly absurd, sometimes not without reason, that dulness is a dignified thing.

Would you know, my youthful reader, how to earn the
high estimation of the great majority of steady-going old
gentlemen? I will tell you how. You have, in the
morning, attended a public meeting for some religious or
benevolent purposes. Many speeches were made there.
In the evening you meet at dinner a grave and cautious
man, advanced in years, whom you beheld in a seat of
eminence on the platform, and you begin to discourse of the
speeches with him. Call to your remembrance the speech
you liked best — the interesting, stirring, thrilling one
that wakened you up when the others had wellnigh sent

you to sleep — the speech that you held your breath to
listen to, and that made your nerves tingle and your
heart beat faster, and say to the old gentleman, ' Do you
remember Mr. A.'s speech? Mere flash! Very superficial. Flimsy. All figures and flowers. Flights of
fancy. Nothing solid. Very well for superficial people,
but nothing there for people who think.' Then fix on
the very dullest and heaviest of all the speeches made.
Fix on the speech that you could not force yourself to
listen to, though, when you did by a great effort follow
two or three sentences, you saw it was very good sense,
but insufferably dull ; and say to the old gentleman,
' Very different with the speech of Mr. B. Ah, there
was mind *there !* Something that you could grasp !
Good sound sense. No flash. None of your extravagant
flights of imagination. Admirable matter. Who cares
for oratory ? Give me substance !' Say all this, my
youthful reader, to the solid old gentleman, and you will
certainly be regarded by him as a young man of sound
sense, and with taste and judgment mature beyond your
years. And if you wish to deepen the favourable impression you have made, you may go on to complain of the
triviality of modern literature. Say that you think the
writings of Mr. Thackeray wearisome and unimproving ;
for your part, you would rather read the sermons of Doctor Log. Say that *Fraser's Magazine* is flippant : you
prefer the *Journal of the Statistical Society.* You cannot go wrong. You have an unerring rule. You have
merely to consider what things, books, speeches, articles,
sermons, you find most dull and stupid : then declare in
their favour. Acknowledge the grand principle of the
dignity of dulness. So shall the old gentleman tell his
fellows that you have ' got a head.' There is ' something

in you.' You are an 'uncommon fine young man.' The truth meanwhile will be, either that you are an impostor, shamming what you do not think, or a man of most extraordinary and anomalous tastes, or an incorrigible blockhead.

But whatever you may be yourself, do not fall into error in your judgment of the old gentleman and his compeers. Do not think of him uncharitably. If he made a speech at the meeting, you may be ready to conclude that the reason why he preferred the dull speech to the brilliant one is, that his own speech was very, very dull. And no doubt, in some cases, it is envy and jealousy that prompt the commonplace man to underrate the brilliant appearances of the brilliant man. It must be a most soothing thought to the ambitious man of inferior ability that the speech, sermon, or volume which greatly surpasses his own shall be regarded by many as not so good as his own, just because it is so incomparably better. It would be a pleasing arrangement for all race-horses which are lame and broken-winded, that because Eclipse distances the field so far, Eclipse shall therefore be adjudged to have lost the race. And precisely analogous is the floating belief in many commonplace minds, that if a discourse or composition be brilliant, it cannot be solid; that if it be interesting, this proves it to be flimsy. No doubt brilliancy is sometimes attained at the expense of solidity; no doubt some writings and speeches are interesting whose body of thought is very slight; which, as Scotch people say, *have very little in them*. But the vulgar belief on this matter really amounts to this: that if a speech, sermon, or book be very good, this proves it to be very bad. And as most people who produce such things produce very bad ones, you may easily see how willingly this belief is accepted by most people. Still, this does

not entirely explain the opinion expressed by the old gentleman already mentioned.   It does not necessarily follow
that he declares the speech of Mr. A. to be bad simply
because he knows it was provokingly good, nor that he
declares the speech of Mr. B. to be good simply because
he knows it was soothingly bad.   The old gentleman may
have been almost or even entirely sincere in the opinion
he expressed.

By long habit, and by pushing into an extreme a belief which has a *substratum* of truth, he may have come
to regard with suspicion the speech which interests him,
and to take for granted, with little examination of the fact
of the case, that it *must* be flimsy and slight, else he
could not take it in so pleasantly and easily.   And all
this founds not merely on the grand principle of the dignity of dulness, but likewise on the impassable nature of
the gulf which parts instruction from amusement, work
from play.   Work, it is assumed as an axiom, is of the
nature of pain.   To get solid instruction costs exertion:
it is work : it is a painful thing.   And the consequence
is, that when a man of great skill and brilliant talent is
able to present solid instruction in a guise so attractive
that it becomes pleasant instead of painful to receive it,
you are startled.   Your suspicions are aroused.   You begin to think that he must have sacrificed the solid and
the useful.   This cannot be work, you think : it must be
play, for it is pleasant.   This cannot be instruction, you
think : it must be amusement, for it is easy and agreeable
to follow it.   This cannot be a right sermon, you think,
for it does not put me asleep : it must be a flimsy and
flashy declamation : or some such disparaging expression
is used.   This cannot be the normal essay, you think, for
you read it through without yawning; you don't know

25

what is wrong, but you are safe in saying that its order of thought must be very light; the fact that you could read it without yawning proves that it is so. You forget the alternative, that solid and weighty thought, both in essay and sermon, may have been made easy to follow, by the interesting fashion in which they were put before you. But stupid people forget this alternative: they never think of it, or they reject it at the first mention of it. It is too absurd. It ignores the vital difference between work and play. Try a parallel case with an unsophisticated understanding, and you will see how ingrained in our nature is this prejudice. Your little boy is ill. He must have some medicine. You give him some of a most nauseous taste. He takes it, and feels certain that it will make him well. It *must* be medicine, he knows; and good medicine; because it is so abominably disagreeable. But give the little man some healing balm (if you can find it) whose taste is pleasant. He is surprised. His faith in the medicine is shaken. It wont make him well; it cannot be right medicine; because to take it is not painful or disagreeable. A poor girl in the parish was dying of consumption. Her parents had heard of cod-liver oil. They got the livers of certain cod-fish and manufactured oil for themselves. It was hideous to see, to smell, and to taste. I procured a bottle of the proper oil, and took it up to my poor parishioner. But it was plain that neither she nor her parents had much faith in it. It was not disgusting. It had little taste or odor. It was easy to take. And it was plain, though the girl used it to please me, that the belief in the cottage was, that by eliminating the disgusting element, you eliminated the virtue of the oil: in brief, that when medicine ceases to be disagreeable, it ceases to be useful. There is in human nature an inveterate tendency to judge so. And it was this inveterate tendency, much more than any spirit of envy or jealousy, that was at the foundation of the old man's opinion, that the dull speech or sermon was the best; that the interesting speech or sermon was flimsy. All the virtue of the cod-liver oil was there, though the nauseous accompaniments were gone; and solid thought and sound reasoning may have been present in quantity as abundant and quality as admirable in the interesting speech as in the dull one; but it is to be confessed the *à priori* presumption was the other way. There must be something — you don't know what — wrong about the work which is as pleasant as play. There must be something — you cannot say what — amiss about the sermon which is as interesting as a novel. It cannot be sound instruction, which is as agreeable as amusement; any more than black can be white, or pain can be pleasure. *That* is the unspoken, undefined, uneradicable belief of the dull majority of human kind. And it appears, day by day, in the depreciatory terms in which stupid, and even commonplace, people talk of compositions which are brilliant, interesting, and attractive, as though the fact of their possessing these characteristics were proof sufficient that they lack solidity and sound sense.

Now, the root of the prevalent error (so far as it is an error) appears to me to lie in this; that sound instruction and solid thought are regarded as analogous to *medicine;* whereas they ought to be regarded as analogous to *food.* It may possibly be assumed, that medicine is a thing such in its essential nature, that to be useful, it must be disagreeable. But I believe that it is now universally admitted, that the food which is most pleasant to take, is the most wholesome and nutritious. The time is past in which philosophic and strong-minded persons thought it a fine thing to cry up a Spartan repulsiveness in the matter of diet. Raw steaks, cut from a horse which died a natural death; and the sour milk of mares, are no longer considered the provender upon which to raise men who shall be of necessity either thoughtful or heroic. Unhappily, in the matter of the dietetics of the mind, the old notion still prevails with very many. And there is something to be said for it; but only what might also be said for it in regard to the food of the body. For though, as a general rule, the most agreeable food is the most wholesome, yet there is an extensive kingdom into which this law does not extend; I mean the domain of sugar-plums, of pastry, of crystallized fruits, and the like. These are pleasant; but you cannot live upon them; and you ought not to take much at a time. And if you give a child the unlimited run of such materials for eating, the child will assuredly be the worse for it. Well, in mental food the analogy holds. Here, too, is a realm of sweets, of devilled bones, of curaçoa. Feverish poetry, ultra-sentimental romance, eccentric wit and humour, are the parallel things. Rabelais, Sterne, *The Doctor* of Southey, the poetry of Mrs. Hemans, the plays of Otway, Marlowe, Ford, and Dekker, may all, in limited quantity, be partaken of with relish and advantage by the healthy appetite; but let there not be too much of them; and do not think to nourish your intellectual nature on such food alone. No child, shiny with excessive pastry, or toothaching and sulky through superabundant sugar-plums, is in a plight more morbid and disagreeable than is the clever boy or girl of eighteen, who from the dawn of the taste for reading, has been turned into a large library to choose books at will, and who has crammed an inexperi-

enced head and undisciplined heart with extravagant fancies and unreal feelings from an exclusive diet of novels
and plays.   But, setting aside the department of sweets, I
maintain, that given wholesome food, the more agreeably
it is cooked and served up, the better; and given sound
thought, the more interesting and attractive the guise in
which it is presented, the better.   And all this may be,
without the least sacrifice of the sound and substantial
qualities.   No matter what you are writing — sermon,
article, book — let Sydney Smith's principle be remembered, that *every style is good, except the tiresome.*   And
who does not know, that there have been men who, without the least sacrifice of solidity, have invested all they
had to say with an enchaining interest ; and led the reader
through the most abstruse metaphysics, the closest reasoning, the most intricate mazes of history, the gravest
doctrines of theology, in such fashion that the reader was
profited while he thought he was only being delighted,
and charmed while he was informed !

The thing has been done ; of course it is very difficult
to do it ; and to do it demands remarkable gifts of nature
and training.   The extraordinary thing is that where a
man has, by much pains, or by extraordinary felicity,
added interest to utility, — given you solid thought in an
attractive form, — many people will, and that not entirely
of envy, but through *bonâ fide* stupidity, at once say that
the interesting sermon, the picturesque history, the lively
argument, is flimsy and flashy, superficial, wanting in
depth, and so forth.   Yet if you think it unpardonable in
the cook, who has excellent food given to prepare, to send
it up spoiled and barely eatable, is it not quite as bad in
the man who has given to him important facts, solemn
doctrines, weighty reasons, yet who presents them to his

readers or hearers in a tough, dry, stupid shape? Does
the turbot, the saddle of mutton, cease to be nutritious
because it is well cooked? And wherefore, then, should
the doctrine or argument become flimsy because it is put
skilfully and interestingly? I do believe there are people
who think that in the world of mind, if a good beef-steak
be well cooked, it turns in the process into a stick of bar-
ley-sugar.

To this class belongs the great majority of stupid
people, and also of quiet, steady-going people, of fair
average ability. Among the latter there is not only a
dislike of clever men, arising from envy: but a real
honest fear of what they may do, arising from a belief
that a very clever man cannot be a safe or judicious
man, and that a striking view cannot be a sound view.
Once upon a time, in a certain church, I heard a sermon preached by a certain great preacher. The congregation listened with breathless attention. The sermon
was indeed a very remarkable one; and I remember
well how I thought that never before had I understood the magic spell which is exerted by fervid eloquence. And walking away from church, I was looking
back upon the track of thought over which the preacher
had borne the congregation, and thinking how skilfully
and admirably he had carried his hearers, easily and
interestedly, through very difficult ground, and over a
very long journey. Thus musing, I encountered a very
stupid clergyman who had been in church too. 'Did
you hear Mr. M——?' said he. 'It was mere flash;
very flimsy; all flowers. Nothing solid.' With wonder
I regarded my stupid friend. I said to him: Strip
off from the sermon all the fancy and all the feeling;
look at the bare skeleton of thought: and then I stated

it to the man. Is not *that*, said I, a marvel of metaphysical acuteness, of rigorous logic, of exact symmetry?
Cut off the flash as you call it; here is the solid re-
siduum; is *that* slight or flashy? Is there not three
times the thought of ordinary humdrum sermons even
in quantity, not to name the incalculable difference in
the matter of quality? On this latter point, indeed, I
did not insist; for with some folk quantity is the only
measure of thought; and in the world of ideas a turnip
is with such equal to a pineapple, provided they be of
the same size. 'Don't you see,' said I, with growing
wrath, to my stupid friend, who regarded me meanwhile
with a stolid stare, 'that it only shows what an admirable preacher Mr. M—— is, if he was able to carry a
whole congregation in rapt attention along a line of
thought, in traversing which you and I would have put
all our hearers asleep? You and I might possibly have
given the thought like the diamond as it comes from the
mine, a dull pebble; and because that eminent man
gave it polished and glancing, is it therefore not a diamond still?' Of course, it was vain to talk. The
stolid preacher kept by his one idea. The sermon
could not be solid, because it was brilliant. Because
there was gleam and glitter, there could not be anything besides. What more could be said? I knew that
my stupid friend had on his side the majority of the
race.

It is irritating when you have written an essay with
care, after a great deal of thought, to find people talk
slightingly of it as very light. 'The essays of Mr.
Q—— are sensible and well written, but the order of
thought is of the lightest.' I found these words in a
review of certain essays, written by a man who had

evidently read the essays. Ask people what they mean
by such vague phrases of disparagement; and if you
can get them to analyze their feeling, you will find that
in five cases out of six, they mean simply that they can
read the compositions with interest? Is *that* anything
against them? *That* does not touch the question whether
they are weighty and sound. They may be sound and
weighty for all that. Of course, that which is called
severe thought cannot, however skilfully put and illustrated, be so easily followed by undisciplined minds.
But in most cases the people who talk of a man's writings being light, know nothing at all about severe thinking. They mean that they are sure that an essay is
solid, if they find it uninteresting. It must be good if
it be a weary task to get through it. The lack of interest is the great test that the composition is of a high
order. It must be dignified, because it is so dull. You
read it with pleasure; therefore it must be flimsy. You
read it with weariness: therefore it must be solid. Or,
to put the principle in its simplest form — the essay
must be bad because it is so good. The essay must be
good, because it is so bad. Here we have the foundation principle of the grand doctrine of the dignity of
dulness.

And, by hosts of people, the principle is unsparingly
applied. An interesting book is flimsy, because it is
interesting. An interesting sermon is flimsy, because it
is interesting. They are referred to the class of light
literature. And it is undignified to be light. It is
grand, it is clerical, it is worthy of a cabinet minister,
it is even archiepiscopal, to write a book which no one
would voluntarily read. But some stupid people think
it unclerical to write a book which sensible folk will

read with pleasure.   It would amuse Mr. Kingsley, and I am sure it would do no more than amuse him, to hear what I have heard steady-going individuals say about his writings.   The question whether the doctrines he enforces be true or not, they cared not for at all.   Neither did they inquire whether or not he enforces, with singular fervor and earnestness, certain doctrines of far-reaching practical moment.   *That* matters not.   He enforces them in books which it is interesting and even enchaining to read ; and this suffices (in their judgment) to condemn these books.   I have heard stupid people say that it was not worthy of Archbishop Whately to write those admirable *Annotations on Bacon's Essays*. No doubt that marvellously acute intellect does in those *Annotations* apply itself to a great variety of themes and purposes, greater and lesser, like a steam-hammer which can weld a huge mass of red-hot iron, and with equal facility drive a nail into a plank by successive gentle taps.   No doubt the volume sometimes discusses grave matters in a grave manner, and sometimes matters less grave (but still with a serious bearing on life and its affairs) in a playful manner.   But on the whole, if you wished to convey to a stranger to the archbishop's writings (supposing that among educated people you could find one) some notion of the extent and versatility of his powers, it is probable that, of all his books, *this* is the one you would advise the stranger to read.   ' Not so,' said my friend Dr. Log.   'The archbishop should not have published such a work.'

Who ever heard of an archbishop who wrote a book which young men and women would read because they enjoyed it ?   The book could not be dignified, because it was not dull.   Why did the steady old gentlemen

among the fellows of a certain college in the university
of Cambridge, a good many years ago, turn out and
vote against a certain clergyman's becoming their head,
who was infinitely the most distinguished of their number, and upon whose becoming their head every one had
counted with certainty? He was a very distinguished
scholar, a very successful tutor : a man of dignified manners and irreproachable character. Had he been no
more, he had been the head of his college, and he had
been a bishop now. But there was an objection which,
in the minds of these frail but steady old gentlemen,
could not be got over. *His sermons were interesting!*
His warmest friends could not say that they were dull.
When he came to do his duty as select preacher before
the university, the church wherein he preached was
crowded to excess. Not merely was the unbecoming
spectacle witnessed of all the pews being filled ; but it
could not be concealed that the passages were crowded
with human beings who were content to stand throughout the service. The old gentlemen could not bear this.
The head of a college must be dignified ; and how could
a man be dignified who was not dull, even in the pulpit ? The younger fellows were unanimous in the great
preacher's favour ; but the old gentlemen formed the
majority, and they were unanimous against him. Some
people suggested that they were envious of his greater
eminence : that they wished to put down the man who,
at a comparatively early age, had so vastly surpassed
themselves. The theory was uncharitable ; it was more
— it was false. Jealousy had little part in the minds of
these frail but safe old men. They honestly believed
that the great preacher could not be solid or dignified,
because he was brilliant and attractive. They never

heard his sermons; but they were sure that something must be wrong about the sermons, because multitudes wished to hear them. Is not the normal feeling after listening to a sermon to its close, one of gentle, unexpressed relief? The great preacher was rejected, and an excellent man was elected in his stead, who could not fail to be dignified, for never mortal was more dull. Cardinal Wiseman tells us very frankly that the great principle of the dignity of dulness is always recognized and acted on by the gentlemen who elect the pope. Gravity, approaching to stolidity; slowness of motion, approaching to entire standing-still; are (as a general rule) requisite in the human beings who succeed to the chair of St. Peter. It has been insinuated that in the Church of England similar characteristics are (or at least were) held essential in those who are made bishops, and, above all, archbishops. You can never be sure that a man will not do wrong who is likely to do anything at all. But if it be perfectly ascertained that a man will do nothing, you may be satisfied that he will do nothing wrong. This is one consideration; but the further one is the pure and simple dignity of dulness. A clergyman may look forward to a bishopric if he write books which are unreadable, but not if he write books which are readable. The chance of Dr. Log is infinitely better than that of Mr. Kingsley. And nothing can be more certain than that the principle of the dignity of dulness kept the mitre from the head of Sydney Smith. I do not mean to say that he was a suitable man to be a bishop. I think he was not. But it was not because of anything really unclerical about the genial man that he was excluded. The people who excluded him did not hesitate to appoint men obnoxious to more serious charges than Sydney Smith. But then, whatever these men were or were not, they were all dull. They wrote much, some of them; but nobody ever read what they wrote. But Sydney Smith was interesting. You could read his writings with pleasure. He was unquestionably the reverse of dull, and therefore certainly the reverse of dignified. Through much of his latter life the same suspicion has, with millions of safe-going folk, thrown a shadow on Lord Brougham. He was too lively. What he wrote was too interesting. Solid old gentlemen feared for his good sense. They thought they never could be sure what he would do next. Even Lord St. Leonards lost standing with many when he published his *Handy Book on Property Law.* A lord-chancellor writing a book sold at railway stations. and read (with interest, too) in railway carriages! What was the world coming to? But it was quite becoming in the great man to produce that elaborate and authoritative work on *Vendors and Purchasers,* of which I have often beheld the outside, but never the inside. And wherefore did the book beseem a chancellor? Wherefore but because to the ordinary reader it was heavy as lead. Have not you, my reader, often heard like criticism of Lord Campbell's interesting volumes of the biography of his predecessors? 'Very interesting; very well written; much curious information; but not quite the thing for the first man on the judicial bench of Britain to write.' Now, upon what is this criticism founded, but upon the grand principle that liveliness and interest do not become the compositions of a man in important office: in brief, that *that* is not dignified, which is not dull.

But let us not be extreme. Let it be admitted that the

principle has some measure of truth. There are facts which appear to give it countenance, which really do give it countenance. *Punch* is more interesting than a sermon, *that* is admitted as a fact. The tacit inference is that an interesting sermon must have become interesting by unduly approximating to *Punch*. There is literature which may properly be termed light. There is thought which is superficial, flimsy, slight, and so on. There are compositions which are brilliant without being solid, in which there are many flowers and little fruit. And no doubt, by the nature of things, this light and flashy thought is more interesting, and more easily followed, than more solid material. You can read *Vanity Fair* when you could not read Butler's *Analogy*. You can read *Punch* when you could not read *Vanity Fair*. And the *à priori* presumption may be, when you find a composition of a grave class which is as interesting as one of a lighter class, that this interest has been attained by some sacrifice of the qualities which beseem a composition of a grave class. Let our rule be as follows : If the treatise under consideration be interesting because it treats of light subjects, which in themselves are more interesting than grave ones (as play always must be more pleasing than work), let the treatise be classed as light. But if in the treatise you find grave and serious thoughts set out in such a fashion as to be interesting, then all honour to the author of that treatise ! He is not a slight, superficial writer, though stupid people may be ready to call him so. He is, in truth, a grave and serious writer, though he has succeeded in charming while he instructs. He is truly dignified, though he be not dull. He is doing a noble work, enforcing a noble principle : the noble principle, to wit (which most people silently assume is false), that what is right need not of necessity be so very much less attractive than what is wrong. The general belief is, that right is prosy, humdrum, commonplace, dull; and that the poetry of existence, the gleam, the music, the thrill, the romance, are with delightful wrong. And taking work as the first meridian, marking what is right, many people really hold that any approximation to play (and all that interests and pleases is in so far an approximation to play) is a deflection in the direction of wrong, inasmuch as it is beyond question a marked departure from the line of ascertained right. Let us get rid of the notion! In morals, the opposite of right need not be wrong. Many things are right, and their opposites right too. Work is right. Play is the opposite of work, yet play is right too. Gravity is right: interest is right too; and though practically these two things seem opposed, they need not be so. And as we should bless the man who would teach us how to idealize our work into play, so should we bless the man who is able to blend gravity and interest together. Such a man as Macaulay was virtually spreading the flag of defiance in the face of stupid people holding a stupid belief, and declaring by every page he wrote, that what is right need not be unpleasant; that what is interesting need not be flimsy; that what is dignified need not be dull.

I am well aware that it is hopeless to argue with a prejudice so rooted as that in favour of the dignity of dulness; and especially hopeless when I am obliged to admit that I cannot entirely oppose that principle, that I feel a certain justice in it. Slowness of motion, I have said, is essentially more dignified than rapidity of motion. There is something dignified about an elephant walking along, with massive tramp; there is nothing dignified

about a frisking greyhound, light, airy, graceful. And
it is to be admitted that some men frisk through a
subject like a greyhound; others tramp through it like
an elephant. And though the playful greyhound fashion
of writing, that dallies and toys with a subject, may be the
more graceful and pleasing, the dignity doubtless abides
with the stern, slow, straightforward, elephantine tramp.
The *Essays of Elia* delight you, but you stand in no awe
of their author; the contrary is the case with a charge of
Lord Chief-Justice Ellenborough. And so thoroughly
elephantine are the mental movements of some men, that
even their rare friskiness is elephantine. Every one
must know this who is at all acquainted with the ponderous and cowlike curvetings of the *Rambler*. Physical
agility is inconsistent with physical dignity; mental agility with mental dignity. You could not for your life
very greatly esteem the solemn advices given you from
the pulpit on Sunday, by a clergyman whom you had
seen whirling about in a polka on Friday evening. The
momentum of that rotary movement would cling to
him (in your feeling) still. I remember when I was a
little boy what a shock it was to my impressions of judicial dignity to see a departed chief justice cantering down
Constitution-hill on a tall, thoroughbred chestnut. The
swift movement befitted not my recollections of the judg-
ment-seat, the ermine, the great full-bottomed wig. I felt
aggrieved and mortified even by the tallness and slender-
ness of the chestnut horse. Had the judge been mounted
on a dray horse of enormous girth and vast breadth
(even if not very high) I should have been comparatively
content. Breadth was the thing desiderated by the
youthful heart; breadth, and the solidity which goes
with breadth, and the slowness of motion which goes with

solid extension, and the dignity which goes with slowness
of motion. I speak of impression made on the undisciplined human soul, doubtless; but then the normal impression made by anything is the impression it makes on
the undisciplined human soul. In the world of mind,
you may educate human nature into a condition in which
all tendencies shall be reversed; in which fire shall wet
you, and water dry you. Who does not know that the
estimation in which the humbler folk of a rural parish
regard their clergyman, depends in a great degree upon
his physical size? A man six feet high will command
greater reverence than one of five feet six; but if the man
of five feet six in height be six feet in circumference,
then he will command greater reverence than the man of
six feet in height, provided the latter be thin. And after
great reflection, I am led to the conclusion, that the true
cause of this bucolic dignity does not abide in mere size.
Dignity, even in the country, is not in direct proportion
to extension, as such. No; it is in direct proportion to that slowness of movement which comes of solid
extension. A man who walks very fast is less dignified
than a man who walks very slow; and that which con-
duces to the slow, ponderous, measured step, is a valuable
accessory to personal dignity. But the connection is not
so essential as the unthinking might conclude between
personal dignity and personal bulk. Now, the composition, whether written or spoken, of some men, is (so to
speak) a display of mental agility. It is the result of
rapid mental movements, you can see. Not with massive
heaves and sinkings, like the engines of an ocean steam-
ship, did the mental machinery play that turned off such
a book, such a speech, such an essay; but rather with
rapid jerkings of little cranks, and invisible whirlings of

little wheels.   And the thing manufactured is pretty, not
grand.   It is very nice.   You conclude that as the big
steam-engine cannot play very fast, so the big mind too.
The mind that can go at a tremendous pace. you conclude
to be a little mind.   The mind that can skip about, you
conclude cannot be a massive mind.   There are truth and
falsehood in your conclusion.   Very great minds, guided
by very comprehensive views, have with lightning-like
promptitude rushed to grand decisions and generaliza-
tions.   But it cannot be denied that ponderous machinery,
physical and mental, generally moves slowly.   And in
the mental world, many folk readily suppose that the machinery which moves slowly is certainly ponderous.   A
man who gets up to speak in a deliberative assembly, and
with a deep voice from an extensive chest, and inscruta-
ble meaning depicted on massive features, slowly states
his views, with long pauses between the members of his
sentences, and very long pauses between his sentences,
will by many people be regarded as making a speech
which is very heavy metal indeed.   Possibly it may be;
possibly it may not.   I ought to say, that the most telling
deliberative speaker I ever heard, speaks in that slow
fashion.   But when *he* speaks on an important subject
which interests him, every deliberate word goes home
like a cannon-ball.   He speaks in eighty-four pounders.
But I have heard men as slow, who spoke in large soap-
bubbles.   And of all lightness of thought, deliver us from
ponderous lightness !   Nothings are often excusable, and
sometimes pleasing ; but pompous nothings are always
execrable.   I have known men who, morally speaking,
gave away tickets for very inferior parish soup with the
air of one freely dispensing invitations to the most sumptuous banquet that ever was provided by mortal.   Oh !

26

to stick in a skewer, and see the great wind-bag collapse!

You do not respect the jackpudding who amuses you, though he may amuse you remarkably well. The more you laugh at him, the less you respect him. And, to the vulgar apprehension, any man who amuses you, or who approaches towards amusing you, or who produces anything which interests you (which is an approximation towards amusing you), will be regarded as, *quoad hoc*, approaching undignifiedly in the direction of the jackpudding. The only way in which to make sure that not even the vulgarest mind shall discern this approximation, is to instruct while you carefully avoid interesting, and still more amusing, even in the faintest degree. Even wise men cannot wholly divest themselves of the prejudice. You cannot but feel an inconsistency between the ideas of Mr. Disraeli writing *Henrietta Temple*, and Mr. Disraeli leading the House of Commons. You feel that somehow it costs an effort to feel that there is nothing unbefitting when the author of *The Caxtons* becomes a secretary of state. You fancy, at the first thought, that you would have had greater confidence in some sound, steady, solid old gentleman, who never amused or interested you in any way. The office to be filled is a dignified one; and how can a man befit a dignified office who has interested and amused you so much?

But the consideration which above all others leads the sober majority of mankind to respect and value decent and well-conducted dulness, is the consideration of the outrageous practical folly, and the insufferable wickedness, which many men of genius appear to have regarded it their prerogative to indulge in. You can quite understand how plain, sensible people may abhor an eccentric

genius, and wish rather for sound principle and sound
sense. And probably most men whose opinion is of much
value, would be thankful to have decent dulness in their
nearest relations, rather than the brilliant aberrations of
such men as Shelley, Byron, and Coleridge. Give us the
plain man who will do his work creditably in life; who
will support his children and pay his debts; rather than
the very clever man who fancies that his cleverness sets
him free from all the laws which bind commonplace mortals; who does not think himself called upon to work for
his bread, but sponges upon industrious men, or howls out
because the nation will not support him in idleness; who
wonders at the sordid tradesman who asks him to pay for
the clothes he wears, and leaves his children to be educated by any one who takes a fancy for doing so; who
violates all the dictates of common morality and common
prudence, and blasphemes because he gets into trouble by
doing so; who will not dress, or eat, or sleep like other
men; who wears round jackets to annoy his wife, and
scribbles *Atheist* after his name in traveller's books; and
in brief, who is distinguished by no characteristic so
marked as the entire absence of common sense. I think,
reader, that if you were sickened by a visit of a month's
duration from one of these geniuses you would resolve
that for the remainder of your life only dull, commonplace,
respectable mortals should ever come under your roof.
Let us be thankful that the days in which high talent
was generally associated with such eccentricities are
happily passing away. Clever men are now content to
dress, look, and talk like beings of this world; and above
all, they appear to understand that however clever a man
may be, that is no reason why he should not pay his butcher's bill. How fine a character was that of Sir Walter

Scott combining homely sense with great genius! And how different from the hectic, morbid, unprincipled, and indeed blackguard mental organization of various brilliant men of the last age, was Shakspeare's calm and well-balanced mind! It is only the second-rate genius who is eccentric, and only the tenth-rate who is unintelligible.

But if one is driven to a warm sympathy with the humdrum and decently dull, by contemplating the absurdities and vagaries of men of real genius, even more decidedly is that result produced by contemplating the ridiculous little curvetings and prancings of affectedly eccentric men of no genius. You know, my reader, the provincial celebrity of daily life; you know what a nuisance he is. You know how almost every little country town in Britain has its eminent man — its man of letters. He has written a book, or it is whispered that he writes in certain periodicals, and simple human beings, who know nothing of proof-sheets, look upon him with a certain awe. He varies in age and appearance. If young, he wears a moustache and long, dishevelled hair; if old, a military cloak, which he disposes in a brigand form. He walks the street with an abstracted air, as though his thoughts were wandering beyond the reach of the throng. He is fond of solitude, and he gratifies his taste by going to the most frequented places within reach, and there assuming a look of rapt isolation. Sometimes he may be seen to gesticulate wildly, and to dig his umbrella into the pavement as though it were a foeman's breast. Occasionally moody laughter may be heard to proceed from him, as from one haunted by fearful thoughts. His fat and rosy countenance somewhat belies the anguish which is preying upon his vitals. He goes much to tea-parties, where he tells the girls that the bloom of life has gone for him, and drops dark hints of the mental agony he endures in reviewing his earlier life. He bids them not to ask what is the grief that consumes him, but to be thankful that they do not, cannot know. He drops hints how the spectres of the past haunt him at the midnight hour : how conscience smites him with chilly hand for his youthful sins. The truth is that he was always a very quiet lad, and never did any harm to anybody. Occasionally, when engaged in conversation with some one on whom he wishes to make an impression, he exclaims, suddenly, ' Hold! let me register that thought.' He pauses for a minute, gazing intently on the heavens ; then exclaims, ' 'Tis done ! ' and takes up the conversation where it was interrupted. He fancies that his companion thinks him a great genius. His companion, in fact, thinks him a poor silly fool.

And now, my friend, turning away from these matters, let us sit down on this large stone, warm in the April sunshine, by the river side. Swiftly the river glides away. The sky is bright blue, the water is crystal clear, and a soft wind comes through those budding branches. In the field on the other side I see a terrier and a cow. The terrier frisks about ; solemnly stands the cow. Let us think here for a while ; we need not talk. And for an accompaniment to the old remembrances which such a day as this brings back, let us have the sound of that flowing river.

CHAPTER XIII.

CONCERNING GROWING OLD.

 WAS sitting, on a very warm and bright summer morning, upon a gravestone in the churchyard. It was a flat gravestone, elevated upon four little pillars, and covering the spot where sleeps the mortal part of a venerable clergyman who preceded me in my parish, and who held the charge of it for sixty years. I had gone down to the churchyard, as usual, for a while after breakfast, with a little companion, who in those days was generally with me wherever I went. And while she was walking about, attended by a solemn dog, I sat down in the sunshine on the stone, gray with lichen, and green with moss. I thought of the old gentleman who had slept below for fifty years. I wondered if he had sometimes come to the churchyard after breakfast before he began his task of sermon-writing. I reflected how his heart, mouldered into dust, was now so free from all the little heats and worries which will find their way into even the quietest life in this world. And sitting there, I put my right hand upon the mossy stone. The contrast of the hand upon the green surface caught the eye of my companion, who was not four years old. She came slowly up, and laid down her own hand beside mine on the mossy expanse. And after

looking at it in various ways for several minutes, and contrasting her own little hand with the weary one which is now writing this page, she asked, thoughtfully and doubtfully. — Was your hand ever a little hand like mine?

Yes. I said, as I spread it out on the stone, and looked at it: it seems a very short time since that was a little hand like yours. It was a fat little hand: not the least like those thin fingers and many wrinkles now. When it grew rather bigger, the fingers had generally various deep cuts, got in making and rigging ships : those were the days when I intended to be a sailor. It gradually grew bigger, as all little hands will do, if spared in this world. And now, it has done a great many things. It has smoothed the heads of many children, and the noses of various horses. It has travelled, I thought to myself, along thousands of written pages. It has paid away money, and occasionally received it. In many things that hand has fallen short, I thought ; yet several things which that hand found to do, it did with its might. So here, I thought, were three hands, not far apart. There was the little hand of infancy ; four daisies were lying near it on the gravestone where it was laid down to compare with mine. Then the rather skinny and not very small hand, which is doing now the work of life. And a couple of yards beneath, there was another hand, whose work was over. It was a hand which had written many sermons, preached in that plain church ; which had turned over the leaves of the large pulpit-Bible (very old and shabby) which I turn over now ; which had often opened the door of the house where now I live. And when I got up from the gravestone, and was walking quietly homeward, many thoughts came into my mind CONCERNING GROWING OLD.

And, indeed, many of the most affecting thoughts which can ever enter the human mind are concerning the lapse of Time, and the traces which its lapse leaves upon human beings. There is something that touches us in the bare thought of Growing Old. I know a house on certain of whose walls there hang portraits of members of the family for many years back. It is not a grand house, where, to simple minds, the robes of brocade and the suits of armour fail to carry home the idea of real human beings. It is the house of a not wealthy gentleman. The portraits represent people whose minds did not run much upon deep speculations or upon practical politics: but who, no doubt, had many thoughts as to how they should succeed in getting the ends to meet. With such people does the writer feel at home: with such, probably, does the majority of his readers. I remember, there, the portrait of a frail old lady, plainly on the furthest confines of life. More than fourscore years had left their trace on the venerable head: you could fancy you saw the aged hands shaking. Opposite there hung the picture of a blooming girl, in the fresh May of beauty. The blooming girl was the mother of the venerable dame of fourscore. Painting catches but a glimpse of time; but it keeps that glimpse. On the canvas the face never grows old. As Dekker has it, 'False colours last after the true be fled.' I have often looked at the two pictures, in a confused sort of reverie. If you ask what it is that I thought of in looking at them, I truly cannot tell you. The fresh young beauty was the mother: the aged grand-dame was the child: *that* was really all. But there are certain thoughts upon which you can vaguely brood for a long time.

You remember reading how upon a day, not many

years since, certain miners, working far under ground.
came upon the body of a poor fellow who had perished
in the suffocating pit forty years before. Some chemical
agent, to which the body had been subjected — an agent
prepared in the laboratory of nature — had effectually ar-
rested the progress of decay. They brought it up to the
surface : and for a while, till it crumbled away, through
exposure to the atmosphere, it lay there, the image of a
fine sturdy young man. No convulsion had passed
over the face in death : the features were tranquil ; the
hair was black as jet. No one recognized the face : a
generation had grown up since the day on which the
miner went down his shaft for the last time. But a tottering, old woman, who had hurried from her cottage at
hearing the news, came up : and she knew again the face
which through all these years she had never quite forgot. The poor miner was to have been her husband the
day after that on which he died. They were rough people, of course, who were looking on : a liberal education
and refined feelings are not deemed essential to the man
whose work it is to get up coals, or even tin : but there
were no dry eyes there when the gray-headed old pilgrim
cast herself upon the youthful corpse, and poured out to
its deaf ear many words of endearment, unused for forty
years. It was a touching contrast : the one so old, the
other so young. They had both been young, these long
years ago: but time had gone on with the living, and
stood still with the dead. It is difficult to account for the
precise kind and degree of feeling with which we should
have witnessed the little picture. I state the fact : I can
say no more. I mention it in proof of my principle, that
a certain vague pensiveness is the result of musing upon
the lapse of time ; and a certain undefinable pathos of

any incident which brings strongly home to us that lapse
and its effects.

> 'In silence Matthew lay, and eyed
>   The spring beneath the tree:
> And thus the dear old man replied,
>   The gray-haired man of glee:
>
> '" No check, no stay, that streamlet fears —
>   How merrily it goes?
> 'Twill murmur on a thousand years,
>   And flow as now it flows.
>
> '" And here, on this delightful day,
>   I cannot choose but think
> How oft, a vigorous man, I lay
>   Beside this fountain's brink.
>
> '" My eyes are dim with childish tears,
>   My heart is idly stirred,
> For the same sound is in my ears
>   Which in those days I heard." '

That is really the sum of what is to be said on the subject. And it has always appeared to me that Mr. Dickens
has shown an amount of philosophical insight which does
not always characterize him, when he wrote certain reflections, which he puts in the mouth of one Mr. Roker, who
was a turnkey in the Fleet Prison. I do not know why it
should be so; but these words are to me more strikingly
truthful than almost any others which the eminent author
ever produced: —

'" You remember Tom Martin, Neddy? Bless my dear eyes,"
said Mr. Roker, shaking his head slowly from side to side, and gazing
abstractedly out of the grated window before him, as if he were fondly recalling some peaceful scene of his early youth, " it seems but yesterday that he whopped the coal-heaver down at the Fox-under-the-
Hill, by the wharf there. I think I can see him now, a coming up the
Strand between two street-keepers, a little sobered by the bruising,
with a patch o'winegar and brown paper over his right eyelid, and
that 'ere lovely bull-dog, as pinned the little boy arterwards, a following at his heels. What a rum thing Time is, aint it, Neddy?"'

Here we find, truthfully represented, an essential mood of the human mind. It is a more pleasing picture, perhaps, that comes back upon us in startling freshness, making us wonder if it is really so long ago since then, and our sentiment with regard to time is more elegantly expressed; but it really comes to this. You can say no more of time than that it is a strange, undefinable, inexplicable thing; and when, by some caprice of memory, some long-departed scene comes vividly back, what more definite thing can you do than just shake your head, and gaze abstractedly, like Mr. Roker? Like distant bells upon the breeze, some breath from childhood shows us plainly for a moment the little thing that was ourself. What more can you do but look at the picture, and feel that it is strange? More important things have been forgotten; but you remember how, when you were four years old, you ran a race along a path with a green slope beside it, and watched the small shadow keeping pace with you along the green slope; or you recall the precise feeling with which you sat down in the railway carriage on the day when you first came home from school for the holidays, and felt the train glide away. And when these things return, what can you do but lean your head upon your hand, and vaguely muse and feel? I have always much admired the truthful account of the small boy's fancies, as he sits and gazes into the glowing fire 'with his wee round face.' Mr. Ballantine is a true philosopher as well as a true poet.

'For a' sae sage he looks, what can the laddie ken?
He's THINKIN' UPON NAETHING, like mony mighty men!'

We can all 'think of naething,' and think of it for a long time, while yet the mind is by no means a blank.

It is very easy, in one sense, to grow old. You have

but to sit still and do nothing, and time passing over you
will make you old.   But to grow old wisely and genially,
is one of the most difficult tasks to which a human being
can ever set himself.   It is very hard to make up your
mind to it.   Some men grow old, struggling and recalci-
trating, dragged along against their will, clinging to each
birthday as the drowning man catches at an overhanging
bough.   Some folk grow old, gracefully and fittingly.   I
think that, as a general rule, the people who least reluc-
tantly grow old, are worthy men and women, who see
their children growing up into all that is good and admirable, with equal steps to those by which they feel
themselves to be growing downward.   A better, nobler,
and happier self, they think, will take their place ; and in
all the success, honour, and happiness of that new self, they
can feel a purer and worthier pride than they ever felt
in their own.   But the human being who has no one to
represent him when he is gone, will naturally wish to put
off the time of his going as long as may be.   It seems
to be a difficult thing to hit the medium between clinging
foolishly to youth and making an affected parade of age.
Entire naturalness upon this subject appears to be very
hard of attainment.   You know how many people, men
as well as women, pretend to be younger than they really
are.   I have found various motives lead to this pretence.
I have known men, distinguished at a tolerably early age
in some walk of intellectual exertion, who in announc-
ing their age (which they frequently did without any
necessity), were wont to deduct three or five years
from the actual tale, plainly with the intention of
making their talent and skill more remarkable, by
adding the element of these being developed at a
wonderfully early stage of life.   They wished to be

recognized as infant phenomena. To be an eloquent preacher is always an excellent thing; but how much more wonderful if the preacher be no more than twenty-two or twenty-three. To repeat *The Battle of Hohenlinden* is a worthy achievement, but the foolish parent pats his child's head with special exultation, as he tells you that his child, who has just repeated that popular poem, is no more than two years old. It is not improbable that the child's real age is two years and eleven months. It is very likely that the preacher's real age is twenty-eight. I remember hearing of a certain clerical person who, presuming on a very youthful aspect, gave himself out as twenty-four, when in fact he was thirty. I happened accidentally to see the register of that individual's baptism, which took place five years before the period at which he said he was born. The fact of this document's existence was made known to the man, by way of correcting his singular mistake. He saw it; but he clung to the fond delusion; and a year or two afterwards I read with much amusement in a newspaper some account of a speech made by him, into which account was incorporated an assurance that the speech was the more remarkable, inasmuch as the youthful orator was no more than twenty-four! Very, very contemptible, you say; and I entirely agree with you. And apart from the dishonesty, I do not think that judicious people will value very highly the crude fruit which has been forced to a certain ripeness before its time. Let us have the mature thing. Give us intellectual beef rather than intellectual veal. In the domain of poetry, great things have occasionally been done at a very early age; for you do not insist upon sound and judicious views of life in poetry. For plain sense and practical guidance, you go elsewhere. But in every other department of literature, the value of a production is in direct proportion to the amount of the experience which it embodies. A man can speak with authority only of that which he has himself felt and known. A man cannot paint portraits till he has seen faces. And all feeling, and most moods of mind, will be very poorly described by one who takes his notion of them at second-hand. When you are very young yourself, you may read with sympathy the writings of very young men ; but when you have reached maturity, and learned by experience the details and realities of life, you will be conscious of a certain indefinable want in such writings. And I do not know that this defect can be described more definitely than by saying that the entire thing is veal, not beef. You have the immature animal. You have the 'berries harsh and crude.'

But long after the period at which it is possible to assume the position of the infant phenomenon, you still find many men anxious to represent themselves as a good deal younger than they are. To the population of Britain generally, ten years elapse before one census is followed by the next ; but some persons, in these ten years, grow no more than two or three years older. Let me confess to an extreme abhorrence of such men. Their conduct affects me with an indescribable disgust. I dislike it more than many things which in themselves are probably more evil morally. Such men are, in the essential meaning of the word, *humbugs*. They are shams ; impostures ; false pretences. They are an embodied falsehood ; their very personality is a lie ; and you don't know what about them may next prove to be a deception. Looking at a man who says he is forty-three when in fact he is above sixty, I suspect him all over. I am in doubt whether his hair,

his teeth, his eyes, are real. I do not know whether that
breadth of chest be the developement of manly bone and
muscle, or the skilful padding of the tailor. I am not
sure how much is the man, and how much the work of his
valet. I suspect that his whiskers and moustache are
dyed. I look at his tight boots, and think how they
must be tormenting his poor old corny feet. I admire
his affected buoyancy of manner, and think how the miserable creature must collapse when he finds himself alone,
and is no longer compelled by the presence of company
to put himself on the stretch, and carry on that wretched
acting. When I see the old reptile whispering in a corner to a girl of eighteen, or furtively squeezing her in a
waltz, I should like extremely to take him by the neck,
and shake him till he came into the pieces of which he
is made up. And when I have heard (long ago) such a
one, with a hideous gloating relish telling a profane or in-
decent story; or instilling cynical and impious notions of
life and things into the minds of young lads; or (more
disgusting still) using phrases of double meaning in the
presence of innocent young women, and enjoying their
innocent ignorance of his sense; I have thought that I
was beholding as degraded a phase of human nature as
you will find on the face of this sinful world. O venerable age, gray, wise, kindly, sympathetic; before which I
shall never cease reverently to bend, respecting even
what I may (wrongly perhaps) esteem your prejudices;
that *you* should be caricatured and degraded in that foul,
old leering satyr! And if there be a thing on earth that
disgusts one more than even the thought of the animal
himself, it is to think of ministers of religion (prudently
pious) who will wait meekly in his ante-chamber and sit
humbly at his table, because he is an earl or a duke!

But though all this be so, there is a sense in which I interpret the clinging to youth, in which there is nothing contemptible about it, but much that is touching and pleasing. I abominate the padded, rouged, dyed old sham; but I heartily respect the man or woman, pensive and sad, as some little circumstance has impressed upon them the fact that they are growing old. A man or woman is a fool, who is indignant at being called *the old lady* or *the old gentleman* when these phrases state the truth; but there is nothing foolish or unworthy when some such occurrence brings it home to us, with something of a shock, that we are no longer reckoned among the young, and that the innocent and impressionable days of childhood (so well remembered) are beginning to be far away. We are drawing nearer, we know, to certain solemn realities of which we speak much and feel little; the undiscovered country (humbly sought through the pilgrimage of life) is looming in the distance before. We feel that life is not long, and is not commonplace, when it is regarded as the portal to eternity. And probably nothing will bring back the season of infancy and early youth upon any thoughtful man's mind so vividly as the sense that he is growing old. How short a time since then! You look at your great brown hand. It seems but yesterday since a boy-companion (gray now) tried to print your name upon the little paw, and there was not room. You remember it (is it five-and-twenty years since?) as it looked when laid on the head of a friendly dog, two or three days before you found him poisoned and dead; and helped, not without tears, to bury him in the garden under an apple-tree. You see, as plainly as if you saw it now, his brown eye, as it looked at you in life for the last time. And as you feel these things, you quite unaffectedly and sincerely put off, time after time, the period at which you will accept it as a fact, that you are old. Twenty-eight, thirty, thirty-five, forty-eight, mark years on reaching which you will still feel yourself young; many men honestly think that sixty-five or sixty-eight is the prime of life. A less amiable accompaniment of this pleasing belief is often found in a disposition to call younger men (and not very young) *boys*. I have heard that word uttered in a very spiteful tone, as though it were a name of great reproach. There are few epithets which I have ever heard applied in a manner betokening greater bitterness, than that of *a clever lad*. You remember how Sir Robert Walpole hurled the charge of youth against Pitt. You remember how Pitt (or Dr. Johnson for him) defended himself with great force of argument against the imputation. Possibly in some cases envy is at the root of the matter. Not every man has the magnanimity of Sir Bulwer Lytton, who tells us so frankly and so often how much he would like to be young again if he could.

To grow old is so serious a matter, that it always appears to me as if there were something like profanation in putting the fact or its attendant circumstances in a ludicrous manner. It is not a fit thing to joke about. A funny man might write a comic description of the way in which starving sailors on a raft used up their last poor allotments of bread and water, and watched with sinking hearts their poor stock decrease. Or he might record in a fashion that some people would laugh at, the gradual sinking of a family which had lost its means through degree after degree in the social scale, till the workhouse was reached at last. But I do not think there is anything really amusing in the spectacle of a human

27

being giving up hold after hold to which he had clung, and
sinking always lower and lower; and there is no doubt
that, in a physical sense, we soon come to do all that in
the process of growing old. And though you may put
each little mortification, each petty coming down, in a
way amusing to bystanders, it should always be remembered that each may imply a severe pang on the part of
the man himself. We smile when Mr. Dickens tells us
concerning his hero, Mr. Tupman, that

> ' Time and feeding had expanded that once romantic form; the
> black silk waistcoat had become more and more developed; inch by
> inch had the gold watch-chain beneath it disappeared from within the
> range of Tupman's vision; and gradually had the capacious chin en-
> croached upon the borders of the white cravat; but the soul of Tup-
> man had known no change.'

Now, although Mr Tupman was an exceedingly fat
man physically, and morally (to say the truth) a very
great fool, you may rely upon it that as each little
circumstance had occurred which his biographer has
recorded, it would be a very serious circumstance in the
feeling of poor Tupman himself. And this not nearly so
much for the little personal mortification implied in each
step of expanding bulk and lessening agility, but because
each would be felt as a milestone, marking the progress
of Tupman from his cradle to his grave. Each would
be something to signify that the innocence and freshness
of childhood were left so much further behind, and that
the reality of life was growing more hard and prosaic. It
is some feeling like this which makes it a sad thing to
lay aside an old coat which one has worn for a long time.
It is a decided step. Of course we all know that time
goes on as fast when its progress is unmarked as when it
is noted. And each day that the coat went on was an

onward stage as truly as the day when the coat went off;
but in this world we must take things as they are to our
feelings: and there is something that very strongly ap-
peals to our feeling in a decided beginning or a decided
ending. Do not laugh, thoughtless folk, at the poor old
maid, who persists in going bareheaded long after she
ought to have taken to caps. You cannot know how
much further away that change would make her days of
childhood seem: how much more remote and dim and
faint it would make the little life, the face, the voice of
the young brother or sister that died when they both
were children together. Do not fancy that it is mere
personal vanity which prompts that clinging to apparent
youth: feelings which are gentle, pure, and estimable
may protest against any change from the old familiar
way. Do not smile at the phrases of the house when
there are gray-headed *boys*, and *girls* on the lower side of
forty-five: it would be a terrible sacrifice, it would make
a terrible change, to give up the old names. You thoughtless young people are ready to deride Mr. Smith when
he appears in his new wig. You do not think how, when
poor Smith went to Truefitt's to get it, he thought many
thoughts of the long-departed mother, whom he remembers dimly on her sick-bed smoothing down her little
boy's hair, thick enough then. And when you see Mr.
Robinson puffing up the hill with purpled face and labouring breath, do you think that poor Robinson does not
remember the days when he was the best runner at
school? Perhaps he tells you at considerable length
about these days. Well, listen patiently: some day you
may be telling long stories too. There is a peculiar sadness in thinking of exertions of body or mind to which
we were once equal, but to which we are not equal now.
You remember the not very earnest Swift, conscious that

the 'decay at the top' had begun, bursting into tears as he read one of his early works, and exclaiming, ' Heavens, what a genius I had when I wrote that!' What is there more touching than the picture of poor Sir Walter, wheeled like a child in a chair through the rooms at Abbotsford, and suddenly exclaiming, ' Come, this is sad idleness,' and insisting on beginning to dictate a new tale, in which the failing powers of the great magician appeared so sadly, that large as its marketable value would have been, it never was suffered to appear in print. Probably the sense of enfeebled faculties is a sadder thing than the sense of diminished physical power. Probably Sir Isaac Newton, in his later days, when he sat down to his own mathematical demonstrations, and could not understand them or follow them, felt more bitterly the wear of advancing time than the gray-headed Highlander sitting on a stone at his cottage door in the sunshine, and telling you how, long ago, he could breast the mountain with the speed of a deer; or than the crippled soldier, who leans upon his crutch, and tells how, many years ago, that shaky old hand had cut down the French cuirassier. But in either case it is a sad thing to think of exertions once put forth, and work once done, which could not be done or put forth now. Change for the worse is always a sorrowful thing. And the aged man, in the respect of physical power, and the capacity for intellectual exertion, has ' seen better days.' You do not like to think that in any respect you are falling off. You are not pleased at being told that ten years ago you wrote a plainer hand or spoke in a rounder voice. It is mortifying to find that whereas you could once walk at five miles an hour, you can now accomplish no more than three and a half. Now, in a hundred ways, at every turn, and by a host of little wounding facts, we are com-

pelled to feel as we grow old that we are falling off.   As
the complexion roughens, as the hair thins off, as we
come to stoop, as we blow tremendously if we attempt to
run, the man of no more than middle age is conscious of
a bodily decadence.   And advancing years make the
wise man sadly conscious of a mental decadence too.   Let
us be thankful that if physical and intellectual decline
must come at a certain stage of growing old, there are
respects in which, so long as we live, we may have the
comfort of thinking that we are growing better.   The
higher nature may daily be reaching a nobler development : when 'heart and flesh faint and fail,' when the
clay tenement is turning frail and shattered, the better
part within may show in all moral grace as but a little
lower than the angels.   Age need not necessarily be
'dark and unlovely,' as Ossian says it is; and the conviction that in some respect, that in the most important of
all respects, we are growing better, tends mightily to strip
age of that sense of falling off which is the bitterest thing
about it.   And as the essential nature of growing old ; —
its essence as a sad thing ; — lies in the sense of decadence, the conviction that in almost anything we are
gaining ground has a wonderful power to enable us cheerfully to grow old.   A man will contentedly grow fatter,
balder, and puffier, if he feels assured that he is pushing
on to eminence at the bar or in politics ; and if he takes
his seat upon the woolsack even at the age of seventy-
five, though he might now seek in vain to climb the trees
he climbed in youth, or to play at leapfrog as then, still
he is conscious that his life on the whole has been a
progress ; that he is on the whole better now than he was
in those days which were his best days physically ; that
to be lord chancellor, albeit a venerable one, is, as the

world goes, a more eminent thing than to be the gayest and most active of midshipmen. And so on the whole he is content to grow old, because he feels that in growing he has not on the whole been coming down hill.

The supremely mortifying thing is, to feel that the physical decadence which comes with growing old, is not counterbalanced by any improvement whatsoever. We shall not mind much about growing less agile and less beautiful, if we think that we are growing wiser and better. The gouty but wealthy merchant, who hobbles with difficulty to his carriage, feels that after all he has made an advance upon those days in which, if free from gout, he was devoid of pence : and if he did not hobble, he had no carriage into which he might get in that awkward manner. The gray-haired old lady who was a beauty once, is consoled for her growing old, if in her age she is admitted to the society of the county, while in her youth she was confined to the society of the town. Make us feel that we are better in something, and we shall be content to be worse in many things : but it is miserable to think that in all things we are falling off, or even in all things standing still. A man would be very much mortified to think that at fifty he did not write materially better sermons, essays, or articles than he did at five-and-twenty. In many things he knows the autumn of life is a falling-off from its spring-time. He has ceased to dance ; his voice quavers abominably when he tries to sing : he has no fancy now for climbing hills, and he shirks walks of forty miles a day. Perhaps deeper wrinkles have been traced by time on the heart than on the forehead, and the early freshness of feeling is gone. But surely, in mellowed experience, in sobered and sound views of things, in tempered expectations, in patience, in

sympathy, in kindly charity, in insight into God's ways
and dealings, he is better now a thousand times than he
was then. He has worked his way through the hectic
stage in which even able and thoughtful men fancy that
Byron was a great poet. A sounder judgment and a
severer taste direct him now ; in all things, in short, that
make the essence of the manly nature, he is a better and
further advanced man than he ever was before. The
physical nature says, by many little signs, WE ARE GO-
ING DOWN HILL ; the spiritual nature testifies by many
noble gains and acquirements, WE ARE GOING ONWARD
AND UPWARD ! It seems to me that the clergyman's state
of feeling must be a curious one. who, on a fine Sunday
morning, when he is sixty, can take out of his drawer a
sermon which he wrote at five-and-twenty, and go and
preach it with perfect approval and without the altera-
tion of a word. It is somewhat mortifying. no doubt, to
look at a sermon which you wrote seven or eight years
since, and which you then thought brilliant eloquence, and
to find that in your present judgment it is no better than
tawdry fustian. But still, my friend, even though you
grudge to find that you must throw the sermon aside and
preach it no more, are you not secretly pleased at this
proof how much your mind has grown in these years? It
is pleasant to think that you have not been falling off, not
standing still. The wings of your imagination are somewhat clipped indeed, and your style has lost something of
that pith which goes with want of consideration. Some
youthful judges may think that you have sadly fallen off;
but you are content in the firm conviction that you have
vastly improved. It was veal then : it is beef now. I
remember hearing with great interest how a venerable
professor of fourscore wrote in the last few weeks of his

life a little course of lectures on a certain debated point
of theology. He had outgrown his former notions upon
the subject. The old man said his former lectures upon
it did not do him justice. Was it not a pleasant sight —
the aged tree bearing fruit to the last? How it must
have pleased and soothed the good man amid many
advancing infirmities to persuade himself (justly or un-
justly) that in the most important respect he was going
onward still !

It is indeed a pleasant sight to kindly onlookers, and
it is a sustaining and consoling thing to the old man
himself, when amid physical decadence there is intellectual growth. But this is not a common thing. As a
general rule it cannot be doubted that, intellectually, we
top the summit sometime before fourscore, and begin
to go down hill. I do not wish to turn my essays into
sermons; or to push upon my readers in *Fraser* things
more fitly addressed to my congregation on Sundays:
still, let me say that in the thought that growing old
implies at last a decay both mental and bodily, and that
unrelieved going down is a very sad thing to feel or to
see, I find great comfort in remembering that as regards
the best and noblest of all characteristics, the old man
may be progressing to the last. In all those beautiful
qualities which most attract the love and reverence of
those around, and which fit for purer and happier company than can be found in this world, the aged man or
woman may be growing still. In the last days, indeed,
it may be ripening rather than growing: mellowing, not
expanding. But to do *that* is to ' grow in grace.' And
doubtless the yellow harvest-field in September is an
advance upon the fresh green blades of June. You
may like better to look upon the wheat that is pro-

gressing towards ripeness; but the wheat which has
reached ripeness is not a falling off. The stalks will
not bend now, without breaking: you rub the heads,
and the yellow chaff that wraps the grain, crumbles off
in dust. But it is beyond a question that there you
see wheat at its best.

Still, not forgetting this, we must all feel it sad to see
human beings as they grow old, retrograding in material comforts and advantages. It is a mournful thing
to see : a man grower poorer as he is growing older, or
losing position in any way. If it were in my power, I
would make all barristers, above sixty, judges. They
ought to be put in a situation of dignity and indepen-
dence. You don't like to go into a court of justice, and
there behold a thin, gray-headed counsel, somewhat
shaken in nerve, looking rather frail, battling away with
a full-blooded, confident, hopeful, impudent fellow, five-
and-twenty years his junior. The youthful, big-whis-
kered, roaring, and bullying advocate is sure to be held
in much the greater estimation by attorney's clerks.
The old gentleman's day is over; but with lessening
practice and disappointed hopes he must drive on at the
bar still. I wish I were a chief justice, that by special
deference and kindliness of manner, I might daily soothe
somewhat the feelings of that aging man. But it is
especially in the case of the clergy that one sees the
painful sight of men growing poorer as they are growing older. I think of the case of a clergyman who at
his first start was rather fortunate : who gets a nice
parish at six-and-twenty : I mean a parish which is a
nice one for a man of six-and-twenty : and who never
gets any other preferment, but in that parish grows old.
Don't we all know how pretty and elegant everything

was about him at first : how trim and weedless were his
garden and shrubbery : how rosy his carpets, how airy
his window-curtains, how neat though slight all his furniture : how graceful, merry, and nicely dressed the
young girl who was his wife : how (besides hosts of
parochial improvements) he devised numberless little
changes about his dwelling : rustic bowers, moss-houses,
green mounts, labyrinthine walks, fantastically trimmed
yews, root-bridges over the little stream. But as his
family increased, his income stood still. It was hard
enough work to make the ends meet even at first,
though young hearts are hopeful : but with six or seven
children, with boys who must be sent to college, with
girls who must be educated as ladies, with the prices of
all things ever increasing, with multiplying bills from
the shoemaker, tailor, dressmaker ; the poor parson
grows yearly poorer. The rosy face of the young wife
has now deep lines of care : the weekly sermon is dull
and spiritless : the parcel of books comes no more : the
carpets grow threadbare but are not replaced : the furniture becomes creaky and rickety : the garden walks
are weedy : the bark peels off the rustic verandah : the
moss-house falls much over to one side : the friends, far
away, grow out of all acquaintance. The parson himself,
once so precise in dress, is shabby and untidy now ;
and his wife's neat figure is gone : the servants are of
inferior class, coarse and insolent : perhaps the burden
of hopeless debt presses always with its dull, dead
weight upon the poor clergyman's heart. There is little spring in him to push off the invasion of fatigue
and infection, and he is much exposed to both ; and
should he be taken away, who shall care for the widow
and the fatherless, losing at once their head, their home,

their means of living? Even you, non-clerical reader,
know precisely what I describe: hundreds have seen it:
and such will agree with me when I say that there is
no sadder sight than that of a clergyman, with a wife
and children, growing poor as he is growing old. Oh,
that I had the fortune of John Jacob Astor, that I might
found, once for all, a fund that should raise forever
above penury and degradation the widows and the
orphans of rectory, vicarage, parsonage, and manse!

And even when the old man has none depending upon
him for bread, to be provided from his lessening store,
there is something inexpressibly touching and mournful
in the spectacle of an old man who must pinch and screw.
You do not mind a bit about a hopeful young lad having
to live in humble lodgings up three pair of stairs; or
about such a one having a limited number of shirts,
stockings, and boots, and needing to be very careful and
saving as to his clothes; or about his having very homely
shaving-things, or hair-brushes which are a good deal
worn out. The young fellow can stand all that: it is all
quite right: let him bear the yoke in his youth: he may
look forward to better days. Nor does there seem in
the nature of things any very sad inconsistency in the
idea of a young lad carefully considering how long his
boots or great coat will last, or with what *minimum* of
shirts he can manage to get on. But I cannot bear the
thought of a gray-headed old man, with shaky hand and
weary limb, sitting down in his lonely lodging, and
meditating on such things as these: counting his pocket-
handkerchiefs, and suspecting that one is stolen: or
looking ruefully at a boot which has been cut where
the upper leather joins the sole. Let not the aged man
be worried with such petty details! Of course, my

reader, I know as well as you do, that very many aged people must think of these things to the last. All I say is, that if I had the ordering of things, no man or woman above fifty should ever know the want of money. And whenever I find a four-leaved shamrock, *that* is the very first arrangement I shall make. Possibly I may extend the arrangement further, and provide that no honest married man or woman shall ever grow early old through wearing care. What a little end is sometimes the grand object of a human being's strivings through many weeks and months! I sat down the other day in a poor chamber, damp with much linen drying upon crossing lines. There dwells a solitary woman, an aged and infirm woman, who supports herself by washing. For months past her earnings have averaged three shillings a week. Out of that sum she must provide food and raiment; she must keep in her poor fire, and she must pay a rent of nearly three pounds a year. 'It is hard work, sir,' she said: 'it costs me many a thought getting together the money to pay my rent.' And I could see well, that from the year's beginning to its end, the thing always uppermost in that poor old widow's waking thoughts, was the raising of that great incubus of a sum of money. A small end, you would say, for the chief thoughts of an immortal being! Don't you feel, gay young reader, for that fellow-creature, to whom a week has been a success, if at its close she can put by a few halfpence towards meeting the term day? Would you not like to enrich her, to give her a light heart, by sending her a half-sovereign? If you would, you may send it to me.

It is well, I have said, for a man who is growing old,

if he is able to persuade himself that though physically
going downhill, he is yet in some respect progressing.
For if he can persuade himself that he is progressing
in any one thing, he will certainly believe that he is
advancing on the whole. Still, it must be said, that the
self-complacency of old gentlemen is sometimes amusing
(where not irritating) to their juniors. The self-conceit
of many old men is something quite amazing. They
talk incessantly about themselves and their doings; and,
to hear them talk, you would imagine that every great
social or political change of late years had been brought
about mainly by their instrumentality. I have heard an
elderly man of fair average ability, declare in sober
earnest, that had he gone to the bar, he 'had no hesi-
tation in saying' that he would have been chancellor or
chief justice of England. I have witnessed an elderly
man whom the late Sir Robert Peel never saw or heard
of, declare that Sir Robert had borrowed from him his
idea of abolishing the Corn-laws. I have heard an
elderly mercantile man, who had gone the previous day
to look at a small property which was for sale, remark
that he had no doubt that by this time all the country
was aware of what he had been doing. With the majority of elderly men, you can hardly err on the side of
over-estimating the amount of their vanity. They will
receive with satisfaction a degree of flattery which would
at once lead a young man to suspect you were making
a fool of him. There is no doubt that if a man be foolish at all, he always grows more foolish as he grows
older. The most outrageous conceit of personal beauty,
intellectual prowess, weight in the county, superiority in
the regard of horses, wine, pictures, grapes, potatoes,
poultry, pigs, and all other possessions, which I have

ever seen, has been in the case of old men. And I have known commonplace old women, to whom if you had ascribed queenly beauty and the intellect of Shakspeare, they would have thought you were doing them simple justice. The truth appears to be, not that the vanity of elderly folk is naturally bigger than that of their juniors, but that it is not mown down in that unsparing fashion to which the vanity of their juniors is subjected. If an old man tells you that the abolition of the slave-trade originated in his back-parlor, you may think him a vain, silly old fellow, but you do not tell him so. Whereas if a young person makes an exhibition of personal vanity, he is severely ridiculed. He is taught sharply that, however great may be his estimate of himself, it will not do to show it. 'Shut up, old fellow, and don't make a fool of yourself,' you say to a friend of your own age, should he begin to vapour. But when the aged pilgrim begins to boast, you feel bound to listen with apparent respect. And the result is, that the old gentleman fancies you believe all he tells you.

Not unfrequently, when a man has grown old to that degree that all his powers of mind and body are considerably impaired, there is a curious and touching mood which comes before an almost sudden breaking-down into decrepitude. It is a mood in which the man becomes convinced that he is not so very old; that he has been mistaken in fancying that the autumn of life was so far advanced with him; and that all he has to do in order to be as active and vigorous as he ever was, is to make some great change of scene and circumstances: to go back, perhaps, to some place where he had lived many years before, and there, as Dr. Johnson expresses it, to 'recover youth in the fields where he once was young.' The aged clergyman thinks that if he were now to go to the parish he was offered forty years since, it would bring back those days again : he would be the man he was then. Of course, in most cases, such a feeling is like the leaping up of the flame before it goes out ; it is an impulse as natural and as unreasonable as that which makes the dying man insist within an hour of his death on being lifted from his bed and placed in his easy-chair, and then he will be all right. But sometimes there really is in human feeling and life something analogous to the Martinmas summer in the year. Sometimes after we had made up our mind that we had grown old, it flashes upon us that we are not old after all : there is a real rejuvenescence. Happy days promote the feeling. You know that as autumn draws on, there come days on which it is summer or winter just as the weather chances to be fair or foul. And so there is a stage of life in which it depends mainly on a man's surroundings whether he shall be old or young. If unsuccessful, over-burdened, over-driven, lightly esteemed, with much depending upon him, and little aid or sympathy, a man may feel old at thirty-five. But if there still be a house where he is one of *the boys :* if he be living among his kindred and those who have grown up along with him : if he be still unmarried : if he have not lived in many different places, or in any place very far away : if he have not known many different modes of life, or worked in many kinds of work : then at thirty-five he may feel very young. There are men who at that age have never known what it is to stand upon their own legs in life, and to act upon their own responsibility. They have always had some one to tell them what to do. I can imagine that towards the close of the ten years which Pisistratus Caxton spent in Australia, far away from his parents and his home, and day by day obliged to decide and to manage for himself, he had begun to feel tolerably old. But when he came back again, and found his father and mother hardly changed in aspect; and found the chairs, and sofas, and beds, and possibly even the carpets, looking much as he had left them; those ten years, a vast expanse while they were passing over, would close up into something very small in the perspective; and he would feel with a sudden exultation that he was quite a young fellow yet.

It is wonderful what a vast amount of work a man may go through without its telling much upon him: and how many years he may live without feeling perceptibly older at their close. The years were long in passing; they look like nothing when past. If you were to go away, my friend, from London or Edinburgh, and live for five or six years in the centre of the Libyan desert; or in an island of the South Seas; or at an up-country station in India; there would be many evenings in those years on which you would feel as though you were separated by ages from the scenes and friends you knew. It would seem like a century since you came away; it would seem like an impossibility that you should ever be back again in the old place, looking and feeling much in the old way. But at length travelling on week after week, you come home again. You find your old companions looking just as before, and the places you knew are little changed. Miss Smith a blooming young woman before you went out, is a blooming young woman still, and probably singing the same songs which you remember her singing then. Why, it

rushes upon you, you have been a very short time
away; you are not a day older; it is a mere nothing to
go out sperm-whaling for four or five years, or to retire
for that period to a parish in the *Ultima Thule*. Life,
after all, is so long, that you may cut a good large slice
out of the earlier years of it without making it perceptibly less. When Macaulay returned from India after
his years there, I have no doubt he felt this. And the
general principle is true, that almost any outward condition or any state of feeling, after it has passed away,
appears to us to have lasted a very much shorter time
than it did when it was passing; and it leaves us with
the conviction that we are not nearly so old as we had
fancied while it was passing. And the rejuvenescence
is sometimes not merely in feeling, but in fact and in
appearance. Have you not known a lady of perhaps
three and thirty years married to an ugly old fogy of
eighty-five, who, during the old fogy's life wore high
dresses, and caps, that she might appear something like
a suitable match for the old fogy; but who instantly the
ancient buffalo departed this life, cast aside her venerable trappings, and burst upon the world almost as a
blooming girl, doubtless to her own astonishment no less
than to that of her friends? And you remember that
pleasing touch of nature in the new series of *Friends in
Council*, when Milverton, after having talked of himself
as a faded widower, and appeared before us as one de-
voted to grave philosophic research, falls in love with a
girl of two-and-twenty, and discovers that after all he is
not so old. And I suppose it would be a pleasant discovery to any man, after he had fancied for years that
the romantic interest had for him fled from life, to find
that music could still thrill through him as of yore,

28

and that the capacity of spooniness was not at all oblit-
erated.   As Festus says,

> ' Rouse thee, heart!
> Bow of my life, thou yet art full of spring!
> My quiver still hath many purposes.'

When Sir Philip Sidney tells us that in walking
through the fields of his Arcadia, you would, among
other pleasant sights and sounds, here and there chance
upon a shepherd boy, ' piping as if he would never grow
old,' you find the chivalrous knight giving his countenance to the vulgar impression that youth is a finer
thing than age.   And you may find among the *Twice-
told Tales* of Nathaniel Hawthorne a most exquisite one
called *The Fountain of Youth*, in which we are told of
three old gentlemen and an old lady, who were so enchanted by tasting a draught which brought back the
exhilaration of youth for half an hour, (though it led
them likewise to make very great fools of themselves,)
that they determined they would wander over the world
till they should find that wondrous fountain, and then
quaff its waters morning, noon, and night.   And Thomas
Moore, in one of his sweetest songs, warms for a minute
from cold glitter into earnestness, as he declares his
belief that no gains which advancing years can bring
with them are any compensation for the light-heartedness and the passionate excitement which they take
away.   He says, —

> ' Ne'er tell me of glories serenely adorning
>   The close of our day, the calm eve of our night:
> Give me back, give me back the wild freshness of morning,—
>   Its smiles and its tears are worth evening's best light.'

And indeed it is to be admitted that in a life whose
poetry is drawn from the domain of passion and imag-

ination, the poetry does pass away as imagination flags
and the capacity of emotion dries up with advancing
time.   But the true philosopher among the three writers
who have been mentioned, is Mr. Hawthorne.   *He* shows
us how the exhilaration, the *wild freshness* of the season
when life is at blood-heat, partakes of the nature of
intoxication ; and he leaves us with the sober conviction
that the truly wise man may well be thankful when he
has got safely through that feverish season of temptation
and of folly.   Let us be glad if our bark has come (even
a little battered) through the Mäelstrom, by the Scylla
and Charybdis, and is now sailing quietly upon a calm
and tranquil sea.   Wait till you are a little older, youthful reader, and you will understand that truth and
soberness (how fitly linked together) are noble things.
If you are a good man — let me say it at once, a Christian man — your latter days are better a thousand times
than those early ones after which superficial and worldly
folk whimper.   The capacity of excitement is much
lessened ; the freshness of feeling and heart are much
gone ; though not, of necessity, so very much.   You
begin, like the old grandmother in that exquisite poem
of Mr. Tennyson, ' to be a little weary ; ' the morning
air is hardly so exhilarating, nor the frosty winter afternoon ; the snowdrops and primroses come back, and you
are disappointed that so little of the vernal joy comes
with them ; you go and stand by the grave of your young
sister on the anniversary of the day when she died, and
you wonder that you have come to *feel* so little where
once you felt so much.   You preach the sermons you once
preached with emotion so deep that it was contagious ;
but now the corresponding feeling does not come ; you
give them coldly ; you are mortified at the contrast

between the warmth there is in the old words, and the
chilliness with which you speak them. You hear of the
death of a dear friend, and you are vexed that you can
take it so coolly. But, O my brother, aging like myself,
do you not know, in sober earnest, that for such losses
as these, other things have brought abundant recom-
pense? What a meaning there is now to you in the
words of St. Austin —'Thou madst us for Thyself, and
our hearts are restless till they find rest in Thee!'
You are beginning to understand that St. Paul was right,
when (even in the face of the fact that inexperienced
youth is proverbially the most hopeful) he declared that
in the truest sense 'experience waketh hope.' What a
calm there is here! Passion is no longer the disturbing force it once was. Your eyes are no longer blinded
to the truth of things by the glittering mists of fancy.
You do your duty quietly and hopefully. You can bear
patiently with the follies and the expectations of youth.
I say it with the firmest assurance of the truth of what I
say, that as he grows old, the wise man has great reason
to thank God that he is no longer young. Truth and
soberness are well worth all they cost. You wont make
a terrific fool of yourself any more. Campbell was not
a philosopher, and possibly he was only half in earnest
when he wrote the following verse ; but many men, no
longer young, will know how true it is : —

' Hail, welcome tide of life, where no tumultuous billows roll,
  How wondrous to myself appears this halcyon calm of soul!
  The wearied bird blown o'er the deep would sooner quit its shore,
  Than I would cross the gulf again that Time has brought me o'er!'

The dead are the only people that never grow old. There
was something typical in the arrestment of time in the case
of the youthful miner, of whom we have already spoken.

Your little brother or sister that died long ago remains in death and in remembrance the same young thing forever. It is fourteen years this evening since the writer's sister left this world. She was fifteen years old then — she is fifteen years old yet. I have grown older since then by fourteen years, but she has never changed as they advanced ; and if God spares me to fourscore, I never shall think of her as other than the youthful creature she faded. The other day I listened as a poor woman told of the death of her first-born child. He was two years old. She had a small washing-green, across which was stretched a rope that came in the middle close to the ground. The boy was leaning on the rope, swinging backwards and forwards, and shouting with delight. The mother went into her cottage and lost sight of him for a minute ; and when she returned the little man was lying across the rope, dead. It had got under his chin : he had not sense to push it away ; and he was suffocated. The mother told me, and I believe truly, that she had never been the same person since ; but the thing which mainly struck me was, that though it is eighteen years since then, she thought of her child as an infant of two years yet : it is a little child she looks for to meet her at the gate of the Golden City. Had her child lived he would have been twenty years old now ; he died, and he is only two : he is two yet : he will never be more than two. The little rosy face of that morning, and the little half-articulate voice, would have been faintly remembered by the mother had they gradually died into boyhood and manhood : but that day stereotyped them : they remain unchanged.

Have you seen, my reader, the face that had grown old in life grow young after death? the expression of many years since, lost for long, come out startlingly in the features, fixed and cold? Every one has seen it: and it is sometimes strange how rapidly the change takes place. The marks of pain fade out, and with them the marks of age. I once saw an aged lady die. She had borne sharp pain for many days with the endurance of a martyr; she had to bear sharp pain to the very last. The features were tense and rigid with suffering; they remained so while life remained. It was a beautiful sight to see the change that took place in the very instant of dissolution. The features, sharp for many days with pain, in that instant recovered the old aspect of quietude which they had borne in health: the tense, tight look was gone, you saw the signs of pain go out. You felt that all suffering was over. It was no more of course than the working of physical law: but in that case it seemed as if there were a further meaning conveyed. And so it seems to me when the young look comes back on the departed Christian's face. Gone, it seems to say, where the progress of time shall no longer bring age or decay. Gone where there are beings whose life may be reckoned by centuries, but in whom life is fresh and young, and always will be so. Close the aged eyes! Fold the aged hands in rest. Their owner is no longer old!

CONCLUSION.

AND such, my friendly reader, are my REC-REATIONS. It was pleasant to me, amid much work of a very different kind, to write these Essays. I trust that it has not been very tiresome for you to read them.

There is a peculiar happiness which is known to the essayist. There is a virtue about his work to draw the sting from the little worries of life. If you fairly look some petty vexation of humanity in the face, and write an account of it, it will never annoy you so much any more. It recurs: and it annoys you: but you have a latent feeling of satisfaction at finding how exactly accurate was your description of it; how completely your present sensation runs into the mould you had made. It is a curious thing, too, that there is a certain pleasure in writing about a thing which was very unpleasant when it happened to one. You know how an artist makes a pleasing picture out of a poor cottage, in which it would be very disagreeable to live. You know how a great painter makes a picture, which you often like to look at, of an event at which you would not have liked to have been present. You pause for a long time before the representation of some boors drinking; or of a furious struggle in a guard-room; or of a murdered man lying dead. Now, in fact, you would have

got out of the way of such sights: the first two would
have been disgusting: the last, at least a 'sorry sight.'

It is not quite a case in point, that we look with great
interest and pleasure at the representation of a sight
which it would have been no worse than sad to see.
Such a sight may have been elevating as well as sadden-
ing. I see a figure laid upon a bed: you know it is stiff
and cold. It is a female figure: there is the fixed but
beautiful face. And through the open window I see in
the west the summer sunset blazing, and the golden light
falling upon the pale features, and the closed eyes which
will never open more till the sun has ceased to shine. I do
not wonder that the exquisite genius of the painter fixed
on such a scene, and preserved it with rigid accuracy, and
wrote beneath his picture such words as these:

The sun shall no more be thy light by day; neither for brightness
shall the moon give light unto thee: but the Lord shall be unto thee
an everlasting light, and thy God thy glory.

Thy sun shall no more go down; neither shall thy moon withdraw
herself; for the Lord shall be thine everlasting light, and the days of
thy mourning shall be ended.

But there is in this one respect an entire analogy between the feeling of the artist and the feeling of the essayist: that to both, this world is to a certain extent transfigured by the fact, that to each, things become comparatively pleasing if they would please when described or
depicted, though they might be unpleasing in fact. Not
merely are those things good which are good in themselves: those things are good which, though bad, will
please and interest when represented. It is extremely
certain, that there is a pleasure in writing about what
there is no pleasure in bearing: and here is a happiness
of the essayist. You are grossly cheated, my friend, by

a man of most respectable character. You are worried
by some glaring instance of that horrible dilatoriness, un
faithfulness, and stupidity, which come across the successful issue of almost all human affairs. You are vexed, in
short, at seeing how creakingly and jarringly and uneasi-
ly the machine of life and society manages to blunder on.
Well, you suffer; and you have no relief. But the essayist's painful feeling at such things is much mitigated
when he thinks that here is a subject for him; and when
he goes and describes it. Once, it was to me unrelieved and unalloyed pain to be cheated : or to listen to the
vapouring of some silly person. Now, though still I cannot say I like it, still I dislike it less. I make a mental
note. It will all go into an essay. One gets something
of the spirit of the morbid anatomist, to whom some
peculiar phase of disease is infinitely more interesting
than commonplace health. Interesting wrong becomes
(must I confess it ?) a finer sight than uninteresting
right. You know how country servants rejoice in
coming to tell you that something is amiss : that a
horse is lame, or a pig dying, or a field of potatoes
blighted. It is something to tell about. Perhaps the
essayist knows the peculiar emotion.

I sometimes have thought that the writer of fiction is to
be envied. He has another life and world than that we
see. He has a duality of being. He sits down to his
desk; and in a little he is far away, and away in a
world where he is absolute monarch. It has not been so
with me. In writing these essays, I have not been rapt
away into heroic times and distant scenes, and into
romantic tracts of feeling. I have been writing amid
daily work and worry, of daily work and worry : and
of the little things by which daily work and worry

are intensified or relieved. I cannot pretend to long experience of life; nor perhaps to much. But from a
quiet and lonely life, little varied and very happy, I
have sent out these essays month by month; and I hope
to send out more.

THE END.

CAMBRIDGE: PRINTED BY H. O. HOUGHTON.

☞ Any Books in this list will be sent free of postage, on receipt of price.

BOSTON, 135 WASHINGTON STREET,
OCTOBER, 1860.

A LIST OF BOOKS

PUBLISHED BY

TICKNOR AND FIELDS.

Sir Walter Scott.

ILLUSTRATED HOUSEHOLD EDITION OF THE WAVERLEY NOVELS. In portable size, 16mo. form. Now Complete. Price 75 cents a volume.

The paper is of fine quality; the stereotype plates are not old ones repaired, the type having been cast expressly for this edition. The Novels are illustrated with capital steel plates engraved in the best manner, after drawings and paintings by the most eminent artists, among whom are Birket Foster, Darley, Billings, Landseer, Harvey, and Faed. This Edition contains all the latest notes and corrections of the author, a Glossary and Index; and some curious additions, especially in "Guy Mannering" and the "Bride of Lammermoor;" being the fullest edition of the Novels ever published. *The notes are at the foot of the page,*—a great convenience to the reader.

Any of the following Novels sold separate.

WAVERLEY, 2 vols.	ST. RONAN'S WELL, 2 vols.
GUY MANNERING, 2 vols.	REDGAUNTLET, 2 vols.
THE ANTIQUARY, 2 vols.	THE BETROTHED, } 2 vols.
ROB ROY, 2 vols.	THE HIGHLAND WIDOW, }
OLD MORTALITY, 2 vols.	THE TALISMAN,
BLACK DWARF, } 2 vols.	TWO DROVERS,
LEGEND OF MONTROSE, }	MY AUNT MARGARET'S MIRROR, } 2 vols.
HEART OF MID LOTHIAN, 2 vols.	THE TAPESTRIED CHAMBER,
BRIDE OF LAMMERMOOR, 2 vols.	THE LAIRD'S JOCK.
IVANHOE, 2 vols.	WOODSTOCK, 2 vols.
THE MONASTERY, 2 vols.	THE FAIR MAID OF PERTH, 2 vols.
THE ABBOT, 2 vols.	ANNE OF GEIERSTEIN, 2 vols.
KENILWORTH, 2 vols.	COUNT ROBERT OF PARIS, 2 vols.
THE PIRATE, 2 vols.	THE SURGEON'S DAUGHTER, }
THE FORTUNES OF NIGEL. 2 vols.	CASTLE DANGEROUS, } 2 vols.
PEVERIL OF THE PEAK, 2 vols.	INDEX AND GLOSSARY. }
QUENTIN DURWARD, 2 vols.	

TALES OF A GRANDFATHER. *In Press.*

LIFE. By J. G. Lockhart. *In Press.*

Thomas De Quincey.

CONFESSIONS OF AN ENGLISH OPIUM-EATER, AND SUS-
  PIRIA DE PROFUNDIS. With Portrait. 75 cents.
BIOGRAPHICAL ESSAYS. 75 cents.
MISCELLANEOUS ESSAYS. 75 cents.
THE CÆSARS. 75 cents.
LITERARY REMINISCENCES. 2 vols. $1.50.
NARRATIVE AND MISCELLANEOUS PAPERS. 2 vols. $1.50.
ESSAYS ON THE POETS, &c. 1 vol. 16mo. 75 cents.
HISTORICAL AND CRITICAL ESSAYS. 2 vols. $1.50.
AUTOBIOGRAPHIC SKETCHES. 1 vol. 75 cents.
ESSAYS ON PHILOSOPHICAL WRITERS, &c. 2 vols. 16mo.
  $1.50.
LETTERS TO A YOUNG MAN, AND OTHER PAPERS. 1 vol.
  75 cents.
THEOLOGICAL ESSAYS AND OTHER PAPERS. 2 vols.
  $1.50.
THE NOTE BOOK. 1 vol. 75 cents.
MEMORIALS AND OTHER PAPERS. 2 vols. 16mo. $1.50.
THE AVENGER AND OTHER PAPERS. 1 vol. 75 cents.
LOGIC OF POLITICAL ECONOMY, AND OTHER PAPERS.
  1 vol. 75 cents.

Alfred Tennyson.

POETICAL WORKS. With Portrait. 2 vols. Cloth. $2.00.
POCKET EDITION OF POEMS COMPLETE. 75 cents.
THE PRINCESS. Cloth. 50 cents.
IN MEMORIAM. Cloth. 75 cents.
MAUD, AND OTHER POEMS. Cloth. 50 cents.
IDYLS OF THE KING. A new volume. Cloth. 75 cents.

Barry Cornwall.

ENGLISH SONGS AND OTHER SMALL POEMS. $1.00.
DRAMATIC POEMS. Just published. $1.00.
ESSAYS AND TALES IN PROSE. 2 vols. $1.50.

Henry W. Longfellow.

POETICAL WORKS. In two volumes. 16mo. Boards. $2.00.

POCKET EDITION OF POETICAL WORKS. In two volumes. $1.75.

POCKET EDITION OF PROSE WORKS COMPLETE. In two volumes. $1.75.

THE SONG OF HIAWATHA. $1.00.

EVANGELINE: A Tale of Acadia. 75 cents.

THE GOLDEN LEGEND. A Poem. $1.00.

HYPERION. A Romance. $1.00.

OUTRE-MER. A Pilgrimage. $1.00.

KAVANAGH. A Tale. 75 cents.

THE COURTSHIP OF MILES STANDISH. 1 vol. 16mo. 75 cents.

Illustrated editions of EVANGELINE. POEMS, HYPERION, THE GOLDEN LEGEND, and MILES STANDISH.

Charles Reade.

PEG WOFFINGTON. A Novel. 75 cents.

CHRISTIE JOHNSTONE. A Novel. 75 cents.

CLOUDS AND SUNSHINE. A Novel. 75 cents.

'NEVER TOO LATE TO MEND.' 2 vols. $1.50.

WHITE LIES. A Novel. 1 vol. $1.25.

PROPRIA QUÆ MARIBUS and THE BOX TUNNEL. 25 cts.

THE EIGHTH COMMANDMENT. 75 cents.

Thomas Hood.

MEMORIALS. Edited by his Children. 2 vols. $1.75.

James Russell Lowell.

COMPLETE POETICAL WORKS. In Blue and Gold. 2 vols. $1.50.

POETICAL WORKS. 2 vols. 16mo. Cloth. $1.50.

SIR LAUNFAL. New Edition. 25 cents.

A FABLE FOR CRITICS. New Edition. 50 cents.

THE BIGLOW PAPERS. A New Edition. 63 cents.

FIRESIDE TRAVELS. *In Press.*

Nathaniel Hawthorne.

TWICE-TOLD TALES. Two volumes. $1.50.
THE SCARLET LETTER. 75 cents.
THE HOUSE OF THE SEVEN GABLES. $1.00.
THE SNOW IMAGE, AND OTHER TALES. 75 cents.
THE BLITHEDALE ROMANCE. 75 cents.
MOSSES FROM AN OLD MANSE. 2 vols. $1.50.
THE MARBLE FAUN. 2 vols. $1.50.
TRUE STORIES. 75 cents.
A WONDER-BOOK FOR GIRLS AND BOYS. 75 cents.
TANGLEWOOD TALES. 88 cents.

William Howitt.

LAND, LABOR, AND GOLD. 2 vols. $2.00.
A BOY'S ADVENTURES IN AUSTRALIA. 75 cents.

Charles Kingsley.

TWO YEARS AGO. A New Novel. $1.25.
AMYAS LEIGH. A Novel. $1.25.
GLAUCUS; OR, THE WONDERS OF THE SHORE. 50 cts.
POETICAL WORKS. 75 cents.
THE HEROES; OR, GREEK FAIRY TALES. 75 cents.
ANDROMEDA AND OTHER POEMS. 50 cents.
SIR WALTER RALEIGH AND HIS TIME, &c. $1.25.
NEW MISCELLANIES. 1 vol. $1.00.

Coventry Patmore.

THE ANGEL IN THE HOUSE. BETROTHAL.
    "   "   "   "   ESPOUSALS. 75 cts. each.

George S. Hillard.

SIX MONTHS IN ITALY. 1 vol. 16mo. $1.50.
DANGERS AND DUTIES OF THE MERCANTILE PROFESSION. 25 cents.
SELECTIONS FROM THE WRITINGS OF WALTER SAVAGE LANDOR. 1 vol. 16mo. 75 cents.

Oliver Wendell Holmes.

POEMS. With fine Portrait. Cloth. $1.00.

ASTRÆA. Fancy paper. 25 cents.

THE AUTOCRAT OF THE BREAKFAST TABLE. With Illustrations by Hoppin. 16mo. $1.00.

The Same. Large Paper Edition. 8vo. Tinted paper. $3.00.

THE PROFESSOR AT THE BREAKFAST TABLE. 16mo. $1.00.

The Same. Large Paper Edition. 8vo. Tinted paper. $3.00.

POEMS. A new volume. *In Press.*

A VOLUME OF MEDICAL ESSAYS. *In Press.*

Ralph Waldo Emerson.

ESSAYS. 1st Series. 1 vol. $1.00.

ESSAYS. 2d Series. 1 vol. $1.00.

MISCELLANIES. 1 vol. $1.00.

REPRESENTATIVE MEN. 1 vol. $1.00.

ENGLISH TRAITS. 1 vol. $1.00.

POEMS. 1 vol. $1.00.

CONDUCT OF LIFE. 1 vol. $1.00. *Nearly ready.*

John G. Whittier.

POCKET EDITION OF POETICAL WORKS. 2 vols. $1.50.

OLD PORTRAITS AND MODERN SKETCHES. 75 cents.

MARGARET SMITH'S JOURNAL. 75 cents.

SONGS OF LABOR, AND OTHER POEMS. Boards. 50 cts.

THE CHAPEL OF THE HERMITS. Cloth. 50 cents.

LITERARY RECREATIONS, &c. Cloth. $1.00.

THE PANORAMA, AND OTHER POEMS. Cloth. 50 cents.

HOME BALLADS AND POEMS. 1 vol. 75 cents.

Edwin P. Whipple.

ESSAYS AND REVIEWS. 2 vols. $2.00.

LECTURES ON LITERATURE AND LIFE. 63 cents.

WASHINGTON AND THE REVOLUTION. 20 cents.

Robert Browning.

POETICAL WORKS. 2 vols. $2.00.
MEN AND WOMEN. 1 vol. $1.00.

Henry Giles.

LECTURES, ESSAYS, &c. 2 vols. $1.50.
DISCOURSES ON LIFE. 75 cents.
ILLUSTRATIONS OF GENIUS. Cloth. $1.00.

William Motherwell.

COMPLETE POETICAL WORKS. In Blue and Gold. 1 vol.
    75 cents.
MINSTRELSY, ANC. AND MOD. 2 vols. Boards. $1.50.

Capt. Mayne Reid.

THE PLANT HUNTERS. With Plates. 75 cents.
THE DESERT HOME: OR, THE ADVENTURES OF A LOST
    FAMILY IN THE WILDERNESS. With fine Plates. $1.00.
THE BOY HUNTERS. With fine Plates. 75 cents.
THE YOUNG VOYAGEURS: OR, THE BOY HUNTERS IN
    THE NORTH. With Plates. 75 cents.
THE FOREST EXILES. With fine Plates. 75 cents.
THE BUSH BOYS. With fine Plates. 75 cents.
THE YOUNG YAGERS. With fine Plates. 75 cents.
RAN AWAY TO SEA: AN AUTOBIOGRAPHY FOR BOYS.
    With fine Plates. 75 cents.
THE BOY TAR: A VOYAGE IN THE DARK. A New
    Book. With fine Plates. 75 cents.
ODD PEOPLE. With Plates. *Nearly ready.*
THE BOY'S BOOK OF ANIMALS. With Plates. *In Press.*

Goethe.

WILHELM MEISTER. Translated by *Carlyle*. 2 vols. $2.50.
FAUST. Translated by *Hayward*. 75 cents.
FAUST. Translated by *Charles T. Brooks*. $1.00.
CORRESPONDENCE WITH A CHILD. *Bettina*. 1 vol. 12mo.
    $1.25.

J. G. Lockhart.

SPANISH BALLADS. With Portrait. 75 cents.

Rev. Charles Lowell.

PRACTICAL SERMONS. 1 vol. 12mo. $1.25.
OCCASIONAL SERMONS. With fine Portrait. $1.25.

Rev. F. W. Robertson.

SERMONS. First Series. $1.00.
   "   Second " $1.00.
   "   Third " $1.00.
   "   Fourth " $1.00.
LECTURES AND ADDRESSES ON LITERARY AND SOCIAL
   TOPICS. $1.00.

R. H. Stoddard.

POEMS. Cloth. 63 cents.
ADVENTURES IN FAIRY LAND. 75 cents.
SONGS OF SUMMER. 75 cents.

Anna Mary Howitt.

AN ART STUDENT IN MUNICH. $1.25.
A SCHOOL OF LIFE. A Story. 75 cents.

Mary Russell Mitford.

OUR VILLAGE. Illustrated. 2 vols. 16mo. $2.50.
ATHERTON, AND OTHER STORIES. 1 vol. 16mo. $1.25.

Mrs. Howe.

PASSION FLOWERS. 75 cents.
WORDS FOR THE HOUR. 75 cents.
THE WORLD'S OWN. 50 cents.
A TRIP TO CUBA. 1 vol. 16mo. 75 cents.

Grace Greenwood.

GREENWOOD LEAVES. 1st and 2d Series. $1.25 each.
POETICAL WORKS. With fine Portrait. 75 cents.
HISTORY OF MY PETS. With six fine Engravings. Scarlet cloth. 50 cents.
RECOLLECTIONS OF MY CHILDHOOD. With six fine Engravings. Scarlet cloth. 50 cents.
HAPS AND MISHAPS OF A TOUR IN EUROPE. $1.25.
MERRIE ENGLAND. 75 cents.
A FOREST TRAGEDY, AND OTHER TALES. $1.00.
STORIES AND LEGENDS. 75 cents.
STORIES FROM FAMOUS BALLADS. Illustrated. 50 cents.

Mrs. Crosland.

LYDIA: A WOMAN'S BOOK. Cloth. 75 cents.
ENGLISH TALES AND SKETCHES. Cloth. $1.00.
MEMORABLE WOMEN. Illustrated. $1.00.

Mrs. Jameson.

CHARACTERISTICS OF WOMEN. Blue and Gold. 75 cents.
LOVES OF THE POETS. " " 75 cents.
DIARY OF AN ENNUYÉE " " 75 cents.
SKETCHES OF ART, &c. " " 75 cents.
STUDIES AND STORIES. " " 75 cents.
ITALIAN PAINTERS. " " 75 cents.
LEGENDS OF THE MADONNA. " " 75 cents.

Mrs. Mowatt.

AUTOBIOGRAPHY OF AN ACTRESS. $1.25.
PLAYS. ARMAND AND FASHION. 50 cents.
MIMIC LIFE. 1 vol. $1.25.
THE TWIN ROSES. 1 vol. 75 cents.

Alice Cary.

POEMS. 1 vol. 16mo. $1.00.
CLOVERNOOK CHILDREN. With Plates. 75 cents.

Mrs. Eliza B. Lee.

MEMOIR OF THE BUCKMINSTERS. $1.25.
FLORENCE, THE PARISH ORPHAN. 50 cents.
PARTHENIA. 1 vol. 16mo. $1.00.

Samuel Smiles.

LIFE OF GEORGE STEPHENSON: ENGINEER. $1.00.
SELF HELP; WITH ILLUSTRATIONS OF CHARACTER AND
    CONDUCT. 1 vol. 75 cents.
BRIEF BIOGRAPHIES. With Plates. $1.25.

Blanchard Jerrold.

DOUGLAS JERROLD'S WIT. 75 cents.
LIFE AND LETTERS OF DOUGLAS JERROLD. $1.00.

Miss Cummins.

EL FUREIDIS. By the Author of "The Lamplighter," &c.
    $1.00.

Mrs. Judson.

ALDERBROOK. By *Fanny Forrester.* 2 vols. $1.75.
THE KATHAYAN SLAVE, AND OTHER PAPERS. 1 vol.
    63 cents.
MY TWO SISTERS: A SKETCH FROM MEMORY. 50 cents.

John G. Saxe.

POEMS. With Portrait. Boards. 63 cents. Cloth. 75 cents.
THE MONEY KING, AND OTHER POEMS. 1 vol. 75 cents.

Charles T. Brooks.

GERMAN LYRICS. Translated. 1 vol. 16mo. Cloth. $1.00.

Leigh Hunt.

POEMS. Blue and Gold. 2 vols. $1.50.

Tom Brown.

SCHOOL DAYS AT RUGBY. By *An Old Boy.* 1 vol. 16mo. $1.00.

The Same.   Illustrated edition. $1.50.

THE SCOURING OF THE WHITE HORSE, OR THE LONG VACATION HOLIDAY OF A LONDON CLERK. By *The Author of 'School Days at Rugby.'* 1 vol. 16mo. $1.00.

TOM BROWN AT OXFORD. A Sequel to School Days at Rugby. Parts I to VIII. 12 cents each.

Gerald Massey.

POETICAL WORKS. Blue and Gold.   75 cents.

W. M. Thackeray.

BALLADS. 1 vol. 16mo. 75 cents.

Charles Mackay.

POEMS. 1 vol. Cloth. $1.00.

George H. Boker.

PLAYS AND POEMS. 2 vols. $2.00.

Henry T. Tuckerman.

POEMS. Cloth. 75 cents.

James G. Percival.

POETICAL WORKS. 2 vols. Blue and Gold. $1.75.

Arthur P. Stanley.

LIFE AND CORRESPONDENCE OF DR. ARNOLD.   With fine Portrait. 2 vols. $2.00.

Henry Kingsley.

RECOLLECTIONS OF GEOFFRY HAMLYN. A Novel. $1.25.

Theophilus Parsons.

A MEMOIR OF CHIEF JUSTICE THEOPHILUS PARSONS, WITH NOTICES OF SOME OF HIS CONTEMPORARIES. By his Son. With Portrait. 1 vol. 12mo. $1.50.

Alexander Smith.

A LIFE DRAMA. 1 vol. 16mo. 50 cents.
CITY POEMS. With Portrait. 1 vol. 16mo. 63 cents.

Bayard Taylor.

POEMS OF HOME AND TRAVEL. Cloth. 75 cents.
POEMS OF THE ORIENT. Cloth. 75 cents.

Horace Mann.

THOUGHTS FOR A YOUNG MAN. 25 cents.

Lord Dufferin.

A YACHT VOYAGE OF 6,000 MILES. $1.00.

Owen Meredith.

POETICAL WORKS. Blue and Gold. 75 cents.
LUCILE: A Poem. Blue and Gold. 75 cents.

T. B. Read.

POETICAL WORKS. 2 vols. $2.00.

Arago.

BIOGRAPHIES OF DISTINGUISHED SCIENTIFIC MEN. 16mo. 2 vols. $2.00.

John Neal.

TRUE WOMANHOOD. A Novel. 1 vol. $1.25.

Hans Christian Andersen.

THE SAND-HILLS OF JUTLAND. 1 vol. 16mo. 75 cents.

R. H. Dana, Jr.

To Cuba and Back, a Vacation Voyage, by the Author of " Two Years before the Mast." 75 cents.

George B. Prescott.

History, Theory and Practice of the Electric Telegraph. With 100 Illustrations. 1 vol. 12mo. $1.75.

Captain McClintock.

Narrative of the Voyage in search of Sir John Franklin and the Discovery of his Remains. With Maps and Illustrations. 1 vol. large 12mo. $1.50.

The Same. Cheaper Edition. With the same Maps and Illustrations. 75 cents.

Charles Eliot Norton.

Notes of Travel and Study in Italy. 1 vol. 16mo. $1.00.

Charles Robert Leslie, R. A.

Autobiographical Recollections. Edited by Tom Taylor. With Portrait. 1 vol. 12mo. $1.25.

Wild Sports of India. 75 cents.

Lake House. By Fanny Lewald. 75 cents.

Charles Sumner's Orations. 2 vols. $2.50.

Tyndall's Glaciers of the Alps. Illustrated. 1 vol. $1.50.

Travels, Researches, and Missionary Labors in Eastern Africa. By Dr. J. Lewis Krapf. 1 vol. With Map. $1.25.

Lyteria: A Dramatic Poem. By Josiah Phillips Quincy. 50 cents.

Charicles: A Dramatic Poem. By Josiah Phillips Quincy. 50 cents.

Poems. By Thomas W. Parsons. $1.00.

RECOLLECTIONS OF SHELLEY AND BYRON. By E. J. Trelawny. 75 cents.

LIGHT ON THE DARK RIVER: OR, MEMOIRS OF MRS. HAMLIN. By Mrs. Lawrence. 1 vol. 16mo. Cloth. $1.00.

THE LIFE AND WORKS OF GOETHE. By G. H. Lewes. 2 vols. 16mo. $2.50.

HOLMBY HOUSE: A TALE OF OLD NORTHAMPTONSHIRE. By G. J. Whyte Melville. 8vo. Paper. 50 cents.

MADEMOISELLE MORI: A TALE OF MODERN ROME. 1 vol. $1.25.

THE SEMI-DETACHED HOUSE. Edited by Lady Theresa Lewis. 1 vol. 75 cents.

FRESH HEARTS THAT FAILED THREE THOUSAND YEARS AGO. With other Poems. By the Author of " The New Priest in Conception Bay." 1 vol. 50 cents.

POEMS. By Miss Muloch, Author of " John Halifax," &c. 1 vol. 75 cents.

GUESSES AT TRUTH. 1 vol. 12mo.

ARABIAN DAYS' ENTERTAINMENTS. Translated from the German of W. Hauff. By H. Pelham Curtis. With Illustrations by Hoppin. 1 vol. $1.25.

HYMNS OF THE AGES. With a Preface by Rev. F. D. Huntington, D. D. 1 vol. 12mo. $1.00.
Also a fine Edition, on large paper. 8vo. Bevelled boards. $3.00.

THE CRUSADES AND THE CRUSADERS. By J. G. Edgar. With Illustrations. 75 cents.

ERNEST BRACEBRIDGE; OR, SCHOOLBOY DAYS. By W. H. G. Kingston. With Illustrations. 75 cents.

SWORD AND GOWN. By the Author of " Guy Livingstone." 1 vol. 75 cents.

ALMOST A HEROINE. By the Author of " Charles Auchester," and " Counterparts." 1 vol. $1.00.

RAB AND HIS FRIENDS. By John Brown, M. D. 15 cents.

TWELVE YEARS OF A SOLDIER'S LIFE: A MEMOIR OF THE LATE MAJOR W. S. R. HODSON, B. A. Edited by his Brother, Rev. George H. Hodson. 1 vol. $1.00.

THE LIFE AND TIMES OF SIR PHILIP SIDNEY. 1 vol. 16mo. $1.00.

ERNEST CARROLL, OR ARTIST LIFE IN ITALY. 1 vol.
16mo. 88 cents.

MEMORY AND HOPE. Cloth. $2.00.

THALATTA: A BOOK FOR THE SEASIDE. 75 cents.

REJECTED ADDRESSES. A new edition. Cloth. 75 cents.

WARRENIANA : A COMPANION TO REJECTED AD-
DRESSES. 63 cents.

ANGEL VOICES. 38 cents.

THE BOSTON BOOK. $1.25.

MEMOIR OF ROBERT WHEATON. 1 vol. $1.00.

LABOR AND LOVE: A TALE OF ENGLISH LIFE. 50 cts.

THE SOLITARY OF JUAN FERNANDEZ. By the Author
of Picciola. 50 cents.

WALDEN : OR, LIFE IN THE WOODS. By Henry D. Tho-
reau. 1 vol. 16mo. $1.00.

VILLAGE LIFE IN EGYPT. By Bayle St. John, the Author
of " Purple Tints of Paris." 2 vols. 16mo. $1.25.

WENSLEY: A STORY WITHOUT A MORAL. By Edmund
Quincy. 75 cents.

PALISSY THE POTTER. By Henry Morley. 2 vols. 16mo.
$1.50.

J. T. BUCKINGHAM'S PERSONAL MEMOIRS. 2 vols. $1.50.

THE BARCLAYS OF BOSTON. By Mrs. H. G. Otis. 1 vol.
12mo. $1.25.

SIR ROGER DE COVERLEY. By Addison. From the
" Spectator." 75 cents.

SERMONS OF CONSOLATION. By F. W. P. Greenwood.
$1.00.

SPAIN, HER INSTITUTIONS, POLITICS, AND PUBLIC MEN.
By S. T. Wallis. $1.00.

POEMS. By Henry Alford. $1.25.

ESSAYS ON THE FORMATION OF OPINIONS AND THE
PURSUIT OF TRUTH. By Samuel Bailey. 1 vol. 16mo. $1.00.

POEMS OF MANY YEARS. By Richard Monckton Milnes.
Boards. 75 cents.

BOTHWELL. By W. Edmondstoune Aytoun. 75 cents.

THORPE: A QUIET ENGLISH TOWN, AND HUMAN LIFE
THEREIN. By William Mountford. 16mo. $1.00.

LECTURES ON ORATORY AND RHETORIC. By Prof. E. T. Channing. 75 cents.

A PHYSIOLOGICAL COOKERY BOOK. By Mrs. Horace Mann. 63 cents.

WILLIAM WORDSWORTH'S BIOGRAPHY. By Christopher Wosrdworth. 2 vols. $2.50.

NOTES FROM LIFE. By the Author of "Philip Van Arte- velde." 1 vol. 16mo. Cloth. 63 cents.

ART OF PROLONGING LIFE. By Hufeland. Edited by Erasmus Wilson. 1 vol. 16mo. 75 cents.

SHELLEY MEMORIALS. From Authentic Sources. 1 vol. Cloth. 75 cents.

THORNDALE, OR THE CONFLICT OF OPINIONS. By Wil- liam Smith. $1.25.

JOHN C. FREMONT'S LIFE, EXPLORATIONS, &c. By C. W. Upham. With Illustrations. 75 cents.

MONALDI : A Tale. By Washington Allston. 1 vol. 16mo. 75 cents.

HINTS ON HEALTH. By Dr. William E. Coale. 3d Edi- tion. 63 cents.

SEVEN YEARS. A Volume of Stories. By Julia Kava- nagh. 8vo. Paper, 30 cents.

POEMS. By Mrs. Rosa V. Johnson. 1 vol. 16mo. $1.00.

CHARLES SPRAGUE'S WRITINGS. 75 cents.

OAKFIELD. A Novel. By Lieut. Arnold. $1.00.

A PHYSICIAN'S VACATION. By Dr. Walter Channing. $1.50.

POEMS AND PARODIES. By Phœbe Cary. 75 cents.

LIFE OF EDMUND BURKE. By James Prior. 2 vols. $2.00.

CHURCH AND CONGREGATION. By C. A. Bartol. $1.00.

POEMS. By Matthew Arnold. 75 cents.

POEMS. By Fanny Kemble. Enlarged Edition. $1.00.

ADVENTURES OF TYLL OWLGLASS. $2.50.

LYRIC POEMS, &c. By George Lunt. Cloth. 63 cents.

THREE ERAS OF NEW ENGLAND. By George Lunt. $1.00.

JULIA. A Poem. By George Lunt. 50 cents.

THE MYSTIC, AND OTHER POEMS. By P. J. Bailey. 50 cents.

THE ANGEL WORLD, &c. By P. J. Bailey. 50 cents.

THE AGE, A SATIRE. By P. J. Bailey. 75 cents.

A JOURNEY DUE NORTH. By G. A. Sala. $1.00.

POEMS. By Paul H. Hayne. 1 vol. 16mo. 63 cents.

AVOLIO. By Paul H. Hayne. 1 vol. 75 cents.

SEED-GRAIN. By Mrs. A. C. Lowell. 2 vols. $1.75.

EDUCATION OF GIRLS. By Mrs. A. C. Lowell. 25 cents.

THE PRESERVATION OF HEALTH, &c. By Dr. John C. Warren. 1 vol. 38 cents.

LIFE OF DR. JOHN C. WARREN. By Edward Warren, M. D. Compiled chiefly from his Private Journals. 2 vols. 8vo. $3.50.

In Blue and Gold.

LONGFELLOW'S POETICAL WORKS. 2 vols. $1.75.

   do.   PROSE WORKS. 2 vols. $1.75.

TENNYSON'S POETICAL WORKS. 1 vol. 75 cents.

WHITTIER'S POETICAL WORKS. 2 vols. $1.50.

LEIGH HUNT'S POETICAL WORKS. 2 vols. $1.50.

GERALD MASSEY'S POETICAL WORKS. 1 vol. 75 cents.

MRS. JAMESON'S CHARACTERISTICS OF WOMEN. 75 cts.

   do.   DIARY OF AN ENNUYÉE. 1 vol. 75 cts.

   do.   LOVES OF THE POETS. 1 vol. 75 cts.

   do.   SKETCHES OF ART, &c. 1 vol. 75 cts.

   do.   STUDIES AND STORIES. 1 vol. 75 cts.

   do.   ITALIAN PAINTERS. 1 vol. 75 cents.

   do.   LEGENDS OF THE MADONNA. 1 vol. 75 cents.

OWEN MEREDITH'S POEMS. 1 vol. 75 cents.

   do.   LUCILE: A Poem. 1 vol. 75 cents.

BOWRING'S MATINS AND VESPERS. 1 vol. 75 cents.

LOWELL'S (J. RUSSELL) POETICAL WORKS. 2 vols. $1.50.

PERCIVAL'S POETICAL WORKS. 2 vols. $1.75.

MOTHERWELL'S POEMS. 1 vol. 75 cents.

SYDNEY DOBELL'S POEMS. 1 vol. 75 cents.

WILLIAM ALLINGHAM'S POEMS. 1 vol. 75 cents.

HORACE. Translated by Theodore Martin. 1 vol. 75 cts.